# My Dark Beast

**MY DARK BEAST**

Copyright © 2024 by WildStone Publishing

All rights reserved. Printed in the United States of America. No part of this book may be used or reproduced in any manner whatsoever without written permission except in the case of brief quotations embodied in critical articles or reviews.

This book is a work of fiction. Names, characters, businesses, organizations, places, events and incidents either are the product of the author's imagination or are used fictitiously. Any resemblance to actual persons, living or dead, events, or locales is entirely coincidental.

*For information contact:*
OLIVIA WILDENSTEIN
http://oliviawildenstein.com

Cover design by Fay Lane @faylane14
(Paperback) art inside cover by @Flyora_art & @vinc_ry
(Hardcover) Art on case cover by @pangolin2b
Character portraits by @Zisrael_art
Chapter headers by @Lettersbylila_

Editing by Lexi George & Rachel Theus Cass

# Content Warnings

***My Dark Beast*** is a new adult romance that contains:

- strong language
- sexually explicit scenes
- graphic violence
- Alzheimer's
- alcohol drinking
- abduction of an adult
- addiction to "magical" drugs (off page)
- death of a loved one (off page)

To the man of my
dreams.

# ONE

Oh my god.

I blink at the giant spider perched atop the tangerine rose—a palm-sized fiend with big beady eyes and furry legs. The flexible stem stripper clatters from my fingers, thudding on the scarred wooden table with enough force to make me jump. The spider does not jump.

I consider laying the rose down and backing up extra slowly, but what if it crawls away and vanishes in some dark corner of my parents' flower shop? Or worse, what if it climbs the stairs to my bedroom?

This, right here, is the sort of moment where I miss my intrepid father so damn much. Nicolas Bloom was my hero—my bug-whisperer, my nightmare-slayer, my joke-cracker, my smile-maker. The only thing that ever scared that man was losing my mother. And me, but especially Mom. The greatest love of his life.

I hold the rose at arm's length. It wobbles like a reed as I carefully pad along the grass-green tiles. The chime above the flower shop's glass door tinkles. I assume it's my bestie, Bryn, finally emerging from her six-hour family luncheon, but lo and behold, it's my least favorite customer.

"Hold the door please, Mr. Valenti!"

He frowns at the rose I'll be stabbing into his wife's bouquet as soon as I get rid of the live ornament on top. Shit. What if he cancels his weekly order because of the creepy-crawly? I try to move the flower out of his field of vision when I catch said field of vision leveled on my cleavage. Never have I been so glad for the sleazeball's fixation with my breasts.

"I'll be right back." I step out onto the dusky Boston sidewalk that's getting battered by rain. "Okay, hairy little guy…or girl, time to skedaddle."

The spider doesn't budge. I flap the long stalk. The creature shoots me a scathing look. Across the road, I spot sweet blond Logan pouring a cocktail into a martini glass. I'm very tempted to cross the street and ask him for help. He's from the South, and Southern men aren't scared of insects—I hope.

I place one stiletto on the road, splashing right into a puddle. Ugh. Nothing like city water inside a shoe. I scan the space between the parked vehicles for other pockets of muck before taking another step.

Car beams splash my face and a honk shatters my eardrums. I let go of the rose, which sails through the air, just as a fancy black sportscar narrowly misses reducing me to bumper goo.

Although the almost-collision is essentially my fault, I fire a peeved glower at the driver, who didn't even have the decency to slow as he shot past me. My glower deepens when I read his license plate—*Hadez1*.

I plant my hands on my hips, squinting, even though there's no way I can discern which family member it was. The uncle? The cousin? The little brother? Or the evilest of the bunch—Tarian Hadez—aloof bachelor, prick extraordinaire, and self-proclaimed murderer?

The sleek taillights reflect on the rain-slicked street, painting it crimson like some metaphorical trail of blood. How fittingly macabre for the man said to have killed hundreds of people in his three decades of life, most notably his own father.

Lips smooshed, I return to the shop where Mr. Valenti is patiently waiting for his bouquet, or for another cop at my boobs. Where my mother's convinced the man's a romantic—when she remembers who he is, which lately, isn't all that often—I'm convinced the "happily married" father of three is a cheating weasel.

"Sorry to have kept you waiting." I try to smile but I'm pretty sure it comes out as a facial tic, especially when Mr. Valenti's eyes stray over my large breasts, which I keep strapped down with sports bras when I'm at work.

"How's your lovely mother?"

"She's great." She's not, but like hell am I sharing her decline with this man. I barely discuss it with Bryn, but that has more to do with me not wanting to dwell on Mom's aggressive Alzheimer's.

I splatter droplets on the tiles, which I'm going to have to mop up because a lawsuit would bury us in debt. On the upside, I wouldn't have to run the shop anymore. I shake the selfish thought out of my head. I already lost my father and a little of my mother; I will not lose Bloom's Blooms, their pride and joy.

I sidestep the lacquered lattice screen that Dad converted into a wall of succulents before his death and get back to Mr. Valenti's bouquet. I forgo removing the thorns off his two dozen—minus one—roses, eager to get the man out of my shop.

"Why did you throw a flower at Tarian Hadez?" Valenti calls out.

*So it was Tarian's car...*

An image of the man stains the backs of my lids. All sharp angles, lean muscles, and eyes rumored to match his hair and personality—black like our city's sewers.

Through the lattice screen, I catch Valenti fingering the sepals of the yellow Brassia orchid beside the register. How the plant doesn't shrivel is a miracle. "Why are women so fascinated with that man?"

Because he's filthy rich, filthy powerful, and filthy dangerous. *Murderer-chic*, as I like to say, which eternally wins me an eyeroll from Bryn.

I shrug. "Beats me."

"You just tossed a flower at him."

I cock an eyebrow at Valenti. Does he think I tossed that rose to get Tarian's attention? Gross.

So the prick quits imagining I suffer from hybristophilia, I deadpan, "It was a marketing ploy. I'm trying to land more customers."

"For the flower shop?"

*Eww.* "Yes, for the flower shop."

I'm still grimacing when he adds, "If you need to make a quick buck, I can hook you up with a man who sells pills."

That sets off a whole bunch of alarm bells. "I'd prefer not to get in bed with the mob." I unspool twine from the giant bobbin nailed to the wall and loop it around the stalks before twirling the bouquet in a sheet of brown craft paper.

"It's not the mob. It's the anti-mob."

Sure, and I'm a chihuahua shapeshifter with a penchant for housekeeping.

"You might've heard of them. The Holy Hunters."

I suck in a breath because I *have* heard of the enigmatic militia that's anti-everything Hadez. "I think I'll stick to flowers." I smack our logo sticker on the craft paper. "But thank you. I so appreciate your concern."

There his gaze goes again, down the rabbit-hole of my cleavage. I dash to the register and ring him up. As he swipes his platinum credit card, I stare at the ceiling that resonates with a familiar Food Network jingle heralding the start of a commercial break. Mom watches that channel from dawn to dusk. She used to be a great chef—even wrote a cookbook that incorporated the use of flowers, which was how she met Dad—but these days, she just stares listlessly at the screen.

The payment terminal spits out Mr. Valenti's receipt. I print the customer copy and place it atop the bouquet on the counter. I used to hand it over, but his fingers would always find a way to brush mine.

"Beautiful," he says to my boobs while sniffing his roses. "Take the week to think about my business proposal. Better yet, I'll send him to meet you."

Hell to the no. "Thanks, but my neighbor's a recovering drug addict, so it's best I don't expose her to any of that." I walk over to the door and hip-check it open. Not subtle, I know, but this man doesn't deserve to be treated with tact.

"There's a lot of money to make." He tosses a glance at the dark sky that needles the sidewalk with razor-sharp raindrops. "We can chat about it next week."

"Absolutely. Can't wait."

He lingers on the threshold. "Do you get any time off?"

"Nope."

"You work seven days a week?"

"Yep." If only we didn't need his business, I'd shove him right out.

"That's inhumane."

That's called being a devoted daughter, one who can't bring herself to institutionalize her mother.

"What time do you close?"

I eye the counter beneath which I keep a bottle of pepper spray. I've always wanted to use it. Perhaps the time has come? "Right now, actually."

Valenti studies the placard hanging on the door with our hours of operation, his gaze lingering on the seven-p.m. closing time. It's not quite five-thirty.

"I need to close early. Deliveries." Sadly, I have zero deliveries to make.

Ever since uber-modern Fleur-de-Lys opened two streets

down, giving customers rebates based on their age, Bloom's Blooms has been wilting as quickly as Mom's memory. At the rate we're going, we won't be able to afford rent come October—if we can even hold on until then.

I grip the edge of the door harder, feeling as though the ivy-covered brick walls are closing in on me and the potted plants are siphoning all the oxygen.

Squealing tires jolt me out of my spiral. For some reason, I'm expecting the vehicle to be black and low to the ground, but it's silver. And the person at the wheel isn't some huge angry alien or deity come to complain that my rose blew a hole in his tire or shattered his windshield.

Yes, alien and deity. Those are the two most common descriptors used for the gazillionaires who disembarked from their private jet in Hanscom Field three decades ago and went on a shopping spree across the U.S., snapping up buildings, skyscrapers, malls, fields, warehouses, banks, colleges, and companies.

In my humble opinion, the Hadezes aren't gods or extraterrestrials. They're foreigners with too much influence and wealth, who should return to their enchanted isle across the Atlantic. The one they aptly baptized "Atlantis" after a mine chockful of blue diamonds was unearthed. Images of this fabled trove abound on the internet, even though every drone that's ever ventured over the landmass has been shot down, every boat that's sailed too close to its shores has been sunk, and the tourist industry is nonexistent.

Bryn emerges from the silver bullet of a car, short strawberry-blonde locks swishing against the huge gold hoops speared through her lobes.

"I don't think you can park the car like that," Valenti says to her legs, which are ensconced in black thigh-highs and a leather miniskirt.

Her eyebrows climb up her forehead in time with one corner of her mouth.

The driver behind her diagonal parking job lays on his horn

before swerving around her ride and cursing her out. Bryn flips him off.

I sidle against the shop door and cross my arms over my chest. "Did you rob an Audi dealership?"

She twirls a key fob hooked to a Louis Vuitton charm. "Little gift from Saul."

"Saul gave you a car?"

"Gave one to Macrazy and one to Mom, too." She waggles her eyebrows. "Although Mom's came with a driver."

"Saul? As in Saul Hadez?" Valenti asks, still playing doorstop.

I cut my eyes at the man, silently begging Bryn to get rid of the guy.

She tosses her keys into a quilted leather tote that looks as new as her car. "Managed to snag us the last two STD appointments of the day. Ready, Callie?"

I choke on a startled snort, then mouth in between coughs, *Really? STDs?*

Mr. Valenti clears his throat. "I'd better get going." After a beat, he says, "You should be careful of Saul. Of that whole family." The craft paper creaks against his chest.

"Agreed." I say this before realizing it might give him a reason to stay.

When he opens his mouth, Bryn chirrups, "Give Mrs. Valenti our best." She flashes him her signature beauty pageant contestant smile—lots of lip, a hint of teeth.

In seconds, the man's nothing more than a blur amid the unrelenting raindrops.

Bryn strides into the shop, pushing a damp lock off her face. "Since you couldn't come to the party"—she extracts a bottle of red wine from her tote, making her armload of bangles and beaded bracelets jangle—"I'm bringing the party to you."

"Party? I thought it was a family lunch?"

"It was. Turned into a party, though." Her heels clack as she circles the wall of succulents to the wooden commode. She yanks open a drawer, then roots around for the flower-shaped corkscrew she bought me as a sympathy gift when it became clear that Mom would no longer be running the shop.

"So…" I nod to her silver ride. "The car?"

"A party favor."

"Forget our pressing gonorrhea appointments. Lead the way to the merrymaking."

Snickering, Bryn stabs the top of the bottle with the corkscrew. "Party favors were for future Hadezes only."

My mouth pops in time with the cork. "Your mom and Saul got engaged? They've been dating for all of a minute and a half!"

"True love doesn't wait." She doesn't bother looking around for glasses, choosing instead to tip the bottle straight to her mouth. After a long swallow, she hands it over.

I just hold it against my chest. "You're going to be related to those people."

"Sure am." Her amber eyes sparkle. "I think Bryn Hadez has a nice ring to it, don't you?"

"You never took your dad's last name, yet you're considering taking your stepdad's?"

"I wouldn't be changing it for Saul. I'd be changing it for Malachi."

"I'm still confused."

She spreads her arms. "You're looking at the future Mrs. Malachi Hadez."

"He also proposed?"

"It's a work in progress." She chin-nods to the bottle. "Are you going to drink that or just hug it?"

My best friend wants to become one of *them*? A trailer full of unicorns crashing through the storefront would've surprised me less.

"Oh, and guess who Macrazy's got her eye on?"

Knowing Bryn's scheming half-sister, it could be anyone on Forbes's Billionaires list. "Who?"

"Tarian."

My heartbeats clank against the bottle, vibrating the wine

inside. "Mackenzie's interested in a man who murdered his own father?"

"The girl would marry a convict if he was rich enough." She eases the bottle from my death grip and holds it up. "Do you realize I'm about to earn god status?"

"The Hadezes aren't gods. They're monsters."

"To gods and monsters." She winks at me, and even though she's the one who drinks, it's my head that spins.

My best and only friend is about to play house with the most dangerous men in Boston.

# TWO

**M**y tongue feels as desiccated as the petals I dry to make potpourri, and my brain, as scrambled as the eggs I remembered feeding myself last night.

Oh, god. The eggs. They lurch up my throat.

I toss the sheets off my legs and scramble to my ensuite bathroom just as my dinner makes an unfortunate reappearance.

I didn't drink that much last night, did I?

The fact that I'm asking myself is probably not a good sign. My stomach spasms, and I fold myself anew over the toilet bowl. As the nausea recedes, the night rolls through me in vivid detail.

The empty wine bottle I shared with Bryn.

Finding Mom asleep on the couch and tucking her in.

Cooking scrambled eggs.

Deciding to have one more drink at the bar across the road from the flower shop.

Having the mental wherewithal to lock all the doors and turn on Mom's monitor app.

Bryn reducing her parking ticket to confetti.

Logan pouring brownish drinks in front of us that he dubbed "Atlantitarians."

Snorting at the name, because how could I not?

Discussing the one pro and million cons of Bryn's mother marrying the sixty-year-old, silver-haired Hadez.

Another wave of acid singes my throat and splashes in the toilet. Today is going to hurt. I glance toward my curtains outlined in dull light. Here's to hoping Mom's not awake yet.

I would've heard her. I think.

I throw up twice more before hitting the shower. Since my underwear and sleep tee need as much washing as my body, and our washer-dryer gave up the ghost last year, I don't bother getting undressed.

After lathering and guzzling down water straight from the shower head, I begin to feel a little less like roadkill. The feeling fades when I catch a whiff of my bathroom. I bleach-clean every surface, then brush my teeth and spritz the air with as much perfume as our upstairs' neighbor, Mrs. Fiona, wears to her Irish dance lessons.

After scrounging up a clean thong, I wrap my long hair in a towel and flop back onto my bed. I curse the Hadezes since it's technically their fault I ingested so much alcohol and grab my phone from the charger on my nightstand.

Go, me, for remembering.

I check the video-monitor app to find Mom still blissfully asleep. Then again, it's six fifty-two a.m. I curl onto my side and close my eyes.

I WAKE to the sound of tinkling metal. At first, I think it's part of my dream, but then I hear Mom's cheery voice through my closed window wishing someone a blooming day.

I jump out of bed so fast the room spins. When my papered walls come back into focus, I'm lying spread-eagled on my purple rug.

"What the hell did you put in that cocktail, Logan?" I grumble, forcing my ragdoll limbs to bend.

I suppose a better question would be, what *didn't* he put in there? As I wrestle on a sports bra, I decide "Atlantitarians" should be illegal.

I dial Bryn to make sure she's still breathing, but it goes straight to voicemail. Since she's a fashion influencer, she has no set office hours. Oh, to be her…

I pull on my uniform of black tights, vintage concert tee, and stilettos. The tops are courtesy of my music-obsessed parents, and the shoes, courtesy of Bryn, who gifted them to me after she posted a picture of herself wearing them on her Instagram feed.

I stagger through the apartment, grab a banana and some crackers from the kitchen, then hurry downstairs to find the garlands of fairy lights twinkling amid the fake ivy Dad nailed to the brick walls.

My mother hums as she rearranges a bunch of white roses inside a vase, a smile playing on her lips. She must hear the click of my heels because she looks up.

I wait for the shine to flicker out of her eyes and the smile to topple off her lips, but both stay intact. "Morning, sunshine."

Blood hammers my veins because she recognizes me. I cradle this rare moment of lucidity. "Hi, Mom. What are you doing?"

"Making a bouquet." She arches a brow that barely rumples her smooth forehead. "So? How was last night?" I open my mouth to answer when she adds, "Did you have fun with Lucas?"

The name hurls me back to the boy I dated all through college, the one I assumed I'd grow old with until he up and dumped me right after my father's funeral.

When Mom begins to frown, I blurt out, "The bell chimed. You had a customer?"

She blinks at me, then at the glass door, and I worry the slim ray of sun that peaked through her mental fog has already burned out of existence, but then she returns her honey-brown eyes my way and smiles. "Yes. Mackenzie Fielding just stopped by to order floral decorations for an event she's hosting tonight."

I can't decide whether I'm more stunned that Bryn's sister stopped by, or that Mom actually remembers who Macrazy is, when half the time, she can't locate Bryn in her memories. But then I shake my head and concentrate on the last part of her sentence. "Tonight?"

"Uh-huh." Mom selects three white roses, then a couple stalks of Baby's Breath.

"And you said...?"

"That we'd be honored to take the job."

"Are you sure we have enough stock?" We have plenty of flowers on hand, but an event usually means bunches and bunches of blooms.

Mom's humming again. It's the Rob Thomas song she used to blast through the apartment to wake me up for school. I have mixed feelings about this song. On the one hand, I love it because it was my parents' wedding song; on the other, I hate it because I'm *not* a morning person.

Also, it reminds me of Dad and of how he used to dance Mom around the shop at closing time or around our tiny kitchen after meals. God, I miss him.

"So, what did Mackenzie Fielding order?"

Mom peers up from the white peonies she's adding to her bouquet. "Huh?"

"You were telling me about Mackenzie Fielding dropping by to order flowers for an event?"

A shallow groove appears between Mom's eyebrows. She's fading.

*Please don't fade. Please.*

"You mentioned Mackenzie stopped by?" Gently, I try to joggle her memory, because as much as I love chatting with Bryn, I'd rather not have to phone up the leggy, blonde ex-model-turned-party-planner for the crème de la crème of New England.

The vertical wrinkle vanishes as her thin eyebrows spring apart. "I jotted down her order." She looks around the shop, dark pixie-cut refracting the glow of the faerie lights, then spins, freezing in front of the lattice screen of succulents. The flowers topple from her arms, landing like feathers at her bare feet.

I move to stand between Dad's last contribution to the shop and my wide-eyed mother. Delicately, I wrap my hands around her biceps and smile, even though my heart is pounding a mile a second. Her pupils pulsate as she scrutinizes my angular jaw, my deep dimples, my smattering of freckles, and the hazel eyes that are a perfect mix of hers and Dad's. *Kaleidoscopic*, he used to call them, because they run the gamut from gray-blue to amber by way of green and yellow.

"I'm sorry, but do we know each other?" She frowns, first at my hands, and then at the empty shop.

At the beginning, when she'd ask me that question, I'd answer, "It's me, Mom. Your daughter." Now, I say, "I'm Calanthe." I wait a heartbeat for my name to register, but her eyes remain blank, and her mouth, parted around hastening breaths. I unclasp her arms, aware that my grip is distressing her. "I work here. In your shop."

Her breathing begins to slow. "Calanthe." She breathes out the three syllables of my name with an emotion akin to reverence—*Ka-lan-thee*. "That's Nick's favorite orchid species. Where is that husband of mine?"

My heart cracks, one half shattering onto the green tiles Dad picked to resemble a field of wild grass, the other half hanging by a thread inside my rib cage. "He went out to deliver some orders."

She stares out the shop window, past the round logo decal that's peeling at the edges. "He didn't take the van."

"It was in the neighborhood, Lisa." I hate using her first name.

Absolutely hate it. But I'm a strange salesgirl to her at the moment, and strangers don't go around calling others Mom. "By the way, he asked me to remind you that your favorite show starts in a few minutes. Would you like me to help you switch on the TV upstairs?"

Mom stares at me as though I've just suggested getting matching tattoos of baby hedgehogs. "I have work."

"Actually, that's why I'm here." I force a smile that dents both my cheeks and mood. "So you can take a break."

"It's not even noon."

"Nick wants you to take it easy."

She shakes her head.

"I'd prefer not being fired my second week on the job. Please?"

One tremendously long minute later, the taut line of her shoulders relaxes. "Okay." Her smile returns, but it's tentative and hardly as bright as the smile she gifts me when she knows who I am.

I gesture to the stairs, and she walks ahead of me. Although she insists I don't need to follow her, I don't give her a choice.

After I get her settled on the couch in front of *Diners, Drive-Ins, and Dives*, I fetch the cocktail of drugs Dr. Kim prescribed during our last visit—pills that are supposed to regulate, block, and release different chemicals in the brain. "Your multivitamins."

If Mom wonders why she has to take so many vitamins or why the new salesgirl is giving them to her, she doesn't say anything. Merely swallows them obediently.

I want to kiss her forehead and tell her that I love her, but it would distress her, so I force my shoulders back and walk to the door.

"What pretty shoes. My daughter loves shoes."

I will her to realize that I'm her daughter since she remembers she has one.

She sucks in a breath. "Cactus! Mackenzie Fielding needs cacti for tonight. Lots of them. Can you tell Nick?"

I startle. "Cacti? Are you sure?"

She nods, burrowing into the throw pillows. "The order form is next to the register."

"Okay."

After syncing the monitoring app, I head back downstairs and, sure enough, find an order form. My eyes bug out as I read it over. Mackenzie gave us a ten-grand budget, and according to the stapled receipt, she's already paid half of it. That's more money than we made in the past month.

Not that all of it will go into our bank account since merchandise needs to be purchased, but still…*ten-thousand dollars.*

I look up the delivery address in Brookline to estimate travel time, then bring up Mackenzie's contact to get more details on what she wants because "cacti" is vague.

> ME: Is there a specific species you want, or do you prefer a mix? And what color pots?

> MACRAZY: Color scheme is chartreuse.

Chartreuse? As I look up the word, another message lights up my screen.

> MACRAZY: I need them by six so be there at four.

I have three hours to find ten-grand's worth of cacti and neon-green pots.

FML.

# THREE

After phoning every plant nursery and garden supply shop in my zip code to secure what I need for Mackenzie's big event, I climb up the rickety staircase to old Mrs. Fiona's gabled apartment, bearing a box of glazed donuts.

The woman has a devastating sweet tooth, or rather denture, since most of her teeth jumped ship from frequenting too many pill mills in her youth. She's been sober for years now, and although she's the busiest busybody on our street, she's also one of the most caring.

I knock, then wait as she unfastens her twenty-plus locks, muttering about how this better be important since her Wordle "ain't gonna solve itself."

"Hi, Mrs. Fiona."

She narrows her eyes on the polka-dot box. "Well, spit it out. What do you need, Callie?"

"For you to hang with Mom for a few hours." I raise the box to eye-level. "I have this big delivery and—"

"It's full?"

I crack a smile because I did once present her with a huge box containing a single stale donut. "Twelve. Eleven for you. One for Mom."

She sniffs the air, then pivots on slippers that look fashioned from skinned racoons, snatches her phone from her doily-covered easy chair, and trundles back toward me with a key ring that puts my old high school custodian's to shame.

I'd hug her if I weren't afraid of smooshing the doughnuts on the white eyelet dress I changed into in the spirit of Mackenzie's Wild West party. Sure, I won't be staying, but I thought it was a cute touch to dress the part. I even dug out a pair of cowboy boots and a felt hat to match, both of which were gathering cobwebs inside Mom's closet.

As Mrs. Fiona locks up, I return to the apartment to inform Mom that our neighbor's Wi-Fi is giving her trouble, so she's coming to use ours.

Mom shifts her gaze off the cookbook I set in her lap. Although she doesn't bake much anymore, she still loves flipping through her prized collection. "Our neighbor?"

"Mrs. Fiona. The lady who lives upstairs. The one who listens to her TV a little too loudly."

As Mom glances at the ceiling as though to catch a glimpse of our hearing-impaired neighbor, I slide the bakery box onto the coffee table.

"How you doin', Lisa?" Mrs. Fiona jangles in, keys clinking on the lanyard around her neck.

Mom startles. "Um…"

"I'm Fi, the cranky coffin-dodger from upstairs."

A careful smile warms Mom's face. "A pleasure to meet you, Fi. I hear you're having internet trouble."

Mrs. Fiona and I exchange a look before she focuses back on Mom. "You know us old folks and new technology."

Mom just smiles but I can feel her underlying tension at having a prattling stranger in our midst.

"I'll see you later." I try to kiss her cheek, but she leans away.

"I'm sorry, but…" She studies me so hard her pupils constrict. "I'm sorry, but who—who are you?"

Mrs. Fiona's ample bosom lifts with pity.

Unable to speak around the lump in my throat, I smile at Mom. The second my back is to her, though, the corners of my mouth collapse.

Mrs. Fiona touches the back of my hand with her gnarled fingers. "I've got her."

I nod. "I should be home around seven, at the latest."

"Callie, I've got her," she repeats gently, giving me permission not to feel guilt for sticking her with this frustrating job.

I grab my bag and cowboy hat from the peg by the door, then swing by the store to make sure all the lights are off before heading out to the van.

FOUR HOURS LATER, car crammed with plants that could potentially gore me if I brake too suddenly, I reach a pair of massive gates. I power down my window and jab the call button. It rings once before someone answers, asking me to state my business.

I mention I'm delivering plants for Mackenzie Fielding.

I expect the gates to sweep open, but they don't. Instead, a man wearing a dark suit, sunglasses, and an earpiece walks over and snaps a picture of my license plate before lifting his phone and photographing my face. Although I can't see his eyes behind his dark lenses, I can feel them assessing me and my prickly entourage.

"Calanthe Bloom." He reads off his screen.

That's some serious facial recognition software.

He presses on his screen and the gate motor groans. "You may proceed up the drive and park beside the pink vehicle."

A pink vehicle? Sure enough, at the end of the very long and sinuous driveway, sits an exact replica of Barbie's convertible. The rosy eyesore must belong to the wife of whichever mogul owns the palatial white mansion.

I hope Macrazy doesn't expect her cacti budget to cover more than one, at the very most *two* rooms in that house, because my time frame was too limited to haggle, and my choice of plants, way too selective.

I park beside the Mattel ride and shut off the engine. My boots hit gravel that's so blindingly white, I can't help but wonder if the stones are power washed daily.

As the Jack Reacher-lookalike drives over in a shiny black golf cart—an understandable necessity considering the length of the driveway—I pull open the van's barn doors.

"My platform trolley's not going to be much use on gravel." I nod to the contents of my van. "Any chance I can borrow your arms?"

Said arms look ready to burst from his suit jacket.

He speaks into a mouthpiece in a language that sounds like a mix of Spanish and Arabic.

A minute later, Mackenzie struts out of the mansion along with two more suit-clad bodybuilders. "You're an hour and thirteen minutes late, Calla Lily!"

I grind my molars. "Rush-hour traffic," I lie, detesting the nickname she gave me the year Bryn and I met at a concert. We were six. Joslyn had brought her daughter along because she was having an affair with the drummer and Mackenzie wouldn't babysit; I was there because my parents loved sharing their joy of music with me. "You know how that is."

"I actually don't anymore. I have police escorts everywhere I go, thanks to Saul." One would think *she* was marrying the man. "So what'd you bring us?"

"The best Arizona had to offer." I sweep my arm toward the interior of my van. "Ta da."

Her bony body goes as rigid as the saguaro I had to lay flat in the van. "What. The fuck. Is that?"

"Cacti."

She rips a pair of bug-eyed sunglasses off her pert nose and glares at the poor plants. "I didn't fucking order cacti. I ordered cream and chartreuse *flowers*." She shuts her eyes and looses this high-pitched growly sound that makes me think of a rabid dog in heat. "I'm going to kill my sister."

I plant a balled fist on my hip, my pulse lashing at my skin. "What does Bryn have to do with this?"

Another shrill whiny noise escapes the high-gloss barrage of her lips. "She convinced me you'd be capable of delivering what we needed, but of fucking course, you and your shit-for-brains Mom—"

Before I can evaluate the consequences of hitting Mackenzie in front of three probably armed men, my palm flies into her cheek. Whatever. I'm so riled-up, I'd bowl them all over with the prickly pear if any of them so much as laid a finger on me. "*Do not* talk about my mother. *Ever*."

Cradling her cheek, she hisses, "Dorian, show the vermin and her—"

Something clicks beside me, and I jump, expecting a cocked gun. Instead, I find a sleek black car and a huge male unfolding himself from the driver's seat. I thought the saguaro was impressive until I saw Reacher, but both pale in comparison to the beast in the white button-down and black suit.

Like Reacher, the man wears dark shades that hide his eyes, yet I can feel them lick up my body, from the pointy tips of my cowboy boots to the flouncy hem of my dress. His inspection is unhurried, as though he's counting the number of eyelets that lead up to the modest V of my halter top. He lingers on my collarbone before moving to the loose chin strap of my cowboy hat and halting on my eyes.

I take a minuscule step away—or maybe it's the force of his stare that blows me back. All I know is that one minute I'm standing my ground, and the next, my open van door is digging into my backside.

Tears leak out of Macrazy's eyes. Since the girl has the emotional range of an acrylic nail, they're all for show.

"What's going on?" The newcomer's voice saws through the air, all jagged edges and quiet steel.

I scoot back another quarter inch.

"This is Bryn's little friend. The one who runs that shop, Boom Boom."

"It's Bloom's Blooms," I mutter under my breath, instantly regretting telling these people where I work.

Then again, the logo's on the van and Reacher has my name and picture. I wouldn't put it past him to have downloaded my entire browser history as well as my blood type. I bet he even knows about my fatal scallop allergy and favorite podcast shows.

"She screwed up everything, and now—" More tears drip into Mackenzie's cupid's bow mouth.

"There was a misunderstanding." I barely separate my teeth around the words.

"And you slapped Miss Fielding, why?" The guy's question causes Mackenzie's lips to twitch smugly.

I square my shoulders. "With all due respect, that's none of your business."

Reacher says something in that weird language of theirs that sharpens the stranger's features. I frown because he looks familiar, yet I can't seem to place the pale skin and sweep of black hair, and—

Oh.

My.

God.

I swing my gaze toward his license plate before zeroing back on Tarian Hadez.

Tarian *I-murdered-my-own-flesh-and-blood* Hadez. Tarian *jaywalkers-can-eat-my-bumper* Hadez.

Even though I spent the deposit and a good chunk of the money still owed on the nursery of cacti in my van, I whirl around and shut the doors. I'll run a huge cacti sale tomorrow. Get Logan to supply me with a few bottles of tequila at cost to color the event.

"I'm so sorry, Tarian." Even though I have my back to her, I can hear Mackenzie's pout.

"What's your name, Calamity?" Tarian's voice reverberates down my spine.

I side-eye him. Is he calling me Calamity because our first, and fingers-crossed, last, encounter was slightly calamitous, or because of my outfit?

"I'm no one, Mr. Hadez. Forget we ever met." As I stride over to the driver's side, I toss over my shoulder, "Mackenzie, I'll give your money back to Bryn when I see her. Hasta la vista."

Did I really just say *hasta la vista*? I suppose it's better than, "Don't let the door hit ya, where the good Lord split ya," which is Logan's favorite farewell, Southern beau that he is.

I try to shut my car door, but it won't budge. A glance upward, and my eyes lock with the cause. Well, with the sleek black lenses of the cause.

"You've got my engagement party decorations in your van."

"*Your* engagement?" *He's* getting married? To whom? I glance back at Mackenzie who's watching Tarian as though she wants to lick his firm body, then suck in a breath, because it all clicks. "Oh, wow."

His black eyebrows slant before leveling out anew. "Wow?"

I shrug a shoulder. "You do you."

Tarian's mouth twitches into what I assume is a smile, but it's hard to tell since I can't see his eyes.

"So you seriously want the cacti?"

Stare unwavering, he drops his voice to a throaty whisper. "I seriously want the cacti, Calamity."

"It's Calanthe."

This time, there's no mistaking his lip spasm for a smile because both corners slope up. Tarian Hadez, the man who has people murdered for a living, is smiling at me, and it's utterly terrifying, because predators only smile when they scent their next kill.

Although he draws my door wide, he doesn't add space between where he stands and where I sit. I've never felt more trapped.

# FOUR

"I believe we've already met, Calamity," Tarian says, voice all suave.

I narrow my eyes, running through a few ideas of nicknames for him since he's so intent on giving me one. Not that I'd ever call him any of the ones scrolling through my head out loud. I rather enjoy having my organs on the inside of my body.

"I have a very common face." I mentally flip him off as I jump out of the driver's seat, spraying pebbles onto his shiny black loafers. Serves him right for not moving his clownishly large feet.

"Hmm." He takes a step back, his mouth tilting. "You're the woman who assaulted my car with a rose yesterday."

I scoff. "Assaulted is a bit dramatic."

"So you remember?"

"I remember almost getting run over by an ass—ton Martin." Heat creeps up my neck, which I start to rub manically.

Teeth flash between his very curved lips. "Bugatti, actually."

"There was a spider on the rose," I mumble.

"Poor spider."

"I was trying to save its life." I regret not having worn my tallest wedges because I have to cant my head to meet his stare. "Anyway, I should really get those cacti inside your house before Mackenzie axes me."

My hat slips off, drifting to my shoulder blades, where it settles thanks to the chin strap. After maintaining eye contact long enough to establish that I'm not *intimidated—much—*I head to the back of my van and unlatch the doors.

Mackenzie jerks her fingers off the bleached tips of her long hair. "What are you doing?"

"Mr. Hadez asked me to unload the cacti. I'm unloading them." I scoop out the prickly pear.

Her blue eyes, that aren't the least bit red-rimmed from her fifteen-second crying session, widen. "Saul will hate them, Tarian."

Wait, wait, wait. *Saul?*

"It's your mother's job to please him, Miss Fielding, not mine. Besides, it's my home, therefore, my decorating choices."

I readjust my hold on the flowerpot, realizing I totally misread the situation. No wonder Tarian looked confused with my *you do you* comment, since he's apparently *not* doing Macrazy. "Sorry to interrupt, but where do you want them?"

"Miss Fielding will show you." The owner of the huge mansion and huge shoes shrugs out of his suit jacket, folds it neatly, then tosses it onto the backseat of the golf cart. He threads one gold cufflink out of its buttonhole, followed by the other, and then rolls up his shirtsleeves.

It's not a striptease, yet somehow, the way he drags the whole thing out makes it come across as utterly licentious. The man has really nice forearms—long, roped with lean muscle, and dusted with dark hair. Probably honed to such perfection by beating up innocents and strangling weaker men.

I start to turn away when I catch sight of a trail of ink that runs from his wrist bone to his elbow before disappearing beneath his folded French cuff. Are those words? Sentences? I spy another line on his left arm.

"Calanthe!" Mackenzie clicks her fingers in front of my face, making me jump and stab myself in the shoulder with the prickly pear.

Serves me right for ogling murderers. Macrazy must be rubbing off on me.

I give the bleating blonde my full attention and follow in her stilettos' wake.

Once we reach the gaping front door, she says, "Even though Tarian is being preposterously compassionate, you totally screwed up, so don't expect further business."

That wasn't compassion; that was Tarian thumbing his nose at Saul. Which leads me to wonder if she's deliberately delusional because she wants to see the best in the mob boss, or if she's truly *that* unperceptive.

"Well, damn," I say. "Here I was holding my breath for a partnership."

"Not happening."

Obtuse it is, then.

Her heels click in a foyer paved in matte, beige stone riddled with tiny, natural depressions—travertine. How do I know the name? Because Dad was obsessed with HGTV, and one of the thousands of episodes we watched together featured a home fashioned entirely from this stone. He'd decided that the day he built his and Mom's dream home, it'd be paved and walled in travertine.

My heart squeezes at the thought.

I don't realize I've stopped walking until a deep voice rasps right beside my ear, "The first thing that draws most women's gazes when they step past my threshold is the expensive art on my walls or the breadth of my entry hall, yet you, Calamity, seem enraptured by my floors."

"I was expecting the fires of Hell, or the stones to runneth over with blood."

I think I've stunned the man into silence with my deprecating humor. Truth be told, I wasn't expecting puddles of gore or flames, but I also wasn't expecting a ruthless murderer to have anything in common with my sweet father.

"Ah, that would be my dungeon you're describing. Would you care for a tour after we're done unloading the party ornaments?" He sounds serious but he can't be, right?

I'm racking my brain for a polite way to say *hard pass* when I catch sight of the yellowish green—sorry, chartreuse—flowerpot he supports on one palm. It's not a small pot, which says a lot about his hands. It also says quite a lot about him. I'd never have anticipated Tarian Hadez to lift a finger, much less five.

Maybe I was a little harsh in calling the male with the alluring forearms and solid fingers an asshole.

*He killed his father, Calanthe,* my conscience shrieks. *Don't be fooled. He's probably helping to get you out of here faster.*

Behind him, Reacher is toting four pots as though they were filled with nothing more than ferns, while the two other security guards haul in the saguaro.

"Calanthe!" Macrazy's shrill voice resonates against the two-story ceilings and paint-splattered canvases.

"Coming." With a sigh, I follow Miss Fuchsia Power Suit into another breezy room just off the grand hall. A backlit slab of quartz stretches from one end of the room to the other, surrounded by two dozen chairs.

Tarian may be a private person, but the scale of his manor and slew of furniture speak of a social person. I wonder who, besides those aforementioned women, gets an invitation into this gated mansion. Other Atlanteans? Fellow mobsters?

"Put the cactus over here." Macrazy points a flaccid finger toward the end of the table that's set with goldware, fine bone china, and amethyst wineglasses.

I count eight place settings as I park my cactus on the glowing quartz. Mackenzie shelled out ten grand on flowers for a puny dinner party? Who has that amount of—

*Saul.* Saul does. Or I suppose Tarian, since this is his house.

"It's impolite to stare," Mackenzie hisses after having the two men park the saguaro beside the prickly pear.

I'd bet the house, or rather the shop, that Mackenzie stared a whole lot the first time she strutted in here. "Geez, I'm not casing the joint for a future burglary."

"Glad to hear it." Oddly enough, Tarian is still wearing his sunglasses. Is he worried I may snap a selfie with him that'd reveal the blackness of his soul, since eyes are windows and whatnot, or is there something wrong with his gaze? "But if you were to rob me, what is it that you'd steal?"

What an odd question. Without looking away from him, I say, "Nothing. You have nothing I want."

"Everyone wants something from me."

"I want my father back. Can you bring the dead back to life, Mr. Hadez, or is that not in the realm of your supposed godly powers?"

A choked sound erupts from Mackenzie.

Tarian sighs. "When did he die?"

Did I hope he'd say, *Lead the way to the graveyard*? No. But did I envision he'd ask for details? Also no.

"Two years ago," Mackenzie answers for me. "A heart attack, wasn't it? Oh, wait, no. It was an aneurysm. I remember Bryn mentioning something about his brain bursting."

The outsized dining room fades, and I'm back in the cramped hospital room with Mom and the doctor who's explaining that even though my father's heart still pumps, there's no more brain activity.

I blink out of the nightmarish memory, blink again to whisk away the gathering moisture, and then I walk out of the mansion toward my van and concentrate on getting this day over with. Soon, thanks to the extra sets of arms, Tarian's quartz table resembles the Mojave desert.

I pull my hat off, the chinstrap feeling like it's choking me, and rub my throat. "That's the last of it, Mackenzie."

However much I can't stand the woman, I have to admit that she's talented. Not only has she smashed cookies and sprinkled the crumbs around the cacti to give the illusion of sand, but she's also propped golden candles here and there in the imitation-dunes. The effect is breathtaking. Especially with the sun setting beyond the picture window that gives onto a sprawling garden.

"Do you prefer settling the bill now or stopping by the shop tomorrow?" I ask.

Mackenzie doesn't look up from the hungry flame tipping her gas lighter. "Settle the bill? You got my order wrong, Calla Lily, so there won't be any *bill-settling*. If anything, consider yourself lucky I'm letting you keep the deposit."

I gape. "I spent more than that on what I bought."

"Not my problem."

"Except it is. You accepted the delivery. You owe—"

"Mr. Hadez accepted it. Not me." Her cruel mouth curves into a smile that glitters with candlelight. "You want the rest of your money, go beg him."

I strangle my hat strap. "I'll come by to collect my cacti tomorrow, then." I may be low on cash, but I'm not going to throw myself at anyone's feet, especially not a Hadez's. Tarian would probably shoot me down, and not figuratively speaking.

"Sure. But make sure to arrive before the garbage truck."

"You're planning on tossing them?"

She shrugs a shoulder. "I don't recycle party decorations. Besides, desert-chic isn't in vogue." She backs up to scrutinize her handiwork. "You're lucky I'm amazing at my job. Now, get. The party's about to commence, and you're not on the guestlist."

Macrazy's iciness roots my cowboy boots to the smoke-colored floorboards.

"Shoo." She wiggles her pointed acrylic nails that are as hot-pink as the pantsuit she wears sans camisole.

I'm tempted to claw her beauty-queen face but decide to be the bigger person. I also decide that, although I won't beg anyone for money, I'll ask Reacher to store my plants so I can swing by to collect them come morning.

As I stalk out of the dining room, I collide with Tarian.

"Fuck," he mutters, reflexively banding one arm around my waist to steady me.

I try to extricate myself, but his arm is a steel beam.

"Sorry," I mutter, shooting down the ball of anger scorching my throat like I shot down Logan's Atlantitarian last night. It burns just the same, and combined with the spicy, leathery scent drifting from the vee of skin peeking from Tarian's shirt collar, it makes my head spin and my stomach churn. "Um, Mr. Hadez, you can let go."

He doesn't.

I shove his chest. The male must be dead set on seeing how far he can push me, because there's zero give to his grip.

I crane my neck and bite out, "Please fucking let…" The word *go* transforms into a shallow gasp as my eyes lock on his sunglass-free stare.

# FIVE

My pulse rushes against my eardrums when Calamity gasps. Did my magic—

"They're black," she says, nose scrunched.

"Beg your pardon?"

"Your eyes. They're black."

I find myself inspecting her stare, which is the color of my woods at sunset—a swirl of maple, gold, and green. The pigments eddy as she scrutinizes me in a manner most wouldn't dare. Not if they have any instinct for self-preservation.

"Were you expecting them to—how did you put it earlier?" My gaze slides over the freckles splashed across her cheekbones and the ghost of her dimples before lowering to the seam of her pillowy lips. *Runneth over with blood?*

"No. Maybe." She snags her lip with teeth so white they heighten the coral hue of her mouth. "Since you're never photographed without sunglasses, I thought there might be something wrong with them."

Rumors thrive about why Atlanteans cover their eyes, some nearer to the truth than others. "You study pictures of me?"

"No. I most certainly do not." She wrinkles her nose, yet a flush steals across her neck and cheekbones.

"Now that you've uncovered that my eyes aren't red from lid to lid, won't you stay for dinner?"

Her pulse quickens beneath my forearm, its frenzied nips tiptoeing past her spine and juddering my bones. "I really have to get home." She glances past me at the front door I've left gaping.

"Surely you don't still have a curfew?"

She swings her attention back to me. "Surely, since I'm twenty-four. What I have, though, is someone waiting for me."

"Who?" I ask, before wondering why on earth I care. Because she shot me down, and no one ever shoots me down? Because the idea of her racing home to some idiot makes my blood simmer?

"Someone. Thanks for"—she gestures in the general direction of the dining room—"your leniency."

Her cheeks dimple as though she were biting back words. She must decide she's done with our conversation though, because nothing more comes out of her mouth as she attempts to step back.

I don't make a habit of holding anyone against their will—well, anyone I don't intend to kill—yet I can't seem to let this woman go. If I weren't so worried about spooking her, I'd rake her in closer. The mere fantasy makes my balls tighten and my dick throb against the zipper of my trousers. The last time I experienced such a flood of lust was… I can't even recall.

"Mr. Hadez." Her pupils are so dilated that only a gilded ring of color remains. "Your arm."

The sound of tires crushing gravel reminds me that my family is about to descend upon my home. I suddenly don't want any of them to lay eyes on her. Especially not my younger brother Symeon, who enjoys nothing more than taking things that belong to me. Although I usually let him "win" them, I don't want him to come within an inch of this girl.

"Let me walk you to your—" My jaw clenches in time with every bone and joint in my body.

*No.*

*Fuck.*

Dread paces up and down my spine as my body warms… burns. As the ancient runes that adorn my skin flare.

Calanthe's breath catches and excavates the hollow in her collarbone. I pray it isn't because she can feel the heat of the words that have poisoned my blood since I dropped through the earth's crust and into an enchanted mine thirty years ago.

She smacks my pec, for balance or to get away, I'm not entirely certain. "Please let go."

I shouldn't appreciate her chafed tone or her pointed glower, but I do, because they mean that my brutish manners are to blame and not my wicked magic.

She crooks one arm to reach behind her back. "Seriously."

When her fingers cinch my wrist, I murmur, "I'm trying, Calamity."

"Try harder."

I'd have smiled if trepidation weren't chewing through me.

I will my elbow to bend; it doesn't. I exercise so much pressure on my joint that the bone will undoubtedly pop from its socket. I grit my teeth, desperately trying to smother the surge of magic, but my body stiffens some more. And then…

My nostrils flare as fiery pain gloves my arm and an archaic word lifts off my flesh, swoop by agonizing swoop.

I want to growl and rage. Instead, I stand there, pitiful and useless, imploring our Atlantean goddess not to transfer the rune. I'd rather she take them back, take *all* her cursed words back.

The fear that blanches Calanthe's eyes stops my heart.

*Fuck.* I'm an asshole. I should've released her immediately.

Her fingers skitter off my wrist bone, and her cowboy hat tumbles from her fingers. Although its fall is noiseless, my pulse is so taut that it sounds like crashing cymbals when felt meets travertine.

I thought I understood how to wield my runes like a weapon. I thought I was in control, but either my powers are morphing, or they're beginning to control me. Either way, it's fucking terrifying.

A hiss trips from her lips a second before the fire recedes from my veins, and I manage to release her. She stumbles back, palming her spine where the toxic word gored her. How long will Calanthe have? A week like my father? Two? A year? Will it depend on the word that transferred from my skin to hers?

An apology clings to my flattened lips, but how does one apologize for ending an innocent's life?

"What the hell was that?" She peers over her shoulder.

I've doomed you, that's what it was. I've fucking doomed you because I couldn't set you free.

Since I can't explain what the hell that was to a mortal, I scrub a hand through my hair and feign ignorance. "What was *what*?"

"You"—she licks her quivering lips—"*stung* me."

I want to shove my shirtsleeve back up to see which word deserted me, but the only muscle I seem capable of flexing is my jaw. "Last I checked, I was no wasp."

Her beautiful gaze tapers.

"You should go home. You don't want to keep that special someone waiting, Calamity." Pathetic, I'm aware, but the covetous prick that I am is hoping her special someone is a four-legged mongrel, even though I have no claim over this girl, and she has no future because of me. "Don't forget your hat." My voice is as rigid as my body.

Her glower grows, and in spite of the sun's absence, her eyes flash with that reflective glow only Atlanteans possess. If I had any doubt that my magic infiltrated her blood, it withers like another piece of my rotten soul.

# SIX

One word comes to mind, flashing like the bulbs on a marquee—prick.

Tarian Hadez is a giant one, at that. Yes, *I* ran into *him*, but did he have to hold me? And what the hell did he do to my back? He may claim he isn't a wasp, and I may not believe in supernaturals, but he's a mobster. He probably pricked me with a dirty needle full of drugs or nicked my skin with a hidden weapon.

When I pull my arm out from behind my back, my fingers aren't stained with blood. I'm one-part surprised, one-part relieved, and a trillion-and two-parts confused. Oh, and pissed off. I didn't think anyone could incense me more than Macrazy, but apparently, the beast with the sly eyes and crooked smirk can top her.

Shooting him one last glare, I scoop up my cowboy hat and stride across the beige stone, giving the male a wide berth.

I reach the door just as a midnight-blue car glides into the spot beside Tarian's, streamlined taillights jeweling the obscurity. The purr of the engine shuts off, and two more broad men emerge. I recognize both from the tabloids—Symeon and Malachi Hadez. The brother and the cousin.

I'm not usually one to stare, but I look my fill on my way to my van. May as well since I don't plan to ever set foot anywhere near this family again. Not even if Bryn ends up dating golden-haired Malachi. I itch to call her and warn her away from the lot of them. Maybe Malachi isn't as—whatever the hell Tarian is—but he's nonetheless an Atlantean.

A girl slinks out of the backseat, and for a millisecond, I think it's Bryn, what with her shoulder-length hair that gleams amber like my friend's, but then I see her feed her arm through Symeon's.

Bryn may have a crush on Malachi, but she isn't a fan of Tarian's little brother, who's apparently constantly high and has an ego the size of Boston, suburbs included. The girl is the first to spot me, but her companions are quick to follow.

None of them are wearing sunglasses. Then again, night crawled over the sky while I helped Mackenzie recreate the Arizonan desert on Tarian's giant dining table.

The girl's marked eyebrows arch as she observes me. I want to mutter, "What are you looking at?" but that'd be hypocritical, considering I'm doing the same.

My spine tingles, and although I resist the urge to touch it, it reminds me to haul ass off this property.

When the girl glances toward the mansion entrance, I look over my shoulder, and my gaze collides with Tarian's. He isn't wreathed in shadows, yet the male exudes darkness—like those debonair villains who whisper seductive words as they run the edge of their blades across their victim's neck.

Although the sting of whatever he did has dulled, the memory hasn't. I inject my stare with every last ounce of my fury, then notch up my chin, screw my hat on, and refocus on my getaway vehicle.

Headlights splash me, and my heart lurches to a stop in time with my body.

Instead of jumping to the side, I raise my arms, squeeze my eyes shut, and brace myself for impact. Clearly, my survival instinct needs work.

*Let the driver hit the brakes.*

*Please, let the driver hit the brakes.*

Like the tweaked string of a harp, my spine tenses, vibrates, hurtling adrenaline into my extremities and flooding my muscles until they feel as rigid as bone.

A second later, metal crunches and air whooshes past my shoulders, blowing my hat off and lifting the ends of my hair.

Steam hisses from somewhere. Since it doesn't seem to be coming from me, I crack a lid open.

The hinges of my jaw go slack as I take in the crumpled silver hood that grazes my thighs. I swing my gaze to the windshield, to the puffed airbag that obstructs my sight of the driver, then back down to the craggy metal folded like an accordion, then lower, to the pebbled driveway because, evidently, the car hit something, and that something wasn't me since my thighs aren't made of mortar.

Bryn stumbles out of the driver's side on rickety legs that lend her the gait of a newborn foal. "Callie?"

I can't reel in my jaw. All I can seem to manage is to breathe. I'm even afraid to move, unsure about my balance.

Bryn just stands there, gripping the side of her door, blinking through the lavender smoke that curls out of her destroyed hood. "Oh my god, Callie. I almost ran into you!"

The heat of the puffing engine does nothing to dispel the goosebumps, which zing and spread when a palm connects with the small of my back.

I jolt my head sideways and up, aligning it with Tarian's. "Don't touch me," I snarl.

Slowly, he withdraws his hand, the sharp edges of his ticking jaw silvered by the wreck's headlights. His mouth shifts, but my ears are ringing, so I can't hear what he says. I can only stare dumbly, wondering, *How am I alive?*

Bryn sprints toward me and throws her arms around my neck, imprinting the shape of each bangle and bead into my skin. "I can't believe I almost hit you!" She muffles a sob against my shoulder.

As I pat her back to soothe her, Symeon and his girlfriend approach.

"Are you all right?" I think the redhead's asking me until I notice her gaze locked on Tarian.

Symeon's black eyebrows wing up as he also glances at his brother. There's an air of resemblance between the two—the shady eyes, black hair, and vampiric complexion—but where Tarian's locks are trimmed and artfully controlled, Symeon's are wild and curly. And where Tarian is tall and lean, Symeon is broad and compact. Another notable difference is their fashion style— Symeon, with his short-sleeve white tee and stone-washed jeans, looks ready for a rave; Tarian, for a board meeting.

"Can someone explain to me what the car hit?" I ask.

"A forcefield." Tarian's voice is barely above a whisper, yet it strikes my ears with the strength of a bat, sending my sanity flying right out of me.

Bryn jerks away from me, whisking away her tears with trembling fingertips. "A what now?"

"A forcefield. A barrier made of energy." Tarian raises a hand and flicks his fingers, and the Audi careens into one of the trees lining the driveway.

"Did you—did you—" I swallow, but that doesn't help me digest any of what I've just witnessed and heard. "Did you just move the car with your hand?"

His eyes, which are on me—*again*—seem to glow with some otherworldly light. "With my mind, actually. My hand only gave it direction."

"I told you he was a real god," Bryn hisses into my ear.

My heart, which has been clattering since my near-death experience, pulses out so many beats that its rhythm would probably register as an irregular line on an EKG and set off a bunch of alarms.

Tarian fixes his demonic stare on Bryn. "You crashed your car into a tree, Miss Fielding. You're shaken but fine."

What the actual fuck?

Bryn nibbles on a hangnail. "I can't believe I managed to crash in your driveway."

I gawk at her, then at Tarian, who says, "Most accidents happen in parking lots and driveways."

What the hell did he do to her memory? "You honestly didn't see the tree?"

"I was a little distracted, Callie. A bee attacked me."

My head rears back.

"Okay, maybe it didn't attack me, but it was buzzing around my face, and you know me and insects." She grimaces. "Don't look at me like that."

"Like, what?" It comes out husky, as though her killer bee is currently lodged in my throat.

"Like I'm insane for fearing tiny creatures."

My gaze climbs back to Tarian, who's exchanging quiet words with Malachi. Although I've never thought her insane for fearing bugs—I mean, *hello, spiders*—I do wish she'd muster a modicum of fear for the creatures crowding us. Creatures who look like men, talk like men, yet can mess with people's minds and create freaking forcefields!

Tarian's eyes glow like those of a cat. He's probably about to strip *my* mind of the events that unfolded. I wait for his lips to form more lies, but when they do move, it's to say, "Mal, take Bryn inside."

My shoulders stiffen. Is he sending my friend away to do more than tamper with my memory? And if that's his plan, what chance do I have of getting away before he can flick his fingers and send *me* hurtling headfirst into a tree?

# SEVEN

**B**ryn tucks one of my hands between hers. "Come."

I eye my car, assessing how fast I could reach it while hauling Bryn along, because I'm not leaving her behind with these mind-scramblers.

"Your friend will join you in a minute." Although Tarian speaks to Bryn, his eyes are locked on mine.

"No." I shake my head. "I'm leaving, and so is Bryn."

"I can't, hun. Mom would be—"

"Because she's always there when you need her?" I don't mean to sound caustic, but Joslyn is a terrible mother. "Please come with me. Please."

My desperation furrows Bryn's brow. I think she's about to relent when she glances toward Malachi, who stands shoulder-to-shoulder with Tarian, arms crossed in front of his black button-down shirt. He better not coerce her to go inside. I watch his eyes, daring him to flick on his glowy power.

Bryn refocuses on me. "How about we stay for one glass of champagne and then we leave?"

"No." I clutch her fingers.

Symeon and his girlfriend exchange quiet words in that same language Tarian used with his guard. Probably Atlantean, or whatever their native tongue is called.

"One drink sounds like a fair compromise." Says the man who tossed me out of his house only a moment ago.

"I didn't ask for your input, Hades."

Bryn's eyes pop at my deliberately erroneous pronunciation of their family name, which I find a hell of a lot more suitable for a family of mobsters.

"Why's the party out here?" Mackenzie's screech slices through the tense darkness. "Well, shit, Bryn. Is that your car?" She sticks a hand on her narrow hip. "You've had it for one whole day."

I'm not sure why I'm still surprised that Mackenzie's concern for the Audi's state of disrepair would top her concern for her sister.

"Cars are replaceable. Siblings aren't." Tarian's stringently delivered words level Macrazy's puckered lips. "Thankfully, your sister was unharmed."

Even though I trust him as far as I can throw him—and I *can't* throw him…probably can't even push him—I appreciate the comeback.

Mackenzie gestures to Bryn. "I can see that she's unharmed, which is *why* I commented on the car. Anyway, the bubbly's getting tepid, and no one likes warm champagne." Mackenzie's attention veers to Symeon and his girlfriend. "Oh, Yasmin. *Heyyy.* I'm so glad you could make it!"

"Wouldn't miss Saul's engagement for the world." Yasmin's lips stretch into a smile that lacks warmth. Does she dislike her boyfriend's uncle, or does she dislike the girl in the hot-pink pantsuit? "See the rest of you inside." She tugs on Symeon's arm, and together, they walk toward the mansion entrance, pausing once to pick up something.

That something happens to be my hat. Symeon frisbees it over to Tarian, who whips out his hand and catches it without so much as a glance in its direction. He's either endowed with the best reflexes or some extra godly senses.

Once they've hiked past her, Mackenzie plants herself back in the doorway like some lurid, humanoid version of Cerberus. One would think she owned the house. "Bryn, you remembered to bring the *something blue* for Mom, right?"

"Sym mentioned he'd take care of it."

"You delegated the *one* job I gave you to someone who has an actual job?"

Bryn purses her lips. "He bought a machine to produce lab-grown diamonds, remember? He told us about it at lunch yesterday."

"Your point?"

"He offered to make Mom blue earrings. Ring a bell? Anyway, I'm sure he brought them."

"How about you go *check*?" Could Mackenzie sound anymore passive-aggressive?

Muttering under her breath, Bryn pulls away from me.

"Bryn, please. No. Stay with me. Leave with me."

"I'll call you as soon as I manage to escape, okay?" Bryn shoots me a stoic smile, squares her shoulders, then marches toward the house like a soldier heading into battle.

Tarian murmurs something in Atlantean to Malachi that makes him go after her. He better not have given his cousin an order to murder my friend.

Mackenzie shuffles out of his way but doesn't retreat inside. If I had to take a wild guess, she's waiting for Tarian.

"You should really stop patronizing your sister, Mackenzie."

Her gaze swings off Tarian. "Excuse me, Calla Lily?"

"Bryn has an *actual* job."

"How about you mind your own fuc—" She chokes. "Gah." She coughs, then wheezes. "I think I swallowed a bug."

Clutching her throat, she spins on her heels and canters into the house.

A smug smile seizes my lips. Karma can be such a bitch.

"Calamity?"

"Stop calling me—"

His dark eyes flash like reflective tape. "Your friend crashed her car into a tree. You're too shaken to drive home, so you'll allow me to take you."

My jaw aches from how hard I'm clenching it. "The hell I'll let you drive me anywhere, Hades."

His lashes sweep low, extinguishing the inhuman glow, and then he sighs. "That's what I thought."

"That's what you *thought*?" I repeat stupidly.

"We need to talk. We can either do it out here, in my office, or inside my car while I drive you home."

"I have a car. Besides, I don't accept rides from strangers. Bring my friend back out of your house, and I'll leave. And I'll never speak a word of what I just saw."

Tarian smiles, but it's not really a smile. "You know what *I* don't accept from strangers, Calamity? Their promises to keep quiet about something that concerns me."

My heart stops.

Just stops.

For a second, I think he may have ripped it out of my ribcage and flung it against the tree, but then it starts pounding again, and its frenzied beats flood my mouth with the taste of metal.

"Aren't you curious as to why you resisted my compulsion?"

*Compulsion...* I feel like I've been teleported onto the set of a supernatural TV show. When he tips his head, I wonder if it's too late to pretend like his mind-warping skill actually worked.

I slide my lips together, fold them. Ugh. I'm too desperate to understand to act dumb or indifferent. "I'm listening." I keep my eyes on his, now that I know he can't influence me. "Why am I special?"

Dark smile still in place, he hands me my cowboy hat. Only

when I'm clutching the felt do I realize I've just freed up both his hands. Wringing my neck will be all the easier. Although, considering the breadth of his hands, one would've done the job.

I stick my hat in front of my chest and hold it there like a shield as he shrugs out of his jacket. *Okayyy*…so maybe he's not reaching into his jacket for a gun or a scythe, or whatever other weapon Atlanteans wield. Besides magic, that is.

"The suspense is killing me, Hades."

His eyes gleam, but not with compulsion. Not with amusement either. I'd call it annoyance, but it seems too petty an emotion for a preternatural being.

"The discomfort you experienced earlier…" He rolls up one shirtsleeve, revealing, once again, the black scribbles that abut the hinge of his wrist and vanish beneath the silken cotton. "It was caused by my magic."

"Your *magic* stung me?"

"Yes."

His driveway lights wink out of existence, and I jump. I try to reassure myself that they're motion-activated. That he didn't turn them off to frighten me.

Still, I take a step back. "Why?"

"To kill you."

# EIGHT

"**I**'m sorry, *what*?" Calanthe smooshes her hat against her heaving chest. "Did you just say you want to *kill me*?"

"My magic does, not me. If I'd wanted you dead, I wouldn't have stopped Bryn's car."

"Is that supposed to reassure me?" I don't miss the extra step back she takes.

What am I to do with this girl? I can't let her walk away with the knowledge of us, yet sequestering her in one of my many rooms feels unjust. I may have few scruples, but the few that I have keep me from forcing her to spend her last days with only me for a companion.

I relocate my attention to the runes inscribed on my skin. Even though I expect the empty space, the word that's amiss startles me. I run the charmed sentence through my mind to make sure I'm not misremembering it, but every time, I come up with the same word.

I gaze back at her, perplexed.

"What?" Her voice is more breath than sound.

"Show me your back."

"What? No."

"Now." I reason that it has probably already morphed into an "X" inside a circle like it did on my father's skin, but still…

"You're insane." She starts for her car, and although it's a dickish move, I stop her with a wall of wind that kicks up her long tresses and exposes the vertebrae cloaked in smooth skin. If only her zipper started lower.

She whirls, fury glossing her vibrant eyes. Although I'm the cause of it, I can't help but admire her fire. "I'm not some toy, Hades."

"A glimpse of your back, and I'll let you leave."

"Why?"

"Because something doesn't make sense."

"Something?" She releases a high-pitched snort. "I'd say *nothing* fucking makes sense." I catch her pinching her arm.

"I'm real, Calamity." I take a step toward her. "A nightmare, perhaps, but still very real." I step so close that the hat she holds as a buoy and buffer brushes my chest. "I know it's a lot to absorb."

"You *know*?" Her fury turns maniacal. "You have *no* idea how I'm feeling right now. None."

Unlike Symeon or Saul, I've never derived pleasure from playing with ignorant human minds. Ripping Calanthe's world to shreds, dragging her ignorance through Atlantean muck…it feels fucking awful, but what choice do I have? I infected her with my magic. Until it leaves her body, or her body leaves this earth, she's my problem.

The idea of her dying has my blood running cold.

"You're wrong. I know how you feel because when I fell into the mine thirty years ago—when it gave me magic—I was confused and terrified." I'd been three, yet the memory of that day sits untarnished in the recesses of my mind.

I remember running from the cemetery where my devastated father lay crumpled over Mother's grave, my uncle crouched beside him.

I remember my lungs burning and my muscles cramping.

I remember the scream I released when I'd sunk right through the earth, and the taste of damp when I'd awakened in a cave flecked with glowing blue glyphs.

I remember the searing pain that lit up my skin when I'd touched the luminescent symbols and they'd embedded themselves into my skin.

"Except I didn't stumble into a magical mine, Tarian. I stumbled into *you*." Calanthe's slender throat bobs with a swallow. "You got magic out of your fender bender whereas I get a death sentence, so excuse me if I fail to see any similarities between our situations."

Her retort carries me back to the here and now, to the starlit mortal girl in my driveway, to the word that vanished from my skin. "Perhaps I was wrong about the death sentence."

"Well, *phew*, because I really didn't feel like dying." She scrubs away her tears.

Tears that I triggered.

Fuck.

"Come. I'll show you to a room." I wait for her to walk ahead of me, but she stubbornly stays planted in my driveway, eyes affixed to her van.

"I'm going home."

"I'm sorry, but that's not a possibility."

"I told you, your secret's safe."

"My secret? This isn't just *my* secret. Besides, do you think I'd have shared any of the things I told you if I had any intention of letting you leave?"

Her eyes widen, and she stumbles backward. "You can't force me—"

I slash my hand through the air. A second later, air hisses from her van's tires—all four of them. "I told you, I can't let you leave. Not until I find a way to get my magic out from underneath your skin."

Her complexion fades like the books my mother used to leave on her windowsill.

"You're safe. I'll keep you safe."

"Safe? I'd be safer in a maximum-security prison yard."

I may have smirked but I'm guessing that would only grate her nerves, and I'd prefer an agreeable tenant to an irate one. "Bryn can stay with you as long as you don't tell her what happened between us."

She lets out a startled wheeze. "First off, I don't stay at random people's houses. Plus, she knows how much I dislike your family, so she'll ask questions. Second, my mother's waiting for me."

I don't ask her why she dislikes us. Any sane human would. "Call her. Explain you're taking an impromptu trip."

She tortures her poor hat. "I can't."

"If you forgot your phone—"

"I can't just take off. My mother needs me. She's not—she's not autonomous, okay?"

I frown. "What do you mean?"

"She has Alzheimer's. She can't be left alone. Right now, my neighbor's watching her."

So that's who she wanted to rush home to see.

The relief I experience is ridiculously heady. "I'll drive you home."

"Just like that? You're letting me leave?"

"I'm not letting you leave, Calamity. I'm taking you home."

Her smooth forehead creases. "And once I'm home…?"

"Once you're home, you'll introduce me to your mother, and I'll work my magic."

Her eyebrows jolt upward like a puck on a high-striker. "Your *magic*?"

"I'll cure her."

Her pretty mouth parts, and although there's no sound, my brain conjures up a seductive pop. "You can do that?"

"I can."

"And you'll do it, *why*? Because you feel guilty to have set off my imminent demise?"

"I'll do it so that you return here without fighting me." I don't promise her a long life because I don't understand what the word that transferred off my skin will do to her.

It's hardly lethal like my father's. The vision of his exsanguinated body tangled in the hotel bedsheets creeps back into my mind and lingers there like a grease stain.

Calanthe has gone so still that I worry I've shared the details of my father's death out loud, but then she says, "So if I refuse to come back here with you, you won't help my mother?"

I don't miss the frenzied flutter of her pulse at the base of her neck. "Returning with me isn't an option. Like I mentioned earlier, I can't leave you in the wild. Not with my magic under your skin." I stalk closer, and although her throat pumps out a great many swallows, she doesn't back away. "Your options are simple. You pack a bag, hug your *cured* mother goodbye, and return with me of your own free will, *or* Dorian escorts you to your new rooms immediately, and your mother doesn't benefit from my munificence."

Her panic warps into a charming ferocity. "How dare you call it munificence! You're blackmailing me into submission!"

Although not her intent, my depraved mind fills with images of Calanthe at my mercy. "Option C, I snuff out your life right here, right now, and spare myself the headache of being saddled with you."

Her head rears back.

"So what will it be, Calamity? A, B, or C?"

"I hate you, Tarian Hadez."

Her words spring a cruel smile to my lips. "I killed the only person who loved me, so get in line."

Her nostrils flare, and her pupils bloom so large they overtake her irises. "I need my bag."

"Why?"

"My keys."

"You have me."

"You can open locks?"

"Yes."

"With your mind?"

"Yes." I sweep open the passenger door of my Bugatti. I may have packaged my suggestions as options, but she has none. Whatever she picks, she ends up with me, the god of her misfortune, because my magic, for reasons that elude me, has made Calanthe Bloom *mine*.

# NINE

"She'll need the van." I don't look at Tarian as I speak.

I haven't looked at him once since he stole my freedom. He may have promised to heal my mother, but until he does, I'll hate him with every fiber of my being.

"I'll have it fixed and dropped off before sunrise." The ribbon of darkened road blurs as he grinds down on the gas pedal.

Twice, I thought we were going to get into an accident, but twice, he slammed back into our lane in the nick of time.

As he hooks a turn at full throttle, I grip my forearms, my thumbs digging so hard into the crooks of my elbows that I cut off my own blood circulation. "Do you have to drive so fast?"

"There's nothing I *have* to do. Everything's a choice. I'm choosing to drive fast, the same way I'm choosing to heal your mother, the same way I *chose* to throw my uncle a fucking engagement party."

"The same way you *chose* to ruin my life?" After a tremendously long beat disturbed only by the purr of his engine and the whoosh of the AC, I say, "So you can create forcefields. You can heal untreatable diseases. You can compel people to forget. What other unnatural powers do you possess?"

"I can blind people. I can choke a person without laying a finger on them. I can stop their hearts. I can start a heart too, but only if the departed still have blood in their veins."

My breath jams in my throat. "Is that why you asked me when my father died?"

"Yes."

"Do you really think I'd be delivering cacti if he'd just passed away?"

"People do strange things when grieving."

His profile looks serrated in the glow of his dashboard. "Will you kill me if your magic doesn't?"

His gaze slides off the road. "Humans aren't allowed to know what we can do."

In other words, *yes*. "A lot of people believe you're gods."

"They speculate. They don't actually know."

"What about the humans married to Atlanteans? Are they kept in the dark?"

His lips sketch a dark smile. "Hoping I'll marry you, Calamity?"

Is he kidding? "Not that I care to die, but living with a monster who could kill me without touching me has never been a dream of mine."

"Ouch." His sustained smirk tells me he isn't hurt in the least. "What is a dream of yours?"

"That my father were alive."

His Adam's apple bobs, dimming his smile. "What else?"

"That my mother never had Alzheimer's."

"What else?"

"That I was free to choose my line of work."

"What would you have chosen?"

"Not to run a dying flower shop into the ground."

"Why did you take it over then? Why not sell it?"

"Because besides one another…and me"—my heart releases a pained beat—"that flower shop was my parents' greatest love." It only hits me now that if he manages to cure Mom, she'll realize how badly I've done. I can already picture how disappointed she'll be. *Unless…* "You wouldn't happen to own our building, would you? We could do with a lot less rent."

He eyes the GPS into which he input the store's name and reads the address. "Saul bought that city block."

My pulse quickens. With a cheaper rent, Bloom's Blooms could possibly stay afloat. Even with ultra-competitive Fleur-de-Lys nearby.

"You think he'd be open to lowering our rent?" It's surreal to be negotiating the store's lease when I should be negotiating my freedom, but I may as well get something out of my dire predicament while I still have breath in my lungs.

Tarian presses a button on his steering wheel and asks his car to dial Saul.

A few seconds later, a crisp male voice streams out of the speakers. "If it isn't the host who ran off with the flower girl. You've wreaked absolute pandemonium, Nephew. Mackenzie is inconsolable. She keeps asking what this Calanthe has that she doesn't, and I must admit, I'm exceedingly curious as well."

"The building you own on the corner of Cedar and Pinckney. How much do you want for it?"

My eyes widen in time with my mouth. Does Tarian think I want to buy the building? Unlike him, I'm not made of money, and no bank will ever loan my family a dime considering the state of our finances.

"Who wants it?"

"I do."

Wait, *what*? And I thought I was confused when a car crashed against a wall of air.

Saul snorts. "You do realize you don't have to buy the shop to bed the salesgirl."

Tarian's fingers clench around his steering wheel. "How much?"

"You know how I feel about the Prudential Center."

A nerve twitches beside Tarian's eye. "Call Vic. Have him draw up the papers for a trade."

I still don't understand what's happening. The Prudential Center is… It's the *Prudential Center*. My building is the property on the left of the Monopoly GO square. The Prudential is the one on the right.

"Never thought I'd see the day my nephew would make a shitty business deal for some piece of ass."

Tarian ends the call without further comment.

I gape at him in total and utter shock. Not only didn't he set his uncle straight about his true reason for buying the building, but… "Why would you give up the Prudential Center?"

"I'll put the deed in your mother's name in case anything happens to you."

I study the hard lines of his face that seem infinitesimally harder after his unpleasant chat. "You mean, in case I die?"

He eases to a stop at a red light, and his dark eyes slide to mine. He doesn't nod, but he doesn't need to. Although I won't pretend to know the man, because I clearly don't, I can tell that's what he's thinking.

The reminder of my potential demise causes my spine to tingle. "The beast has a conscience. Who would've thought?"

The light turns green, but he doesn't floor the gas pedal. He keeps scrutinizing me as though *I* were the oddity in the car.

"What?" I realize that I've uncrossed my arms. I'm not certain when that happened or why. I certainly don't feel more at ease in his company. I refold my arms over my chest.

A car honks behind us.

Tarian's left eye twitches, but still, he doesn't look away. "I bought you a building, now show me your back."

Of course he had an angle. "That was a lot of money to lose for a glimpse of my back."

"Now, Calamity."

More honking erupts around us.

Tarian's reaction is to put the car in park.

Right there.

In the middle of the road.

"We'll be pulled over for public indecency."

"Do I look like a give a single fuck?"

"Why do you want to see it?"

He releases a low growl that makes him sound more animal than man.

"Explain what you're looking for, and you get to pull down my zipper." I don't let my mind linger on the fact that this will be the most action I've gotten in months.

He swings his arm toward me, flips it over, and shoves up his folded cuffs, and then he points to a small gap between the line of ink that runs up the inside of his arm. "Because I need to see what the rune I branded you with looks like."

The rune.

Tarian just said *the rune*. That's what they call magical tattoos in those supernatural TV shows. I can't decide whether to scream, laugh, or cry. I settle on squeezing my eyes shut and pinching myself. Again. When the pain dissipates and my lids reel up, I'm still in Tarian Hadez's fancy-ass car.

I inhale deeply. I must exhale more air than I breathed in because I feel lightheaded. "I have a—a—" I attempt to gather my wits, but they must've scattered on Tarian's white gravel driveway. "That's what you stung me with? An enchanted tattoo?"

Tarian unclicks my seat belt. "Your zipper."

Although my body has gone stiff with shock, I somehow manage to swivel on the burgundy leather. I seize the *oh-shit* handle with both hands because this feels like a real *oh-shit* moment.

I start to wonder if he'll shove my zipper down with his magic or if he'll use his hands.

He grips my hair and carries the thick mass over to my shoulder, hitting every inch of skin on the way. When he frees my locks, and they unravel, goosebumps spring up. Instead of going straight for my zipper, he trails his blunt nails down my back, bumping over the curve of each vertebra.

Either he's just as frightened as I am of what he's about to unearth, or he's dragging out the moment to amplify my discomfiture. I'm leaning toward option two.

"Can a stake made of silver or iron or—I don't know—plutonium, kill you?"

The hot puff of his snort punches my shoulder blades, driving more goosebumps to the surface. "Looking for ways to murder me, Calamity?"

"Looking for ways to stay alive now that I know people like you exist, Hades."

He pinches the metal pull and slides it down.

My pulse nips at my skin as though my veins were filled with pop rocks instead of blood. "So?"

"The mineral quarried from our mine can momentarily neutralize an Atlantean's powers, but kill them? Only I'm capable of that." His grave timbre steers my mind toward corners I'd prefer not to visit.

"So it's true? That you killed your father?"

He parts the fabric of my dress, and although it's only my spine he exposes, I feel as though he's stripped me fully naked.

A minute ticks by and still he doesn't answer me.

I glance over my shoulder and find his tapered gaze leveled on the middle of my back. "Well? Do I have a tattoo?"

He bunches the eyelet cotton. "Yes."

"What does it say?"

"*Kemos*." I don't miss the jagged dip of his throat.

"Which means?"

He parts his lips, but the screech of a police siren slams them shut. He pinches my zipper just as blue and white lights skip over us. The cop in the cruiser gestures for me to power down my window.

"Remember that your mother will only be healed if you cooperate." Tarian's rasped threat slips around my neck like a roughened noose.

I toss a muttered, "Screw you," over my shoulder before focusing on the cop and pasting on a cheery smile. "Hi, Officer."

The man holds up a flashlight. "Something the matter with your car?"

I shade my eyes. More like, *something the matter with the driver.* "Nope. Nothing the matter. Isn't that right, Mr. Hadez?"

"Mister—Mr. Hadez's with you?"

"He most certainly is." I press my body into the seat to allow the guy an unobstructed view of my companion.

The cop clicks off his flashlight. "Apologies for bothering you. If you'd like to sit at this intersection a while longer, I can park behind you and divert traffic."

"That won't be necessary," Tarian answers, his voice almost pleasant. "But thank you. I won't forget your serviceability. Have a good night."

"You too, Mr. Hadez. You, too." The officer shuts off his car's flashing lights and zips off.

I wheel back around to face him. "Must be nice to have the law in your pocket."

Like twin gun barrels, Tarian's black eyes lock on my face.

Earlier in the night, the intensity would've made me squirm, but seeing as my sanity went the way of Mrs. Fiona's teeth, I only grow more annoyed. "So, is the word on my spine the one that's missing from your arm?" I try to remember what it read. *Kemo? Kemas? Kemos?*

"It is."

"And what does it mean?"

The left side of his face brightens, whitens as though lit from within, except...except the light isn't coming from him. It's streaming through the windshield.

"Tarian!" I scream as a bus careens toward us, its high beams flooding the inside of the Bugatti.

Instead of whipping the car out of the way, Tarian scoops me out of my seat and whirls me so that my back is pressed to the driver's seat and my front is flush against his. Every bone in his body seems to sharpen and swell as he looses a gut-curdling growl that vibrates through my marrow.

The crunch of metal is nothing like Bryn's car. It's an explosion that rips the air from my lungs and the noise from my ears.

Something thick and hot splashes my face. I pray it isn't brain matter. I try to pull out of Tarian's arms to see, but he's still hugging me to him tightly. That's good, right? That means he's still alive, right?

*Only he can kill Atlanteans.*

Fire erupts around us, a wall of flames that cordons us off from the world.

"Tarian, we need to get out of the car!"

He jerks, stiffens, hinges backward. His shirt is soaked with so much blood that another scream erupts from my boiling lungs.

Although Tarian's lashes flutter, his eyes don't open as his big body slopes and falls, right through the wall of fire. I try to shout his name, but the flames chew up my words and shoot down my throat. Adrenaline propels my body sideways, and I fall where he fell, except I don't land on him. I land on cold, hard asphalt.

I squint, hunting the smoky darkness for the broad shape of his body, but Tarian Hadez is neither sprawled next to me nor is he looming over me.

Tarian Hadez is gone.

# TEN

I wake to rhythmic beeps and muted voices. I recognize one of the speakers but not the others. I wrench my lids open and find Bryn chatting with Yasmin, who vapes by an open window, and Tarian's brother and cousin sitting in matching blue armchairs, sipping coffee or mead or whatever gods drink.

After I get over the shock of being surrounded by so many strangers, I prop myself into a sitting position on rickety arms. "Where am I?" I sound as though I swallowed the flames that engulfed the car last night.

Oh my god, the car!

The accident!

"Tarian," I gasp. "Where's Tarian?"

Bryn lurches toward me, eyes smudged with a mixture of runny mascara and lack of sleep. "Callie! Oh, Callie!" She sinks onto the bed and grabs one of my hands, the whites of her eyes reddening.

Yasmin neither moves away from the window nor stops sucking on her e-cig, but the boys set down their beverages and amble toward me, expressions pinched.

"You gave us quite a scare there, Miss Bloom." Although it didn't strike me last night, Malachi's English is more accented than Tarian's, peppered by British and Spanish inflections.

"Where's Tarian? Is he okay?"

Bryn sniffles. "Why wouldn't he be?"

My eyebrows shuffle toward one another. "Because he was in the car with me."

Symeon flicks his brown gaze toward Malachi.

My gut churns. "Did you guys not know he was with me?"

Bryn whips her gaze toward Tarian's cousin. "She's concussed, isn't she? The doctor mentioned there was a chance of that."

I blink at the lot of them.

"Well, she *was* in a head-on collision." Yasmin flips her hair.

In the cool light of morning, it shines a fiery red, nothing like Bryn's strawberry-blonde, even though their shoulder-length bob is similar. Then again, it's the current trend. I almost chopped off my long curls last month but decided against it, worried that such a drastic change would confuse Mom.

"Considering the state of Tarian's Bugatti, chances are high her brain incurred some damage." Yasmin tucks her metallic vape pen into the designer purse slung across a torso that's so well-proportioned, it seems to have been carved by a plastic surgeon or the hand of God, himself. Which, perhaps, isn't so far-fetched since she's one of them. Right?

I scrutinize her eyes, but they don't gleam. Perhaps they only glow in direct sunlight?

Malachi touches my shoulder, jerking my attention to him. His irises burn a blindingly bright shade of blue. Oh, shit. He's doing that thing. What did Tarian call it again? Completion? Compulsion?

"Tarian lent you the Bugatti because your van had a flat tire. He stayed at home for the party. He's at work now."

The bang of metal.

The crunch of glass.

The cage of strong arms.

The spray of blood. The ooze of it. The taste of it.

The stench of burnt leather and flesh mixed with the scent of *him*—warm spice and male musk.

My heart needles my chest as the evening flashes behind my lids, a cacophony of sound and light and smell that fills the hospital room, along with my wild pulse.

"Must've been scary when that school bus rammed into you in the middle of the night." Symeon rakes his hand through his shaggy black curls, revealing a face not quite as chiseled as his brother's. "There should be a system on the car's ignition or on the steering wheel that can breathalyze..." His voice drifts like his body. He returns to the armchair, a cell phone pressed to his ear. "Vic, I want to file a new patent."

*A patent? A school bus? Tarian lent me his car?* What fresh hell— or absurd version of reality—is this?

Did Tarian ask Malachi to lie about lending me his car? The thought of the dark-haired male whose magic I wear on my spine and beneath my skin makes my gut churn and churn.

"Thank all that is holy there were no kids on that bus." Bryn's weary sigh carries my attention back to her shiny, crimson eyes. "And that you were driving the Bugatti and not the van. God, the van would've folded like an accordion."

I knead my forehead, and although my skin isn't wet with blood, gauze and tape drape across the left side of my face.

"Don't, hun." Bryn seizes my wrist.

Her grip is so lax that I manage to lift a corner of the bandage. When I graze the mosaic of scabs and bubbled blisters beneath, I wince.

Bryn swallows. Audibly. "The doctor assured us there'd be minimal scarring."

"The doctor? I'm in a hospital?"

"Your very own private room in Massachusetts General."

Yasmin approaches, heels clicking on the linoleum. "They brought you into the ER last night, but—" Her eyes, the same green as haircap moss, flick to Malachi before refocusing on me. "But Tarian insisted you lodge in the Hadez wing."

Even though my bones drum, I prop myself up higher. "Can I speak with him?"

The apple in Malachi's throat slides up and down. Twice. "He's impossible to reach when he's at work."

Alarm bells sweep through my mind—maybe because I *am* concussed—nevertheless, my gut tells me the strangers in my room are keeping a secret. Why convince me I was at the wheel? For insurance purposes? Because Tarian asked them to lie? And why are they all here *except* him?

"I'd like to leave him a message then. You know, to apologize for wrecking his car."

"You didn't wreck it." Bryn's headshake is slightly spastic from too much stress and too little sleep. "That drunk driver did, so you don't need to worry about your insurance premium."

My insurance premium is the furthest thing from my mind at the moment.

"And the hospital bills will be entirely covered by the Hadezes." Bryn squeezes my hand and beams up at Malachi as though his generosity was some grand heroic gesture when in reality, it was orchestrated to keep me subdued and under his family's thumb.

"How...generous." I glance around the vast room bathed in sunshine before my thoughts careen to my mother and Mrs. Fiona. They must be worried sick. Well, Mrs. Fiona must be. For once, I hope my mother's oblivious to my existence. "My cell phone! Shoot. I think I left it in the van."

"You did. I have it right here." Yasmin beams with pride as she unlatches her designer flap bag and fishes my jelly green case out.

"Why do *you* have it?"

The rudeness of my enquiry strikes me only when Bryn's pupils tighten in reproof. "She has it because she was the only one *not* out of her fucking mind with stress when that cop called last night."

Yasmin glides the phone toward me, shooting me a smile that's as smooth as the tan leather gloves she wears. In June. Sure the AC is on full blast, but gloves? Maybe she hates touching things in hospitals.

"Thanks," I mumble.

"Don't mention it." She hooks a lock of her red hair and tucks it behind an ear decorated with three blue-diamond studs—quarried from their fabled mine?

Each stone is larger than the solitaire Dad proposed to Mom with, and which she wore until last year when I found her squeezing out a bottle of conditioner on her finger in an attempt to dislodge the ring she claimed was cursed. Why? Because it made her mad and sad.

I tap my screen, which thankfully lights up, even though my battery life is critically low. I'm expecting a bunch of notifications but find none.

"A woman named Fiona Murphy kept calling last night. I took the liberty of answering one of her calls." Yasmin clicks the latch of her bag back into place.

"What did you tell her?"

"That you were involved in a little fender bender, and that you'd be home as soon as the doctors gave you the go-ahead."

"She made me send her proof of life," Bryn adds with a snort.

Sure enough, on my message thread with Mrs. Fiona, there's a picture of me asleep in this very hospital bed. Although Bryn, or someone, fanned my hair out over the bandage, it still shows through the dark strands.

"Here I thought she was into word searches and Irish folklore, but apparently your love for true crime rubbed off on her." In spite of Bryn's attempt to lighten the mood, the walls feel as though they're closing in around me.

"Is Mom—did she tell her?"

Bryn shakes her head. "We decided not to burden Lisa with it."

"Good." I swallow. "Thank you. Both of you. All of you." Do I find their presence odd? Absolutely. But I decide that acting grateful is way wiser than acting suspicious.

"Anyway, I should get going." Yasmin casts a glance over at Symeon, who's still discussing his new business endeavor. "When that one gets an idea in his head, he thinks of nothing else." There's affection in her tone, which leads me to wonder how long they've been together, but a pinch to my spine propels me back to the most pressing matter.

Tarian.

I open up a new contact form on my phone. "So what's Tarian's phone number?"

Malachi produces his own phone and clicks open a message thread. "I'm not at liberty to disclose it. For security reasons," he adds congenially. "But here. Text him from my phone."

I type out a short message full of lies, since I'm supposed to believe I crashed his car, then hand it back. "Thanks for keeping me company, Bee."

"Are you kidding? Where else would I be?" Bryn knuckles her puffy lids as new tears glisten and spill over.

"Celebrating with your mother and sister," I venture.

"Celebrating what? The demise of Saul Hadez's mind?" Yasmin's vivid gaze returns to us, alight with pity. "No offense, Bryn."

"None taken." Although Bryn never badmouths Joslyn or Mackenzie in front of anyone but me, she also never pretends that they're a tightknit family.

Yasmin pivots toward Symeon as he ends his call. "I programmed my number in your phone in case you need anything, Calanthe. Unlike the boys, I'm not hung-up on security."

Malachi shakes his head. "It's called being cautious, Yaz."

She murmurs something—not in English—that makes a nerve twitch beside his eye, then shoots me a smile before hooking Symeon's arm and carting him out of the hospital room.

The air in the room ripens with Malachi's tension.

Bryn must feel it because she quips, "I know we like to do everything the same, but crashing our cars the same night is overkill."

Except *I* didn't crash my car, and neither did she.

I attempt to return her smile, but my lips refuse to bend. "I need to get home. You think you could make that happen, Mr. Hadez?"

"Malachi or Mal, and I don't think that's a good idea. Yet."

"I feel fine."

Bryn shakes her head frantically. "Callie, it's the drugs they've pumped into your system."

My skin prickles. "What drugs?"

"Painkillers. Mostly."

"Mostly?" I cock an eyebrow, not liking the idea of being filled with substances. Especially after Tarian filled me with magic.

Is that how I'm even alive? Or is it because of his magic that I almost died?

"Bryn, could you ask one of the nurses to bring us a fresh pot of tea?" Malachi's eyes don't leave mine as he says it, and I sense the errand is an excuse to get me alone.

I could grab Bryn's hand and refuse to let go; I could insist on pressing an intercom, because a room this modern is surely equipped with a direct line to the nurses' station. I do neither because a small part of me is holding out hope that Bryn's absence will make Malachi miraculously confess to whatever it is he's holding back, because he is clearly holding *something* back.

Once the door snicks shut behind Bryn, he says, "We need to talk, Calanthe."

*Aha!* "Isn't that what we've been doing?" Although my tone is flat, my pulse has escalated, setting off the EKG machine beside the bed.

Malachi doesn't spare the readout a glance. He merely tightens the knot of his arms. "My compulsion didn't work on you."

"Your"—I let out a strangled sound that gets eaten up by the bleating of my heart—"compulsion? Don't even know what that is."

"Look, this can play out one of two ways. You work with me, and you get to leave this hospital room, or you keep up the ignorant act, and I make sure you never set foot outside again. Which do you prefer?"

# ELEVEN

**M**alachi Hadez's ultimatum clangs through my mind and across my vast hospital room, tightening both my rib cage and my lips. I don't like to be threatened. I suppose no one does, but it feels particularly abusive considering the weakened position I'm in.

"Where's Tarian?" I question through gritted teeth.

"The others aren't aware of your immunity to my compulsion, but I could change that. I could call my cousin and tell him. I could call the Atlantean Council and—"

"Where's. Tarian?" I repeat, jaw clenching tighter.

Malachi's nostrils flare. "If we bloody knew where he was, I wouldn't be here."

My breath stutters, and not because of his brusque tone but because of his confession. "He said he was the only weapon that could kill Atlanteans, so he's not dead, right?"

Malachi stays quiet, but a vein throbs along his neck. He's

angry, and I don't think it's with me. "How much has he told you about us?"

"He told me about the mine. And about his runes, after one stung me."

Malachi's pupils dilate.

"He believes that's what made me immune to compulsion."

He clamps his index finger and thumb around the bridge of his nose. Since his shirtsleeves are pressed halfway up his forearms, I get an unhindered view of his skin—his rune-less skin.

"Where are your magical tattoos?" I gesture to his arms while trying to remember if I spotted any on Symeon's. What was Symeon wearing?

The blue tint of Malachi's irises is arresting.

"Look, I'm not asking to see them. I'm only trying to understand—"

"There's nothing for you to understand, Calanthe."

"I wish I'd never taken Mackenzie's job. I wish I'd never bumped into Tarian, but the fact is, *Malachi*, I did. And now I'm fucking stuck in this right along with the lot of you, so spare me your tightlippiness."

He cocks a thick, brown eyebrow. "*Tightlippiness?*"

"The act of being tightlipped."

The corner of his mouth seems to twitch. "You said one of his runes stung you. Can I see it?"

"You show me yours, I'll show you mine."

The knot of Malachi's arms slackens, and he rubs the dark-blond stubble covering his jaw before sliding his hand along his nape and lifting his hair, revealing three swirled words at the base of his nape. "Atlanteans—except for Tarian—wear only one sentence."

I squint to make out the words, but between the fancy swoops and the fact that they aren't in English, I can hardly grasp the letters constituting them. "What does it say?"

"*Jo soc destaiqaz.*"

I wait for him to elaborate. He doesn't.

"Which means?"

"Which means, *I am awakened*. Now show me yours."

"So Tarian *gave* you those words? How? By stinging you too?" Do *I* have magic? Will the word printed on my skin kill me? Where is the harbinger of my death, but also my protector?

"Bryn will be back any moment."

I may remember only fragments of the accident, but I haven't forgotten how Tarian swung me into his seat and cocooned my body with his. The same way I haven't forgotten the feeling of wet on my forehead and the sight of his blood-soaked shirt.

Malachi eyes the door, his impatience tingeing the already ripe air. I sit up further, and my hospital gown—which is loads softer than the ones my father wore during his final days—splits open in the back, revealing my spine.

His enduring silence disquiets my nerves. "What does *kemos* mean?"

"*Kemos*?" Malachi rocks back on his heels, a vertical groove denting the skin above his nose.

"That's what Tarian said right before—" I gulp as the high beams of the bus whitewash my vision. "Before that bus barreled into us. It wasn't an accident, was it?" My insight rushes out on a breath.

"No. It was no accident."

"Who?"

"It'd be swifter to compile a list of who doesn't wish us harm."

My heart gives a hard shudder as the memory flares, but on the heel of my horror is anger. "Is the bus driver dead?"

"Yes."

"So the driver was human?"

"Yes."

"Did he have any beef with Tarian?"

"The man was a school bus driver, Calanthe."

I burrow back against my pillows. "Maybe Tarian cut funding to his school bus association or something."

"Tarian only ever gives funding."

I toss my hands up because nothing makes sense. "You said it wasn't an accident!"

"It wasn't."

"Are you saying…?" The beats in my chest slow as the muscle hardens. "Are you saying that it was orchestrated by—"

Of course, Bryn picks that moment to saunter back into the room. "Sorry it took me so long. Mom called, and well, she had a lot to say about nothing. Anyway, I ordered tea and lunch for three. Unless you're leaving, Mal?"

"I have to—"

"Stay," I interject. "He has to stay. You have lots of paperwork to help me fill out. *And* you were going to help me find a solution for my mother, remember?"

Malachi looks thoroughly confused, but like hell am I letting him abandon me and my mounting question pile.

"Tarian mentioned an experimental treatment for Alzheimer's. He said my mother was the perfect candidate for the trial and he was going to take care of it himself. Since he's so busy with work, I'd appreciate it if you could help me."

"I'm sorry. I'm not sure what trial Tarian was referring to."

Is he being daft on purpose? "Her brain. He mentioned he—I mean, the treatment—could heal her brain."

Bryn's eyes widen. "Oh my god, Callie! Really? That's amazing!" She tips her head to the side.

"What?"

"I'm a little surprised you discussed your mother with Tarian."

"Your sister mentioned my parents."

Her mouth puckers. "Ugh. Always sticking her nose in places it doesn't belong. I'm sorry."

Since she's standing close to my bed, I catch her hand and squeeze it. "You've got to stop apologizing for your sister and mother's mistakes, Bee. We are only responsible for our own mistakes, all right?"

"Okay, Gandhi," she says with an eyeroll. "Now, tell me more about this treatment."

"There's not much more to tell, really." I swing my attention toward Malachi, who stands on the other side of my bed. "You think you could make it happen?"

"No. Tarian has connections I don't."

I take it to mean that Tarian's magic is more powerful than his, which hurtles my mind right back to what he said earlier, about the Atlanteans' magic being dependent on Tarian's.

Apparently, the man I owe my insane evening to is the big cheese of deities.

"When he's not as busy at work, maybe you can remind him, Mal?" Bryn asks, giving my hand a squeeze back.

He nods.

"Can you call Mrs. Fiona and see if she can stay with Mom one more night?" I need a minute—more like twenty—with Malachi.

"Of course." Striding toward the tufted blue chairs, Bryn fishes her phone out of her cropped leather jacket pocket and dials my home.

I can't believe my room has a living room inside.

*Focus, Callie. Focus. You have one point five minutes until Bryn returns.*

"I know you don't trust me, Malachi—it's not like I trust you— but I need to understand a few things." He doesn't nod, but I plow ahead anyway. "Do I have magic now too?"

"No."

"But I thought—"

"You'd have needed to be in the mine with Tarian."

*Okay...* "So he's what, a conduit?"

"Yes."

"And you can't heal my mother?"

"No."

My theory about his powers must've been accurate. "The bus driver was compelled, right?"

He gives the faintest flick of his head.

"So Tarian was godnapped by one of your people?" I whisper.

He stays perfectly still and perfectly silent, which I interpret as a *yes*. After all, what would freak out a god more than the most powerful one getting abducted?

"You understand why I can't let you leave?" Malachi asks instead.

"Because I know too much and therefore cannot be released into the wild because mere mortals aren't allowed to know about you?"

"Yes. But it's also for your protection."

*Oh.* "Except I'm not an Atlantean, which an Atlantean would know."

"Perhaps, but you were with Tarian, and you're alive."

From where she sits on the arm of the tufted chair with the phone pinned to her cheek, Bryn gives me a thumbs-up. The gesture is so at odds with my hushed conversation that I want to tug on the roots of my hair and yell, *Is this really my life?*

"The instant whoever abducted him learns that you're alive"—Malachi's voice is so low I have to strain to hear him—"they'll come for you."

"Why?"

"Because Tarian could've saved himself, but instead, he depleted his powers to save you. Which an Atlantean would know."

# TWELVE

Lunch is brought into the room.

I barely touch it because my stomach is as knotted as my brain. On top of confusion and complete shock, I now have to contend with guilt. I don't think that was Malachi's intent when he explained that Atlantean magic works like a well, one that runs dry when too much is drawn out, but that eventually replenishes itself.

"It's really kind of you to stick around, Mal." Bryn's gaze strokes up his wide shoulders and corded neck to his light-brown mane streaked with strands of gold.

She liked him before, but his "compassion" has undoubtedly made him skyrocket in her esteem and heart.

"I'm only here because Tarian couldn't be," he finally admits.

Well, color me surprised. He's not even pretending to be considerate, and for that reason alone, Malachi Hadez rises in *my* esteem.

His phone chirps. "Excuse me. I need to take this." He pats his mouth with his napkin, then slinks toward the window, keeping his back to us.

Bryn leaps up from the armchair and plods over to me. I've told her to go home and change out of the purple satin dress and sheer eggplant tights she wore to her mother's engagement party, but she refuses to leave my side. She's even asked the nurses to bring in an extra cot for tonight, incredible friend that she is.

She wheels away my overbed table and plops down on the mattress. "Okay, spill."

My heart stops before taking off at a brisk pace that makes my pink hospital gown vibrate. "Spill what?"

"What's the deal between you and Tarian?"

"The"—I lick the sweat dotting my upper lip—"deal?"

"He lends you his car. He puts you up in the fancy wing of the hospital. He tasks his cousin with ensuring you're well taken care of."

The tightness in my chest dissipates with each one of her remarks.

"You did only meet last night, right?" Her lips curve into a brazen smile. "You're not hiding some secret, torrid affair from me?"

I choke. "No affair. Promise."

Bryn presses a glass of water into my hand, and I gulp down the chilled contents.

"He only lent me his car because my tires were flat."

"Uh-huh."

"What's *uh-huh* supposed to mean?"

"He could've lent you a number of cars, but he gave you *his*."

"It's a car, Bee."

She shakes her head, smile firming. If only I could explain that the unfortunate transference of one of his runes incited him to take an interest in me, just like it spurred him to save me. A rune which Malachi has yet to translate. I tried looking it up on my cell phone, but unsurprisingly, Google doesn't offer Atlantean translations.

"Father sends you his best." Malachi slides his phone into the back pocket of his gray slacks as he returns to us.

Yeah right. Saul's probably out of his mind with worry for his nephew and hates me for being the reason he was taken.

"Also, I've arranged for your mother to be transferred to the room next to yours."

"No! She can't be in hospitals! Hospitals trigger her." The last time we went to visit my father, the day his doctor informed us there was no more hope, not only did I lose him, but I also began to lose her. "She needs to be at home." Which is where I need to be as well, even though I understand why that's not a possibility. "Could you find her an around-the-clock nurse until I'm *healed*?" It breaks my heart to saddle her with a stranger, but it's unfair to lay all this responsibility on Mrs. Fiona.

Bryn bites her lip. "Can you afford that?"

What choice do I have?

"I heard there's an intern looking for work experience to flesh out her resume," Malachi says. "She's not looking to get paid."

There exists people who want to work full-time for free?

Malachi rolls his neck. "The downside is that she might not be as highly trained as—"

"Did she finish nursing school?" I ask.

"Not yet, but I hear she's top of her class."

"When can I meet her?"

"I'll see if the hospital can send her up."

AN HOUR LATER, Electra Serran, a raven-haired girl with one blue eye and one brown one saunters into my hospital room. She seems a little young and not especially *nursey*, but it's late, she wants to work for free, and both Malachi and the on-call doctor who escorted her up to my room vouch for her competency. So I hire her.

Malachi informs Bryn that his chauffeur is idling downstairs. "It would probably be best that you introduce the new recruit to Mrs. Bloom."

Bryn looks about as excited by this task as I am to pull hair out of the drain.

"Grab me some clothes?" I call out before she swings out of the room with a huff.

As she trails her, Electra arches an eyebrow Malachi's way, which hefts up my own eyebrows.

The second the door shuts, I ask, "Is she good at her job or in bed?"

Malachi chokes on a cough. "Excuse me?"

"The supermodel nurse."

Disgust warps his features. "She's a kid, Miss Bloom."

I may have misread the situation, but there's definitely some familiarity there. "Why are you helping me, Malachi?"

He scrubs a hand down his face. "Because Tarian isn't only my cousin. He's my best friend." His wrought tone and raw confession make me regret having asked him whether he banged the nurse.

"Any news?"

"Father's called a council meeting. Hopefully, we'll get answers tonight."

Silence settles between us. Not the awkward type. No, this silence is introspective.

"I'm sorry Tarian didn't save himself," I finally say.

He sighs. "And I'm sorry I can't heal your mother, but I can heal your face. If you'll let me?"

What he's really asking is whether I trust him, and I decide that I do, so I nod.

Delicately, he peels off the tape and the gauze. I wince when fresh air hits my wound. I don't ask how bad it is because I don't want to know. I saw the size of the bandage when I went to the bathroom earlier—it runs from my hairline to my chin. I'm surprised the fire didn't singe off my eyebrows or my hair, but by some miracle, both were spared.

Malachi hovers his palm over the scabbed side of my face. When needles of fire snap-crackle against my flesh, I bear down on my molars. Thankfully, the discomfort lasts only mere minutes.

I raise my hand and touch my cheek that's as soft and smooth as velvet. "Thanks for the facial."

He smiles but his amusement topples off his lips almost as quickly as it appeared. If someone had kidnapped Bryn, I too would be as tense as a high-voltage cable. I hold on to the hope that Tarian will be found quickly.

"Why would one of your people abduct him?" I ask.

"Jealousy. Cupidity. Power. Tarian's blood is extraordinarily potent." He redresses my cheek. "Keep the bandage on until the doctor removes it, all right?"

"Why did Tarian kill his father?"

Malachi's somber expression turns downright fierce. "You shouldn't believe everything you read in the papers."

"I didn't read about it. Tarian told me himself." Well, he'd hinted at it, repeatedly. Unless he didn't mean his father when he mentioned he'd killed the only person who loved him? Maybe he meant an old flame?

Malachi's voice is almost a growl. "The rune that transferred onto Barak's skin didn't drain him of blood, only of magic."

"Transferred?" My mind lights up like our street during the holidays, making connections left and right. "So he stung Barak too?"

"Yes. You're the second person he's ever stung."

"Why? I don't have magic."

"It's not something he can control."

"They're *his* runes."

"It never happened before Barak, and it hasn't happened since, either. But then, he hasn't dared touch anyone in the past five months. I'm surprised he touched you."

Five months? How lonely. "I bumped into him."

"I suppose that makes more sense."

"So how did Barak die?"

Malachi inhales slowly, exhales even slower. "He was bled to death."

"Why?"

"Because our blood holds magic."

"Except his didn't have any more magic, correct?"

"He may no longer have had his own runes, but he wore one of Tarian's, which means my cousin's magic was circulating through his veins."

"Like it's circulating through mine?"

He nods.

"Was it the same word I wear?"

"No."

"So *kemos* doesn't mean *drain me* or anything like that?"

"*Kemos* means *mine*."

"*Mine?*" I gasp. "What? As in your fabled mine?"

"In Atlantean, the word for mine is different."

"So mine, as in I'm Tarian's *property*?"

His eyebrows hug. "Were you upside-down when he read it?"

"Yes, I was demonstrating my proficiency at headstands." Before he thinks I'm being serious, I say, "Of course not. I was sitting in his car. It was right before we were hit. Why?"

"Show me your back again."

I sit forward and let him part the dahlia-pink gown.

Malachi's shoulders become alarmingly geometrical beneath his black button-down.

My skin prickles with goosebumps. "Well, go on. I freaking hate suspense." Ironic for a true crime junkie, considering most of the episodes I listen to are cold cases.

"At least it's still a word."

"As opposed to…?"

"On my uncle, it transformed into a symbol. A circle with an 'X' in the middle."

"Maybe because the man had magic and I don't, so there's nothing to 'X' out of me?"

"Perhaps."

"So what word do you read?"

"*Somek*, which contains the same letters as *kemos*, but reversed. What are those called again? Palindromes? Ambigrams?"

"I don't know, Mal. How about we just call it malevolent word-play?" I'm exasperated, not by him but because the cards I hold have changed. "What does *somek* mean?"

"Slumber."

Not that *mine* made much sense, but *slumber* makes even less sense.

I force my lids extra-high. Malachi may claim Tarian didn't cause his father's death, but what if he's wrong? And what if the rune on my spine will kill me in my sleep?

I am *never* shutting my eyes again.

# THIRTEEN

I yawn.

Bryn pauses the movie we're watching on the hospital room's flat-screen to look over at me from her cot. "Okay. Lights out, sleepy head."

"No!" I sit up and shake my head to joggle my brain awake. "No. Don't feel tired."

"You've been yawning for the past three hours. And frankly, I'm dead." She tosses the remote on the little table she's pulled up beside her bed. "Like more dead than after those Atlantitarian cocktails Logan whipped up. Geez, those were lethal. He says *hi* by the way. Oh, and he promised to check up on Lisa. He's the sweetest." She tucks her hands under her pillow, lids already clasped, hair fanned around her head like sunflower petals.

I want to beg her to stay awake, to keep *me* awake, but that would be unfair, especially after the night and day I've put her through. I climb out of bed and decide to pace the hallways.

Nothing like a little blood pumping through my veins to stave off sleep.

Except...

Except the glass doors that lead to the hallway are sealed shut, and since they're sanded down, I can't see anything through them.

Malachi takes my security very seriously. Too seriously.

I don't like the idea of being locked-in, not even for my protection. I knuckle the glass and call out a loud, "Hello!"

No answer.

I head back into the bedroom and pick up the phone on my bedside table. I speed-dial the nurses' station.

A chirpy voice picks up. "What can I bring you, Miss Bloom?"

"I wanted to stretch my legs, but I'm not sure how to open the sliding doors outside my room."

"I apologize, but Mr. Hadez sealed them himself, and they can only be unsealed with his thumbprint."

My heart pumps harder. Here I liked Malachi, but I'm not so certain that I do anymore. "What happens if there's a fire? I can't leave?"

"If there's a fire, I'll be able to access the emergency bypass."

"Can you access the emergency bypass now? I'm feeling very claustrophobic."

"I left some Xanax in your bathroom when I stopped by to take your vitals earlier. That will help calm you."

I'm not putting more drugs into my system. "What if I want cupcakes?" I start hyperventilating, which works wonders to clear my body of fatigue.

"Do you want cupcakes?"

No. What I want is for those doors to be open. "Yes."

"I'll put in a request with Mr. Hadez's assistant to have some delivered when he comes back in the morning. Is there a particular flavor you'd like?"

"What if he doesn't come back in the morning?"

"Then it would have to wait until the afternoon, but he said he'd be back in the morning. In any case, your refrigerator and cupboards are stocked with plenty of meal options and drinks."

I traipse over to what looks like a closet, but which hides a fancy kitchenette fashioned from auburn wood and stainless steel. Wireless phone tucked under my cheek, I open all the cupboards, finding fancy jars of pickled condiments, plump olives, fatty tuna in oil, organic jams, and sundried tomato spreads. Plural. I count four different types.

"Any special flavor for the cupcakes?"

"You really can't get some tonight?"

"I really can't. How about I ask for a variety box?"

My pulse keeps increasing until it feels as though my heart has migrated in the vicinity of my throat.

"Can I help you with anything else?"

"Magazines. I'd like magazines." I pant as though I've run a 10K.

"You have a tablet in the room on which you can download any magazine. Any book as well. Perhaps take the Xanax, Miss Bloom?"

"Perhaps call Mr. Hadez and tell him I don't appreciate being caged," I grit out.

"I'll leave a message with his assistant. Try to rest now." And then the nurse hangs up.

I knead my temples, but the giant Band-Aid is in the way so I rip it off, and although stripping it angers my skin, its absence brings me some relief. I riffle through the fridge and unearth a mini champagne bottle. Preferring alcohol to drugs, I uncork it and drink it while I pace my bedroom.

Once the alcohol hits my bloodstream, I grab the tablet off its charging station and download ten magazines, ranging from *Cosmo* to *Southern Living* to *National Geographic*, then drape my body over the armchair and start reading, combatting my sinking lids by changing position often.

The tablet screen blurs and then slides off my lap. I reach for it, but my hand meets air.

"Give a warm round of applause to our next contestant, Calanthe Bloom. Born and raised in our very own Hadeztown. Florist by day, sleuth by night. Cupcake amateur. Calanthe can most often be found in the condiment aisle of..." The announcer's voice fades to a dull buzz as I raise my arm to shade my eyes.

Like a starlit sea, round tables dripping with candlelight and orchid arrangements spill around me. And sitting around those tables are women in sparkly gowns and men in tuxes. I spin on myself as everyone claps.

What the actual hell?

Behind me is a line of girls with puffy gowns, puffier hair, and pageant sashes bearing the names of their home countries. I drop my chin to peer down at my body. My sleep shorts and boxy tee are gone, replaced by a layered buttercup dress sprinkled with pink sequins. Over the scratchy tulle sits a satin sash that reads *Hadezworld*. I'm no stranger to odd dreams, but this one takes the cake.

Wait! I almost give myself whiplash from how fast my head snaps up. I didn't want to sleep! I *can't* sleep.

My heart's clamor is as deafening as the spectators' applause. I'm trying to power myself out of this dream when a beam of light drapes over the audience, over a man who sits alone at a table set for many.

"Tarian?" I exclaim.

His dark eyes gleam like the satin lapels of his tuxedo jacket as he scoots his chair back to better face the stage. "Yes, Calamity?" A microphone must be hooked to his starched shirt collar because his voice booms against every stemmed glass and gilded molding.

As the faceless audience keeps cheering, I shake my head, my waterfall curls brushing against my bare arms.

This isn't real. *Not real.* As though I've pressed some magical pause button, the audience freezes midclap.

"Becoming Miss Universe..." His eyes dance with a smile. Surely a mocking one. "Is this one of your dreams?"

I snort. "No."

"You'd win."

It's so fucking absurd that I laugh. "Yeah, sure."

The heat of his gaze burns a path across the dim room and sinks into my skin. "You'd win." His tone brooks no argument.

His vote of confidence is kind, albeit unnecessary since I don't even care to enter a beauty competition. I leave those to the Fielding women, all three veterans in the pageantry domain.

"I like the dress."

A choked sound hurtles past my lips. "It's yellow. With pink sequins."

Tarian drops his elbow on the table and cradles his head on two long fingers. "Am I not allowed to like you in yellow dresses with pink sequins?"

I wonder why my subconscious desires Tarian's affection when conscious-me certainly doesn't. I feel like Alice in Wonderland. *Calanthe in Hadezland.*

"You read the word wrong by the way."

His black eyebrows writhe beneath a glossed curl. "Did I?"

"According to Malachi, it says *somek*. Which means—"

"I'm well acquainted with the meaning of *somek*, Miss Bloom." Even though the spotlight still bathes him, his expression darkens. "When, do tell, did you expose your back to my cousin?"

His tone rings with…*jealousy*? Odd. Then again, everything about this dream is odd.

"You make it sound as though I flashed him." My quip does little to smooth his expression. "Which I didn't, in case you were wondering. Though you probably weren't, since you're not even real," I ramble.

He must have a kink in his jaw because he keeps working it from side to side. "Show me. Show me the rune again."

I dig through the springy folds of sequined yellow until I locate the zipper underneath my armpit. I tug it down, letting the bodice fall away from my ribs. God, it feels good. Since I'm wearing some fancy white lacy bustier bodysuit, and this is not real life, I step out of the dress.

Tarian leans back in his chair and manspreads. "You'll have to come nearer, Calamity."

In a pair of hot-pink heels I'd drool to own in real life, I approach the edge of the stage and scan the area for stairs. Finding none, I sit and hop off, then amble around the sea of tables.

His eyes flash like opals when I reach him, and his throat dips with a painfully slow swallow. "Turn." His voice is gravel, and it scrapes across my exposed skin, coating it in goosebumps.

"Say *please*."

His surprise at my demand is swiftly superseded by amusement. He spreads his thighs wider as though to welcome me closer. "Please, Miss Bloom, turn."

As I indulge him, I hear the chair creak and the expensive fabric of his suit rustle. And then I feel his fingers brush the exposed skin between the white bra strap and scoop bottom. My rune warms under his scrutiny, thrusting the blood faster through my veins. I've had vivid dreams, but this one's next level.

"K." He traces the letter with one fingertip. "E." He follows the swooping shape. "M." Another agonizingly languid caress. "O."

My skin warms with a blush that spreads like dripping paint from my cheeks to my neck, across my collarbone and fluttering chest.

"S." When he strokes the last letter, a shiver seizes my body. "*Kemos*," he murmurs thickly, his breath glancing over my skin.

Forgetting I'm not a contortionist, I hook my hair and try to peer over my shoulder but obviously see nothing, besides the rune's glow.

Tarian's hand settles on the indent at my waist, even though his gaze wanders lower, across the globes of my ass. I try to step away, but his fingers tighten.

"Don't move, Calamity."

"I know this isn't real, but still, my backside's in your face. Even my ex never got this up close and personal with that part of my body."

"His loss." He raises the hand still flush with the tablecloth to the single button keeping his jacket closed and unfastens it, and then he leans forward some more, knuckles trailing the rounded shape of my behind. "My gain."

*Whoa. Whoa. Whoa.* All the blood in my body converges between my legs, beating against my tender flesh, dampening the fabric between my thighs. When his nostrils flare, I worry he can smell my arousal.

I haven't been with anyone in a long time, but fantasizing about Tarian Hadez…? I have no words to describe the insanity of this delusion. "I can't believe I'm having a dirty dream about you."

His half-lidded gaze tracks up the curves of my body before settling on my face. "Best fucking dream I've ever had." His knuckles pause on the cleft between my legs before leisurely gliding upward. "You are a siren, Calanthe Bloom." His knuckles trail back down. "*My* siren."

His desire to possess me sends another hard shudder through my body. He presses an open-mouthed kiss to the dimples at the base of my spine, right above the scooped band of the bodysuit's bottom, then drags his hot tongue upward and swirls its tip over the rune he burned into my spine.

My head falls back on a moan, my long curls draping over Tarian's upturned face. He fists them, brushing them out of his way.

To think I resisted sleeping.

He suddenly gasps against my wet skin. I wheel around just as his spine slams into the rungs of his chair, and his head flies sideways as though someone had socked him in the jaw. He snarls, but it's cut short by an acute inhale that stiffens his body and makes his eyes roll to the back of his skull.

When he tips off his chair and crashes to the floor, I scream.

# FOURTEEN

ool hands cup my cheeks. "Callie, wake up. Wake up."

My lids shoot up to find Bryn's sleep-rumpled face staring down at me. "It was just a nightmare." Her thumbs stroke my cheekbones. "Oh, sweetie. Don't cry. You're okay. You're okay."

I squint at the dusky hospital room.

"That's why you were resisting going to sleep."

My stinging gaze slams back into Bryn's.

"Because you were afraid to dream about the accident?"

I don't say anything. I'm not sure I could speak even if I tried, since my throat feels wadded with gauze.

"You're safe, Callie. You're safe and—" Her voice drifts away, along with her palms. "And you're healed. *Wow.* Incredible."

*Crap. The bandage.*

"The Hadezes' private doctor can really work miracles." Her eyes glitter with wonder. "Maybe he's a god, too."

I don't refute her claim.

My rune stings and throbs. I sit up and hinge my elbow to reach under my boxy sleep tee. My intent is to soothe the burn, but that intent flies out the window when my fingertips encounter dampness. Am I bleeding?

Bryn's expression sharpens. "What?"

"Nothing. I just—" I slip my hand free and lift it, expecting… something. The pads of my fingers are damp, but not with blood. "Bathroom. I need the bathroom." With Bryn's help, I wrench my aching body from the armchair and stride to the ensuite.

I shut the door in her concerned face. Guilt worms through my breastbone, but I can't very well expose my tattoo. She'd ask when I got it, why I didn't immediately tell her about it, and what the hell it means.

I stand with my back to the mirror and hike my T-shirt up, then squint at the black rune that's no longer glowing like it was in my dream, but that nonetheless shines where dream-Tarian tongued the skin.

Except Tarian wasn't real. His mouth wasn't real. His touch wasn't real.

I sidle up to the mirror to decipher the word. The font is so fancy, I can barely make out the letters, but I'm pretty certain I read *somek*. Since the image in the mirror is inverted, it could very well be *kemos*.

My pulse pounds a mile a minute. Perhaps I could strap myself back up to the EKG machines. Surely my blood pressure would set off a code-red or black, or whatever life-threatening rhythms are called, and it would activate the emergency bypass, and the doors would unseal, and—

The bathroom door swings open. I drop the hem of my T-shirt, but not fast enough.

Bryn stands there with a hand on her hip. "What the hell? You got a tattoo?"

*Shit.* I gape at her like a turkey at Thanksgiving. "It's, um… temporary."

"Oh." Her hand slips off her waist as she pads closer. "Let me see."

Gnawing on my lip, I tug the T-shirt back up.

Her forehead ruffles. "*Somex*. Or is the X a K? Looks more like a K, actually."

So Malachi is right and Tarian is wrong.

"What does it mean?" Bryn asks.

My heart palpitates inside my mouth. "Sleep." I wait for her to connect the word to the Atlantean tongue.

"In what language?"

I expel a breath, glad she didn't guess. I wouldn't have known how to explain selecting a word that belongs to people I dislike.

"Callie?" she prompts me.

"In Old English," I blurt out.

"Old English? But mostly…why *sleep*?"

"I've been suffering from insomnia."

"So you immortalized your condition by getting its archaic spelling tattooed on your spine?"

"*Temporarily* tattooed."

"Still weird, Callie. Even for you."

"I was looking for cures and found this, um, doctor who claimed it'd help."

She releases my shirt. "Well, next time you meet up with your woo-woo healer, ask him to add the words *keep me safe*, all right?" Bryn pushes her hair off her haggard face. "Remember that Chinese symbol Mackenzie got inked on her hipbone? The one she thought meant *love* but actually meant *queef*?"

Thoughts of Tarian and of my predicament momentarily wane. "How could I forget? Never laughed so hard in my entire life."

Bryn cocks her head to the side. "What if *somek* actually means *horny kangaroo*?"

I snort. "It'd explain the dream I just had."

Her head straightens so briskly her neck cracks. "You woke up yelling bloody murder. What the hell sort of deviant fantasy were you having?"

The corners of my mouth fall in time with my gaze. *Shit. Shit. Shit.* I scrutinize the two rectangular white pills tucked in a tiny plastic cup beside the sink—the Xanax I was instructed to take. "Um. I, uh— It just ended oddly."

"But it began nicely?"

I shrug. "It was all very weird. I was competing in a pageant. My dress was hideous. Yellow puffy tulle with pink sequins."

She grins.

"And there was this guy in the audience. And we started discussing my tattoo. He kept insisting it was some other word, so I pulled off my dress to prove it wasn't."

"Naughty Callie. Who was the guy?"

"No one." I say this much too quickly.

"Spit it out."

Why does she have to know me so well? Without meeting her gaze, I say, "Logan."

"Liar." I'm about to insist it was our favorite barkeep when her tone turns cautious. "It wasn't Malachi, was it?"

My eyes snap back to hers. "No." I shake my head. "Promise."

Relief that I'm not crushing on her crush returns a brazen smile to her lips. "So, who?"

Heat rises to my cheeks.

"Was it Tarian?"

I try to school my features and shape the word *no*, but before I can manage either, Bryn snaps her fingers, and although the click of her middle finger against her thumb is low and doesn't sound like a gunshot or a car crash, I jump.

"I knew it! There was *a lot* of sexual tension between the two of you."

Heart still beating messily, I roll my eyes. "Tension, yes. Sexual, no."

My rune prickles as though to clamor, *Liar!* Yes, Tarian and I shared a moment in the car when he unzipped my dress, but it was nothing compared to the attention he lavished on me in my dream. My skin tightens at the mere memory of his phantom tongue tracing the letters on my spine.

"You mentioned it ended badly. What happened?" Bryn asks.

Any and all lingering lust for dream-Tarian vanishes, and I shudder. "He dropped dead."

Her lashes pull up so high they skim her browbone. "How?"

"Don't know." My stomach hardens and my breath comes fast. "It was so scary, Bryn."

"Oh, sweetie." My friend erases the distance between us to hug me. "It wasn't real. He's fine."

Except he's not. He may be a god, but he suffers like a mortal, in reality and in my dream.

She pulls away but keeps her palms anchored to my shoulders. "When Malachi comes back, we'll phone his cousin so you can see that he's fine. Maybe he'll even stop by to check up on…"

Bryn's voice fades into white noise as the car accident replays inside my mind, followed by my dream—and not the sexy part, but the one where he collapsed off the chair. I try to remind myself that he's a mob boss, that he brought this upon himself, but then Malachi's theory that Tarian was kidnapped for his magic supplants my vengeance hypothesis.

"Bee, do the Hadezes have enemies? Besides the Holy Hunters?"

Her lips quit shifting for a breath and her brows kiss. "Why?"

Instead of explaining the reason behind my newfangled interest, I shrug. "Just thought you'd know. Now that you're an insider and everything."

Her eyebrows level out. "It was an accident. The bus driver was drunk—"

"I realize I wasn't being targeted."

She studies me a moment. "But you think Tarian was." She doesn't formulate this as a question.

"The man controls the country."

Her pupils spread.

"Look, I'm not saying it was. I was just wondering if you've overheard anything about friction with another Atlantean family, that's all."

"The Hadezes don't gel with any of the families from their home island. Not *one*. Mom says it's because they're so much more powerful financially, socially, and"—she drops her voice—"magically." I slide my lips from side to side, which leads Bryn to add, "Yes, yes, I know you don't believe that last part." She shoots me a grin. "Unless you've changed your mind now that you've met Tarian. He is *quite* bewitching if you like your men dark, handsome, and brooding."

"Which I don't."

"Clearly." Her smile turns wicked.

Before our conversation can completely derail, I say, "There mustn't be friction with *all* the other families since Yasmin and Symeon are dating."

"Oh, Saul loathes Yasmin's parents, but she hates them too, so Stepdaddy's fine with them dating. Tarian, on the other hand, doesn't trust her. Not that Symeon cares. He and Tarian get along about as well as Mackenzie and I do."

How much bad blood exists within that family?

My skin pebbles as a realization strikes me: less than ten percent of crimes are committed by strangers. What if Tarian's abductor isn't only someone close to home but someone *from* his home?

# FIFTEEN

Unlike Bryn, who tumbles back into Morpheus's arms the second her head hits the pillow, I can't sleep, my mind much too busy playing detective to shut down.

I don't write out my hypotheses of who could've taken Tarian and why, worried a paper trail would end up in the wrong hands, but I research every godly player on my phone's browser. Tarian's uncle, his brother, and his cousin, then Yasmin and her family.

There's much more to read about the Fablez clan than there is about the Hadezes. Firstly, Yasmin's family is ten times the size of Tarian's, and secondly, each member is remarkably popular. The seventy-something matriarch is the brains behind a stem-cell renewal technology that can regrow tendons and damaged organs. Her six children went on to concoct ointments and miracle pills to smooth out skin and melt fat. The members of the third generation —Yasmin's—are either finishing up their studies or interning at their family company, patenting cures of their own.

Now that I believe in magic, I can't help but wonder what goes into the Fablez family's cosmetic and medical products, especially since I've spotted their signature Mediterranean-blue jars in my mother's bathroom. What if their wrinkle cream penetrates into more than superficial tissue?

Anger spikes through my veins but it's quickly doused by the reality that if Fablez products caused Alzheimer's, there'd be an increase in cases, and to my knowledge, there hasn't been. Unless Yasmin's family is hiding the data…?

Between my lack of sleep and the adrenaline triggered by my dream-nightmare, my conspiracy theories proliferate, taking on such epic proportions that I deep dive into my internet browser to research every single product that has come out of the Fablez factory. Unsurprisingly, zero side-effects are listed.

I let out such a shrill snort that Bryn stirs. I'm conflicted between waking her so I can talk her ear off about my theories and not involving her in my investigative work. As she flips onto her stomach and her breathing evens out, I redirect my thoughts to the original reason for my research: understanding who godnapped one of Hadeztown's favorite bachelors.

Considering the Fablezes' success, I don't see what they'd have to gain from abducting their fellow Atlantean. Then again, Atlanteans don't seem immune to the very human condition of forever craving more.

I return to my initial belief—that the crime was committed by someone close to Tarian—and examine his relatives until I go cross-eyed. I blink to clear the blur. When my lids pull up, I'm standing in my dusky flower shop, a bunch of roses clasped in my arms, and through the store window, I see *him*.

Although sunglasses shade his eyes, and it's full dark out, I know he sees me too, because his mouth softens around that silly nickname he's given me: *Calamity*.

"Why do I always dream of you?" I murmur.

He watches me, and I watch him. He looks so real. So…tangible.

He stalks closer to the door. "You see me, don't you?"

My heart catches when he wraps his long fingers around the knob. I don't know in what direction this dream will go. Will those fingers stroke my body again, or will they staunch an oozing wound?

He twists the knob, but the door doesn't open. It doesn't even rattle. My subconscious must not want to let him in. My subconscious is smart.

Tarian glares at the handle, then at me, and then over his shoulder at something the night conceals. When his attention swivels back toward me, his forehead is slick with sweat. "Let me in, Calamity."

I don't; I can't. I stand like an ice statue, my quickening breaths fluttering the crimson petals of the roses I hug. I don't want trouble, and Tarian Hadez is trouble.

"Calanthe, please. We need to talk, and we need to do it now before—" He jolts, his inhale catching.

My gaze drops to his middle, expecting to find blood soaking the white fabric of his shirt, but no stain appears this time. Only smoke; it curls off his suit, slowly chewing through the fabric.

"Is your suit on *fire*?"

My rune flares, heating my frozen spine and glazing my nape with cool sweat that absorbs into the boxy shirt I wore to sleep. I look past the bouquet I hug, at my legs that are bare, save for microscopic cotton shorts. Although relieved I'm not naked or bedecked with some hideous gown, I do wish my dream-self had elected to don leggings.

Tarian slams his palm into the glass door, jolting my gaze off my skimpy apparel. "Calamity," he bites out. "Let. Me. In." His jacket is gone, reduced to ash.

"I don't think that's a good idea."

As the smoke wreathing his body consumes the white fabric, it reveals acres of bullet-pocked, bruised skin that leak not red but blue.

*Just a dream,* I remind myself. *No one's shooting at him. No one's coming after him.*

Unless he broke free in more than just my dream?

"I need you." His fractured entreaty delivered with such despair hits me square in the heart.

I toss the roses aside and head to the door, already reaching for the... I pitch my gaze to his shaded one. "There's—there's no handle!"

He lunges backward. "Move!"

"Why?"

"Because I don't want you to get hurt."

"Then don't come near me."

That stills Tarian. I think he closes his eyes, but the sunspecs shading them are so opaque that I may just be imagining it. "I can't."

My forehead grooves some more.

His chest lifts. Falls. Lifts again. "For some reason, I can't *not* seek you out, Calamity. I believe it's because of the rune. I believe it ties us together. I believe it ties you to me."

"The word says *sleep.* Not *mine. Sleep.*"

"Well, I'm fucking dreaming of *you,* not of anyone else. So same fucking shit, Calamity."

In normal circumstances, I'd be stunned by how many bad words a person can string together at once, but I find something else way more alarming. "Not to burst your delusional bubble, Tarian, but you're in *my* head. You're starring in *my* dreams."

He opens his mouth, probably to counter my remark, but his retort fizzles like the muted lights inside the shop. "They're here." His voice is barely above a whisper. "I can hear them. They're here." The distress painting Tarian's features rivals the glow of his runes...their *blue* glow. "Help me figure this out, Calamity."

"How?" How does a mere mortal help the most powerful man in Boston—in the fucking universe? "I have no power."

"You're wrong."

"Are you saying I can use the rune you seared into my back?"

"Yes."

"How?"

"Let me in, and I'll teach you."

My mind is a wild place after dark. Since I want answers, even if my subconscious will be making them up, I step aside. And then Tarian is running, his huge, bruise-webbed body slamming into the glass. The faintest crackle appears where his shoulder connects with the clear barrier. He lunges back and rams himself against the fissure anew.

My rune smolders harder as he grunts and pummels. "This isn't real," I whisper to myself, kneading my temples. "These meetups aren't real. I'm in the hospital, and Tarian's in— Where is he? Where are you?"

"I don't fucking know." He puts all his weight behind his next body check. This time, shards of glass tumble onto the green tiles at my feet. He watches them settle, muttering, "Get out of the way so I don't injure you further."

His words punch into me, increasing the hammering behind my ribs. Utterly silly since my mind is making him say all these things. Real-Tarian doesn't actually care about me. Real-Tarian barely knows me.

"Calanthe," he growls.

On legs that feel all at once wooden and woolen, I back up. As Tarian widens the hole with his bare hands, ribboning his skin, I finally hear what he's hearing—voices garbled by an incessant hiss. As though a pipe has burst on the street. As though *all* the pipes have burst.

More smoke swirls through the cracked glass, carrying the scent of sulfur and something else, something sickly-sweet, like rotten blooms. I swing my watery gaze around the shop, seeking out the source of the stench, but none of the bouquets are coated in mold. I stumble back a step, and my bare heel sinks onto something sharp. I suck in a lungful of air that constricts my stinging throat and throttles my whimper.

Releasing a litany of curses, Tarian beats on the door until the pane is nothing more than twinkling dust and then he steps past the metal frame and crunches over the carpet of glass and roses.

His thighs are bare. Bare and bulging. Only a thin piece of fabric sheathes his private parts. He lifts bruised, wet knuckles to my cheek, and although he must be painting me with his blood, I don't recoil.

"Where?" His rapid inhalations smack the tip of my nose as he pushes away my hair to inspect my skin.

"Where, what?"

"Where did I get you?"

"You didn't—"

"Where?"

"My foot."

Relief smashes into his distress. "Which foot?"

"The right one."

He crouches. "Hold on."

I just have time to smack my palm against one hard, glowing shoulder before he boosts my foot. As he pulls the glass free, I notice black fabric has materialized over my legs—the leggings I so wanted.

Fucking weird.

Everything is so fucking *weird*.

He scoops me into his arms.

"What the—?" I hook my hand around his neck as he spins and runs, right toward the brick wall covered in ivy and fairy lights. Doesn't he see it? "Tarian!" I choke, curling my head into his big body.

Not real. Not real. Not real.

But glass hurt, so bricks surely will too.

"Tarian, stop." My cheek, my nose, my forehead are slick with the blue substance coating his chest. "Stop!"

He doesn't.

Cold air whips up my hair and blasts my skin. Unless he's running in place, we should've collided with the wall. I peep.

There's no wall. No shop, either. We're sprinting down a dark tunnel illuminated solely by the cyan glow of Tarian's runes.

Suddenly, he jerks, and my body soars out of his grip.

"Calamity," he roars, whipping one arm out to break my fall, but I drop…and drop. "Find me!"

I hit the ground so hard it knocks my teeth together.

"Callie?"

Something groans and clicks. Probably my battered skeleton. I blink my eyes open to find my cheek pillowed on the linoleum flooring beside my bed. I flop onto my back and look up at Bryn, who's crouched next to me, then past her at…at…

"What a brutal manner to wake up, Miss Bloom." Saul Hadez sets a pastel bakery box on the bed.

I sit up so fast my head spins. I smack my palms against the floor, then scuttle backward to prop myself against something solid—the wall.

One of Saul's dark eyebrows wings up over irises as crystalline blue as the liquid basting Tarian's chest. "Perhaps she's not ready."

"For what?" I whisper.

"To go home, Callie," Bryn explains, tightening the belt she added to a pair of high-waisted denim shorts she must've snagged from my closet yesterday. "The doctor gave you the all clear." She still wears the Counting Crows sleep tee, but she's knotted the hem, transforming it into a fashionable crop top.

"I can go home?"

Saul's index finger tap-taps his beige linen trousers. "If you feel well enough."

The news Saul delivers shortens my breath. If I'm being allowed to leave the hospital, then that means…

That means I'm no longer at risk of being kidnapped and used.

That means Tarian is free!

# SIXTEEN

"You were very lucky, Miss Bloom. I don't believe I've heard of many people surviving a head-on collision virtually unscathed."

I'm very much scathed. Malachi may have repaired my skin, but the accident left a glaring wound on my sanity.

"I'd like to speak with Tarian." I should heave myself off the floor, but I'm still attempting to catch my breath and decelerate my heart rate.

"I'm afraid he's in the middle of a meeting." Saul smooths his silvering strands. "I can have him call you once he gets off work."

I can't tell if he's lying, and the fact that I can't read him bolsters my distrust of him. "Please do. I feel simply awful about his car."

Saul's irises gleam in the sunlight streaming through the partially lowered blinds. "Nothing to feel awful about. It wasn't your fault, Miss Bloom."

No, it certainly wasn't. Was it Saul's? "Congratulations, by the way. I hope I didn't ruin your special evening, Mr. Hadez."

He responds with a chin nod, probably too well-mannered to admit that, between the cacti and the accident, I completely wrecked his engagement dinner.

Bryn lifts the lid off the bakery box. "Yum, cupcakes. Thanks, Saul."

"You'll have to thank the nurse, sweetheart. I was merely tasked with ferrying them from her desk to your bedroom."

I balk at the term of endearment. I never pictured Saul as a man who'd nickname someone *sweetheart*. Then again, I've rarely pictured Saul Hadez saying or doing anything. The sole Hadez who entered my thoughts before I met the notorious family was Tarian, and that's only because he seemed the most elusive of the bunch.

Bryn plucks out a giant frosted thing that she walks over to me. "Eat. You need the sugar."

My stomach spasms. "Not blue."

"They all taste the same, hun."

"Please, Bryn. Any other color."

"All right, weirdo." She returns to the box and swaps it for a pink one.

I'm still not hungry, but I know Bryn won't let me off the hook until I fuel my body, so I bite off a huge chunk of frosting.

"Is that—is that blood?" Bryn's voice is a raucous whisper.

"Blood?" My stomach folds in on itself. "Where?"

She points to the crimson smear—*crimson*, thank fucking god—on the linoleum. "Did you cut yourself when you fell out of bed?"

Chills pucker my skin.

It can't be…

Can it?

I twist my leg to peek at my sole, and the cupcake drops from my fingers, frosted side slicking down the outside of my bare thigh before landing noiselessly beside me.

I blink. The thin, angry line reddening the curve of my heel doesn't vanish. I blink again. Still there.

Which means…

Absurd.

Impossible.

After my pageant dream, my rune was damp where Tarian's tongue had swiped. Now my heel is bloody where dream-glass carved my skin.

I squeeze my lids shut, cradle my forehead between my fingertips, and rock like a crazy person, because clearly that's what I've become—*insane*.

My dreams are real.

I stop rocking as my shock is trampled by another emotion—mortification.

I stripped down to my underthings in front of a virtual stranger.

A stranger who I let lick my skin and fondle my ass.

My one and only hope is that none of it was real for Tarian.

Oh, god, what if it was?

My wish to speak with him becomes a vital need. My eyes fly open, and I pop my mouth wide to ask Saul to phone him immediately, but my demand withers at the sight of the face poised in front of mine.

For a moment, I think it's my mother, and I want nothing more than to burrow inside her arms, but Mom's eyes are as pale as heartwood, not deep brown like this woman's, and her hair is shorter, spikier, and she wears skinny jeans and silken camisoles, not lavender scrubs.

The nurse presses my hands away to hover a digital thermometer over my forehead. "No fever."

Saul and Bryn stand behind her. Where Saul's eyes are as hard as polished aquamarines, Bryn's are soft with worry.

What if none of this is real? Maybe I'm in a coma. Or maybe, I didn't survive the crash. This could be the afterlife. But if this is the afterlife, where's my father? Am I in some sort of limbo realm where my soul is getting evaluated before it can reach its final destination?

The nurse cups my shoulder, stilling the tremors racking my body. "Miss Bloom, I'm going to administer—"

"No drugs." Although my brain feels unmoored, swishing from left to right, clanging against my temples, I need a clear mind to figure out what's real and what isn't.

"Callie, just take the medication." Bryn crouches beside me. "It'll help."

"No." Using the wall for support, I stand. My foot throbs, reminding me of the wound that sparked my sanity's tailspin. "I'll take a Band-Aid if you have one, though."

If the cut is real, then the flower shop is in shambles. Unless that's not how my cursed sleep works?

"Mr. Hadez, I understand your nephew isn't the sort of man who appreciates being disturbed, but I need thirty seconds of his time."

On a sigh, Saul extricates a cell phone from his suit pocket and dials a number. "Hi, Ursa. I have a young lady who'd like to speak with Tarian. Can you put him through?"

I blink at Saul, stunned that he indulged me, but even more so by what this call truly means: that Tarian is safe.

"Tell him it's of the utmost importance." Saul's gaze doesn't waver off mine as he speaks to someone who I assume must be Tarian's assistant. "Thank you." He extends the phone.

I stare at it a full beat before seizing it and putting it to my ear. Silence pours from the receiver. Out of the corner of my eye, I notice Bryn speaking in hushed tones with the nurse.

"Hello?" I ask.

Nothing.

I pull the phone away from my face and glance at the darkened screen, then thumb it. It doesn't show any call in progress.

Before I can inform Saul that the call must've dropped, he steps nearer to me, giving the nurse and Bryn his back, and snares my gaze with his preternatural blue one. "You spoke with Tarian. He told you to head back to your little shop and forget about whatever happened between the two of you."

Irises now dull, he reaches out for his phone and wrests it out of my white-knuckled grip. My chest is a chaotic mess of heartbeats and snappy breaths. Fearing he'll detect my immunity to his compulsion, I blink until my eyes water, then swipe at the moisture with my fingertips.

"Sorry. Stray lash." I point to my eye, then poke at it, pretending to search for the irritant. "I'll be right back." I whirl toward the bathroom and manage one step in its direction before Saul's low voice halts me.

"What did my nephew say, Miss Bloom?"

Saul's question makes me freeze, save for my pulse.

Feverishly batting my lashes to enflame my eyeballs and produce tears, I glance over my shoulder, grit my teeth, then tip up my chin. "He told me to move the fuck on. Like I want anything to do with him and his overinflated ego anyway." With a haughty snort, I swipe at my wet cheeks and spring toward the bathroom.

Only once I have a wall between me and the supernatural manipulator do I drop the act and attempt to understand why Saul would fake a phone call—because Tarian isn't safe, or because he doesn't want to talk to me? And Malachi. Why did he keep the rune transference to himself? Because he doesn't trust his father?

Although I had a whole slew of suspects, Saul's name slithers to the top of my list. He has the most to gain from his nephew's disappearance. With Tarian gone, he has one less Hadez to contend with.

Who's next? Symeon? Or is it me? What if Saul suggested I go home to dispose of me without anyone noticing?

# SEVENTEEN

Saul, Bryn, and I exit through the underground parking lot in which two chauffeured vehicles await. Although Malachi claims I'll be safest at the hospital, if anyone is after me, what will stop them from going after Mom? The teenage nurse Malachi vouched for? Old Mrs. Fiona?

Although I'm certain my upstairs neighbor would give them hell—maybe attempt to suffocate them with her pungent perfume, or choke them with her lanyard—if Tarian was taken by Atlanteans, by his own uncle no less, she wouldn't stand a chance. Besides, I need to see what's become of the shop. If the window's whole, it'll prove that my dreams, however strange, are merely in my head.

"Tarian's driver will drop you off at home." When Bryn takes my arm to come with me, Saul says, "Bryn, sweetheart, we're having a family lunch."

"I should stay with Callie—"

"Your mother would be exceedingly disappointed."

"My mother's always disappointed."

Saul's mouth hardens into a tight, disapproving line. Is he cross with Joslyn or with Bryn? "They serve the freshest oysters and lobster in all of Massachusetts."

Although my friend enjoys seafood, she's not the type to be lured by her stomach. Now, if he'd mentioned an all-you-can-buy shopping spree…

Before Bryn can refuse, he adds, "I'm trying hard to be a family, and my son won't come if you don't. You're the only Fielding he can stand."

Because the other two are selfish witches. How does he not see that?

"Please," he adds quietly.

I know Bryn will capitulate before the sigh even whistles past her teeth, but then she glances my way, and doubt weakens her resolve.

"Your friend will have medical care at home." At my peaked eyebrows, Saul adds, "Joslyn mentioned that your mother wasn't *well*. I took the liberty of arranging for a nurse so both you and your mother will have round-the-clock care."

Dread unspools inside my stomach. What if this second nurse is a spy? Or worse, one of them?

"I appreciate your thoughtfulness, Mr. Hadez, but I already hired someone, and I can't afford two nurses. Besides, now that I'll be home, round-the-clock care is totally unnecessary."

"I'll call my hire and tell her to give yours leave."

I don't like that idea one bit. "No."

"Then you'll have two. I'll pay for both. My treat."

I clench around the straps of the giant handbag stuffed with most of my wardrobe. This is all too convenient.

"Hun, you need a break." Bryn squeezes my arm. "Take the break. Besides, that candy striper you hired looked painfully incompetent."

Saul's eyes glow. "Wait for me in the car, Bryn." He gestures to the one behind him. "Miss Bloom, be gracious and accept my nurse."

I flip him off—in my mind. "A second set of hands is so welcomed," I grit out, which creates a furrow between his brows. When he roots around the shadows cast by the bill of my favorite baseball cap, I smack an obliged smile on my face. "That was really considerate of you, Mr. Hadez. How can I ever repay you?"

"It's my pleasure to help people in need." Saul plucks sunglasses from his jacket pocket.

*People in need?* I feel like he's just smooshed me under his loafer sole and kicked me to the curb. *We're not beggars*, I want to growl. Realizing that speaking my very pissed off mind will only make Saul suspicious, I pivot and stalk toward the car Bryn didn't get into.

Tarian's driver, the one built like a golf cart, already has the door propped open. I mumble a quick *hello* before settling onto the beige backseat. The door suctions closed, and although I'm aware it hasn't siphoned out the oxygen, I find it suddenly difficult to breathe.

By the time he pushes on the ignition, my lungs feel like wet tissues—crumpled and unusable. I start to reach for the handle when the locks all click shut.

My anger morphs into panic. "Open—the door. Can't—can't breathe." I pray my voice penetrates the privacy screen between him and me.

My fingers scrabble over the black glass partition, desperately seeking an intercom button. *Damn it, Tarian! Why do you have to own such a fancy-ass chauffeured car?*

When my vision turns grainy and gray, I forgo trying to communicate with Reacher and reach for my door handle, only to find that there's none in this goddamn car.

As my heart pumps savagely, Mom's face flashes in front of my eyes, then Tarian's. Heat blasts against my face as though the flames that chewed through the Bugatti are now chomping through this car. Splinters of panic pierce my heart and flood my mouth with the taste of metal.

"Stop!" I raise my fist to rap on the privacy window when Reacher guns the car up the exit ramp, throwing me back into the seat, and the world becomes as noiseless and black as a moonless night.

MY ARM JIGGLES. Once. Twice.

Color floods the backs of my lids, and the sound of someone laying on their car horn rushes through my eardrums.

"Miss Bloom?" Another jiggle. "We've arrived at our destination, Miss Bloom."

I snap my eyes open and jolt into a seated position, then scramble against the car door Reacher isn't gripping. Nausea slams into me, followed by another rebellion of heartbeats.

Because I'm going to be sick, I thumb the window control button. Instead of powering it down, though, it unlatches my door. I flail sideways. Reacher claps my denim-clad thigh, just managing to keep my ass anchored to the backseat.

Nausea rolls out of me and soils the road. The acrid sting dampens my lashes as my stomach heaves anew and releases another wave of bile.

A cab swerves around my gaping passenger door, the driver tossing out a, "Do you have a death wish, lady?" before speeding off.

*No.* I have a life wish.

Once the spasms calm, I pull myself back upright, dragging the door along with me. Reacher dangles a wet wipe in front of my face. I wonder if he made them appear out of thin air, because what grown, childless man carries around wipes? Maybe he's Atlantean and conjuring up disposable washcloths is his superpower?

I take it from him and shakily raise it to my lips, wiping away the taste of my panic. "Th-thank you."

"I should take you back to the hospital."

"No. I'm fine." I need to get my mother out.

"You just threw up."

Balling the wipe, I say, "Motion sickness."

"Are you certain, Miss Bloom? You fell asleep the second we left the hospital parking lot."

I didn't fall asleep; I passed out. I don't correct Reacher, because I much prefer he believe I was calm enough for a snooze.

I adjust my forest green baseball cap, tugging the brim low. "Thank you for the ride."

He nods, then backs up to let me out. I start to scoot forward when I catch sight of Bloom's Blooms storefront.

# EIGHTEEN

**O**ur door isn't broken.

"Everything all right, Miss Bloom?" Reacher peers between me and the shop.

*No,* I want to scream. Everything is all wrong. I'm having fucking dreams about your fucking boss that feel fucking real but clearly aren't!

I'm not one for cursing, not even inside my mind, so this says a lot about my anxiety level. I squeeze the bridge of my nose as I work on slowing my breathing before I can pass out—again—from hyperventilation.

"Stay in the car." Reacher studies me through his dark lenses. "I'll go collect your mother."

*Collect my mother?* Not only would the sight of this colossus in black traumatize her, but also—and most importantly—*why* does he want to get her? To trap her inside with me and drive us out to a landfill?

When he starts to close the passenger door, I slap my palm against it to keep it open. "I feel fine. Besides, my mother won't react well to the likes of you." Imbued with a nervous energy, I leap out of the car and streak across the pavement.

"Miss Bloom?"

I whirl around to find Reacher holding out my bag. It's no rifle, yet I stare at it as though it were.

Pressing my hand against my heart to wrangle its harried beats, I snatch the bag from his meaty fingers, squeaking out a, "Thank you."

As I root around for my keys, Reacher's gaze ceaselessly sweeps my street. Is he expecting danger, or is he making sure he isn't the last person seen with me before I vanish from the face of the earth?

When my fingers finally encounter metal, I slide the key between my index and middle fingers. I really wish I'd had the presence of mind to ask Bryn to grab my can of pepper spray from underneath the register. Though, would tear gas even manage to find its way beneath sunglasses? And would it hurt an Atlantean, whose eyes aren't even human?

"Did you find your keys?" He's staring straight at them.

"No need to stick around."

"I was told to escort you inside."

"I'm good. Thanks for the ride, Reacher."

"Richard?"

*Crap.* I snare my bottom lip between my teeth, trying to recall what Tarian had called him but between the accident and my frayed nerves, it doesn't come back to me. "I forgot your name."

"It's Dorian." His lips curve with a very small smile—microscopic really, and totally chilling. "But you can call me Richard."

If I weren't stressed out of my mind, I may have smirked at the misunderstanding, but honestly, I don't have a single smirk in me. Besides, if he ends up gunning me down, I may prefer to think of him as Richard, since Reacher's a hero and all.

He lowers his aviators to reveal irises that glimmer like prisms. "Please open the door, Miss Bloom."

Ugh. If I don't abide, he'll know I'm immune to his magic.

Mouth puckered, I jam my key in the lock and twist, then step inside. "Door's open. Job accomplished. Thanks a mil."

I try to shut the door, but he palms it open.

"My boss would want me to make sure you're safe."

My keys rattle in my white-knuckled grip. "Which boss is that?"

"Tarian."

"What about Saul?"

"Not my boss."

"Yet you came to fetch me on his behalf, didn't you?"

"Not my boss," he repeats, his pitch so low that it barely makes it to my ears.

"Speaking of your boss—"

"If you want to speak of my boss"—he nods to the shop—"we'll do so indoors."

The oxygen sliding down my lungs is so barbed it feels like I'm inhaling thorny rose stalks.

"*Now*, Miss Bloom. Before we attract too much attention." He must read the anguish in my stare, because he adds a soft, "I won't let any harm befall you. I swear it on your god."

"I don't have a god." I used to, but that god took Daddy, so He and I are on the outs.

"Well, you still have my word. And know that I neither give it liberally nor often."

"Tell me one thing. Is Tarian safe?"

A woman pushing a stroller gawks at the hulking male crowding me before swerving around us and wheeling her baby across the street.

"No," he finally concedes. "And you aren't either. Which is why I'm here."

"To keep me from getting gunned down?"

He nods. Is he saying, *Yes, that's right, I'm here to act as your shield and armor*, or is the nod a prompt to let him in? Can I trust him? I want to, but Saul—whom he claims he *doesn't* work for— made him drive me here.

"We're sitting ducks out here," he murmurs.

I flick my eyeballs left and right, then squint at the windows of every building lining the street. Though I don't spot any sunglasses-clad gang of nefarious Atlanteans, I don't breathe any easier. How can I when I'm sharing air with a man who could crush my skull between his pinkies?

Reacher's square chin grazes his corded neck. "Please help me find Tarian, Miss Bloom."

His quiet entreaty, coupled with his fretful timbre, is my undoing. Hoping I'm not leading my killer inside, I finally step back. The chime's tinkle drops me back into last night's psychosomatic trip…or whatever the hell it was. Maybe Reacher will know. I'm dying to discuss my connection to Tarian with someone, and who better than a fellow Atlantean? What if all new gods can hang out in their sleep? And yes, I'm aware I'm not Atlantean, but I've clearly become *something*.

After we enter the shop, Reacher flicks the lock, which flicks my erratic pulse. I back up toward the display table, the cut on my foot throbbing as hard as my heart. There's no glass on the floor, yet the backs of my lids shimmer with its memory.

"Get your mother so we can head out."

"Where is it you want to take us?" Tucking my bag between my arm and rib cage, I approach a glass vase that's bound to do *some* damage if lobbed at someone's head. Right?

"To a safehouse."

"They take witnesses to safehouses."

"Your mother, Miss Bloom. Please go collect her." He divests himself of his sunglasses, revealing eyes as clear and blue as the sky beyond the windowed facade. I'm guessing he's going to try to influence me again, but his eyes don't spark with anything more than frustration.

"Why did Saul tell me Tarian was back at the office?"

When Reacher slips his hand inside his jacket pocket, I grab the vase. Although it weighs a fucklot, and my arms are shaking like cymbals, my grip doesn't waver.

"I'm just putting away my glasses. You can set the flowers down."

"Not until you tell me what the hell's going on. What am I witness to?"

"Tarian Hadez's abduction." Reacher's teeth barely separate as he speaks. "Once we reach the safehouse, I'll tell you everything I know."

"Why should I trust you?"

"Because Saul wants to use you as bait to lure the people who took his nephew, and if they come for you, you'll want me at your side."

"So Saul didn't kidnap him?"

"No."

"Are you certain?"

The stairs creak, and I jump, whipping myself in the face with wilted petals.

In two strides, Reacher's at my side. "Get under the table," he murmurs, striding past me and around the wall of succulents, a gun gleaming between his fingers.

Another creak.

What if it's Mom? I'm about to hiss, "Put the weapon away," when I think, *What if it's Tarian's kidnapper? Or that second nurse Saul hired?*

I set the vase down, then crawl under the table. Heart thundering, I fish my phone from my bag and type out 911. I hover my finger over the dial button just as a woman's legs appear—too skinny to be Mrs. Fiona's and too tall to be Mom's.

A gasp sounds, and I think Reacher's shot her, but then the woman hisses, "Fucking finally. I've been phoning you nonstop."

Though I didn't recognize the legs, I recognize the voice; it belongs to that teenage nurse. No wonder Malachi wanted me to hire her. Is she even a nurse?

# NINETEEN

**D**orian lowers his gun. "What the hell are you doing here, Elle?"

Not only does he know Electra, but he has a nickname for her?

"Mal called."

"Consider yourself *uncalled*."

"Not your decision to make, big brother."

*Brother?* I grind my teeth. Of course Electra is one of them. Stupid, stupid me for thinking I'd employed a regular nurse.

"I thought you were another one of those asshole hunters." She steps down the rest of the stairs, then rounds the wall of succulents, short black hair swishing around her tanned face.

I try to spot similarities between the two Atlanteans, but they look nothing alike. Not that all siblings have to resemble one another, but still… Why am I wasting a minute on the genetic makeup of two strangers?

After a quick glance around the shop, she casts her gaze to the table I'm hiding under. "Miss Bloom." Her odd-hued eyes take on that inhuman glow. "*You* hired me, not Malachi Hadez. Dorian and I have never met. No Holy Hunters stopped by. And you're under the table because you dropped an earring."

As I pretend to search for freaking jewelry, I clench my molars to the point of chipping enamel. I'm so fucking furious with Malachi that I want to snatch Dorian's gun and shoot the siblings in the toes.

"No earring." Anger tightens my pitch, making the words snap like darts off my tongue. As I crawl out from under the table and straighten, I ask, "Where's my mother?"

Electra scrutinizes me as though I was a land lobster. "Upstairs. Watching a cooking show with that crotchety neighbor of yours."

"Awesome." I shuffle past her, or rather attempt to.

She steps into my path. "It's best you don't go upstairs at the moment."

"Why?"

Electra side-eyes Dorian. I don't think new gods can communicate without words, but these two seem so attuned to one another that maybe I'm wrong. "It's...messy."

"Did you throw a rave in my absence?"

She snorts. "Yeah, it was your mother's idea." My eyes must bulge, because she says, "There was no rave."

Even though she said Mom and Mrs. Fiona were looking at the TV, my heart begins to hammer anew.

"Just tell her, Elle," Dorian says softly. "Miss Bloom should know since she's going to help us find Tarian."

Electra blinks at Dorian, then hisses something in Atlantean— probably her displeasure at roping me into their secret society's secrets. I'm not certain what Reacher replies, but it makes Electra swing her attention back my way.

"Your neighbor's the reason it's messy," she ends up saying. "She didn't like the looks of Saul's new hire, so she phoned up the clique that hates our people."

"You told Mrs. Fiona where you were from?"

"Of course not."

"Then—"

"She caught Ines speaking in our tongue on that nanny cam you installed."

I take it Ines is the other gun-for-hire Saul passed off as a nurse.

"We weren't aware we had an audience." She tips me a look that says, *You could've informed us about the recording device.*

I'm so glad I didn't. "I'm surprised she had the Holy Hunters' number." And also that she'd recognize Atlantean. I didn't.

"She apparently saw an ad for their hotline on TV. Anyway, she let four of them in about an hour ago. We killed three; Ines left with the last."

Dorian's jaw slackens. "She—left?"

"Yep." Electra's eyelid twitches.

"Why would she leave with a Holy Hunter?"

His sister studies her nails with inordinate interest. "We assumed the sect might be involved in Tarian's disappearance. What better way to find out than visiting their Headquarters?" Electra shrugs. "I'm sure we'll hear from her soon."

Dorian mutters beneath his breath, then sweeps his cell phone from his jacket, and dials someone. "She's not picking up."

"She's probably busy torturing him or something." Shrug. "You know Ines." Shrug.

Electra's definitely holding something back. Is it something she doesn't want me to know or her brother?

He puckers his lips. "One more reason to get out of here." He glances my way. "Is there anything more you need from upstairs? Besides your mother?"

"Mrs. Fiona. We're not leaving her behind."

Electra opens her mouth to protest.

"If you want me to cooperate, she comes with us. End of fucking story." I start toward the stairs, but Electra snaps out her arm to keep me in place.

"Let Dorian get them. Like I mentioned earlier, it's messy."

He grumbles as he climbs the stairs.

I recall her saying only one Holy Hunter left. Which reminds me that the three others are dead. Will blood start seeping through the ceiling?

"I know my brother's built like an ox, but he has an unparalleled way of putting people at ease."

I bet she's referring to his compulsion, and I almost say something about it, but neither Electra nor Dorian know I can resist it. Only Malachi is aware of my immunity. Interestingly enough, he hasn't divulged it to the siblings.

Dorian draws open the door at the top of the stairs, hurtling a sickly-sweet gust through the shop. It throws me a decade in the past, to a time when I set my hair on fire while blowing out my birthday candles.

"Is something burning?"

"Just the corpses." Electra's incredibly calm, as though incinerating dead bodies is an everyday occurrence. And maybe it is in her world but it's definitely not in mine. "I heaped them inside Mrs. Murphy's bathtub, so the fire won't spread to the rest of your building. Don't worry."

A manic chuckle sputters from my mouth. Is she fucking serious right now? "You set fire to people, and you're expecting me to stay chill?"

"Those *people* wouldn't have hesitated to eliminate you." A ray of sunlight bends through the shop window and illuminates her face, yellowing her brown iris and cooling her blue one. "Your mother and neighbor are *safe*. I kept them safe," she grits out, her arm still blocking me from racing after Dorian.

My chest trills with panicked beats. Does she expect a medal? If that other Atlantean had just spoken in English, Mrs. Fiona wouldn't have gotten spooked. "You think they're involved in his abduction?"

Electra slides her lips together. "Though I would've preferred not to be ambushed by that merry band of zealous dickheads, I'm hoping it'll serve us."

I inch away from her and toward the register to grab the pepper spray. "Didn't you"—I'm about to say *compel*, but thankfully, swap it out for—"interrogate the survivor?"

Her cheeks flex as though she's crunching down on a mouthful of walnuts still in their shell. "He was resistant to my interrogation methods." When I lean over to filch the spray, she tilts her head to the side. "What are you doing?"

"Grabbing some cash." I drop the can inside my bag, then pop open the register.

"You're not gonna need any money."

"Well, I'd prefer not to leave it behind."

When I start toward the stairs, Electra says, "Dorian will be down in a second."

"I need my EpiPen." And probably a fresh Band-Aid for my foot, which is stinging almost as much as the rune on my back.

"Seriously, don't venture up there. I'll get you a new one."

"I don't go anywhere without it."

Surprisingly, Electra doesn't whip out a forcefield to keep me corralled inside the shop. Then again, her brawny brother is upstairs, so she mustn't fear I'm going to slip away. I grip the banister and start climbing just as the door opens and Dorian appears with my mother on one arm and Mrs. Fiona on the other.

"Callie, baby." My mother's delicate features tremble with a mixture of trepidation and relief. "Get out. The building's on fire."

Dorian gives the slightest shake of his head to let me know it's not true.

"This fine young man came to succor us." Mrs. Fiona pats Dorian's beefy arm, gazing up at him as though he was God himself. If only she knew he was an Atlantean.

"Sweetie, go, go, go." My mother gives a jerky nod in the direction of the exit. "Smoke inhalation is just as dangerous as flames."

Just as she says this, the smoke detector blares, and the sprinklers gush. Electra's localized fire must've spread. Unless one of the Hunters survived and climbed out of the bathtub? The thought must strike her mind, because she races past me.

"Go!" Mom cries out.

I startle, and my injured foot catches on a puddle. As I flail forward, I shoot my arms up to protect my head from cracking against the tiles.

*Splash.*

My lips part around a startled gasp that shoots salty liquid down my throat. Another splash whitens the water around me, then an arm bands around my waist and hefts me up from behind. I try to lock eyes with my lifeguard, but my hair curtains off my sight.

How much freaking water did our sprinkler system dish out?

I grip the forearm that's so corded with muscle I assume it's Dorian's, until I detect the cyan glow of runes.

# TWENTY

The second my head tears through the surface, I retch out a mouthful of—of *sea water*?

"You're really living up to that nickname, Calamity." The deep voice is warm and feather-soft, and although it touches only the shell of my ear, I feel it everywhere.

I close my eyes and murmur, "This is a dream. Only a dream. Not real."

"It is a dream." Tarian presses one large palm against my navel and swivels me. "But it's also real."

"Except dreams aren't real."

"You used to think supernatural beings weren't real, but you've come to terms with the fact that some of us have magic."

I keep my lids shut and count down from ten.

"I'm afraid this isn't a game of hide-and-seek, Miss Bloom."

"…three…two…"

"Still here." His rasp strikes the tip of my nose, boosting my heart's tempo.

Sure enough, when I raise my lashes, the chiseled planes of Tarian's face come into perfect focus.

"Impossible." My foot stings then, reminding me that many senseless things are evidently possible.

Before I can think better of voluntarily touching him, I snake one of my hands out of the water and skim my fingers across his jaw. Yes, I can feel his arms and chest and legs, but those could possibly be Dorian's appendages and my crazed mind is pasting on Tarian's imaginary face.

Unlike Tarian, Dorian sports no beard, yet bristly stubble tickles my fingertips. I snatch my hand away as though the Atlantean has electrocuted me. Breath sawing through my lungs, I gape at the male keeping our bodies afloat.

"Though I do love to swim"—Tarian moves us forward with one powerful stroke—"I prefer to do so with far less clothes." He reaches out and grabs ahold of a metal ladder.

"This is insane." I shake my head to drive some sanity back into my brain. "*I'm* insane."

He takes one of my hands and gently wraps it around the ladder. "You're not insane, Calanthe."

"We're meeting in a dimension that isn't real."

"It's real to us." He wraps my other hand around the side rail.

I finally manage to snap out of my daze and power my body up the steps. Once aground, I watch Tarian heave himself out of the indigo surf, his white button-down plastered to the broad mantel of his shoulders and the slabs of muscle beneath.

The man is a beast. It seems ludicrous that he could've been captured, and even more so that he hasn't yet been able to break free.

Tarian drives his fingers through his black locks, springing sea water from them like those models in Italian cologne commercials. I can't help but stare at the swollen muscles flexing beneath the see-through fabric that covers unmarred skin. Has he mended in the real world also?

Thinking of his old wounds makes my heel sting again. Nothing like salt water on a fresh cut to clear the mind. "Everyone's looking for you, Mr. Hadez."

"Tarian. I'm not your boss."

I grip the hem of the Bon Jovi shirt I put on earlier and wring it out. "You may not be my boss, but you're still a stranger."

"I think we're past being strangers, don't you?" He tips his head to the side. "Unless you allow strangers to lick your skin?"

Though soaking wet, I'm suddenly about ready to fan myself. At this point, my clothes may dry on their own. "It's not a usual occurrence, no." I'm about to add, *But it didn't actually occur*, when my mind whispers, *The rune on your back was wet with his saliva.* "Back to your whereabouts. Where are you?"

His eyes dim so fast that I regret having brought up reality. No, that's not true. I don't regret it, because the faster we locate him, the faster I will be free of *my* new reality, and the faster I get my mother back.

"Where are you?"

"At my house in Martha's Vineyard." A lock of black hair flops into his bottomless eyes, tangling into his ridiculously thick lashes. "With you."

"I mean in real life. Where are you?"

His lips thin. "Don't fucking know."

"How come you can't break free?"

"Because my powers won't fucking regenerate."

Guilt pokes at my chest, tightening my grip around the sodden gray fabric and rumpling my nose.

His lashes lower a fraction. "What's with the look?"

I drop my gaze to my waterlogged sneakers, glad Bryn had the foresight to select practical shoes that wouldn't slide off during my inter-dimensional travel. I would've hated ruining or losing a pretty pair of stilettos. Although, would I have lost them, or would I have been beamed back in the real world, outfit intact?

Why am I even thinking about shoes at a time like this? Because it's my brain's mechanism for coping with the heavy dose of responsibility I feel for Tarian's abduction?

I snare my bottom lip and nibble it, but then I sigh and decide to face my tormented conscience straight on. "Malachi explained that you used up your powers to save me."

"Malachi?" Tarian dips his head and his voice. "As in, my cousin Malachi?"

"Yes. When I woke up in the hospital, he was there. Remember? I showed him my rune."

"The hospital?"

Did I forget to mention I'd been brought to the hospital during our last dream? "Your uncle had me discharged this morning."

A vein throbs so hard at his temple I worry it may rupture. Can dream-veins rupture? *Your dream-foot bled,* my mind reminds me. Bleeding makes me think of the way we parted in real life. I shudder as the scarlet smear blooms across my vision.

"Where are you? And who are you with?"

His nervy tone does wonders to cleanse my mind of the memory. "I'm with Dorian."

"Good."

"He's trustworthy?"

"Entirely. Him *and* Malachi."

"What about Dorian's sister? Electra? Do you trust her?"

I'm guessing my nipples are drilling holes into Bon Jovi's name because his gaze is currently planted there. Where most men's attention feels sleazy, Tarian's doesn't. Could be because the man has already worshipped my curves, so staring at my rack is really not all that scandalous.

"You can trust her."

"Do you trust Saul?"

"No."

"Dorian doesn't think your uncle is behind your abduction."

Tarian studies my mouth for almost a full minute after I've finished talking, like he's trying to parse out my words. He gives his head a shake and steps nearer, casting me in his shadow. "You're shivering. Let's get you into some dry clothes."

I try to conjure some from the ether, but my wardrobe stays unchanged. "I made leggings appear last time."

His brow furrows.

"What? I did." I try again. Nothing. "Why isn't it working?" I grit out.

"It's the first time I've shared this sort of connection with another person, so I don't know."

"So these communal psychosomatic trips"—I gesture between him and me—"aren't a usual Atlantean power?"

"No." His exhausted smile reaches deep into me, thawing all those places hardened by resentment and fear. "They're not."

His hand comes up to my face. For a heartbeat, it hovers, but then his fingers snare one of my wet locks and slots it behind my ear. More goosebumps pour over my skin at his proximity. I should really step back, but I really don't want to.

"Actually…" He returns his hand to his side. "I think I understood something." Suddenly, his wet suit trousers and button-down morph into a white linen shirt and a pair of low-hanging gray slacks.

I gasp. "Did I just do that?"

"No." His smile reaches into his dark irises, and although it doesn't brighten them, it makes them shimmer. "I did."

I picture a simple sundress. My skin prickles as my wet clothes are replaced by…*not* a sundress.

"Hmm…" A boyish grin spreads over Tarian's face. "So that's how it works."

I perch my hands on my hips and mock-scowl. "Seriously?"

"My dream, Calamity." His shiny gaze drinks in the outfit he's clearly conjured up. "My fantasy."

# TWENTY-ONE

I'm still uncertain why my magic bonded me to a stranger, but I'm grateful it chose this girl. If it had welded me to someone like Mackenzie Fielding… Perish the thought.

I would've shunned sleeping. I may even have bartered with my persecutors—offered them my complete cooperation in exchange for a bedside vigilante tasked with slapping me anytime my lids drooped.

Perhaps Gaea picked Calanthe because She knew what Fate had in store for me and took pity on my soul. Or perhaps *I* picked her. Though Father was a great believer in soulmates, I never adhered to the sappy concept of twin souls, but what if this woman does belong to me?

I stab my wet hair with my fingers again and shake my head. *This isn't a romantic connection, you bloody idiot. This girl isn't your soul's salvation, solely your body's.*

If only I could puzzle out where said body is being kept. This is what I should be focusing on instead of playing dress-up with my dream girl. Though, I'd dare anyone in my situation to concentrate on logistics in this woman's presence.

As my hand falls back to my side, my gaze takes another whirl around her luscious curves. What I wouldn't give to shape them with my hands. To feel the flutter of her pulse and the velvet of her skin under my palms.

My cock kicks against my zipper, aching for what lays beneath her black string bikini. I start to reach out to… I don't even know what I planned to do. Tow her to me without her consent? What sort of beast have I become? I ball my fingers and let them drop back to my side, and then I take a good, long breath and tell my dick to stand down. But the poor chap doesn't get the memo. He merely keeps hardening and leaking as the sun bounces off the thin gold chain that wraps around Calanthe's neck before dipping between her breasts and tying around her waist.

"I can't wait to be in charge of our next dream." Even though she doesn't look all that peeved, her hands are still bolted to her hips. "I have the perfect outfit in mind for you."

"Yeah?" Arousal dropkicks my voice a full octave.

I'm not sure if she senses my attraction, or if it's the weight of my attention that's affecting her, but her skin breaks out in goose-bumps, and one of her hands lifts to her chest. Oh, to be that hand.

She toys with the bodychain. "Is this type of jewelry common in Atlantis?" Her tone is perfectly smooth, unlike her movements.

"Not that I'm aware of." To avoid getting chafed by my zipper, I readjust myself. I have to do it again when her hazel eyes sink to my crotch and her pupils dilate. I end up easing the strain by swapping the constricting trousers for gray sweatpants. "I probably spotted something of the sort on a magazine cover."

If she wonders why I changed clothes, she doesn't ask. Merely says, "I didn't take you for a *Vogue* type of guy."

I smirk. "The pilots stockpile them on our jets for my uncle's merry-go-round of girlfriends."

"Your uncle's, huh?" Although she sounds almost blasé, her pulse nips at the skin of her neck. "What do *your* girlfriends read? *The New Yorker*? *Good Housekeeping*?"

The corners of my lips quirk up some more. "This may come as a surprise, Calamity, but I don't keep women around long enough to learn their reading preferences. As for the few women who've traveled with me, they're there for business meetings. My time is precious, so if they spent any of it flipping through glossy magazines, they'd be out of a job."

A faint groove forms between her brows.

"What?"

"Nothing."

"You're clearly thinking something."

"When you say *long enough,* how long are we talking?" She tucks a wet strand behind her ear.

"I don't date."

"Are you saying you've *never* had a girlfriend?"

"Girlfriends require time and energy. I've none to give."

Her pupils are still blown, but this time, it isn't desire that dilates them; it's surprise. "You've got none to give, or you're epically selfish?"

My gaze sinks back to the part of the chain buried between her breasts. "Selective loneliness is a luxury, Miss Bloom."

"What you call a luxury, I call depressing."

"I was attached and look how that turned out for my father."

She sighs. "He didn't die because you loved him, Tarian."

"I'm aware my love didn't off him, Miss Bloom. I'm aware my fucking magic is to blame."

Instead of recoiling, she narrows her eyes. "Malachi said it wasn't."

I grunt, then stare over Calanthe's head at my father's first U.S. acquisition—a white clapboard mansion that reminded him of our home back in Atlantis. Reminded him of Mom. When Symeon and I divvied up his assets, it was the sole property I requested, only to find out that Dad had already put it in my name. Astonishingly, Symeon didn't fight me for it. Then again, Father bequeathed him the 60-meter yacht he kept in Cape Cod, so my brother assumed he'd gotten the better asset.

"You pasted a rune on my skin," Calanthe is saying, "and I'm still alive."

"For now…"

Her cheek dimples. Since she isn't smiling, I assume she's biting the inside of it. "If I survive, though, it'll prove you're not a killer. Well…not that sort of killer. You've probably murdered plenty of people." She flicks her fingers. "Which I don't want to hear about."

"Did you assume I was going to offer you a play-by-play of all my killings?"

She snorts, but her expression wavers when I don't crack a smile.

"I don't kill and tell, Calamity." I add a wink that seems to fluster her further.

She reaches for that marvelous chain I summoned. The minute I break free, I'm having a jeweler recreate it. It's the least I can do after having upended her life. Hopefully, she'll accept my gift and wear it.

What if she wears it for another man? As I scrutinize the gold quivering against her deep tan, my lids twitch. My jealousy is surely some perverse result of the word that lifted off my skin and tattooed hers, yet I can't seem to beat it back down.

"Turn," I bark. "I want to check the rune."

"You know, the word *please* has never shrunken a man's testicles."

"*Please*, Calamity," I drawl, "show me your back."

As she pivots, she scoops up the wet mass of her hair and carries it over her shoulder. "Why immediately, Hades."

I hate that she refers to me as the god of the underworld, even in jest, because it reminds me that I have that sort of power over her delicate human life.

Her rune glows. Her *unchanged* rune. I keep expecting the letters to warp into that hateful "X," marking her for death.

The exhale I let out is so potent that it makes her peek over her shoulder. She hitches up an eyebrow.

With a dark smile, I proclaim, "Still mine, Calamity."

She frees her hair, concealing the word. "How come it only reads that way to you?"

"Because the powers that be decided you belonged to me."

She rolls her eyes. "I meant, why does it read *sleep* to Malachi?"

Like the first time we discussed this in the pageantry dream, I'm hit with a visual of my cousin leering at Calanthe's bare back, and it causes every tendon in my neck to strain. If the letters had been lined up the same, what thought would've gone through his head? Would he have assumed she was his? I grip my nape and squeeze it to relieve the growing pressure.

"Tarian?" Calanthe's expressive eyebrows quirk, prying me out of my caveman thoughts.

"I don't know, but aren't you glad?"

"Glad that a second Atlantean doesn't think I'm a thing to be possessed? Yeah, I'm glad."

"I don't think of you as a thing."

As she pivots back toward me, she holds my stare, assessing the veracity of my reply. "The rune you stung your father with. What was it?"

Her question feels like a punch to the gut. I immediately see the five letters that lifted off my right bicep and settled on my father's shoulder the last time he and I ever touched. Five little letters that transformed into a symbol that stole his magic and immortality.

"*Itfir.* It means *withdraw*." My ribs ache as violently as my mood. "It started with his runes. A week later, it withdrew every last ounce of blood from his veins."

Horror makes her eyes glisten like the ocean hemming in my private pier. "Your father bled out?"

"No. He *dried* out."

She pales. "Did it read differently to Malachi?"

"No. He saw the 'X.'"

"So if it morphs into a symbol, I'm a goner? It really gives new meaning to becoming someone's ex." Her dimples poke free. "I still don't get something. Why are you so convinced you killed him if all you did was withdraw his magic?"

I cross my arms. "Didn't you hear the part about me withdrawing his blood?"

"You said that happened a week later."

"We have several pints inside our body. It must've been gradual."

She sighs, and the sound smacks of so much pity that I take a step back. It's my least favorite emotion to stir in people. For almost a month after Father died, I stopped talking to Malachi because of his exhausting compassion.

"Tarian, you assume your magic rid him of blood, but you don't actually know that it did."

I stay mute. I'm not having this debate again. Especially not with someone who barely understands the sort of magic I wield.

"Fine." She expels a second sigh—a frustrated one this time. "But explain this to me. Since I had no magic to begin with—no magical sentence to smother—how come you were so convinced branding me would trigger my death?"

"Because my magic is toxic, Calanthe. My runes have only ever corrupted and killed. Maybe the word won't outright exsanguinate your body, like it did to my father, but it won't leave you unscathed."

I'm suddenly back at the construction site I was visiting with Malachi when we received Saul's call. The one informing us that the call girl my father would meet on Thursday afternoons had arrived for their tryst to find my father dead. Malachi had jumped to the conclusion of foul play; I hadn't.

"Can we chat about something else? *Anything* else. Honestly, I'd even prefer hearing all about Mackenzie's skincare regimen again than discuss my malign magic."

Calanthe blinks, and then a smile softens her expression. "*Again?*"

The dinner Saul roped me into so I could meet Joslyn hadn't been a barrel of laughs, but when her eldest joined us after a meeting with a client in the very same restaurant, it had become downright tedious. Malachi—the sympathetic Hadez—had been kind enough to appear invested in her monologue on serums and face creams; I hadn't even bothered. I cannot fake interest, for the life of me.

"I would've paid good money to watch that conversation play out." Calanthe is still smiling, and although it's no spell, the simple curl of her lips unknots the tension festering inside my body.

"Help Dorian locate me, and I'll sit down with both you and Mackenzie to chat about wrinkle balms."

She releases a startled laugh that's so throaty and fresh, the sound sinks straight into my dick. "Deal. Never thought I'd look forward to spending any time with Mackenzie, but I literally cannot wait."

I'm suddenly impatient for this sit-down myself. Not only does it mean I'll be free, but also, it means that Calanthe and I will meet again, this time wide awake.

A warm breeze kicks her honeyed wildflower scent toward me, and fuck if it isn't the headiest fragrance I've ever inhaled. I'd blame my craving on the magic binding us, but Calanthe Bloom had my mind and body's full attention the minute she tossed that rose at my car. The only reason I hadn't hit the brakes and gotten out of the Bugatti was *because* of my body's reaction. I avoided temptation like my uncle avoided celibacy.

"Okay, Hades. Let's make the most of our time together."

My mind drops into the gutter as I picture her grabbing her bathing suit ties and tugging.

She clicks her fingers in front of my face, and I blink away from the pretty black bows. "Concentrate."

"I am," I rasp.

"On the words coming out of my mouth, because concentrating on my hips isn't going to help me find you."

"True, but it's going to make the search-and-rescue a lot more agreeable."

Her freckles darken with a lovely blush, and then her lips part around words I don't catch because the world is tipping, tipping…

She reaches out and grabs my arm to steady me. "Tarian!"

I don't hear my name as much as I read its shape on her lips. I try so hard to stay with her, but like a pendulum, I swing sideways again, and then I crash out of the dream and back into an airless dark room.

An airless dark room that rocks.

# TWENTY-TWO

I gasp awake.

"Callie? Oh, Callie." Old Mrs. Fiona's panicky voice rattles my brain. "Cor blimey, child." She shudders. "When you fell down those stairs…"

I blink at her lined face, at the bruise-hued pockets beneath her eyes, then blink around me at the bedroom done up in fifty shades of gray, with blackened steel finishings and sleek light fixtures that cast a warm glow over the otherwise cool bedroom.

Mrs. Fiona pads barefoot toward the open door and yells, "Hey, G.I. Joe, Calanthe's lucid!"

I assume G.I. Joe is the moniker she came up with for Dorian. Sure enough, he barrels through the door a second later. As he nears, I prop myself up in the king-size bed, my forehead screeching. I start to raise my hand to touch it when I notice that my hair and clothes are damp. As I touch the cotton, my mind vaults back to Tarian and the ocean we tumbled into. Well, *I* tumbled into; *he* dove in after me.

I know our Martha's Vineyard swim didn't actually happen, yet I pinch the collar of my T-shirt and carry it up to my nose. The whiff of brine that punches up my nostrils suspends my pulse. Our sprinkler system isn't hooked up to the ocean, yet I smell like the inside of a conch shell.

"You banged your head pretty hard. Nurse Serran applied some butterfly stitches." Dorian nods toward my forehead where, sure enough, six small strips have been pressed onto a tender piece of skin.

I'm about to ask why she didn't just heal me with magic when I remember that neither Dorian nor Electra is aware that Tarian marked me, and that Malachi filled me in on all things Atlantis.

As my fingertips drop to the slate-hued sheets that are darker where I lay, I glance around the elegant bedroom that's devoid of personality. No knickknacks grace the sleek black dresser, no clothes are piled on the gray armchair parked beside the bed, no books grace the shelving unit, no paintings adorn the walls.

I take it we're in the safehouse, but since Mrs. Fiona's present, I don't outright pronounce the word, afraid to spook her. I wonder what she was told.

"Where are we?" My voice sounds rough, as though I'd been intubated.

"In an apartment that this young man has kindly put at our disposal." Mrs. Fiona latches onto her braid that looks more lilac than its usual pinkish-gray. "I left the stove on while I was colorin' my hair, and, well..." She tracks her veiny hands down to the scrunchie which she always matches to her outfits—it's yellow like her blousy top today. "My apartment caught fire and the flames spread to yours. Oh, Callie, I'm so sorry."

I level an eloquent look at Dorian. I hate that he's convinced her that she's at fault. She may have phoned up that anti-god bunch, but she didn't start a fire.

"Your mother's nurse is helpin' me with all the insurance

filing. Apparently, all will be covered, and you and Lisa will be compensated for any loss of business."

My anger surges at her guilt. "Where's Mom?"

"In the kitchen. Bakin' a cake with Electra."

I toss the sheets off my legs and start to rise when Dorian says, "Mrs. Murphy, could you give me and Callie a minute?"

Mrs. Fiona glances my way, and although she doesn't ask whether I want to be left alone with him, she does linger beside the door until I nod.

Dorian shuts it behind her. I wish he hadn't, but if Mrs. Fiona hears anything she's not supposed to, he'll scrub her mind some more, and I want that less than I want to be in a room with Tarian's giant bodyguard, however much Tarian trusts him.

"Malachi's on his way," he says.

"Wonderful. Will Saul also be dropping by?"

"No one else but Malachi is aware of where I've brought you."

"Where did you bring me?"

"Somewhere safe."

"I got that, but *where* is this *somewhere safe*? Are we even still in Boston?"

"We are. I was going to take you to Tarian's house, but Electra was concerned it would be the first place the people who took him would look, so we brought you here, to our parents' apartment."

"Your parents? Are they here?" I'm not sure why I feel the need to whisper.

"They moved back to Atlantis four months ago. They've never actually lived here. Electra uses the place, though."

I give the sterile room another once-over, then inhale deeply. Even the scent is sterile—a mixture of cleaning products and air-conditioning. Either Electra's a neat freak or she doesn't spend much time here.

"Who did you tell my mother and Mrs. Fiona you were?"

"I told them I was your new landlord's site supervisor."

"My new landlord, huh?"

"Tarian's lawyer informed me of a contract he was drawing up between Tarian and Saul for the ownership of your building?" His voice lilts like it's a question.

What exactly is he asking? If it's true? Or is he evasively enquiring why on earth Tarian would prefer my diminutive brick building over the Prudential Center?

He crosses his arms and peers down his nose at me.

"Spit it out, Reacher."

"How long have you known Tarian?"

"I met him a few minutes after I met you."

"Then why is he purchasing your building?"

Since I can't exactly share Tarian's true reason without revealing my rune, I skirt the truth with a ridiculous reply. "He preferred I owe *him* rent?"

Sure enough, Dorian snorts.

"Look, when we find him, you can grill him to your heart's content. But I really don't see how that's important right now. Especially since the transaction didn't even go through. If anything, it proves that..." My eyebrows pinch, tugging at my newest wound. "It proves that Saul didn't abduct his nephew."

"We've already discussed Saul's innocence, Miss Bloom."

"Yes, yes, I remember." I flutter my fingers. "But I wasn't convinced. I am now, though." Saul sounded very excited about the trade. "Actually, who inherits Tarian's estate should he never resurface?"

"He can't die." Dorian tenses. Even his pupils seem to tense at his faux-pas. After all, he's just revealed his boss's immortality to a human. "Because I won't let that happen," he adds, casting his attention on the smoke-gray floorboards.

"I do." The deep voice springs both Dorian's and my gaze to the doorway, to the male darkening it. "I inherit everything."

# TWENTY-THREE

I was so concentrated on solving the mystery of Tarian's disappearance that I didn't even hear the door open. Then again, neither did Dorian, and he has enhanced senses, doesn't he?

Malachi shrugs before ambling deeper into the bedroom, stopping a foot away from the bed. The man has motive to kill his cousin, nevertheless my pulse doesn't hasten and my gut doesn't churn. My insides may not be criminal detectors, but I genuinely can't picture placid Malachi at the helm of such an atrocious operation.

He runs a hand through his mussed locks. "I know how that looks, Calanthe, but I don't covet more things or more magic."

Dorian's lids spread wide at the mention of magic.

"She knows about us." Malachi glances over his shoulder at Dorian before returning his attention to me. "One of Tarian's runes transferred to her skin."

My jawbone is so tight that my gums ache.

"She can't be compelled, but only Tarian and I are aware of that. My father and Symeon aren't. We'd like it to remain this way."

A flush of anger creeps up my skin. "*We*? I would've preferred that *no one* found out." I hate that Malachi tossed my ace to the wind.

Dorian's expression fills with…pity? He must think I'll incur the same fate as Barak. I realize I've squashed that macabre thought. Especially since the rune I wear hasn't metamorphosed.

"Dorian and Electra will keep our secret." Malachi stabs his hands into his jeans' pockets and ambles closer to the bed.

"*My* secret." I'm aware I sound petulant, but I would've appreciated being consulted on the matter.

Malachi's exhausted eyes blaze a path toward me, mollifying my sulkiness. "Calanthe, I want to find my cousin before it's too late."

I scrutinize the taut lines of the Atlantean's face and tauter lines of his body. "Tarian trusts you and the Serran siblings with his life." When I catch Malachi's eyebrows slanting, I drop my gaze to the bedsheets, because that's a lot of knowledge for someone who's spent a handful of minutes with the man. "He told me this when he was driving me home." My tendons all but grind from the force I exert to make eye contact. "Right before we got plowed into." My mind floods with memories of the collision, and I crimp the sheets.

"What else did my boss share with you?" Dorian demands.

"That unlike you, he doesn't trust Saul."

My revelation furrows Malachi's forehead. "He told you all this the evening he drove you home?"

My grip freezes on the steel-gray sateen. "We were discussing Joslyn and Saul's shotgun engagement."

"My cousin isn't one to discuss family or his feelings with strangers."

"He was planning on sequestering me in his house, so he wasn't all that concerned about secrecy."

Malachi regards me steadily a moment longer. I see the moment he decides to trust me—his chest rises and falls with a long sigh and his forehead smooths. "My father may be going through some midlife crisis, especially since Barak died, but he wouldn't hurt Tarian."

I decide to discard Saul as a suspect for the time being. "What about Symeon? Could he have done this?"

"Tarian gave him almost everything he received from their father," Malachi says, "so I really don't see what more Sym would want."

I cross my legs and peel my back off the tufted headboard. "You said it had to be another Atlantean since the driver was compelled. Could it have been Symeon's girlfriend?"

"Her grandmother heads the council since Barak passed away." Malachi rubs the stubble on his jaw. "Although Catalina Fablez denies any involvement, Yasmin's convinced her family's involved. She flew home to get us proof."

"What about the Holy Haters?"

"*Hunters*," Malachi corrects. "They're human, Calanthe. They can't compel anyone. Besides, Ines just broke out of their dockside warehouse, and—"

"Broke out?" Color seeps into Dorian's cheeks. "What do you mean *broke out*?"

"Electra didn't tell you?" One of Malachi's eyebrows rises out of alignment. "She stunned Ines so they would take her back to their Headquarters and they could find out whether the Holy Hunters had Tarian."

"*They*? Was Ines on board with this?" A vein bulges on Dorian's temple. "Are you fucking kidding me, Mal?" He grumbles something in Atlantean before gritting out in English, "You shouldn't have called my sister. You shouldn't have involved her."

"Because you really think Ele would've sat back and waited by the phone for news?"

"What did Ines say?" I ask to redirect the conversation.

"They don't have him. Apparently, they were aware of the abduction and glad for it, but none of their factions has claimed the capture."

"And we trust them?" I ask.

"We trust no one," Dorian grits out.

I think of everything Tarian told me when we rendezvoused in his dream. "Tarian mentioned that minerals from your mine neutralize your powers. Could they have—I don't know—stabbed him with a giant blue diamond?"

Dorian pushes the long sleeves of his black tee up to his elbows. "His heart would've pumped it out."

"Not if they're continuously bleeding him," Malachi says quietly. "That would keep him weak."

My spine prickles as I picture his wan body hooked to tubes that unremittingly siphon out his blood. Could that be why he was taken? "Back at the hospital, you said that Atlantean blood holds magic. What could the captors do with Tarian's?"

Dorian harrumphs. "What can't they do with it would be a better question."

"Atlantean blood can be used for anything, from curing fatal illnesses and rejuvenating cells, to temporarily enhancing the physical abilities of humans." A deep breath whooshes through Malachi's lips. "Depending on the injected dose, it can also end someone's life. Tarian's blood—according to ever-curious Symeon —can do all that, times a trillion."

"In other words, Tarian's blood is a weapon of mass destruction if used for evil," I muse aloud. "Or the cure for all illnesses if used for good?"

"It can only be used for good if the blood is freely given," Malachi explains.

Which it isn't since Tarian isn't even conscious. Their pool of suspects just got a hell of a lot wider. "Which Atlantean desires to take over the world?"

Malachi sighs. "Gaea would punish any Atlantean who tried to extract his blood without Tarian's permission."

"Gaea?" I ask.

"She's the goddess of the mine," Dorian explains.

I wonder if Tarian's the one who baptized the higher power that created this enchanted mine or if She gave him her name. *Thoughts for another day, Callie. Concentrate.* "How would She punish them?"

"They'd lose their runes. It was Her way of making sure no one could turn against Tarian," Dorian says.

"Fact or theory?" I ask.

"That's what the verse on his left arm says," Malachi replies. "So, fact."

"What if they hired a human to do the dirty work?" I ask.

"A drop of Tarian's blood on their skin would poison a mortal." Dorian's voice has slipped to a hoarse timbre.

"Heavy-duty gloves exist," I remind him. "Not to mention there are machines nowadays. No one would have to be in direct contact with his skin."

A nerve feathers Malachi's jaw. "I suppose we can't rule it out."

Malachi and Dorian revert to Atlantean. I catch two words: *Holy Hunters.* I'm guessing they just floated back onto the list of suspects.

"By the way, how did Symeon find out the potency of his brother's blood without losing his runes?" I ask.

"Tarian let him experiment with a couple drops once." Dorian's eyes flash with anger. Clearly, he was against this.

Even though I feel as wired as a coffee junkie, I'm extremely tempted to feign exhaustion so I can meet up with Tarian and divulge what I've learned, hoping he's acquired some information of his own. He may not be in mortal danger, but the longer they have him, the more magical blood they're able to collect.

I'm about to shoo Malachi and Dorian out of the bedroom when my mother screams. The sheets tangle around my legs as I rocket out of bed and slam into Malachi, who grips my biceps to steady me.

When another shrill yell resounds, I push away from him and scramble out the door, then cut through a sleek living room, toward a kitchen that's all stainless-steel and sapphire glass. My mother stands with her back to the stovetop, a bread knife covered in batter clutched between her hands. It bobs as she screams at both Electra and Mrs. Fiona to get back.

I stand in the doorway. "What's going on in here?"

"Who are *you*?" Her wild gaze vaults to me, tarrying on the butterfly Band-Aids on my forehead. "Where am I?"

The head-on collision hurt less. "At your and Nick's new home." My father's name holds as much magic as a rune to my mother.

Like a switch, it flicks something inside of her, and she lowers the knife.

"Someone bought the flower shop. Nick used the money to purchase this apartment, Lisa." I nod to the raven-haired Atlantean. "Electra is your new housekeeper."

Electra side-eyes me. Was she expecting me to refer to her as a nurse? Doesn't she realize that the term would agitate my mother who, at the moment, isn't aware anything's wrong with her?

"Mrs. Fiona is our—*was* your neighbor back at the flower shop. She came by to pay you a visit."

"I missed ya, Lisa. New owners are young and moderately agreeable." Mrs. Fiona offers my mother a smile so wide it displays all the chiclet-like teeth of her dentures.

Mom's slender throat bobs over a swallow, and although she doesn't return Mrs. Fiona's enthusiasm, she does give her the teensiest nod before moving her attention back to me. "And you? Who are you?"

"I'm the salesgirl." My heart aches, tender like the gash on my foot, raw like the one on my forehead. "Nick hired me to help with deliveries."

"You just said we sold the shop."

*Right.* "Nick needed the van, so I drove it over from the shop. He went to drop off some farewell bouquets to Bloom's Blooms most loyal customers."

"Such a kind man"—I catch Mrs. Fiona knuckling away a tear —"that husband of yours."

"Yes." Mom finally smiles. "I hope he thought to bring the Valentis tangerine roses."

I hate that she remembers them but not her own daughter.

Footsteps sound behind me, scrunching her face anew. I'm guessing Dorian and Malachi decided to join the party. I could pass them off as movers—especially Dorian—but I don't want to overwhelm my mother. Without glancing over my shoulder, I hold my hand out in the universal stop gesture before pressing my palm to the doorframe. Both men halt.

I amble nearer to my mother, making a great show of sniffing the air and *not* staring down at the knife dripping batter onto her white sneakers. "What are you making? It smells delish."

Mom's face softens at my compliment—gone is the wariness, and in its place, shines pride. "Nick's favorite. Banana bread."

My ribs ache because it *was* Dad's favorite. It was also the first cake my mother ever taught me how to bake. "He'll love that." My voice has gone thick, but my mother doesn't notice my grief since her full attention has returned to the stainless-steel bowl. "I don't think it'll be ready to slice up for a while still."

At her frown, I nod to the knife. She studies it with a furrowed brow before finally resting it inside the sink. As the blade clinks against metal, Mrs. Fiona expels a breath. I do too. Even the walls surrounding us seem to quiver with a sigh.

"Here." Electra brandishes the whisk. "It'll be easier to stir with this than with that bread knife."

The edges of Mom's pixie-cut glisten amber in the glow of the recessed spotlights beaming down from the ceiling. "Why would I use a knife to stir batter?"

Electra cocks a brow. "That's what Mrs. Murphy and I were trying—"

"Out," I interject. "They were trying it out. They couldn't locate a spatula, so they experimented with a knife."

Forgetting the use of everyday objects has been happening more often lately. I understand Electra isn't a licensed nurse, but I did mention this recent development during the "job interview."

My mother shakes her head and takes the whisk from Electra. And then, she finally smirks. "A knife is useful to ribbon in the dollops of Nutella my daughter loves adding, but unless you enjoy your cake lumpy, I suggest you stick with a whisk, ladies."

The ball of grief in my throat grows so spiky it feels as though I gulped down a barrel cactus. To think, if Tarian hadn't been abducted, Mom would've been rid of her Alzheimer's.

"How about I make us some tea, and you can give me and Mrs. Murphy some more kitchen pointers?" Electra slides a deep drawer open and extracts a glass teapot, glass mugs, and a decorative tin. "Jasmine okay, Calanthe?"

Even though the rest of the apartment is bare, the kitchen has clearly been stocked.

"Calanthe?" My mother releases the whisk, and the wire loops sink into the pale-yellow batter. I think she's about to remember me when she says, "My daughter's here?"

Pity crosses Electra's gaze; Mrs. Fiona's too.

"She's unpacking her boxes," I say. God, it hurts. Each and every time.

My mother begins to whisk the batter, the metal clinking rhythmically against the sides of the bowl. "Callie?" I'm about to repeat that she's unpacking when my mother glances over her shoulder at me. "Are we adding Nutella today or not, baby?"

My battered heart leaps, and the spikes on the lump forever lodged in my throat recede. "Absolutely, Mom."

I swallow and pivot toward Electra.

Before I can ask her for the chocolate spread, she says, "We don't have any, but I'll order some now."

"Or Callie and I can head to the supermarket?" My mother

wipes her hands against her jeans. "Sweetie, can you get my cell phone and bag?"

Electra's odd-hued eyes flash.

Before she can try to compel my mother not to leave the apartment, I bounce in front of her. "Let's go after we drink some tea."

I loop my arm through my mother's and tug her toward a little dining nook set up beside a picture window. I expect Electra to instruct us to sit elsewhere, but a glance outside reveals we're at the top of a high-rise with a sprawling view of the North End. I'm guessing we're out of sight all the way up here.

I end up not having to convince my mother to stay in the apartment, because an hour into our tea, she forgets all about the Nutella.

Forgets all about me.

With Mrs. Fiona's help, we settle her on the couch in front of The Food Network. Although I can tell she wonders why her employee is hanging out inside her new home, she doesn't ask me to leave, merely side-eyes me from time to time, the same way she side-eyes Dorian, who Mrs. Fiona explains is the right-hand man of Bloom's Blooms' new owner.

"Who's here *why*?" Mom whispers to Mrs. Fiona.

Even though she's guarded around me, she seems perfectly at ease around Mrs. Fiona. And yeah, it hurts, but at least she trusts *someone*.

"He's waiting for Nick, Lisa. Needs some more documents signed for the—what was it you called it?"

"Ten-thirty-one," Dorian says, without missing a beat.

Note to self: the man is a fantastic liar.

I nod for him to follow me into the kitchen, where I line a loaf tin with parchment paper and pour my mother's batter into it. "Where's Malachi?"

"He went to check some things out."

My skin breaks out in goosebumps. "By *things*, you mean the *Holy Hunters*?"

"Ines wanted to meet."

"Still can't believe your sister handed her over to the Double Hs. Should I be worried?"

"Catchy. And"—his mouth puckers as though he'd bitten down on a lime wedge—"no. Electra and Ines have a complicated relationship." He ousts a breath that speaks of a very profound complication. "But to answer your question, you can trust my sister to keep you safe."

I'm not completely sold. Perhaps it's because she's already deceived me. I'm saved from overanalyzing this by Mrs. Fiona who calls out for water. I grab three bottles from the fridge. Before walking them over to the couch, I ask, "Any chance you can heal my forehead and foot?"

"Right. You know about our magic." A smile alleviates the tension on his face as he lifts his palm and splashes heat onto my bandaged skin. "Can't believe you had us fooled."

My lips curve. "I didn't know if I could trust—" My spine prickles, burns. Shit, shit, shit. Before I faint at his feet a second time, I jog out to the living room, calling out, "I'll be right back," even though there's a distinct possibility that I might be gone for quite some time.

The world grays so fast that I flop into the armchair and toss the water bottles at Mrs. Fiona. I see her Wordle booklet flying off her lap and then I see nothing.

# TWENTY-FOUR

When I come to, I'm standing in front of a bay window that frames an infinity pool, and beyond the pool, sprawls a vast starlit ocean. I know exactly where I've landed before I even catch Tarian's reflection.

"I felt it this time," I say, meeting his steady gaze in the dark glass.

He sits in a leather armchair, one ankle propped on his opposite knee, a crystal tumbler of something amber—whiskey, maybe? —clasped between his long fingers. "What is it you felt?"

The floor-length white silk dress I wear shimmers in the glass. "You, calling me back to this limbo plane. My rune got really hot. Like it caught fire."

I glance over my shoulder, discovering that my spine is fully exposed save for a slender gold chain wrapped around my waist. It looks sewn into the silk, but I can feel it roll over my skin, the same way I can feel the chain shiver between my breasts. I fathom it's the same accessory Tarian trussed me up in last time.

"I'm sorry, Calamity." The ice cubes in his drink click together, soft like the jazz music playing in the background.

"I didn't tell you to get an apology. Besides, I'm currently stuck in an uber-modern high-rise. This place and this view are a pleasant escape."

The ice cubes clink again. "What do you mean *stuck*?"

"Dorian decided to hide me in his parents' place." I turn away from the picture window, the sole of my foot still tender. I'm about to ask whether he could heal me when I get sidetracked by my footwear.

Crystallized sandals peek out from underneath the hem of my dress, tinsel-bright against the patterned navy rug that unspools like a dark wave under the sleek living room furniture. A pinch of my skirt reveals glittery straps that coil around my calves like diamond vines.

"Are you sure you're not poring over those fashion magazines the pilots keep in your jets?"

Tarian's enduring silence urges me to glance up. I find him thumbing his lower lip as he regards my exposed legs from knee to painted white toenails. Although his brazen scrutiny makes my chest prickle with a blush, it emboldens my own stare, which I drag over his seated figure. The fine wool of his tailored suit glimmers sapphire over his white button-down.

"What was your question?" His rasp draws my spine straight.

"You're obviously getting your fashion inspo from somewhere." I release my skirt, which settles like spilled milk over my legs. "I assume your source is the magazines you *apparently* don't flip through."

"Symeon was just a baby when our mother passed away. He had such trouble falling asleep that according to Father..." His voice drifts, and my heart aches for him, because I sense the pause was caused by the ever-present ache of loss. "According to Father, I'd tell my brother long-winded bedtime stories about ancient kings and queens in faraway lands." He gestures to my dress. "I have a very vivid imagination, Calamity."

"I see that." I tilt my head sideways, which sends my unbound locks whooshing over my shoulder. "By the way, why do you insist on calling me that?"

"Calling you what?" His eyes take another leisurely stroll over my curves, which press against the cool silk.

Though the fabric contains zero stretch, it somehow doesn't crease around my figure. The dress is gorgeous, if a tad more revealing than I'd favor in real life, but this isn't real life. This is a safe—sort of—fantasy bubble.

"Calamity. Is it because I'm at the root of your recent misfortune?"

His gaze jounces to my face.

"Or is it because I wore a cowboy hat and boots the first time we met?"

"Let me make one thing clear, Miss Bloom. I don't blame you for my recent misfortune." He unhooks his foot from his knee and rises from his seat, all six feet and many inches of him.

Although the heels he picked for me are tall, I still have to crane my neck as he approaches.

"Don't you even dare contemplate such a thing." He stops a foot away from me, his dark eyes perusing my upturned face, lingering on the freckles splashed across my nose. "As for your nickname, when I was a child, my father and I would watch Westerns. I think that's why he chose to immigrate here, to the U.S."

I can't help but think, *Wrong state*. But I suppose, right country.

His eyes tighten on my collarbone. "I was fascinated by the character of Calamity Jane. That woman didn't shy away from danger. Stood up to the biggest, baddest men."

"Sorry to break it to you, Hades, but you need to retire the nickname. I may have sharpshot some daring words your way when we met, but that was because I was pissed off. Not because I was brave."

A smile slashes Tarian's brooding expression.

"Not to mention I don't know the first thing about rifles. Unlike Bryn. She's the rifle whiz, thanks to her dad. He takes her to a shooting range before each one of his deployments."

Although Bryn and her dad aren't super close, what with my best friend being the result of a ripped condom and Delta Lynch visiting her in Boston a grand total of twice a year, the man still recognized her as his kid and video-calls her as often as he can from wherever he's stationed.

"He's a distinguished sniper in the U.S. Army." Considering the data Dorian had on me, I imagine Tarian knows all about Bryn's genealogical tree. "You should call *her* Calamity."

His mouth twists with a scowl. "Your nickname's not up for grabs."

Weird ass, moody man. "Fine. Whatever. Call me Calamity until the end of days. Well, until the end of *my* days, since that'll probably come before any apocalypse."

His temper sharpens.

Probably shouldn't have reminded him of what he set in motion. Before he can blow a dream-gasket, I ask, "So, does the military eat out of your hands like the police?"

"No."

Tarian's comment blows a frown across my brow.

"They tried to establish a base in Atlantis. You can imagine the council's reaction and answer."

I'm guessing it was a resounding no, the same way I'm guessing that blowing off the military chafed many egos. "Because of the mine?"

"Yes."

"Don't *you* have to be present for the mine to *awaken* people?"

"I do, but our rocks hold power."

The pool of people intent on harming Tarian keeps getting wider and deeper. "You think they'd quarry it?"

"No one can penetrate the mine without me, but they could coerce one of my people to go fetch them some rocks. I imagine, or rather *hope*, Gaea would strike them down or seal off the mine."

"You hope… So you don't actually know?"

"No one has ever tried to excavate the mine without my permission. As for entering, Symeon tried to take one of his girlfriends once. She died before he could finish lowering her into it."

I scrunch up my nose.

"How about we discuss less tragic matters? For example, what can I pour you?"

Although my synapses are firing at full speed, I set his case aside for when I get back to reality. "Can we drink in dreams?"

He lifts his glass to his mouth to prove that we can.

"What's in your glass?"

"Macallan '75."

"Hmm. I'd love the same thing."

"I didn't peg you as a whiskey drinker, Calamity." He's so close that the expensive fragrance of his drink melds with that of his skin, creating an intoxicating blend that has me inhaling long and deep. "Here." He hands me his glass.

I carry it to my mouth and take a hit of the liquor that's so smooth, it slips down my throat like sweet smoke. "I'm not much of a whiskey connoisseur, but it was my father's favorite drink. Whenever he got a really good bottle, he'd let me sample it."

I take another measured swallow before handing the glass back and licking my lips, because seventy-five years was damn good to the grains of malted barley.

"He would've loved this one." My throat begins to sting, and not because of the liquor.

One glance into Tarian's face has all thoughts of my beloved father fleeing from my mind. The god's eyes have gone full black, like a predator about to strike. Or like a man in pain. I'm suddenly afraid he's about to teeter out of this dream.

"Are you okay?" I touch his forearm. "Tarian?"

Tendons twitch beneath the fine wool, roiling against the pads of my fingers.

After an interminable stretch of silence, he says, "Have another taste, but don't swallow immediately."

His instructions give me pause. "Why?"

"To experience the full flavor."

"All right," I take the glass back. "But then we need to discuss why you tipped out of the last dream, deal?"

His gaze presses into mine. "You've got yourself a deal, Miss Bloom."

I take a sip and hold the alcohol, allowing the whiskey to coat my palate and baste my tongue. As the flavor intensifies, Tarian's hand snakes around my waist. I'm so startled by his touch that I gulp down the liquor too fast. The burn in my throat pales in comparison to the one skipping along my waist and sinking into my veins.

Tarian crooks a finger beneath my chin, forcing my gaze back to his, and then he lowers his mouth to mine and pries my lips wide. My heart pounces as he sweeps his tongue against mine, seeking leftover droplets of his Macallan.

"Delicious," he murmurs, straightening his head and licking his own lips.

I gape at him, wondering if he's talking about the whiskey or me. What am I going on about? Of course he means his whiskey. Right?

He cups my fingers around the tumbler and carries it to his mouth. After taking a deep pull, he winds his free hand through my hair and tugs at the thick mass.

"Tarian, we should…"

His pupils are so blown that his eyes have become twin pools of ink.

"We should…" I fail again to finish my sentence, much too entranced by the intensity of his stare and the feel of his fingers in my hair. Never has a man looked at me this way. Touched me this way. Like he wants to devour and possess me.

He slants first his head and then his mouth. Once he's collapsed the space between our bodies, he trickles whiskey onto my tongue, and the flavor of it…of him…explodes against my palate and rib cage.

His thumb ventures off my pulse point and caresses my throat as I swallow everything he feeds me. I've never tasted anything as addictive as this man. I curl my hand around his neck to deepen this kiss, if this is even what's happening. What if it's some strange Atlantean drinking ritual?

In case he doesn't want to keep his mouth welded to mine, I release his neck and pull away. His palm flattens on the small of my back, and his lips widen mine. Definitely a kiss.

I can hardly believe that the man crushing me to him—a literal god—could desire *me*, a plain and lowly mortal. Then again, I'm the only person he can currently interact with. If he'd been connected to Mackenzie, his mouth may very well have been fused to hers right now. The thought sours my stomach and rumples my nose.

Tarian must feel my grimace because he pulls back. Although his grip around my hair slackens, he doesn't let go. I sense he wants to say something, but he stays quiet, his heavy brows beating down against his thick eyelashes.

I kick Bryn's sister from my thoughts. She's not here. She doesn't get to poison this dream. She doesn't get to intrude on the sexiest kiss of my existence.

I reach between us and dip my finger inside the dregs of umber, and then I paint my mouth with it. "I don't think you've properly experienced the full flavor of your vintage, Mr. Hadez."

The shift in his expression is gradual and so very subtle that if I blinked, I would've missed it. But I don't blink. I keep my gaze steady as his eyebrows unhurriedly level out and the corners of his mouth crook into a seductive smirk.

"Is that right, Miss Bloom?"

When I suck on the tip of my finger, his smile vanishes and his palm scoops me in so close that the hard ridge of his cock bites into my abdomen, imprinting his desire into my skin. He grumbles something in his language before taking the glass from my hand and flinging it aside.

The rug is so plush it buffets its fall. I suddenly picture Tarian lowering me to that rug and—

"Callie?" Bryn's voice explodes between my temples.

How am I hearing her? Did Tarian bring her into our dream? Can he do that? I arch my back to stare around us, but the living room is bare of anyone but him and me.

"What is it? What's going on?" Tarian's nostrils flare with wild breaths.

"Callie, wake up." Bryn's slim hands shape my cheeks.

"No," I murmur. "No." I don't want to wake up. I don't want to leave Tarian.

"What is it, Calamity?" Tarian's timbre is as harsh as the heart that beats in time with my own.

"Bryn. I think she's waking me up." The words stutter out of me a second before my body stutters out of his arms.

# TWENTY-FIVE

**B**ryn's eyes sparkle like the whiskey I just slicked across my lips. "You've *got* to give me the name of that witch doctor."

Did I just dive headfirst into another dream or is my best friend actually present and *actually* asking me about a— "Witch doctor?" I croak.

As she sits back on her heels, I scrub a hand down my face. My heart skips a very long beat when I catch the scent of Tarian's cologne on my fingertips. To think that a minute ago, I was with him, in his house in Martha's Vineyard. That his hands were on my body, and mine on his. And—

"The dude who inked your back so you could sleep better. I *need* his name." Bryn's voice snaps me farther away from Tarian, farther away from the hot crush of his lips and the even hotter press of his tongue.

I honest to goodness never thought I'd prefer the company of a virtual stranger—let alone a Hadez's—to the company of my best friend, but as I stare at Bryn, I desperately wish I were gazing into much darker irises.

"Yoo-hoo. Callie?" she singsongs, fluttering her fingers in front of my face.

My disenchantment balloons. Granted, I'll see Tarian again soon. After all, we humans do spend a third of our lives sleeping.

Will we kiss when we meet again, though? We probably shouldn't. At least not until we've figured out where he is.

But once he's free, will he still want to kiss me? He'll have his pick of women. Not to mention that I may or may not be dead at that point, depending on the evolution of my rune.

I probably shouldn't even want to kiss Tarian Hadez. After all, he's a dangerous man, and I'd really appreciate a serene life. One that doesn't require a bodyguard or safehouses or lying to my best friend.

"Your occult-healer-slash-tattoo-artist," Bryn says, pulling me out of my turbulent thoughts. "What's his name?"

My scalp prickles with the force of someone's attention. A glance over my shoulder reveals that this someone is Dorian. Mrs. Fiona is in attendance as well, but she's dead to the world. Her snores are so loud they jostle her ample chest, which in turn, jostles her lanyard of keys. I start to smile, glad she feels comfortable enough in this remote apartment to nod off, but the empty seat beside her freezes my expression.

I spin back around. "Where's my mother?"

Dorian steps away from the giant window overlooking the night-dark city. "I moved her into one of the bedrooms after she nodded off. One would think that she, too, visited a magical tattoo parlor."

I don't take the bait. If that was his intent. Maybe it was just an observation.

Bryn gives my thigh a slight squeeze. "Clearly, whatever the healer did worked. Dorian told me that you've slept through the afternoon."

He inclines his chin infinitesimally lower. If he tips it down any farther, it'll end up knocking into his Adam's apple.

My cheeks prickle from his enduring scrutiny. "Well, I *was* concussed."

Does he know I've been dreaming about his boss? Did I moan or utter Tarian's name during my impromptu nap? God, I hope not.

Bryn dents her lip with her front teeth. "Maybe we should get you back to the hospital and have the doctors run new scans on your brain."

I sit up and shake my head. "That's unnecessary, Bee."

"But what if it's not the tattoo?" she murmurs.

"It's the tattoo. I swear, my brain is fine." I can't say as much for my blood, which is now laced with Atlantean magic. And not just any Atlantean's, but Tarian's.

I lick my lips, and my heart gives a hard kick when I taste him and his Macallan.

"Callie?" Bryn stamps her palm on my forehead. "Are you sure you're okay? Your cheeks are really flushed."

"Yep. Totally fine. Just hot." I stretch my arms over my head.

"What does this magical *tattoo* of yours say?"

I jump at the nearness of Dorian's voice. For a hulking man, he's mastered the art of creeping up on people.

Bryn glances up at where he now stands, right behind the sofa. "Sleep, in Old English."

The male's brow furrows. Mine, too, but for a whole other reason. I assumed Malachi would've told him all about the word on my spine. Apparently not.

"I don't remember that word being on Tarian's—"

I clear my throat to interrupt Dorian.

But it's too late. Bryn heard him. "Tarian?"

"Forget I mentioned Tarian, Miss Fielding." Dorian's eyes must be glowing because my friend's mouth puckers.

I dig my nails into my palms, wishing Malachi had kept her

away from me. Speaking of which. "Where is your future step-brother?"

"He went to check if any rats got into my apartment. I was too terrified to look. That's why I was asking about your woo-woo healer."

"Um." I knead my temples. "I'm not seeing the connection between the sleep doctor and your rats."

"I'm getting to it." She gets to her feet, rubbing her palms against her high-waisted jeans. "So, I called him after I got your message about a sleepover."

A message I never sent since I'm all out of cell phones. I wonder who sent it? Did Electra bring my bag here? Is she piloting my device?

"Anyway, while we were driving over, I got a call from my super. Apparently, my building's infested with rats, so one, I'm here to stay until every rodent is caught, and two, I don't think I'll *ever* be able to sleep again. I mean rats, Callie. Not cute, fluffy mice. *Rats.*"

Is this murine swarm another lie? "Since when do you find mice cute and fluffy?"

"Since I learned about the gang of crimson-eyed rodent squatters." She wrinkles her nose. "Just, yuck."

It suddenly strikes me that she hasn't asked me why I relocated to the high-rise. "I take it you've heard about the flower shop?" I remain cryptic to ferret out what exactly she's been told.

Her gaze perches on Mrs. Fiona. "Fires are so scary."

I wait to see if she'll mention the Holy Hunters.

She doesn't. But she does say, "Mal told me Tarian personally sent his people to fix up your building, so it should be like new in no time."

She smiles; I don't, because that's just another lie.

Bryn gestures around her. "In the meantime, how lucky were you—*we*—that Dorian here had an empty apartment on hand?" Discreetly, she adds, "He's not making you pay rent or anything, is he?"

"We haven't discussed—"

"*He's* not." Dorian's evidently invested in our conversation. "It's my pleasure to house Calanthe and her family."

"Either way, it's so generous." Bryn flashes him a smile that feels a little brittle. For all her adoration of the Hadezes, she doesn't seem quite so taken with Tarian's bodyguard. "How's Lisa doing?"

"She's...adjusting." The knife incident brightens my memory but darkens my mind. "I told her that Dad sold the shop and bought this place. In case she mentions something along those lines when she wakes up."

"She must've been terrified when the fire brigade blasted into the shop."

"Her nurse was with her," ever-attentive Dorian replies. "Electra kept her calm."

"Thank God for Electra." Bryn does not sound grateful for her at all. Then again, she did tell me, after their shared car ride yesterday, that she thought I'd made a mistake hiring her. That she was too young and probably going to spend her work hours surfing social media.

"Where *is* Electra?" I glance around the dim living room, then toward the softly lit kitchen, straining to detect the presence of another soul over the purr of the air conditioning unit and the rumble of Mrs. Fiona's snores.

"She's taking a breather," Tarian's bodyguard says.

I tilt my head toward him. "Perhaps you should take one, too."

As he extracts his cell phone from his pocket, Reacher shoots me an eloquent look that says he'll sleep once his boss is found. If only I could speed this up. If only Tarian had glimpsed a face or recognized someone's voice—some detail that could lead us to him.

"Mal and I picked up some Thai food on the way over. It's in the kitchen." Bryn tips her head toward the bright entryway, untangling the braided friendship bracelet I wove her back in middle school from a tennis bracelet made with diamonds that shine as blue as Tarian's runes—another present from the Hadezes? "Hope you're hungry 'cause the man ordered everything on the menu." When my stomach rumbles, Bryn's lips quirk. "I take that as a 'yes.'"

On my way to the kitchen, I try to slide my hand through my hair. I must've shifted around a whole lot during my little sleep spell, because my curls are atrociously tangled.

"Shoot." Bryn pats the back pocket of her jeans. "I think I forgot my phone in Mal's car. Can you text him?"

"I…um. I left mine in Mom's room. Don't want to wake her."

"Let's hope he spots it and brings it upstairs." As we start popping the lids off takeout containers, she says, "Everything's scallop-free."

"Thanks, Bee."

We plate large spoonfuls of sweet-smelling deliciousness, then carry our plates to the little table that's been cleared of the tea Mrs. Fiona brewed earlier. "Has Tarian visited?"

I choke on a forkful of rice noodles, then cough until I've cleared my airway. Bryn springs out of her seat and scans the kitchen, fear sparkling in her eyes. "Where's your EpiPen?"

I shake my head to reassure her that I'm not having an allergic reaction. "Just…went down…the wrong…way."

She expels a raucous breath and drops back into her seat, her hand slipping over her heart that's pummeling her crop top. "Thank God," she whispers. But then she repeats, "You have your EpiPen on you though, right?"

"Forgot it at the flower shop." When her eyes well with renewed worry, I reach over and clasp her hand. "I'll ask Dorian to pick it up once he gets off his call."

She glances down at my plate. Before she can suggest boiling some pasta, I remind her that she asked for scallop-free food. There's no reason a Thai restaurant would try to poison me. Unless it's owned by Atlanteans.

My appetite vanishes as swiftly as it appeared, and I push back in my seat. "Maybe I'll wait until he retrieves my EpiPen."

Bryn kicks off her teal suede heels, then bends one of her legs and gathers it against her chest. It's her favorite way to sit, but she doesn't do it very often anymore, what with her wardrobe consisting mostly of skirts and dresses. Not to mention that whenever her mother or sister catch her sitting this way, they both scowl and remind her that she's a lady, not a trucker. Which has always struck me as odd since I've never seen a trucker sit with one leg propped up.

She swirls a spring roll in sweet sauce. "Remember when Logan's hamster got loose in the bar?"

I press the tip of my tongue against my chipped front tooth. "How could I forget? My body still bears the mark of that night."

It bears the mark of another night, too. I suck in a breath when my spine begins to tingle.

"What made you think of"—I clench my teeth as the rune prickles a little more sharply—"*that*?"

My poor friend will have a meltdown if I pass out at the table.

"The rats in my apartment," she says.

I desperately try to focus on the story of our ridiculous freakout that she's taking great pleasure in rehashing. The one that led to my damaged enamel and her sprained ankle, courtesy of a spilled cocktail, stilettos, and an uncoordinated attempt to flee the bar.

I sit up in my seat so the sensitive skin on my back doesn't rub against the rungs of the chair. *Not a good time, Hades. Not a good time.* But it isn't like he can hear me.

The warmth rushing through the letters becomes so strong that I jerk up and fake a yawn. "I'm feeling super sleepy again."

"But you just woke up."

"From a nap." I press my palms on the sleek table and stand. "I'm just going to go lie down for a bit. Ask Dorian for my EpiPen?"

In my mind, I streak through the apartment toward the bedroom I woke up in earlier. In reality, I hobble, skimming my fingers along the wall to keep myself upright.

A hand wraps around my elbow—Bryn's. "Callie, you're scaring me."

"I swear I'm fine. Just exhausted. From the car crash. The move. Mom. It's been a lot."

My friend's pupils tremble and stretch until they take over her face, the apartment...*everything*.

# TWENTY-SIX

**C**alanthe reappears beside me on the upper deck of the *Amapola*, my father's…*no*, not my father's, my *brother's* yacht. After all, Father left the boat he named after Mother to Symeon.

"Before you vanished…" I lean my hip against the guardrail and start to cross my arms but wince because the skin over my runes is tender from whatever torture my asshole captors are inflicting on my body. To curb the pain, I breathe in long and deep and picture my revenge. My mind fills with the crimson slick of all the bodies I will disembowel and—

"Before *I* vanished…?" Calanthe prompts, cutting off my vindictive deliberations.

"Before you vanished, you asked me whether I'd picked up on anything useful."

She blinks as though surprised that's what I'm leading with. I suppose we should discuss what happened earlier, and we will, but I don't know how long we have before someone from her world calls her back.

"And?" Her voice is a little breathy and a whole lot husky, which fades the urgency of what I planned on telling her.

*Fuck.* What was I about to tell her?

"Tarian?"

When her lips shape my name, the pulse clipping my eardrums becomes an insistent buzzing.

She clicks her fingers, succeeding in scooping my attention off her mouth. "Useful tidbits?"

*Right.* I readjust my suit trousers, then raise my gaze back to her vibrant one. "I'm being transported."

"To Atlantis?"

"I don't know. All I've figured out is that I'm inside a large vehicle." The *Amapola* rocks as I say this, causing Calanthe to stumble into the guardrail.

I sweep my hand to buffer her collapse with a forcefield, but my powers fail me. I do manage to catch her elbow, but not before her hip bites into the varnished wood and a muted hiss falls from her lips. I hate how pathetic and weak I've become, in the real world and in this one.

Through gritted teeth, I say, "They've got me strapped down, and it isn't to keep me from breaking loose."

Because I can't. I can barely regain consciousness.

Before I can crush her elbow, I release her and turn toward the ocean bathed in fake moonlight, shimmering over a fake wake, produced by a fake ship. I grip the guardrail, my knuckles going white with rage that I'm someone's prisoner.

A spot of warmth blooms on my shoulder blade, and I pivot. At my growl, Calanthe jumps. I catch the downward arc of her arm and realize *she's* the one who prodded my skin.

The violence burning in my veins extinguishes. "Touch me again—"

"I won't!" She thrusts her stare onto the teak deck. "I'm sorry. I shouldn't have. Sorry."

I shackle her wrist and park her hand on my nape. "Again, Calamity. Touch me *again*." I wait until her fingers curl around my skin. When after several seconds, they don't, I add the word she so loves to hear cross the barrier of my lips, "Please."

Like some magical switch, my plea bends her delicate fingers. I wait until her grip strengthens and I'm certain she won't let go before I lower my hand to her waist, wishing a T-shirt wasn't in the way. I consider making it vanish, but instead, I crook my hand beneath the hem and stroke up the side of her rib cage.

As I soak up her softness, I close my eyes and bury my nose into her hair. "You feel so fucking good." The scent of salt and wildflower nectar that lifts off her sinks into me, filling all the deadened places inside my soul. Slowly, I come back to life, my senses tingling and my blood warming with something other than the visceral need to kill. "I'm sorry to have dragged you into my hell."

She snakes her arm around my middle and takes a step forward, slotting her body into mine. And then she twists her head and presses her cheek against my chest.

Against my dark, bestial heart.

"The last person to hug me perished," I find myself telling her.

In spite of my warning, she doesn't let go. "From a hug? How hard were you holding them?"

My lips bend into a sad smile that declines as the scene of that fateful evening replays in my mind.

"Are you talking about your father, Tarian?"

I am.

"If you are, your hug didn't kill him."

"Still, you shouldn't be hugging me, Calanthe."

"I'm already marked."

"What if my magic stings you again?"

She shrugs. "Pass on a neater word this time. Preferably, something that doesn't make everyone believe I suffer from narcolepsy."

The corners of my mouth hook back up. Although I can't see her face, I somehow know she's smiling too. My intrepid dream girl.

"No person outside of my family has ever hugged me." I want her to know that I don't make a habit of getting close to people. "Until you."

"Tell me about your mother."

I swallow at the mention of the woman who gave birth to me but never got to raise me. Probably for the best. I can't imagine she would've been proud of the man I've become.

"I was three when she died, so my memories are scarce, but according to my father and the thousands of pictures and videos he took, I spent a good deal of time in her arms."

A particular reel of her—*us*—plays out. I'm sitting astride her hip, one short leg hooked over her pregnant belly, one pudgy hand fisted around her long black hair as she hums and stirs something in a giant pot. My father asks her what she's making. She looks over her shoulder at him and smiles, blinding the camera with her radiance. *Why…your favorite dish, my love.*

I try to block out my father's answer, but it echoes between my temples, unbidden, *You're my favorite dish.*

As a teen, I'd gagged, which had made him laugh. As an adult, I'd arched a brow. What I wouldn't give to hear him chortle over my disgust one last time.

"I never understood how he could live with a ghost." I take another hit of Calanthe's nectar-sweet scent. "I would've gone mad staring at a face I could no longer touch."

"After Dad died, Mom threw away every picture frame in our house. I couldn't decide if she'd done it because she couldn't remember him, or because she remembered him too much."

I smooth my hand through the soft waves of her hair.

"I rescued them from the trash and stored them in a box under my bed. Every time she asks me where the pictures are, I put them back up. And when I feel her fade, I stash them away. Living with a ghost is painful, but the alternative…removing them from your sight, *erasing them*…it's so much worse, Tarian." Her already husky voice thickens with grief.

Grief my selfish, whiny ass put there. "I wish I could've brought him back for you."

Her arms tighten around me as though she might drown in her sorrow if she doesn't cling to something solid. But how solid is a man who exists only in her dreams?

"Bring back my mother. Once you're free"—her voice catches—"promise to bring her back?"

I hate that it sounds like a question.

"I already promised you that I would." I catch the wild lengths of her hair that the wind is kicking up and wrap them around my fist to keep them from flogging the parts of her I can't shield.

After a beat of easy silence, she asks, "Any theories on why your magic marked *me*?"

I sigh. "I imagine it's because I touched you."

She picks her head off my chest to peer up into my face. "I get that you're not big on hugs, but surely I'm not the only person you've touched in three decades?"

"I don't touch people often. Or allow them to touch me." I relocate my palm to the small of her back.

Clouds scurry over the moon like locusts, painting the world around us in shadows that dim but don't dull the emerald-copper gleam of Calanthe's irises.

I try to think of *why* her. And why Father? Why would my runes choose to hurt two people who didn't deserve pain? I'm suddenly glad I didn't lay a finger on Dorian or Malachi. I would've hated infecting them. Saul, on the other hand…I banish the cruel thought. My uncle may be exasperating, but he's not a malevolent man.

"Until this last winter, my magic had never acted up." The memory of Father's gasp as my rune seared his skin rattles my heart. "You'd think I would've grasped its intricacies by now, but either it's evolving, or I've been in denial about who controls whom this whole time."

"Can I see your markings?" She traces the swirls that start at my nape, making them heat and beat as though she was running a lit match over my skin.

I'm aware that she can't control my magic, that the frenzied prickle is an illusion, a fabrication of my mind, like this dream, yet worry pools in my gut. I bring her hand up to my face, then flip it over and inspect every square millimeter of her fingers for a renegade glyph. When I can't find one, my ribs loosen.

"What are you doing?" Her pupils throb in time with my pulse.

"Checking that I didn't curse you again."

"Do you really think you could in this dimension?" She pulls her fingers away from mine and studies them.

"I don't particularly care to find out." I stuff my hands into my pockets to keep myself from pawing at her again and stare out at the vast black ocean. "How long has it been?"

"Since?"

"Since the car accident. How long?"

"Two days. We're coming up on the third one."

If my magic follows the same pattern as it did with my father, then she has four days left before it snuffs out her life.

Her dark eyebrows crouch, darkening her bright stare. "Did your father ever use his magic for evil?"

"What?"

"Did he ever try to hurt you or someone else?"

"No!" Fury whets my tone, making her recoil. "My father was a good man. A fucking saint."

She snares her bottom lip with teeth that glow as white as the veiled moon.

"Why? Did someone imply that he may have?" My mind shoots straight to Symeon. My brother was always so quick to find fault in the man who only ever had his children's wellbeing at heart.

When Symeon overdosed on some crap that was supposed to enhance his powers, crap he'd bought off Yasmin's cousin a couple years back, my father had sat at his bedside for weeks on end, only taking breaks when I'd come to replace him.

"No. No one implied anything. I'm just trying to understand why your powers would delete someone's... Did he ever try to take your blood without your consent?"

"No."

She purses her lips.

"My father was a fucking saint, and I'm the fucking devil."

"A devil doesn't save people. You saved me, Tarian. And not just once, but twice. First when Bryn almost ran me over, and then from the school bus. Maybe your goddess marked me so I could return the favor. And yes, I'm aware that sharing dreams with Dorian or Malachi would've been more useful since I'm human and weak and all that, but—"

Before I can think better of touching her—*again*—I snatch her chin and tip her head up to rope her stare. "You're not weak."

Her lips tighten in disagreement.

"You're *not*."

"I got you kidnapped."

When she tries to avert her eyes, I tip her head a little higher. "Not your fault."

Her eyes slam back into mine, flashing with a fire that drags me into her orbit as though I were nothing more than a hapless moth. "You depleted your powers to save my mortal life so stop pretending like I'm not at fault."

I don't deserve this woman's mercy. "I fucking branded you!"

Her nostrils flare. "Yeah, with the word *mine* or *sleep*, or whatever." She unscrews her face from my fingers, leaving my skin cold.

"I'm not your savior, Calamity. I'm your executioner. You'd do well to remember that."

She shoots me an eyeroll. "Well, I'm still going to try to save your grumpy Atlantean ass, so help me out. Wake up and collect something I can carry back to Dorian and Malachi. In other words, stop dreaming of me, Tarian."

Except I don't want to stop dreaming of her. Calanthe's become my lifeline. The light at the end of my murky tunnel. "Have Dorian search all vehicles belonging to Atlanteans. Vans. Trucks. Planes. Ships."

She nods.

"Actually, tell him to delegate this task to someone else. I don't want him to leave your side. Not for a bloody second."

She frowns. "How exactly am I supposed to do that?"

"You say: *Dorian Serran, Tarian commands you not to leave my side.*"

"Sure. That'll work."

"The man's loyal to a fault so he'll do as I say."

"You do realize that I'll have to give him some context? Explain how I'm hanging out with you in my sleep?"

"He can know. Malachi, too. No one else, though."

"Tarian, they may be endowed with some freaky powers, but they're bound to think that I'm a few sandwiches short of a picnic."

"Excuse me?"

"It's an expression that Logan uses on the regular. It means, to be crazy."

"Who the hell's Logan?"

"The owner of the bar across the road from the flower shop."

My runes blaze. She blinks at the ones she can see, their cool glow highlighting her freckles.

"And you see him on the regular, *why*?" I grind out.

She frowns. "Because he's a really good friend. Why did you just light up like a firefly?"

I stab my hands into my trouser pockets. "My jailors must be torturing me." When her nostrils flare with horror and her expression fills with pity, I almost regret my lie. "Distract me by telling me more about this Logan?"

"We met five years ago when he opened up shop. He, Bryn,

and I spend a lot of time together. And get this…" She cranes her neck to look up at me, a smile titillating the curve of her lips. "He invented a cocktail named *Atlantitarian,* after you. I drank it the night before we met. Gave me the worst hangover of my life. Tell you what, once all this is over, I'll take you to the bar and treat you to your namesake."

My jaw clenches. "Can't wait."

"Logan will be totally starstruck. I mean, he thinks you're scary and dislikes you because his boyfriend has the hots for you, but I'm sure he'll change his mind when he meets you in the flesh."

The blood swooshing through my veins must not be reaching my brain, because it takes several seconds for all she says to penetrate. *His boyfriend.*

I don't realize I've spoken it out loud until she adds, "Yeah. People find you attractive. Go figure."

I stare at her. Her expression is so impassive that I can't decide if she's teasing me or not. "Do I repulse you?"

"Believe it or not, I don't make a habit of kissing men who repulse me."

"About that kiss…"

She stares at my mouth, as though waiting to see what I'll say or do next.

I itch to reach out for her. To cup her cheek, fist her hair, and guide her lips to mine. Because I care about her safety, I keep my hands buried deep inside my pockets. "It was a mistake. One we shouldn't repeat."

She's suddenly staring everywhere but at my face, which makes me feel like a giant prick. "You're right."

No. I'm wrong.

I'm wrong, but I'm afraid that my nefarious magic and I will only end up hurting her more. "Go, Calanthe."

She clasps her lids, squeezing them so tightly that they ruck the delicate skin around them.

A glumness settles over me, rotting the barely beating muscle in my chest. "Go and—"

"I'm fucking trying." When she finally pierces me with a look, I don't miss the sheen of anger and tears glossing her magnetic stare.

Her expression almost makes me abandon my resolve to keep my hands off her body, but it's for the best.

A minute slips into two before she huffs, "It's not working. Probably because it's your dream, Mr. Hadez."

The use of my surname widens the rift I cleaved between us.

"Let. Go."

I fist my fingers before they can grasp her side of the rift and tow it back toward mine. My father's bloodless body flashes inside my mind, slapping me with common sense, reminding me that this will be her fate if I reach for her.

Even though returning to reality is the very last thing I crave, I close my eyes and will my body away from the *Amapola*...away from Calanthe.

When I open them again, the ocean's gone, but Calanthe is still there. And this time, we aren't alone.

# TWENTY-SEVEN

I drink in the peaked roof crafted from folds of burgundy fabric and the crowd swanning about the giant tent. Clearly, I haven't been returned to my bed.

Unless…

Unless I have and this is my dream? Instead of asking Tarian, I try summoning shoes. When none appear over my socks, I get my answer: Tarian's the one who catapulted us into this glitzy big top.

I cross my arms, refocusing on the man who just called the kiss *he* initiated a mistake. I'm aware that my reaction is totally childish, especially since I don't even like the man, but am I immune to the sting of his rejection? Nope.

"Don't you want to be saved?" I ask him.

"What sort of question is that?"

"If you don't free me from la-la land, then I can't exactly tell Dorian where to look for you."

He stabs a hand through his coiffed locks that shine as blackly as the satin lapels of his tuxedo and onyx bowtie.

"I imagine someone from the real world will eventually shake me awake, but *eventually* could be in a couple hours from now, and however much I enjoyed *The Greatest Showman*, I don't think now's the time to join the circus."

A nerve feathers his jaw.

"Look, I tried to wake up but couldn't, which means that you, Mr. Hadez, need to find a way—"

"Tarian." Another tick of his jaw. "Stop calling me Mr. Hadez."

I purse my lips and tighten the knot of my arms. "How about we discuss your preferred—"

"You could've at least worn a hat, Tarian." A man in emerald tails and a top hat sidles over to us. Because of the pasted-on handlebar mustache, it takes me a second to realize it's Malachi.

When Tarian neither acknowledges his cousin's advice nor removes his attention from me, I begin to frown. Did he not hear him?

Malachi's eyebrows gather in the shadows cast by the brim of his velvet headpiece as he gives me a cursory once-over. "And you are?"

"A figment of your cousin's imagination," I reply sweetly.

Malachi blinks, then looks between Tarian and me. "Do you have a name, *figment of Tarian's imagination*?" His voice carves over the brass band's upbeat tune.

Yes, there's a live band. There are also waiters dressed like circus entertainers toting wicker vendor trays overflowing with miniature popcorn bags and bite-sized cotton candy.

"Sure do. It's Calanthe. Calanthe Bloom."

Recognition doesn't fire across dream-Malachi's expression. How odd. Then again, is it any odder than being locked inside someone's dream? I glare at this someone; he glares right back. But our eye-jousting is cut short when Malachi inserts himself between us.

The blond god nods to my socks. "I'm heading to the dressing room to grab my broody cousin a prop. Come with me. We can unearth something for you to wear."

"I'm not planning on staying." I try to catch Tarian's attention, but Malachi takes a step nearer, effectively sealing away the ringleader of this slumber circus.

"I'm afraid you're not going to be able to go anywhere for the next hour, Miss Bloom. Boston's getting battered by the biggest blizzard since 1978."

How convenient. Especially taking into account that it's almost summer back in the real world. "Well, then, lead the way to this magical costume closet."

Here's to hoping that walking away from Tarian stabs this new dream in the bud and sends me sailing home.

As we cross the lively space, I let my gaze wander over the room again. Over the bandmembers perspiring beneath the beams of the stage lights, their brass instruments shimmering like the guests' costumes and jewels. Over a skinny performer bending his limbs at unnatural angles to fit inside a teeny treasure chest. Over a female bodybuilder with rouged cheeks and glittery eyelashes, toting around a wine bottle twice as large as the pirate chest on stage.

"So how did you and my cousin *actually* meet?" Malachi asks, tearing my attention off the strongwoman and her Nabuchodonosor.

Since this isn't real, I decide to let my imagination run free. "In a synagogue. I was there for a conference on the reproduction of cuttlefish in the Dead Sea."

Both of Malachi's eyebrows hitch up.

"I got my dates mixed up, because I arrived right in the middle of a Bar Mitsvah."

"That my cousin attended?" Skepticism modulates his pitch.

"Obviously. Do you really picture that man signing up for a talk about squids?" I add a grin that trips off my lips when the rune on my spine heats.

"I must agree that a conference on the subject of squid mating wouldn't get Tarian away from the boardroom." Malachi's soft snort is drowned out by the crowd's applause when the contortionist succeeds in stuffing himself inside the chest. "I'm honestly a little surprised he attended a Bar Mitsvah. Whose kid did you say it was for?"

"I didn't." Heat bursts from my rune. I force my lips into a smile before Malachi can spot my discomfort. "I wasn't on the guest list, remember?"

"Right." His expression dances with amusement. "So, are you a marine biologist?"

"No. Just a wildlife enthusiast." Which is actually not a lie. I like my nature documentaries just as much as my true crime podcasts.

The corners of Malachi's mouth slope a little higher. "If you ever do find out how squids make babies"—he seizes a fold in the tent wall and hoists it up—"especially in water that's too hot and salty for most creatures, you'll have to tell me all about it."

I'm glad to see that fake-Malachi isn't a gullible dimwit. "Never thought I'd meet a fellow squid fan."

"It's not the squids I'm a fan of." He winks.

All right, then. Things just got weird. Well, *weirder*. Even though Malachi isn't real, the guilt that floods me feels extremely real.

I consider returning to the devil I know, but when I stare back in Tarian's direction, I find a tall, skinny blonde all but glued to his front. Although his eyes are on me, or maybe they're on Malachi—hard to tell from the distance and subdued lighting—he's not pushing away the woman in the hot-pink leotard giving him a vertical lap dance.

Why would he? This is his fantasy, after all. Everything and everyone in this dream is of his making. I start to twist back toward Malachi when the crowd shifts, and I spy the blonde's footwear. I have zero reason to be jealous, yet the sight of the crystallized sandals strapped around her bony calves is a punch to my bruised ego.

*They're just shoes, Calanthe. Not even real ones. Not even yours.*

When Tarian's fantasy girl swivels to snatch a champagne flute from a nearby vendor tray, my hurt sharpens into a whole other emotion. I narrow my eyes on the Atlantean's and shake my head in disgust, then duck beneath his cousin's arm and arrow straight for a rack bursting with color and glitter. The least the asshat could've done was not stick Mackenzie Fielding in *my* shoes, which I'm aware, aren't mine, but *still…*

My fingers shake as I trace the sequined sleeve of a black jacket adorned with gold shoulder tassels. "Your cousin and the blonde in the pink gymnast suit, are they a thing?"

"I don't think so. Are you and he a *thing*?"

I glance over my shoulder at the man ambling toward me. He may look and sound like Malachi, but he definitely doesn't act like him.

"No." I hold his stare, waiting for…I'm not even sure what. Tarian to snap me out of this dressing room and away from his captivated cousin?

When that doesn't happen, I tug the jacket off the hanger. May as well change into something that hasn't soaked up dream-sea water and real-sweat. Surprisingly, or perhaps *un*surprisingly, I know the cropped tailcoat will fit me before I've even tossed off my rumpled tee and done up the rhinestone buttons over my sports bra.

"You'll find shoes in the corner." Malachi gestures toward the back of the dressing room, his gaze traveling down my body with a hunger I recognize, because it's the same hunger which had animated Tarian's features before he replaced me with Bryn's sister.

"Don't forget that prop for your cousin." My tone is as tight as the jacket confining my breasts, which unlike Mackenzie's, aren't perky and the perfect handful, as she so loved to point out when I hit puberty and sprouted boobs that, for years, wouldn't stop growing. Here I'd thought my numerous ice cream therapy sessions with Bryn dissecting the reasons for Macrazy's body-shaming had evicted my insecurities, but I'm apparently still chockful of them.

I select shoes that are the furthest things from the delicate, crystallized pair Mackenzie's wearing and plop my ass down on the lid of a closed wooden chest to zip them up. Just like the jacket, the patent leather thigh-highs mold around my shapely legs to perfection.

"That's right." Malachi rifles through the shelf laden with top hats and wigs and countless other props that seem better suited for an S&M gathering than a Barnum & Bailey-themed bash.

As he pulls out a leather whip, I stand up and smooth my palms down my black leggings. "Probably best not to give that man a torture device." The heels on my boots are so tall that our faces almost align.

Malachi flashes me a crooked grin that makes the curl of his mustache rise. "This isn't for him. Besides"—he presses the fall hitch to the inside of my ankle, then waits, as though to see how I'll react—"whips don't only procure pain."

I'm so stunned that I don't move a muscle. Even my eyelashes have stopped fluttering, but then Bryn's face floods my mind, and with it, a sobering amount of guilt.

If Malachi had been *anyone* else, I might've given this fantasy flirtation room to grow, if only to stop thinking of Tarian and Mackenzie, but make-believe or not, I could never do that to my friend. Just as I'm about to step back, a deep voice freezes my retreat.

"Unless you're interested in being popped in the balls with that thing, I suggest removing it from her fucking body."

Malachi and I both startle at the intrusion.

I shoot Tarian a frosty smile. "How about you let me decide how Malachi's whip kink plays out?"

"Fuck." Malachi tosses the whip aside. "Sorry, Tarian. I thought you were with the blonde." He backpedals toward the tent flap. "I'll just let myself out."

Tarian doesn't watch him leave, too busy drinking in my ring-leader getup. I can't tell if he's repulsed or aroused. Not that I care.

I scoop up the whip and tap it against my open palm as I stroll toward him. "Speaking of *the blonde,* where is she?"

"Is that why you want me to release you from my dream? So you can screw my cousin?"

Genuine shock stills my tapping. "Excuse me?"

His eyes twitch. Both of them. "What were you doing in here with him? What did I interrupt?"

The audacity of this man!

I taper my gaze on his and rap the tip of my whip against his chest. "Nothing that concerns you, Hades."

He grips the whip but doesn't tear it from my fingers. The only thing he does is use it to reel me into his too-big and too-hard body. "Has the word I branded onto your back slipped your mind?"

My threadbare good humor crumbles like potpourri. "*You* didn't brand me with it. Your magic did. You know"—I rise onto my toes to breathe my next words straight into his ear—"the magic you can't even control." It's a low blow, but lord, does his ego deserve some leveling.

He turns his face toward me so suddenly that I rock back, yet his nose still bumps mine, his mouth still brushes against mine. "Don't fucking taunt me."

"Or what? You'll wring my neck?" I should put a mile between our bodies. Instead, I keep perfectly still to show the beast that he can roar all he wants, I'm not intimidated. "Murdering the only link you have to the real world—to your reliable cousin—would be incredibly dumb."

Was bringing up Malachi necessary? *No.* Did it feel good? The memory of Mackenzie trying to climb Tarian bangs into my mind. *Absolutely.*

"Calamity." His growl vibrates my lips that are still entirely too close to his.

I swallow down the rough sound before gritting my molars

and feeding him mine, "Let me out of this nightmare." I tighten my grip on the whip. "Let me go."

I don't think he'll let me—even though that's what I want…the *only* thing I want—but I'm wrong. Tarian Hadez releases the whip, and I stumble into the stretched canvas.

"Don't. With Malachi. Don't." The force of his brutal stare impales my body to the fabric wall.

I should confess I have no interest in Malachi, but liars don't deserve honesty, so I square my shoulders and stalk through the tent flap. I'm half expecting to finally tumble back into my bed, but naturally, Tarian Hadez isn't done playing with me.

# TWENTY-EIGHT

The landscape of Tarian's dream has, once again, changed. For the creepier this time. I am surrounded by complete darkness and silence. It's so quiet that when I spin around, I can hear the soles of my high-heeled boots crunch over gravel.

"Where are we now?" I grumble as a low whoosh fills the darkness.

Shit. Where the hell *did* I land?

"Tarian?" I call out.

Twin rods of light suddenly carve up the darkness and glaze the sequins on my jacket, making me glimmer like a disco ball. When the squeal of metal stabs my eardrums, the whip tumbles to the railroad tracks. Even though I'm conscious that the vehicle bulleting toward me isn't real, adrenaline drenches my system, and I lunge sideways, screeching Tarian's name. The man has got to wake up before I become the figurehead of the incoming train.

I trip on the track. Of course I do. My heel clips the outer rail and somehow gets jammed between the metal. Little rocks plink into my body as I wiggle my foot to unbolt my heel. But the damn thing's stuck. I scrabble to find the zipper of my boots, only to discover it's disappeared. Just like the circus tent. If this is Tarian's way of punishing me for talking back, then by god, the man's wicked.

He's a mob boss, I remind myself. A mob boss with supernatural powers and a grudge.

"Tarian?!" I hunt the crushing darkness for the man in charge of this nightmare. "Tarian, I swear to never badmouth you or your magic again!"

The lights draw closer.

"Come on, Tarian! Don't murder me over your wounded pride. You're better than that."

Please be better than that.

The train is still advancing while I'm very much *not*.

I hinge at the waist and skim the ground for a rock I can use to snap my heel. The only thing I come up with is a handful of teeny pebbles.

"Help!" I scream, hoping this isn't another one-on-one dream with Sleeping Beauty. Please let there be a cast of extras on the set of this nightmare. "HELP!"

But no one comes to help. I grip the patent leather around my thigh and try to rip it. When that doesn't work, I try to stretch it. Fail. Fail. Fail.

I glance up, estimating I have a handful of seconds left before I become worm food. Because Tarian is all about atmosphere, numbers light up the darkness. *20. 19. 18.* A countdown.

I spend three precious seconds cursing the deviant god, then another five wriggling my foot.

When single digits appear, I throw my entire body weight into a whirl. Something snaps. The pain that ensues is so sharp it whitewashes my vision. Did I just fracture my own ankle?

*7. 6. 5.*

Sweat pours down my temples and neck in rivulets.

I'm going to die.

For half a second, I think, *Good. I'll be free of Tarian's twisted magic and back in Dorian and Electra's penthouse.* But then, I think, *Wait. No. Everything that happens to me in Tarian's dreams is real. If I get smooshed beneath the train of his wrath, I get smooshed for real.*

I don't want to die. "Tarian, make it stop! I beg you! Make it stop!"

Fire erupts in the middle of my back, so sharp and hot, it eclipses the agony lancing up my calf. Is Tarian removing my rune? Calling on it? Carving it deeper?

When the number '2' flashes to '1', I tip my body sideways and smack into the ground. The impact severs the heel of the shoe, and I roll, once, twice. And then I lay there, wherever *there* is, staring up into a starless sky as the train barrels past me, its velocity kicking up the ends of my hair and plastering them to my damp forehead. Even though my ankle and spine are hotbeds of pain, my pulse finally eases.

My mood, though, that's a whole other story.

"Tarian Hadez, mark my words"—I pant—"if your captors don't find a way to kill you"—another labored breath—"I will."

The screeching of metal is suddenly replaced by the crackle of a feminine voice. "We are pleased to announce that Delta Train 666, with direct service to Atlantis, will arrive at Platform 66 in six seconds. Please stand clear of all doors."

Seriously, Tarian? The devil's number? And a train with direct service to Atlantis? The imagination on that one is manifestly boundless.

I close my eyes and picture Mom, Bryn, the penthouse. I even picture Dorian and Electra, hoping that visualizing where I want to be will magically transport me there. Do I consider clicking my heels? Absolutely. That is, until the stabbing pain in my foot shoots up my leg and my heel shouts, *Do not click me!*

When I open my lids, I'm still stuck in Tarian's fantasy world.

Growling in frustration, I grip handfuls of pebbles and hurl them at the entrenching darkness. "Fuck you! Fuck. You!"

Careful not to jostle my tender ankle, I turn onto my side, then dig my palm and forearm into the gravel, and hoist my tattered body into a seated position. Huffing and puffing, I force my hair off my forehead just as new high beams gouge the darkness.

Although the train will probably go off the rails and crush me, I feel no fear. There's no room for that emotion amid the irritation and rancor. Forget dressing Tarian up in a Richard Simmons' leotard. Once I see that bastard again, once *I'm* in charge of our dream, I will ship him to a scorching desert and stake him to a saguaro with extra-large needles while I suck down margaritas from a nearby paddle pool.

A figure detaches itself from the abounding darkness and crunches over the gravel toward me. Although I can't see much of the person yet, I catch the supernatural glow of eyes, the mussed curls of dark hair, and the breadth of wide shoulders.

"Enjoy the show?" I spit out.

"What show would that be?"

The tenor of the voice jolts me. Not Tarian, but definitely male. Who has he dropped into this nightmare now? The man steps nearer and, although he shares many features with the maker of my misfortune, he's not him. Not the man to blame.

"Symeon?"

"Have we met?" Like illusory-Malachi, illusory-Symeon has no clue who I am.

"No."

"But you know my name?"

"The Hadezes are a notorious bunch."

A smile tugs at his slightly lopsided mouth. "I suppose we are. Need a hand?"

More like a crutch, but I suppose a hand will do until I can find a wall to lean against. When I nod, he reaches down. My brand, which had gone pleasantly cold, flares anew. I grit my teeth against the discomfort as Symeon lifts me and sets me on my feet—well, foot. I keep the other one off the ground. It strikes me that it's the same foot that got sliced up on a shard of glass. At least that's convenient.

I hiss as the fire in my spine spreads to the skin surrounding it. "Any chance you know where I can find your brother?"

"He's on his way to Atlantis."

I blink at him. I know this is a dream, but could there be truth in it?

When Symeon lets go, I clamp my fingers around his bicep. "Sorry. I think I broke something." I nod to my foot.

He studies it.

"You wouldn't be able to fix it for me, now, would you?"

"I'm not a cobbler."

"I didn't mean the shoe. I was talking about my bone."

"Not a doctor, either."

"But you're an Atlantean. You have powers."

He tilts his head. "Powers?"

"Forget it. Happen to know where I can—" I growl as what feels like a scorching knife carves into the whorls of my rune to make the word sink deeper. Is this some sick way of Tarian's to remind me that I'm his?

"Where I can?" Symeon prompts just as the train chugs into the station.

"Find a chair?"

His crooked mouth curls into a smile. "I do, actually."

He helps me hobble up a set of stairs that wasn't visible in the dark—or didn't exist until now—then leads me toward a train wagon that has no doors or windows.

I dig my heels in. *Heel.* Singular. Although it doesn't stop Symeon, it slows him down. "I don't want to get on the train."

"Everyone wants to go to Atlantis."

"Not me." I shake my head. "The only place I want to go is home."

The loudspeaker crackles anew. "You have sixty-six seconds to board the train, Miss Bloom."

I startle at hearing my name. God only knows why, since this is Tarian's dream, and Tarian, unlike everyone else, knows who I am.

A new countdown begins. I really, *really* dislike countdowns.

The metallic body of the train mutates to glass, making me forget all about my countdown loathing.

Bryn sits in a vintage diner booth, in front of a seven-tiered wedding cake that looks like it dropped straight out of *The Knot* magazine. "Callie, you made it to the cake tasting!"

Hearing my name on her lips rattles me. And yes, I'm aware of how wacky that is in the grand scope of Tarian's dream. Not only is there a *wedding cake tasting*, but also, and strangest of all, the company Bryn keeps...

*Why in the world would you toss Yasmin Fablez and Delta Lynch into your dream, Tarian?*

# TWENTY-NINE

I study Sergeant Delta Lynch's profile, from his shaved scalp that gleams as though dipped in clear polish, to his brown eyes trained on the ceiling of the train car, to the navy lines of ink representing the latitudes and longitudes of all his past battles that scroll out of his short-sleeved olive tee and cover half his bicep.

I try to recall Tarian's reaction when I mentioned Bryn's father the time we discussed his little nickname for me. Did I utter Delta's name? Is that what stirred a memory of the man? Clearly, considering the level of detail, Tarian and Delta are familiar with one another. I suppose Atlanteans keep a detailed file on their enemies, and since Delta is part of the U.S. military, he's considered persona non grata in Atlantis.

Yet here he is, on Wacky Wagon 666 with direct service to Atlantis.

Since dreams originate in our subconscious and reveal our

greatest fears, I'm guessing that having Delta, aka the military, visit the hallowed island preoccupies Tarian immensely. The same way Joslyn and Saul's nuptials preoccupy him, hence a wedding cake. As for Yasmin, he must not be a fan of—

Malachi mentioned she was flying home because she thought her family was behind the abduction. Could that be true, and that's why she has a starring role in Tarian's subconscious? Unless her home is in Atlantis? Maybe she was one of the few families that didn't emigrate.

My pulse crackles like the loudspeaker prompting me to board Delta Train 666. I may be a little salty with Tarian for being trapped inside his mind *and* for my damaged ankle, but I suddenly wonder if he's trying to send me a message through all these seemingly incoherent sequences.

What if the vehicle he's on *is* a train?

What if they broke *his* ankle?

What if the military and the Fablez family *are* behind the abduction?

I'm dying to wake up so I can fill Dorian and Malachi in on all my hypotheses, but what if Tarian has more to show me?

"Get your ass on this train, girl!" Bryn kicks her feet onto the table and crosses them at the ankle.

She's wearing sneakers. Granted, fashionable ones, with leopard-print stars, but *sneakers*. In the many years I've known Bryn Fielding, never has she *ever* worn a pair of shoes not equipped with heels.

"Go. He needs you," Symeon murmurs as the bodiless announcer counts down the seconds.

I know the brothers don't have the best relationship, but there must be fraternal love if Tarian depicted Symeon as compassionate.

"Do you have any idea where he is, Symeon?"

The male's pupils shrink, then dilate, then shrink again. And then he averts his gaze, heightening my frustration. I have to remind myself that Tarian doesn't know where his physical self is being kept, so why in the world am I expecting an answer from dream-Symeon?

"Will you come with me?"

He takes a step forward, hits an invisible wall with a bang, then staggers back, taking me along with him. Thankfully, he catches himself before either of us goes down.

"Seems like I'm not invited." His thick eyebrows descend over his eyes, casting shadows over his wrought expression. "Yasmin?"

She doesn't lean past Delta to look at Symeon, doesn't even acknowledge him.

"Yasmin!" he yells again, his eyes darkening further. "Don't do this."

The disembodied voice counts down the seconds. "Twenty-four. Twenty-three."

I know this isn't real, nevertheless the flash of pain that crosses Symeon's features at Yasmin's snub is tangible. Did Tarian toss in a breakup because he's not a fan of his brother dating Yasmin? After all, dreams also expose our deepest desires.

"Seventeen. Sixteen. Fifteen," the voice continues.

"Come on, Callie. Get on!" Bryn pats the banquette.

Because one injury is more than enough for one evening, I reach out the hand I don't have clamped around Symeon's bicep to check for an invisible partition.

When my fingers sink through air, I turn to him. "Maybe I can lead you through—"

Symeon flickers right out of existence.

Well, all right then. Symeon's not meant to get on the train.

"Callie, hop on already," Bryn exclaims.

I glance over my shoulder, hoping I'll spot Tarian, but there's only darkness beyond the platform. "Please let this not be a roller-coaster. I'm really not a fan." I wince as I totter aboard.

As soon as I step onto the linoleum, the countdown stops, and the glass wagon warps back into metal. Thankfully, the train doesn't leave the station immediately, giving me enough time to hop on one foot to Bryn's side.

"What happened to your shoe?" she asks.

"Caught my heel in the train tracks and had to tear it free. Tore up my ankle in the process." As I drop onto the banquette beside her, I nod to the others. "Sergeant, Yasmin."

Unlike Symeon, Yasmin smiles and says, "Excited for the trip, Calanthe?"

I startle that she knows who I am, whereas Tarian made me a stranger to Malachi and Symeon. Not that dreams are logical, but shouldn't there be some consistency? "I didn't know they allowed tourists to enter Atlantis."

She toys with her vape pen. "They don't, but you're special."

*Because of my rune?* Although the people around me aren't real, I keep my query to myself.

The train finally moves, but instead of shooting straight forward, it swerves to the left and then it rocks, jostling my poor ankle. Sweat bleeds down my neck as a fresh wave of pain shoots into my calf.

My fingers close around the edge of the table as I brace myself for God—*Tarian* only knows what. When the train doesn't topple and explode, I let my head loll back and groan in relief. And then I stretch out my aching leg and close my eyes, taking a moment to tune out the craziness.

Without opening my eyes, I ask, "How do you know Tarian, Sergeant Lynch?" I'm so glad to be sitting that I don't even care if this train takes me deeper into the underworld.

"Another hit," he murmurs.

I open my eyes, about to ask him what exactly was hit when I get sidetracked by the ceiling. Unlike the spotless metallic walls, the sheet of metal overhead is festooned in bright graffiti. Slashes of pinks, blues, oranges, and yellows overlap and crisscross, show-casing the same sequence of letters and numbers—'CVN-666'.

"What the heck is 'CVN'?" Someone's initials, maybe?

The wagon rocks, and I go skidding into Bryn, who's swirling her finger inside the tiered monstrosity's frosting, unfazed by the rocking.

"You've got to try this wedding cake. It's to *die* for."

Even if I wanted to indulge in fake cake, the cocktail of pain and queasiness has doused my appetite. "Maybe later," I say, wondering why Tarian is dreaming of my best friend glutting herself on frosting. Because he's hungry?

The thought digs its claws into me and fills me with anger on his behalf. He probably *is* being starved, which explains the insane playground that is his mind. I mean, trains that rock? Circuses? Delta Lynch?

"So 'CVN-666'? Any idea what that stands for?" I ask my odd array of travel companions.

Yasmin sucks on her e-cig, then blows out vapor. The white curls slither around the ombré cake and punch up my nose, amplifying my nausea because they smell like exhaust fumes. "The Club of Very Naughty people?"

Bryn snorts, scooping frosting off the cake with her index finger. "I'd go." She sucks off the frosting. "I can be naughty."

My gaze slingshots between my friend and her father. Their relationship might not be traditional, but to go so far as to discuss sex clubs…?

*Calm your tits. It's a freaking dream, Calanthe.*

Yasmin shrugs, which makes her deep cashmere V-neck sweater collapse off one of her shoulders. "Perhaps it's a TV channel?"

What if it's the channel that Tarian's abductors are watching? Or listening to? It must definitely hold meaning for Tarian if it's plastered all over this place.

Bryn scrapes up some more frosting. "Oh my god, this cake. Gah. It's crack."

From the gluttonous way she eats, I wonder if the wedding cake is, in fact, laced with drugs.

"More." Delta Lynch steeples his fingers on the table and inclines his head. "More!"

I jump at his brusque tone. More cake?

Although the frosted dessert stands between us, if I lean away from Bryn, I have a direct line of sight on the sergeant, and from what I can tell, he's not snacking away on the cake. So is he telling his daughter to eat more?

"No. No more." Yasmin swipes Lynch's gaping mouth with her pinkie.

Is that blood? Is he bleeding? Is she?

She leans forward, reaching up to readjust the toppled bride and groom figurines on the cake. In the process, her pinkie collects some frosting. She licks it off, and I gape because her fingertip doesn't bleed but it's black. From a birthmark? Spilled ink? I squint but get sidetracked by the red hair of the bride statuette and her miniature metallic vape pen. I shoot my attention to the groom who's a perfect replica of—

A hand grabs my sprained ankle and jerks it to the side. I howl in pain, then whimper when unbearable heat envelops my skin.

"Quiet her before she wakes up the whole house, Dorian," a familiar voice commands.

I blink. Find Dorian looming over me, palm pressed to my lips. "Sorry," he murmurs.

My nostrils flare as my ligaments and bone reknit. Oh god, oh god, oh god...I want to plunge my foot in a vat of ice. My entire leg.

Just as suddenly as the heat engulfed my skin, it vanishes. Along with the pain.

"There. All better." Malachi releases my ankle, then stands from his crouch and crosses his arms. "Now, how about you explain how one breaks a bone while lying in bed?"

# THIRTY

I didn't physically plummet out of Tarian's dream, yet the shock of being back in the real world feels like I jumped out of an airplane without a chute.

As Dorian reels his palm back, his hopeful gaze searches mine. "Your rune, it does something more than make you sleep, doesn't it?"

I sit up, then run my hands down my face. I don't need a mirror to know I look as worn out as the two Atlanteans looming over me, since all the sleep I'm getting these days is most definitely *not* restorative.

"Calanthe?" Malachi's haggard tone flicks my attention to his face.

I'm suddenly back at the circus, back in that dressing room with him, and heat engulfs both my neck and that part of my leg he'd prodded with his imaginary whip. I squeeze my eyes shut to push away the awkward memory. When I feel somewhat cooler, I

196

lift my lids. This time, I stay firmly in the here and now, with the version of Malachi who has zero interest in whip-play or in me.

I sit up and gather my legs into my chest. My relief at seeing my feet deathtrap-free is muddied by the realization that I'm down a T-shirt. I find it puddled on the floor. It dawns on me that when I tossed it off in my dream, I must've pitched it off in reality. Even though I'm wearing a concealing sports bra and not lace underwear, I tug the sheets higher around me.

"Calanthe?" Malachi bites out my name, his jaw flexing in time with the muscles in his forearms.

I snap my gaze over the rest of the room. "Where's Bryn?" I have every intention of telling Dorian and Malachi all I know, but I need to make sure my friend isn't within earshot, because I don't want them screwing with her mind.

"She's safe." Every tendon in Dorian's neck bulges.

"That wasn't my question. My question was—"

"Dorian calmed her down after she ran out of your bedroom shrieking that something was wrong with you." Malachi kneads his nape as though his runes were prickling. "Electra said you screamed, then proceeded to babble. Something about cake, Delta, and the number six."

I narrow my gaze on the hulking bodyguard. "How exactly did you calm her down, Dorian?"

The glance the men exchange heightens the pulsing behind my ribs.

I'm about to reiterate my question when Dorian says, "I compelled her to forget."

"What else did you do to her?"

"I asked Elle to drive her home."

"The home Bryn thinks is overrun by rats?"

Malachi presses his lips together. "Dorian cleared that up."

"The infestation or the lie?" A vein throbs so hard in my neck that I half expect it to rupture. "If your mind games cause any lasting damage to her brain, I will—"

"You'd do well not to threaten us, Miss Bloom." Malachi's tone has dropped so many octaves that I can barely hear him over the hysterical thudding of my pulse. "After all, your mother and your neighbor are still here. Under *our* protection."

I taper my eyes on the blond Atlantean who's apparently not as charming as he passes himself off to be. "If you want to find your beloved cousin, Mr. Hadez, then you keep protecting my mother and Mrs. Fiona, and you don't fucking hold their safety over my head."

We stare so hard at one another that his irises begin to glow. Possibly mine, too. Who knows? Sure, Malachi said I didn't have any power, but Tarian said I might. Could've been to placate me, but also could've been the truth.

Dorian murmurs something in Atlantean that snags Malachi's attention away from me. After he's finished talking, Malachi's nostrils flare with a harsh exhale.

"Sorry. I haven't been able to sleep since Tarian was taken, and it's catching up with me." His eyes are not only rimmed crimson but also smudged with shadows. "Please, Calanthe. Please help us."

His broken plea thaws me out. "Fine." Here goes everything. "Don't judge and *don't* interrupt."

Where Malachi gives a slow nod, Dorian's is jerky. Their tangible anticipation is daunting because what if all the discombobulated events I'm about to relay are merely figments of Tarian's eccentric imagination?

"The rune on my back connects me to Tarian in my sleep."

The spastic batting of both gods' eyelashes crumbles my lingering reservation that meeting up in dreams was an Atlantean power. It isn't that I didn't believe Tarian— Actually, it's exactly that. The male's a stranger who dwells in my mind, and I barely trust my own mind as it is.

"Where is he?" Dorian breathes out.

"He has no clue. He can't seem to wake up."

Malachi curses under his breath while Dorian stays stock-still and silent.

"He thinks he's being transported somewhere because he can feel a rocking motion. He wants you to check any and all vehicles owned by Atlanteans."

Dorian rushes to the sleek metal and granite desk next to the empty bookcase and snatches a palm-sized tablet. As he types, I slide my lip between my teeth, running my nighttime excursion under a magnifying glass, weighing what has value and what doesn't.

Malachi begins to pace, clearly at the end of his rope. "What else?"

"I think…I think that maybe—"

He jerks to a stop and whirls on me. "Maybe *what*?"

I don't mean to create suspense. I'm just trying to decide if I should voice my hunch. What if it leads them on a wild goose chase?

"The last dream I had was particularly *eventful*." I stare at the outline of my foot under the sheets that was raw with pain only minutes prior. "After my ankle broke, Symeon guided me toward a train—Delta Train 666—with direct service to Atlantis. Since trains can't cross the Atlantic Ocean, I thought that maybe Tarian could've heard a Delta Airline announcement?"

"Symeon?" Malachi grabs his cell phone from the back pocket of his slacks while Dorian pounds away on the tablet.

"Wait. Don't call him, Malachi. Just wait. There's more."

"Talk!" Forget being at the end of his rope. Malachi is in freefall.

"I don't know how this fits in with the rest, but Yasmin was getting married and not to Symeon. He looked really hurt by this. Could they have broken up?"

Malachi spears his hair. "They very well could have, but how is that relevant—"

"The school bus that plowed into us the night Tarian was taken. You said the person was compelled. What if—what if Yasmin was the one to compel him, and that's why she left? Because she knew she'd get caught?"

Dorian has stopped typing. Malachi has stopped breathing.

"I know the Fablez family claims not to be involved, but what if *she* is? After all, she handled my cell phone."

Dorian lowers the tablet. "She was at the house when we got the call about the accident."

"Which makes for a great alibi," I point out.

Malachi resumes pacing. "Except we can't compel humans over the phone."

"Not even with FaceTime?"

"No." Tarian's cousin shakes his head. "Electronics stifle our power."

That's both reassuring and aggravating. "Actually, I was meaning to ask, how do you know the guy was compelled?"

"He was driving a school bus in the middle of the night," Dorian says.

"Someone might have paid him to do that."

"He had no criminal record, and his death… He didn't die from the impact." His mouth thins. "His heart exploded."

"People die from heart failure every day."

Malachi stops pacing. "It didn't fail, it *exploded*."

All right, then. Compulsion, it is. I'm about to ask if he could've been compelled in advance, but who could've anticipated our trip to the flower shop? "Could someone have bugged Tarian's car, then warned a friend he'd driven off the property sans backup? That's a possibility, right?"

Malachi cracks his knuckles. "Dorian, call up Catalina and ask her if her granddaughter made it home."

"I don't think that's a good idea." The bodyguard's tone is borderline gentle, as though he senses he's about to get blasted out the window. "If Catalina's involved, it'll only tip them off that we're onto them."

Silence. Tense, heavy, all-consuming silence soaks the room.

"Look up every ship, train, car, and plane registered to the Fablez family. I'm going to go find Symeon." Malachi starts toward the door.

"Malachi, one more thing," I call out.

He spins back around.

"When I was sitting inside the train, there was this sequence of letters and numbers: 'CVN-666'. I'm not sure what they mean. Maybe someone's initials and birth year? Maybe an abbreviated address?"

Dorian inputs the code into his tablet. A half second later, he snaps his neck straight. "Are you sure that's what you read?"

"Yes. Why? Did you get a hit?" I try to peek at the screen of his tablet, but it's gone dark. Or maybe it's only visible to Atlantean eyes? Wait, don't I have Atlantean eyes now?

"It's not the Fablez fleet we should be looking at, Malachi." A crazed smile jostles Dorian's lips. "CVN-666 is an aircraft carrier. A U.S. aircraft carrier."

That's why Delta was in my dream! Not because he's marrying Yasmin, but because it was Tarian's subconscious way of telling me that the Fablez are in bed with the military.

The pastel light of a new dawn leaks around the curtain's edges. How fitting.

I throw the sheets off my legs. "How do we find the vessel?"

"*We* don't do anything," Malachi snaps.

"But—"

"Calanthe, you need to stay put. Not only are you our only link to Tarian, but also, my cousin will have my head if anything happens to you." Malachi's voice is soft again, but not the rest of him. The rest of him vibrates with nervous energy. "Dorian, find out the location of the carrier." He raises his cell phone to his ear and barks, "Elle, where are you?" Silence. "Well, fucking hurry."

Is he calling her back so that she can babysit me while he and Dorian lead the search and rescue, or will she go with them?

Tarian's demand that Dorian stay with me twirls through my mind. I smother it. If they took the god of all gods so easily, snatching a lone lesser god will be a breeze. Dorian and Malachi need to stick together.

I brew a pot of coffee while the men plot their hostile takeover at the kitchen table. They're draining their mugs when Electra barges into the apartment, cheekbones flushed as though she's just run up all sixty flights of stairs. Or is it eighty? How far up are we?

"What did I miss?" She pushes a lock that escaped her hair tie behind her ear.

As Dorian fills her in, her eyes grow as wide as the dish on which someone plated Mom's banana bread. I nibble on a slice, but the flavor sours my stomach and stings my eyes because it reminds me acutely of Dad. I push the plate away and down a full glass of water to rinse away the lingering tang of my sadness. I'm going to need to eat at some point, but truth is, I'm not even hungry. All I am at the moment is a jumbo ball of stress.

Malachi nods to the front door, and Dorian gets up.

As the men trundle past us, Electra grips Dorian's hand and squeezes it. "Keep him safe," she murmurs, this time in English.

Does she mean Malachi or Tarian?

Although I still don't trust her like I trust the other two, as long as she's fighting on our side, I'll give her the benefit of the doubt.

*Our side.* Never thought I'd be siding with Atlanteans. Then again, I never thought I'd be dreaming of one.

I hear the echo of that entreaty Tarian murmured in the in-between: *"Find me."*

*I'm trying, Tarian.*

As the door snicks shut and Electra bolts it, I send up a prayer to whoever's up there that the information I gave Malachi and Dorian is correct.

"You better not be leading them into a trap." Electra's distrust stings.

The irony isn't lost on me that I can be hurt by a feeling that's mutual. "I want him found just as much as you do, Electra. More so, even, because I want his rune off my skin."

"He wasn't able to lift the one he gave his father." She pours herself a mug of coffee and carries it over to the table where I sit. "What makes you think he'll be able to remove the one on your skin?"

My chest prickles with… I'm not even certain with what. Unease? Worry? "So, either I die when the week's up, or I'm stuck dreaming of Tarian for the rest of my life?"

"I could think of worse fates."

I gasp. "Than dying?"

"No. Than dreaming of Tarian Hadez." She smirks, which ferries heat into my cheeks. "That's what I thought."

"What is it you thought?"

She eyes the banana bread, breaks off a chunk, and flicks it into her mouth. Once she's done chewing, she says, "That you're not too bothered by your predicament."

"I'm very bothered by it."

"Hot and bothered. Not the same thing."

"I'm—I'm—" …speechless.

"Immune to his dark charm? Haven't met a single woman immune to that man's charm. Besides myself, that is." She breaks off another piece of the banana bread. "Your mom sure knows how to cook. I don't think mine ever opened a fridge in her life. Actually, that's not true. She opened it daily to grab the syringes she stashed inside."

"Syringes?"

"Of my blood."

"Your mother collected your blood?"

She takes a bite of cake, then chases it down with a sip of coffee. "My mother was human. I wasn't."

"So she *bled* you?" I'm appalled. *Horrified* on her behalf.

"Once a week till I was ten. She'd make good money selling it on the black market. When she wasn't injecting it into herself, that is."

"Didn't it make her sick?"

"It did, but the high was worth the pain, apparently."

"Your father didn't stop her from bleeding you? *Dorian* didn't stop her?"

"The Serrans are my adoptive parents. My real father walked out before I was born." She takes another bite of cake as though she wasn't in the middle of recounting her dysfunctional child-hood. "The only thing I know about the man is that he's Atlantean—because *enchanted blood*—and fucking careless since my human mother knew all about my blood's miraculous properties."

I study her oval face, her long-lashed heterochrome eyes that are as destabilizing by their intensity as they are by their hue. "You said it stopped when you were ten. What happened then?"

"The council was cracking down on the illegal use of Atlantean blood. Malachi was in charge of North America since that's Hadez territory."

She makes the family sound like kings.

"He found my mom, which led him to me. He took me away. Brought me into his home and taught me how to use my powers so I would never again suffer abuse." She breaks off another chunk of cake, but this time she doesn't eat it, just plays with it, reducing it to crumbs. "He tried to find my father, but either the man didn't want to be found, or he didn't want to claim me as his. Or he's dead. Long story short, Saul wasn't pleased that his adult son had picked up a stray, so he insisted that Malachi find me a more appropriate living situation. I was supposed to live with Ines"—she imitates slicing her neck—"but she didn't want to be saddled with a ten-year-old, so I ended up with Dorian's family."

Well, that just tugged on every heartstring I possess. It also clears up her devotion to Malachi, her lack of resemblance to Dorian, and her antipathy toward Ines. "I can't believe people actually inject themselves with someone else's blood."

She shoots me a close-lipped smile. "Modern-day vamps."

She's so cool and collected for someone who endured so much trauma. Did she bury it deep, or did she overcome it? Also, I remember thinking she was young when I hired her, but I'm only now realizing *how* young she is. Is she even twenty?

Recalling Dorian's surprise the day he saw her in Bloom's Blooms, I ask, "I assume you don't work for Malachi full time?"

She pauses. "I would if my pain-in-the-ass brother hadn't forced me to go to college."

"College, so you're…?"

"Nineteen."

"What are you studying?"

She rubs her index finger and thumb together, peppering the smooshed piece of cake with crumbs before lifting both to her mouth and sucking off the residue. "Petrology and mineralogy."

"Planning on lab-growing your own Atlantean mine?"

She snorts. "Can you imagine?"

"I assume you've visited it?"

"I have."

"And?" I lean my elbows on the table and link my fingers underneath my chin. "Does it look like those AI photos floating around social media?"

"It's even more breathtaking. In my humble opinion, it puts all the other wonders of the world to shame. It's cavernous, with a well of light where Tarian fell. And phosphorescent. And the walls hum."

"Tarian told me it killed one of Symeon's girlfriends."

"One? More like three. And the dickhead blamed his brother each and every time. Told him that the reason Atlanteans were persecuted and hated was because we were too cliquey and that we needed to *convert* more people to our *religion*." She air quotes the words 'convert' and 'religion.'

"What happened between the brothers that created such a rift?"

"Barak happened." She sighs. "He favored Tarian. I don't think he meant to, but the fact is, he did. I was hoping his death would bring them closer."

I don't have to ask whether it did because I know that it hasn't. "How's he taking Tarian's *absence*?"

"He apparently sort of…checked out."

"What do you mean?"

"He's not answering his phone. Saul said he found him drugged out of his mind yesterday."

Because Tarian's gone or because Yasmin dumped him? *Did*

she dump him? One more question for my teetering pile. Here's to hoping Tarian is at the root of his anguish and not some girl.

Unless…

Unless it isn't anguish but guilt eating at Symeon. Could one brother have doomed another?

# THIRTY-ONE

The sun rises and sets with zero news from Dorian or Malachi. The only thing we receive is a large order that Electra placed for markers, mandala coloring books, and origami after I explained that doing arts and crafts relaxes my mother.

"What did you tell Bryn after you took her home last night?" I ask as I reheat the Thai takeout.

Electra lowers the paperback that arrived with the rest of the stuff earlier today. When I spotted the fluffy romance in the box, I was certain she'd selected it for Mom, but apparently, romance is Electra Serran's jam. Who would've guessed the leather-wearing, gun-toting Atlantean enjoyed meet-cutes? Certainly not I, who'd pegged her for a thriller-lover like me.

My instincts are plainly tawdry.

"I told her that you'd taken your mother out of state to visit a prominent neurologist recommended by the Hadezes."

I bob my head. "Good." At least Bryn wouldn't be too worried if she tried to contact me, and I didn't immediately pick up. As the glistening rice noodles spin in the microwave, I ask, "Do you think she's safe?"

"Why wouldn't she be? She's not a target."

"But she's close to me. And Delta Lynch is her father." Dreaming of him may have been symbolic, but the fact remains that he was there, and that Tarian somehow knows him.

"Delta Lynch?"

"He's a sniper in the U.S. Army."

"Her father works for the fucking military? Are you serious?" She shuts her book with a snap. "Did you tell Malachi?"

"I…" I rack my brain. "I don't remember." I toy with my super soft locks, courtesy of Electra's miracle conditioner. "Shit. Did I?" I drop my voice so that Mrs. Fiona and Mom don't risk hearing me over *Dirty Dancing*, which is currently blaring in the living room. "Do you think it's important? We already know—*think* the Army's involved. Besides, I expect your brother's aware of Bryn's genealogical tree. He knew everything about me when I arrived for the flower delivery. Your brother will have run a background check on Bryn, right?"

Electra tightens her ponytail, then taps on her phone screen that displays an impersonal picture of a twilit cove. "You're probably right."

She opens up an encrypted chat and types out a message. I assume it's to warn Dorian in case he isn't privy to the fact that Bryn is related to a person who may or may not like Atlanteans. I can't imagine that the *entire* U.S. military hates gods. Maybe he's one of the few that doesn't crave their power and destruction.

"Any news?"

With a sigh, she says, "No."

"No news, good news?" I venture.

She purses her lips and stands from the island stool she's warmed all day. "No news, *no news*."

"They're not alone, Electra. The council sent backup."

"Yeah."

My reminder does squat to reassure her.

As I take the bowl of noodles out of the microwave and zap a beef dish, she asks, "Where's your rune?"

I hike up the back of my white tank top to reveal the word that hasn't heated all day. I should be glad about this since it means Tarian's awake, and if he's awake, then there's a high chance his body is fighting off whatever his captors pumped into his system, but anxiety mucks up my positivity.

"How does it work? Your dream connection?"

I pull the clingy fabric back down. "If he dreams, the rune heats and transports me into his subconscious. If I dream, I transport him into mine. The dreamer is in charge of the dream, if that makes sense."

"What do you do in your dreams?"

I turn toward the microwave. "We mostly talk."

"About?"

"About his abduction. Last night was the first time he showed me anything remotely useful though. *Hopefully* useful," I add under my breath. "I wish we could call Malachi and Dorian for news."

"They're off the grid."

I spin in time with the little platter inside the microwave. "I know. I can reach out to Tarian."

"You can fall asleep on demand?"

I chew on my lip. "Not usually, but maybe I can take a sleeping pill...or two."

"Don't think we have any. Besides, it may be best not to distract him, in case he's mid-escape. Sure, my brother could carry him, but that would slow them all down."

I hadn't even considered that.

Even though I'm a ball of crackling nerves, I prefer to be a highly caffeinated ball of nerves to avoid falling asleep, so I head over to the coffee machine. "Want a cup?"

"Sure."

Her phone vibrates on the island. I jump, and the coffee capsule I was about to insert inside the machine slips from my fingers and falls at my feet.

Electra frowns, which jostles my wild nerves some more. "It's Symeon."

"Maybe he has news?"

Her eyebrows stay low as though she wasn't quite convinced. The phone vibrates twice more before she finally accepts the call. "How can I help you, Mr. Hadez?"

Her eyes flick to mine.

When the sea of white expands around her irises, my tongue begins to throb from my heightened pulse. "What? What's happening?"

She says nothing, neither to me nor to Symeon.

"Electra?" The rune on my back begins to heat. Or maybe I'm so cold all over that it feels hot.

I become lightheaded and sway, and although I grip a drawer handle, I don't succeed in staying upright. The jangle of cutlery is the last thing I hear before I gasp awake in...

In someone's bed.

# THIRTY-TWO

A large hand rests on my midriff, atop the thin white fabric of my tank top. I trail that hand to a forearm ornamented with runes.

Oh. My. God.

Literally.

Well, not *my* as in *mine*. Tarian may believe I belong to him, but I have no such delusions. The man belongs to Atlantis and the Atlanteans. Not to me.

His ridiculously long lashes are fanned out against his high cheekbones, and pieces of his hair are artistically matted to his forehead. Pretty forward of the man to stick me in his bed after calling me a mistake and breaking my ankle.

As he sleeps, my eyes sweep over the runnels bordering his spine, over the sharp edges of his shoulder blades that look as though they could sprout bat wings, over the globes of his ass enclosed in short and very tight black briefs, over the dark hair peppering his muscled thighs and legs. Clearly, Tarian's only vices are whiskey and fast cars. And possibly guns, although who needs weapons when one *is* a weapon?

I'm about to wake him when I decide to peruse him some more. Not his body, mind you. One trip over the playground of quilted muscle and man-skin was quite sufficient. I absolutely don't need to further imprint this male into my corneas, or he'll be all I see when I finally meet Mr. You-Are-Not-a-Mistake.

This time, my attention is entirely focused on the scrawled sentence that burgeons at his nape and curves over his bladed shoulders before veering down his arms. The string of consonants and dotted vowels splinters on the slope of his right shoulder, then once more, on the top of his bicep where the script curls toward the inside of his arm.

Although maybe I'm imagining the second break. I start to crane my neck when he stirs. I think he's about to wake up but I'm wrong. He remains blissfully immobile, flopped onto his stomach, thick arm caging me.

How strange to think they were given to him by some magical rock. How strange that magic actually exists. Will I ever find it normal? I probably won't need to because, best case scenario, Tarian jacks his rune, along with all my memories; worst case scenario, he ships me to the underworld.

I banish the glum contemplation by focusing wholly on my surroundings—navy walls decorated with framed maps, white wooden beams, bronze and glass light fixtures, a navy rug with a thin pattern of white lines and matching curtains that bracket a giant window. I suppose the moonlit body of water beyond could be any body of water, but I sense this is the view from his home in the Vineyard. Does he keep returning here because it's his haven or because it's somehow connected to his abduction?

My pulse skitters to a stop as I recall Electra's expression. What if Tarian isn't on a military vessel sailing to Atlantis? What if he's under house arrest in his own home?

"Tarian?" My voice competes with the lazy whir of the wooden ceiling fan that spits air onto where we lay, on his rumpled navy sheets. "Tarian?" I give his arm a small shove in order to, one, wake him and, two, break his hold on me.

He hums. Instead of lifting, his fingers skate over to my waist and grip it.

"Tarian, up." I thrust on his arm again.

He finally shifts his heavy body, but he takes mine along, and I end up on my side, facing him.

"Found you." His sleep-coarsened timbre sends chills skittering over my bare arms, chills that exacerbate when the callused pads of his fingers begin to stroke the edge of my ribs.

"I'm not the one missing. Besides, this isn't a game of hide-and-seek." I poke his arm. I make zero progress in getting out from under his thumb and other fingers.

"I lost you, Calamity. I walked out of that circus tent, and you were gone."

"Um. No. I was still stuck in that dumpster fire of a dream. Which got worse, by the way. I broke my ankle, then had to sit in a weird-ass diner train with Bryn, her dad, and Yasmin."

His gaze vaults open and levels on my legs that poke out from a pair of frayed denim shorts.

"You didn't mean to break any of my bones, right?"

His attention veers back to my face. "How could you even suggest that?"

"Because it happened in *your* dream."

His eyes grow pitch-black, and his exhales roughen, striking the tip of my nose. "You vanished when you walked out of that dressing room. Just—vanished. I thought you'd gotten lost in the maze, but after trudging through it for fucking hours, I assumed someone back home had shaken you awake."

"No such luck."

His fingers tighten around my waist.

"My ribs aren't made of steel, He-Man."

His eyebrows slant. "What?"

I nod to his hand. "Your grip. It's"—*confusing*—"uncomfortable."

"Shit." Tarian jerks his palm off my body, then collapses onto his back, every muscle in his torso rippling from the momentum. "When I touched you just now…" He peers at his forearm. Like on his shoulder and bicep, there's a gap in the magic verse. "I didn't sting you again, did I?"

"No." I'm about to ask him whether he really thinks it could happen in this realm when I remember that I *really* broke my ankle. I'm guessing anything is possible.

"Is it still broken?"

I look away from his arm. "What?"

"Your ankle? Is it still broken?"

"No. Malachi fixed it."

His jaw pops as though he's trying hard to contain his temper. Is he angry that his cousin expended energy and magic to fix my bone? "I would never deliberately hurt you, Calamity."

*Ah*, so that's what's got his briefs in a twist.

The mattress dips again.

"I hope you know that." Tarian's stare is so intense it dents my flesh and does weird stuff to my blood.

*Mistake. Mistake. Mistake.* The word he used blares like a car alarm between my temples.

I lower my gaze to his Adam's apple that bobs as he repeats, "You trust me, right?"

"I trust you want to be found."

"That's not what I asked."

"You don't need my trust. All you need is my cooperation." I vault off the bed, combing my fingers through my hair, which is still phenomenally supple thanks to my new Atlantean friend and her miracle conditioner.

I wonder if Electra wigged out when I hit the kitchen floor. But most of all, I wonder what Symeon said that blasted open her lids.

"You're wrong." Tarian's temper ripens the air.

"Fine." I stroll toward one of the maps. "I trust you didn't *mean* to break my—" I gasp, because the ink drawing *is* a map, but not of landmasses and oceans.

I swing back around to find Tarian stalking toward me like some furious predator. I recoil, suddenly not so certain about his intentions toward my bones. What if dream-Tarian isn't in control of himself? My body's reaction makes him stop in his tracks and tautens every jagged line in his body, of which he has many.

When after a tension-filled minute, he hasn't tried to bridge the gap between us, I relax and refocus. "Why is this aircraft carrier important to you?"

A groove forms between his brows. "What aircraft carrier?"

I knuckle the glass enclosing the blueprint. "This one. CVN-666."

When I twist around, I find he's stepped closer, stopping a hairsbreadth away from me. I never gave that expression much thought until now. Until the triangle of dark hair that arrows down to his navel brushes against my bare arm, coaxing out goosebumps.

I step to the side before he can scramble more than my flesh. "So?"

His long-lashed gaze tapers on the one-dimensional ship design.

"Is that where you are?"

"I don't fucking know where I am since I can't seem to fucking wake up." His runes flare, gilding his upper body in light like some fallen angel.

Perhaps the boy who fell in the mine was a little angelic, like children often are by virtue of their innocence, but the man who rose out of that pit in the ground is all ruthless devil. One that will unleash hell upon the world when he awakens.

"In your last dream, 'CVN-666' was plastered all over the ceiling of the train, so it has to hold some significance for you. It has to be some clue."

A nerve feathers his jaw. "Symeon was obsessed with military vessels as a kid, so I organized a tour of an aircraft carrier.

Happened to be this one. When we got home, he drew *this* on his tablet. All from memory." He nods to the design behind the glass. "I had it printed and framed. When Dad purchased the *Amapola*, Symeon was very unimpressed and said he should've bought a warship instead." His tone has softened, but nothing else. "He also said that, someday, he'd build a private vessel as large as this one and live on it. That's his dream. To live on the water and create, create, create."

What if he's not creating, but bleeding, bleeding, bleeding? Symeon's broken expression in Tarian's last dream heaps a brickload of guilt atop my shoulders. Why am I so quick to suspect him of ill-intent? Because the brothers have beef with one another? Because he's related to Tarian, and most crimes are committed by a family member?

*Most murders*, my mind corrects. *Not abductions*. I don't have the faintest clue about kidnapping statistics.

"Your brother called Electra before I was transported here," I find myself saying.

Tarian pins me with his midnight stare. "Is he all right?"

"I don't know."

"What did he say?"

"You zapped me out of there before I could find out." I hesitate to tell him about Electra's perplexed expression, but what if I misread her face? I don't want him to think his brother is involved if he isn't. Besides, the man I met in Tarian's dream was considerate and sad, not guilty and cruel. Then again, the light cast on dream-Symeon was all Tarian-engineered.

"What are you hiding from me, Calamity?"

I jump at his accusation. "Nothing."

His eyes become reflective even though no sunbeam bends into them. "Tell me what's on your mind."

I cross my arms and boost my chin. "Are you seriously trying to compel me?"

He snuffs out the glow with a sweep of those enviable lashes.

"I… Yes." He rubs the back of his neck. "My apologies, but…but if you think my brother's involved, you need to tell me."

I roll my lips together. "Dorian and Malachi should've reached the aircraft carrier by now so we'll—"

"Dorian? He fucking left you?" His fury is so thick I think I might choke on it.

"Electra stayed behind."

"Electra isn't Dorian. Electra's a kid!"

"She's not a kid, Tarian. Besides, she's an Atlantean."

"I asked you to keep Dorian at your side!" His anger chisels the already harsh lines of his face.

"Can you stop yelling at me? I did what I thought was best for you, okay?" I perch my hands on my hips and square my shoulders. "You're the one in danger, *not* me. *You* need him and he needs *you*. So does Malachi. So do all your people."

He pivots away from the blueprint, his broad body tossing a shadow over mine. "If anything happens to you, Calamity—"

"You lose your instrument of communication with the outside world. I'm aware." I conjure a smile that's all artifice. After all, who'd rejoice at being someone's tool? I suppose I could think of myself as a weapon, which is loads better for the self-esteem.

"That's not—" He pauses. "You're not—" He rams his fingers through the raven mess atop his head and growls.

If only it could make him look like a deranged scientist instead of a tormented god. *Ugh*. Out of all the men in Boston, why did I have to go and develop a crush on the singularly most frustrating one?

"You're not some means to an end. You're my fucking salvation, Calamity."

"To be someone's salvation, one must do some salvaging. And yes, I am actively trying to find you, but as of now, you're still missing. Unless Dorian and Malachi are with you?"

"I'd be awake if they'd found me."

"In your last dream, you included Bryn's father. Do you think he might be involved?"

"Who's Bryn's father?"

My head rears back in surprise. Considering the level of detail with which he depicted the man, I thought for certain that Tarian had met him, and more than once, at that. "His name's Delta Lynch. *Sergeant* Delta Lynch."

Tarian goes deathly still.

"You do know him," I murmur.

"Sergeant Lynch is Bryn's father?"

"Yes. If you didn't meet him through Bryn, then who introduced you?"

He cracks his knuckles and pops his jaw. "My brother."

# THIRTY-THREE

Even though I've had my doubts about Symeon's involvement, all roads seem to lead back to him.

"What brought a sniper and an Atlantean together?" I'm not sure why I feel the need to whisper. It isn't as though anyone can eavesdrop in this realm. At least anyone real.

"Blood." Tarian's gaze goes unfocused, as though he's traveled back in time. "A few months back, I got a call from a club owner in South End. He said he had my brother. I thought he meant he was holding him for ransom but soon found he wasn't looking for remuneration. He just wanted to avoid getting into trouble with the cops and with my family.

"Anyway, he found my brother when he was tossing out the trash. When Dorian and I arrived, Symeon still hadn't come to. He was riddled with bruises and track marks. The owner assumed Symeon had OD'd and begged me not to kill him. I promised I wouldn't if he told me who Symeon had met with. He drew a blank, even when Dorian used compulsion, which led us to ask for the bar's camera footage."

"Let me guess. The man he met with was Delta Lynch?"

"The man he met with wore a baseball cap and a black hoodie. Never once looked at the camera. Clearly, he knew exactly where it was. My brother handed him a nondescript gym bag and his companion handed him two vials. Since they weren't on Sym's person when we found him, we assume it was the reason he was jumped."

"What do you think was in there?"

"Drugs." The lack of hesitation in Tarian's response leads me to think this isn't an assumption but a hard fact. Sure enough, he adds, "After I healed the worst of his contusions, and Sym finally came to, he confirmed he'd taken some strong shit."

My eyes widen. "Symeon exchanged his blood for drugs? Aren't you all filthy rich? Couldn't he have paid for it with cash?"

Tarian offers me a smile as thin as a razor blade. "Because of his drug habit, Father kept Sym on a tight leash. Now that he's gone"—a hard swallow jostles his throat—"the role of conservator fell on me."

My heart is jackhammering, propelling so much blood through my system that my pulse thunders at my temples. Not only did Symeon have motive to kill his father, but he has motive to do away with his brother. "Tarian, are you thinking what I'm thinking?"

"If you're thinking my brother is an absolute idiot who needs a stint in rehab, then yes."

"I'm thinking your brother's way past idiot. I'm thinking he's a murderer, and that your capture—"

"My brother isn't a killer, Miss Bloom."

Is Tarian obtuse or did I tragically misread the situation?

"*I* killed my father. *Me.* How many times do I have to fucking repeat this?"

I narrow my gaze on the growly male, a few choice replies gathering on the tip of my tongue. I rein them all in, deciding not to debate a subject he's so hellbent on contesting since it will get us exactly nowhere.

"What did the council have to say about your brother's side-hustle?" I ask instead.

"The punishment for selling Atlantean blood is death. Symeon and I may have our differences, but he's my brother." His gaze tightens on mine. "Understood?"

"If by 'understood,' you're implying 'keep your trap shut' or you'll permanently shut it for me, yeah, I *understood*." I eye the door. If I weren't so scared of where I'd end up, I would stalk out of this bedroom and let the thickheaded male stew in his *woe is me* mood.

"Symeon wanted out. I got him out, which is how Sergeant Lynch and I came to meet." A beat of silence passes. "My brother isn't a bad kid."

Is he trying to convince me or himself? "Why didn't he just compel Bryn's father to forget about their transaction?"

"When humans have our blood in their system, they become resistant to compulsion."

"Are you saying that Delta Lynch was using Atlantean blood?"

"Yes."

I didn't think Bryn's father was the most outstanding male specimen—after all, he didn't even try to raise his daughter—but I also didn't imagine he'd be the type to shoot himself up with performance enhancing fluids.

"Malachi mentioned you allowed Symeon to test your blood." Can he see all the neon arrows pointing to his brother? Because they're all I can see.

"A drop of it. Is there a reason you're bringing this up?"

*Yes. To open your freaking eyes!* "What exactly did he do with it?"

"He didn't use it on himself, if that's your question. He tested it on a mouse."

"And you know this for a fact?"

His nostrils flare with irritation. "I trust my brother."

I keep rubbing the sore spot. "Was anyone present?"

"His lab technicians."

What if he kept the vial to use at a later date? Like, a four-day ago date? "Why didn't you go?"

"I was in the middle of negotiating a consequential deal."

"That you couldn't reschedule?"

"Too many players involved."

Perhaps I'm wrong, but it sounds a lot like Tarian didn't even try to fit the experiment into his agenda. I mean, he's Tarian Hadez. Anyone willing to do business with his family would bend over backwards to accommodate the man. This, obviously, leads me to wonder about his reasons for not attending. It couldn't be complete disinterest, could it? Though he could've already known what would happen because he'd done his own experimenting.

"Any chance you figured out a way to ship me out of your dreams?" I muse, dying to return to Electra to hear what Symeon called to say.

Floorboards creak, then hinges groan. Tarian ropes my waist and propels me behind his back. My heart goes haywire. I try to quiet it by reminding myself that whoever just entered this realm isn't real. But then I remember the acute pain of breaking my ankle.

Whoever stands beyond my shield of taut flesh, roiling muscles, and glowing runes might not be real, nevertheless, they can inflict *real* pain. What if it's Symeon? What if all my theorizing has made Tarian bring him here?

I peek over Tarian's massive shoulder just as a male voice murmurs, "Hello, Son."

# THIRTY-FOUR

Barak Hadez. That's who stands in the entrance to Tarian's bedroom—or whoever this room belongs to. Perhaps it's not even a real room.

I shuffle out from behind Tarian's back and meet his deceased genitor's deep brown eyes. Like Tarian, they're fringed with such thick lashes that they tint the irises black. Another thing he bequeathed to his eldest son is his stature—both men are broad through the shoulders and narrow through the waist. If Barak's hair weren't so grizzled, he could've passed for Tarian's twin.

"Saul told me you had a special someone in your life. About time, wouldn't you say?"

My skin prickles when Barak's ghost smiles.

"Aren't you going to introduce us?"

I glance up at Tarian who stands frozen beside me, jaw so sharp it could clip lilac stems. The only part of him that moves is his Adam's apple, which rolls with swallow after swallow.

"Tarian?" I touch his hand. His fingers are stiff and cold.

I feel like an actress propelled in front of a camera with no direction and no script. What do I do? Introduce myself to our fantasy visitor?

Nibbling on my lip, I decide to do just that. I stalk toward the door and hold out my hand. "Pleasure to meet you, Mr. Hadez. I'm Calanthe Bloom."

Barak doesn't hesitate to clasp my fingers. Instead of shaking my hand though, he carries it to his mouth and presses his icy lips to my knuckles. "Calanthe. A genus of flower if I'm not mistaken?"

"An orchid."

"My wife is also named after a flower. Amapola. Poppy, in your tongue."

His use of the present tense rattles me until I recall that they're both not of this world anymore. What if there truly is an afterlife, and they've found one another again? Tears form as I think of my own departed father. I suddenly wish I was in charge of this dream, so I could include him, so I could touch him once more.

With a smile, Barak lets go of my hand. "You'll join us for dinner, I hope." He scratches a spot on his bicep.

"Dinner?" I croak. For all my blinking and swallowing, the grief of my loss has sunk its thorns into my heart.

"Amapola and Saul have prepared a veritable feast." He's still thumbing his arm.

"Saul cooks?"

"Yes. My mother was over the moon when one of her boys took an interest in her recipe books." A crooked smile slides along his lips. "Amapola wasn't as lucky. Neither Tarian nor Symeon showed any interest in spending time at the stovetop."

A new ball of grief lodges itself inside my throat. This time, though, my sadness is for Tarian, for the boy who could not possibly learn anything from his mother because he lost her too early on.

"Shut the door," Tarian commands, his voice low yet somehow resonant.

I glance over my shoulder at him. Find him staring hard at his father. "All right." When I twist back around, all the joviality has leached from Barak's features. Even though this is all make-believe, I can't help myself from trying to curtail his pain. "We'll be down in a minute, Mr. Hadez. As soon as Tarian's put on some clothes."

Barak's eyes soften, and he backs up. "We'll be waiting."

As soon as the door snicks shut, Tarian breathes out a harsh, "Fuck."

I turn to find him clutching the roots of his hair. As he tugs, he falls to his knees and hunches over, whispering words I can't understand. My heart breaks for him. For this dream of his that shows a version of the present that doesn't exist.

I pad over to where he's collapsed and kneel in front of him. He releases his hair, and his palms scrape down his stricken face before slapping his thighs. He stares at me, and I stare back. I'm not sure what to do with this broken version of Tarian. I'm not sure how to handle him. I'm not sure how to fix him.

He gives his head an abrupt shake, as though to drive away the darkness I allowed into the bedroom. It unsettles his mussed hair and sends a black lock stumbling across his brow. I consider just sitting back on my heels and offering him my quiet company until his heart scabs over, but the gleam of his eyes combined with the bobbing of his throat has me leaning over and wrapping my arms around him.

When I pillow my cheek against the hollow of his collarbone, he shudders. I expect him to push me away with a gruff reminder that his runes might rub off, or that he doesn't want my pity, but he doesn't move, and he doesn't growl. He's all ragged breaths and tattered pulse, slumped shoulders and clammy skin. Even his runes have gone cold and dark.

He lets me hold him. And then he's holding me back. Clasping me with both arms and spreading his knees to slot my body nearer.

"I hate this." His words both warm and ice my scalp.

I don't think he means my embrace, otherwise he wouldn't be reciprocating, but since he doesn't elaborate, I do venture, "My hug?"

"No, Calamity." His arms tighten as though to stress his reply. "I hate being subjected to living in the fantasy worlds concocted by my mind. I hate having no control over what happens. I hate the constant reminder of everything and everyone I've lost." He inhales slowly, then exhales even slower. "My parents. My freedom. My free will." Another breath flutters my hair. "But mainly, I hate that I've dragged you into this. That I keep dragging you into this. That I can't fucking figure out how to *stop* dragging you into this."

I sigh. "Believe it or not, I don't hate it. I might not have *loved* how your last dream ended, but all in all, this connection adds a certain layer of..." I riffle through my mind for a word that will properly encompass all the strangeness of dream rendezvousing with a man who isn't just a man and who's way less despicable than anticipated. I come up with, "...*intrigue* to my day-to-day existence."

After a solid minute of silence, he rasps a quiet, "Thank you."

"For enjoying your crazy?"

I feel the curve of his mouth against my scalp. "For enduring my *crazy*. For not despising me."

"I think we have a real chance at friendship, you and I."

In some wild corner of my heart, I *actually* believe this, but then I recall a high school shooting podcast I listened to during a flower run with my father a decade ago. Although the survivors banded together to take down the shooter and then reunited for interviews years later, none of them ended up staying in touch.

I'd asked my father why that was, and he'd replied with a sigh that people often drifted apart after shared trauma because being in one another's company reminded them too acutely of what they'd withstood.

Will that happen to Tarian and me if we ever manage to disconnect ourselves from our communal dreaming? Will he expel me from his life because I'll forever remind him of his worst nightmare?

I don't realize I'm torturing my lip until his thumb pops it free from my teeth; the same way I didn't realize he'd released me. I sit back and fold my hands into my lap, then wring them together.

"A penny for your thoughts?" His timbre sinks into my skin and settles beside his lingering scent and heat.

The same thumb that was on my mouth is now hooking the black strand slashing his forehead and pushing it out of his eyes. His expression is soft, the only soft part about this man. Although I aim my gaze at my hands, it scampers along my thighs toward the hardening bulge prodding my knees.

*Look away.*

Look. Away.

Ugh. I really need to get laid. I close my eyes and swallow, my mouth feeling suddenly as dry as plaster. "The going rate for my thoughts is way more than a penny, Hades." I try to smile but am too flustered to muster the required curl of lip.

"You drive a hard bargain."

This time, I do smile. I still don't open my eyes though, too worried they'll zip right back to that part of his anatomy barely contained by his black briefs. The mere thought of it has heat swarming my cheeks and crawling up my legs. I'm going to be doing a lot of swiping right the minute Tarian's retrieved, and I get my hands on my phone.

I start to inch backward when two palms land on my thighs, pinning me to the navy rug. My eyes open and become consumed by the play of tendons and veins bulging against the tops of Tarian's large hands.

"I'll give you a hundred grand for your thoughts." Has his

voice deepened? Is that even possible? "You know I'm good for it, Calamity."

I finally raise my gaze to his. Even though there's hardly any demarcation between pupil and iris, I don't miss how the black dots expand and take over the dark, dark brown. "I was thinking about school shootings."

"*Huh.*" Although his hands don't climb higher up my legs, his thumbs begin to tread against the inside of my thighs, and lord if that doesn't heat me up everywhere. "Is it working?"

"Working?" My voice is thready. What's working? Working at what? I try to make sense of his question, but I'm greatly distracted by those thumbs.

A corner of his mouth kinks as he tugs on my knees. "Working at staving off your attraction."

I gape at his cocky grin, then at the flesh hardening into a bone between his thighs. "That wasn't—" When his thumbs resume their caress, I shackle his wrists to keep him from rubbing away the thin patina of my restraint. "Stop before we make *another* mistake."

That stills his assault.

"I get you want to feel something other than loss at the moment, but you don't get to use me for that." I pare his palms off my inflamed skin. "As for school shootings, I wasn't thinking about them to *cool off*. I was thinking about them in regard to the possibility of an enduring camaraderie. I was thinking how shared trauma will probably drive us apart instead of together, because it's easier to move on when you're not always looking at a reminder of the most grievous time in your life."

He straightens, and out of the corner of my eye, I catch him readjusting himself. "Yet you saved the pictures of your father. Wasn't his death traumatic?"

"I don't see what his death—"

"You kept pictures of him the same way my father kept pictures of my mother. You're not the type of person who disposes of reminders in order to *move on*."

"You're right. I'm not. But you are, Tarian."

His eyebrows slide low over his eyes, streaking his expression with more darkness. "Although I agree that friendship will not be in the cards for us, I don't agree with your reasoning."

"Do share *your* reasoning."

"I could never be friends with someone like you."

My jaw slackens before zippering shut. "Like *me*?" Saul's throwaway *people in need* comment resurfaces. Is that how Tarian perceives me?

"Yes, like you. A woman I'm dying to fuck." Violence and intimidation sculpt his smile. "You should get off your knees, Miss Bloom, because I have *a lot* of pent-up frustration."

After recovering from his brutal honesty, I smile sweetly. "And I have *a lot* of teeth."

His eyes are pitch-black with lust, none of which dissipates at my threat. If anything, my little comeback seems to swell both his lungs and cock.

As I get to my feet, I snap, "Don't confuse me with a puppet, Tarian. Everyone else in these dreams might not be real, but I am. You don't get to shout out *mistake* one second, then *blow me* the next."

His jaw ticks.

Even though I have zero desire to explore what lies beyond the doors of his mind, I can't bear to stay in this room a second longer. And not because I don't trust Tarian, but because I don't trust him not to find a way to unpick my resolve and yank on the delicate thread keeping it darned to my ego.

I inject steel into my spine and trek back toward the door. As the knob turns in my slick hand, I prepare to enter a new dimension, but Tarian is manifestly not done with this dream cycle.

He's suddenly right behind me, palming the door wider, his harsh breath pelting the back of my head as he takes in his family's version of the *Last Supper*.

If I shut the door and pull it back open, will the Hadezes still be there, crowded around the round table set for eight but occupied by only six people?

Even though Tarian's not pressed up against me, I can feel the feverish vibrations of his heart against my spine. Honestly, I'm not entirely certain how his heart's even still working; mine would've gone still if I'd been in the presence of my father.

I slide my lip between my teeth and contemplate our two options: close the door or go out there. Actually…"How about you stay in the bedroom and shut the door behind me?"

"And leave you to face my perverse mind alone again? No."

Never has someone's personality given me so much whiplash. "Will you be okay?"

I note that he's magicked himself a button-down shirt, gray wool slacks, and black dress shoes. I almost ask him to weave me some footwear, but what if he gives me the crystallized, wrap-around sandals again, the ones he later bequeathed to Macrazy? Pride keeps me barefoot.

"Come on you two." A woman with long raven hair and sapphire eyes pats the seat beside hers. "The food's getting cold."

Although we've never met, I know immediately that she's Amapola, and not because Tarian is her spitting image—because he isn't—but because there's something inherently similar about mother and son. They're like the same art model painted by two different artists—one crafted with dainty brushstrokes and subdued light, and the other, with blunter strokes and dramatic illumination.

A second woman sits at the table. I assume she's Malachi's mother, even though her eyes are green instead of blue, and her locks, a shade of blonde that's so pale it appears almost white. Coloring aside, though, mother and son look identical with their angular mouths, straight noses, and marked brows that sit low over their eyes.

I try to remember what Bryn told me happened to her. As I comb through the cobwebs of my memory, callused fingers lock around mine. I blink up at Tarian, but he's not looking at me or at our fused hands. He's staring at the members of his family.

*You odd, mercurial man.* I give my head a slight shake and squeeze our palms together in solidarity. He and I may never be friends, but at this precise moment in time, I'm all he has.

I wait for him to take the first step. Once he does, I release the doorknob and follow.

Barak gestures to the free seat between Malachi and Saul. "Calanthe, you'll sit between my brother and nephew."

Tarian's hand tightens around mine. "No." He nods to the seat Barak has just offered me. "She'll sit beside me. Sym, scoot."

Symeon doesn't react, much too transfixed by the black wax pooling around the tapered candle holder on his dinner plate. As he swirls a long finger through the melted wax, I squint to see if he's drawing anything worth memorizing, any clue I can use in case Malachi and Dorian come home emptyhanded.

If only Tarian had pulled me into this dream a minute later, I could've heard what Symeon had to say. Perhaps he *does* have Tarian and called to state his terms?

"Her place is over there, sweetheart." Amapola's voice is all at once soft and coarse, like linen sheets swaying in a torpid breeze.

I try to slip my fingers from Tarian's, but he clamps down on them with a muttered, "No."

"It's just a dream—"

"You're not fucking sitting next to Malachi." His teeth don't even separate as he speaks. "You're sitting next to me. End of fucking story. Sym, move!" He grips the back of his brother's chair and pulls, but it doesn't budge, much like his brother, save for the hand with which he carves the wax.

As Tarian growls and jostles Symeon's chair, my gaze cartwheels around the table, my skin pebbling as I notice that everyone has a candle holder on their plate. Unlike Symeon's though, Malachi's candle burns bright. So does Saul's. So does the candle on the plate between them. Everyone else's has liquefied. Actually, the one on Tarian's plate is only half melted.

A deeper chill seeps into my bones. "Tarian?"

"What?" he snaps.

Since I'm not the cause for his foul mood, I don't take offense. "The candles, what do you think they represent?" I gesture to the eight wide-rimmed gold plates.

As he swivels his head, a frown creases the smooth skin between his eyebrows. He squeezes my hand some more and backs up. Well, attempts to. His palm remains glued to the back rungs of Symeon's chair. He expels a slew of choice words in a mix of English and Atlantean, then flexes his bicep and leans his weight into his heels.

"I'm stuck. I'm fucking stuck." He releases my fingers to grip his forearm. He must be calling on his magic because his shirt-sleeves glow.

"Maybe if I sit in the seat between Malachi and Saul, it'll unlock your—"

"Don't move. And don't touch anything on that table!" His frantic tone makes me jump. "And don't touch anyone, either." He glowers at Malachi. "Fuck. We should've stayed in the bedroom."

As fresh guilt worms itself through me, I toss a glance at the door that led us here only to find it gone. I decide to keep this discovery to myself, sensing Tarian's incensed enough as it is.

While his son struggles to break free, Barak fists his wife's long hair and carries it off her neck, then bows his head and presses a kiss to the gentle slope of flesh. The act is so sweet that I don't immediately remark the absence of runes. I glance at Barak's neck —bare. I fling my attention to Symeon's—bare.

I stride around the table, my breath catching and releasing in my lungs.

"What?" Tarian all but barks as he yanks on his arm so hard, I half worry he'll dislocate his shoulder or break a bone.

"The runes. Malachi and Saul have them, but no one else, Tarian." It has to mean something, but— My heart holds still. "Is Malachi's mother Atlantean?"

"Yes. She was."

*Was…*

My blood feels like it's oozing out of me and puddling around my feet. I fling my attention back toward Tarian, but my eyes hook on Symeon, whose finger is still indolently swirling through the gooey mess.

"Lovely thing, aren't you?" The crystalline blue eyes Saul shares with his son shimmer like the flame atop his candle. "Are you keeping her, Tarian?"

"Don't fucking touch her!" Tarian's alarmed tone rips through me, causing my body to jerk.

Saul chuckles. "I wasn't asking for myself, Nephew. You know I don't like my women too green." He points to Malachi. "I was enquiring for my son."

Tarian squares his shoulders, no longer trying to break free of Sym's chair. "Calanthe isn't interested in your son, Saul."

Apparently, Tarian feels very strongly about this matter.

Granted, I *don't* have an interest in Malachi. What I do have an interest in is speaking for myself. Nevertheless, I understand that Tarian's not himself at the present moment, so pointing this out would do more harm than good.

With a sigh, I remind him, "This isn't real, Tarian."

The runes on his body flare so bright that he outshines the four candles that have yet to flicker out. "Feels bloody real."

"Huh." Saul tilts his head to the side, his silver hair gleaming like the platinum diamond chain wrapped around his dead wife's neck. "Never thought I'd see the day you'd keep anyone, my boy."

Tarian glowers at his uncle. "Can you come back here, Calanthe?" After a tense beat, he adds a gruff, "Please."

Even though I'm thoroughly weirded out by the whole scene, I find it sweet that he softened his command with a *please*.

Just as I set off toward him, Malachi snares my wrist and pulls. Before I can dig my heels in, I tumble right into his lap. Tarian roars, and the blood-curdling sound bangs against the black glass tabletop, rattling the plates and flustering the four flickering wicks. His chest lifts with such exacting pants that one of the buttons on his shirt pops.

"If you truly care about this girl, then you'd leave her to Malachi." Saul nods to his son who appears downright cherubic in comparison to the snarling devil. "After all, she's safer with him than she will ever be with you."

"Except I don't want to be with Malachi. No offense, Mal." I propel my body forward to pare myself away from the cousin, but I'm stuck, and not because he's holding me down. My ass is just tacked to his thighs, the same way Tarian's hand is taped to his brother's chair.

"Calanthe, please. Come back to me."

"I'm trying." With one hand, I grip the cold edge of the table. With the other, I shove against Malachi's chest.

"Are you really?"

"No, I'm giving him a lap dance. The moment called for one," I deadpan. "A little help, Malachi?"

But Malachi doesn't aid me. He just keeps provoking Tarian by running his fingers through my hair and down my arm. I really, *really* wish Tarian would stop imagining that his cousin is attracted to me.

I shove against Malachi's chest again, but again, I'm unsuccessful. "In real life, your cousin isn't interested in me, Tarian."

His nostrils flare.

"Seriously, he isn't." I hunt the table for a knife to cut through the trousers keeping me down. "You're in charge here. You're making him do this. *You*." I find a spoon.

Actually, I find ten spoons.

Twenty.

They keep appearing on the table in every size and style, from demitasse to ladles.

A song suddenly blares between my temples—Alanis Morrisette's "Ironic."

Fitting. "Any chance you could conjure up a knife, or even better, a pair of scissors?"

The song grows louder, and it momentarily stills my escape attempt, because it transports me to another table, to another time. To Mom asking Alexa to play her music louder while flipping pancakes. To Dad snipping the stem off a white rose and tucking it inside a napkin. Every Sunday, I'd get a white rose, music loud enough to wake the dead, and a feast of a breakfast.

God, I miss the ruckus.

The singing.

The laughter.

The white rose in full bloom.

The smell of pan-fried dough and warm syrup.

Alanis's gravelly voice grows louder, as though my mother's here, spinning the volume dial on Alexa. It drowns out whatever Tarian is trying to tell me.

I point to my ears. "I can't hear you over the music!"

I see him mouth, *What fucking music?*

I press my palms over my ears, and it stifles the sound.

If it isn't playing in my head, how come Tarian—

Dots of gray and white crimp the edges of my vision, crumbling the sight of Tarian, of Symeon, of the wax-filled plates. I blink. When my lashes sweep up, I'm lying in my borrowed bed in the Serrans' apartment, under a blanket of crisp sunlight.

I sit up so suddenly that my hands slip off my ears, and Alanis's voice punches my eardrums, along with my mother's.

I managed to get back!

I managed to break out of Tarian's consciousness!

Anxiety plucks at my relief until it's as bare as a leafless stalk. I hate that I abandoned Tarian to the dark machinations of his mind. I consider going back but returning won't set him free. What will is sharing all the clues I've gathered with people who can actually do something about it.

I race out of the bedroom, tripping on my very own feet when I see Mrs. Fiona and Mom singing along to the lyrics of "Ironic" that scroll across the TV screen.

Mom grins. "Fi, I think we woke my daughter."

"We probably woke the dead, Lisa." Mrs. Fiona smiles, and it pleats her entire face. "Sorry, Callie."

*My daughter. My daughter. My daughter.*

I want to stay here and soak up her lucidity, to store it for all the moments when she won't recognize me, but Tarian needs me, and I need Electra. "Where's your nurse, Mom?"

"Right here." Electra bursts from a room across the living area, rubbing the sleep from her eyes.

I arrow toward her, take her by the elbow, and lead her back the way she came.

Even though Mrs. Fiona and Mom are intoning a new karaoke song, I kick the door shut to keep our conversation private. "It's Symeon. Symeon did it!"

Electra mustn't be fully awake because she blinks. Repeatedly. "Did *what*?"

"He kidnapped Tarian."

She sighs, then tightens the ponytail she must've slept on, because half her hair is hanging out of it. "Maybe."

"There's no 'maybe' about it. He's involved!"

Electra shuts her eyes, and tears snake out. She chases them away with quivering fingers.

My heart catapults against my spine and remains pinned there. "What? Why are you crying? What happened?"

Her throat bobs around another swallow. "He's dead, Calanthe."

All my organs go cold, as though someone's flicked a switch on the pump propelling the blood through my veins. I graze my chest to make sure the muscle beneath still beats, and though it does, the rapid thuds do nothing to drive away the chill of Electra's news.

"I thought… I thought he couldn't die."

"When we lose our runes, we lose our immortality."

Their plan wasn't to drain Tarian! It was to rob him of his magic!

I failed him.

I failed the Atlanteans.

I failed the mine and its goddess.

I. Failed.

# THIRTY-SIX

I stare daggers at the empty space on Malachi's lap where Calanthe was sitting mere seconds ago. I'm so fucking angry I could sock him in his pretty jaw. To think that he's with her in the real world.

Unless he's with me?

I shake my head, discarding my foolish optimism. If he'd gotten me out, I'd be awake, because he would've found a way to purge my system of whatever chemical or weapon is paralyzing both my body and mind.

My skin feels like rubber and stone. My heart, too. What I wouldn't give to be free. What I wouldn't give for Calanthe to know me as a man instead of a victim.

The patch of skin that used to carry Calanthe's rune prickles. If only I could stroke it to make her appear, but that's not how it works. To bring her to me, I must think about her. Visualize her. I must want to hold her. I must *want* to be with her.

Besides my freedom, she is all I want.

When the tingle transforms into a burn, I slam my lids shut and concentrate on the spreadsheet I studied during my last boardroom meeting. I picture the endless rows of numbers until I've snuffed out my selfish desire. I refuse to carry her back into my tortured mind. I refuse to watch her straddle my cousin—even if I'm the asshole who perched her there.

"You can let go, Tarian." Symeon's voice snaps my lids wide.

I'm still attached to his chair. I'd almost forgotten about my quandary. But suddenly, I do forget about it because something else takes precedence over my predicament—the rest of my family is gone. The dinner table is gone. The rooftop, gone. The floor, gone. The walls of my Vineyard house, gone. Only my little brother remains, slumped in his chair, his neck craned so far back that I have a direct line of sight to his upturned face.

I suck in a breath and spring my fingers off his backrest. "The fuck is wrong with your eyes?"

He spins, or rather his chair rotates, as though propped on a whirling podium display. "You should know, Tarian."

"I should know?" My throat tightens, beating back the horrified wheeze threatening to tear free. "Why? Because it's my dream?"

"No." Symeon's bleached eyes roll over me. "Because you made me like this."

I squeeze the bridge of my nose, willing myself away from this time and place. *It's all in your head. All in your fucking head.*

"Can't even look at me, can you?"

I thought I'd reached the zenith of this nightmare when the ghosts of my parents appeared, but then Malachi raked Calanthe onto his lap. Since she was real and my parents weren't, that part had struck me as far worse. But again, I was wrong. *This*—my brother's sightless eyes—is the ultimate high point, or rather, abysmal point of this nightmare.

"Not real," I murmur to myself.

"Sadly, it is, Brother. You're poison. Everything you touch withers. Look at what you did to Father."

I lose my shit and send my fist sailing into his jaw. My brother's head snaps sideways, droops. I reassure myself that what I've just punched is my subconscious, not Symeon. I rub my knuckles, waiting for his neck to straighten and his fake mouth to spout more of my real guilt, but his lips don't move. The silence prompts my mind to return to our last heated interaction on the morning after Yasmin's million-dollar birthday celebration.

I gave that party ten minutes of my time. I spent nine of those getting accosted by a parade of Atlantean toadies and one on cornering Yasmin to ask her—*politely*—to cut my brother free from her web.

The following day, Symeon had popped by my office to rip me a new one. As he complained about my meddling and called me a disrespectful bastard, I'd slid over the picture of Yasmin cozying up to a man who wasn't my brother. Sym had planted both his palms on my desk and had leaned over. But not to stare at the picture—he'd barely spared it a glance; he leaned over to better spit in my face, *"Stay out of my life before you ruin it like you ruin everything and everyone."*

I hadn't raised my voice or my fist that day; I'd merely reclined in my office chair and observed his reddening complexion and feverish stare with the calm of a man used to zealous outbursts.

*"You know, I used to envy your magic, but now... Now I pity you for it, because all it's done is make you miserable."*

For a full minute, I'd considered telling him that his girlfriend had propositioned me, and not only before she'd hooked up with him but twice more after that. He might have been able to overlook an affair with a human, but her interest in me? That would've ground his ego to dust.

Preferring not to needle his ever-present insecurities, I'd ended up saying, *"You should ask Electra out on a date. She's sweet."*

He'd released an ugly laugh. *"Wouldn't that be convenient? You could control me through her since she's at your beck and call."*

The only reason I'd suggested Electra was because she was a nice girl.

*"A shame she's so obsessed with Malachi, huh?"*

*"Just find someone else, Sym. Yasmin isn't with you for the right reasons."*

*"Maybe I'm not with her for the right reasons. Ever consider that?"*

I hadn't considered that my brother could have an agenda, but I suppose that dating a Fablez came with its perks, what with their wealth and the tight leash I kept him on. He'd left before I could ask him how much money he owed Yasmin, intent on keeping him out of the wretch's debt. More importantly, though, he'd left before I could explain that all I did for him came from a place of love, because even monsters are capable of love.

Calanthe's face scores the backs of my lids, and my skin blazes. Not just the blank flesh between my runes, but all of me. I loathe how violently I burn for that woman, because like Symeon pointed out, I'm destructive.

I'm poison.

Worse than poison, because there exists no antidote to my toxic magic. I cripple and kill, and although killing cripples me with remorse, I'm obliged to fucking endure.

"Don't you think I rue the day I infected Father, Sym?" I murmur to the hallucination before me. "I would give up everything I own and am to get him back. Every cent. Every rune. Every breath in my lungs and every beat of my cold, cruel heart."

I wait for Symeon to challenge my noble avowal, but he keeps quiet, and his silence irks me far more than any shout.

"Sym?" I crouch in front of him.

His head still droops, hanging at an impossible angle, marble eyes wide and unblinking.

My pulse stutters. I latch onto his shoulders and shake him. "Sym!"

My brother doesn't awaken, and neither do I.

# THIRTY-SEVEN

**D**ead.

I can't seem to accept it. I was just with Tarian. He can't be dead. This must be another dream.

I pinch myself. My skin stings where I tweaked it. Not a dream.

Tarian's dead. I wasn't able to save him.

I bite down on my knuckles to keep my scream from rocking the penthouse and alarming my mother.

He needed me, and I failed him.

If only he'd stung Malachi with his dreaming rune. His cousin would've gotten him out, because unlike me, Malachi isn't some weakling mortal.

Electra's phone vibrates on the foot of the unmade bed. As she whirls on her heel to grab it, my gaze snaps to her nape.

I pop my teeth off my fist and gasp, "If he's dead, how do you still have your runes? Gaea let you keep them?"

She cocks one eyebrow. "I don't see the connection between my runes and his death."

"He's the link between—I assumed—" I suck in a breath that feels loaded with an absurd amount of oxygen. "*Youmeant-Symeon!*" I see his liquefied candle, his plateful of black wax. Tarian's alive, but his brother isn't. "But…he called you, didn't he?"

"It wasn't Symeon, Callie."

*Callie.* It's the first time she's used my nickname. I'm aware it's an odd thing to remark on at a time like this, but isn't that how the mind works? Hooking on to absurd things in the face of tragedy?

I give my head a little shake to make room for Symeon.

Symeon, who's gone.

*Oh, Tarian.* How devastated he'll be.

"It was the fisherman who recovered Sym's body off the coast of Nantucket." My furrowed brow makes her add, "The caller."

"Symeon drowned? I thought…" I slip a lock of hair behind my ear. After shaking, my fingers are now stiff. "I thought Atlanteans could only die at the hand of another Atlantean?"

"He didn't die from drowning. His body was found floating in a life raft, exsanguinated like Barak's."

My stomach lurches. "Because he got too close to the truth?"

"Because he got too close to Tarian." I almost miss Electra's reply, because her voice is extra low, and her attention, wholly trained on her phone.

When I catch the name *Ines*, I fall back a step. I thought Electra didn't trust her fellow Atlantean. What is she doing writing to her? And yes, I'm aware Dorian doesn't think Ines is involved, but Tarian's bodyguard also trusts Saul…

Electra tucks her phone into the back pocket of her skintight jeans. Did she just free her hands to grab her gun? My sleep-starved mind becomes a wild place, crackling with a gazillion possibilities that spike my adrenaline.

I scan the room for a makeshift weapon, but the furniture's all built-in and there are no framed pictures to unhook, no books to lob. Not even the paperback she was reading yesterday is present.

My gaze snags on a white charger cord plugged in beside the bed. Could I rip it out of the socket before she feeds me lead?

As I start creeping toward it, I keep my eyes level with her hands which have yet to reappear from behind her back. "So Symeon found Tarian?" Is it me, or do I squeak like a rubber duck clutched in the hands of an overexcited kid?

"Yes." Her hands reappear.

I startle backward and smack my tailbone into the sleek bookshelf, jostling both my vertebrae and her eyebrows.

"Callie? What's wrong?" Her hands are empty.

I start to relax until I remember she has power at her fingertips. Power she could use to blow me out of this high-rise. I grip the shelf, my nails digging into the dark wood. "Tarian's been found?" I try to keep my pitch even but fail.

"No."

My confusion peaks higher.

"What's going on with you? You look like you've seen a ghost."

If I lunged, I could grab the cord, but that would put me right in front of the window.

Electra takes a step in my direction. Heart clocking my ribs, I fling myself toward the nightstand and snag the cord, then straighten, clutching it as though it were some magical lasso.

One of her black eyebrows quirks up. "Planning on charging something?"

*Yes, you. If you come any closer…*

"Are you in possession of a phone I'm not aware of? If you are, you need to hand it over so I can disable it. Unless you *want* to be fished out of the ocean next?"

My eye twitches.

"Callie?"

*Don't call me that,* I want to shout, but instead, I say, "I thought you didn't trust Ines?"

"I don't."

"Then why were you messaging her?"

"Ah." A crooked smile pitches up a corner of her mouth. "The cord isn't for some clandestine phone, is it?"

She raises her palm, and I throw myself onto the bed, then roll off the other side, whacking into the ground. I leap back up, about to tear into her neck with my makeshift weapon, when an invisible wall descends between us.

"First of all, calm the fuck down. I'm on your side, all right?"

My pulse is so unhinged, I taste metal.

"Second of all, I was messaging Ines because Saul wants you to attend the memorial. I said, 'Thanks but no thanks.' And not because Malachi and Dorian both yelled at me to keep you out of sight, but because I think using you as a lure is a shit idea. If Symeon managed to find his brother, then so can we."

All the adrenaline drains out of me. "You could've led with that."

"You jump to conclusions pretty damn fast."

I toss the cord on the bed, then sink onto the mattress beside it. "Malachi and Dorian are back?"

"They're in the Vineyard with Saul and Catalina Fablez, who just flew in from Sweden." Her gaze goes to the window, to the slice of river dotted with sailboats and sunlight.

"You said Symeon was found off Nantucket." My skin crackles with goosebumps. I thought Tarian's backdrop came from a sentimental attachment but now realize its significance is more immediate. "Does that mean Tarian is there, too?"

"He's not on the aircraft carrier." She conceals a smirk between her teeth. "Dorian and Malachi had fun with that visit. They did learn that Delta Lynch recently retired, so if he's involved, it isn't on the military's behalf."

I wrinkle my nose. "I honest to goodness didn't send them there on a wild goose chase."

"I know. *They* know." The smirk breaks free. "As for Tarian, we've got the island surrounded, so if he's still there, we're going to find him."

I slip my index finger past my lips and nibble on a hangnail as

I recall the redhead vaping in the train wagon and her effigy planted in that monstrous cake next to Delta's likeness. "Is Catalina Fablez here to offer support to her granddaughter for her boyfriend's passing?"

"No, to Saul. Yasmin's MIA. Never made it home to Sweden."

My pulse picks up speed like Tarian's swaying train. "Could *she* have killed Symeon?"

Electra shakes her head. "No."

Maybe the intake of Atlantean blood gives mortals the power to end a lesser god's life. "Delta Lynch?"

"No, Callie. Tarian killed his brother."

# THIRTY-EIGHT

I attempt to make sense of Electra's assertion, but it just doesn't track. When I told Tarian earlier about my suspicions, or rather, *convictions*, he'd defended his little brother tooth and nail. "Are you sure?"

Although Symeon deserved to be punished for his involvement, I'm shocked that Tarian went so far as to kill him. Even blinded with rage and disappointment, I can't picture my dream companion snuffing out his brother's life. On the upside, it means Tarian finally woke up, even if he has yet to break free.

Electra slides her phone back out of her pocket and taps the screen, then pinches an image to blow it up. "Here."

I frown at the marble plaque, then gasp when I decipher the symbol emblazoned on it—an "X" enclosed in a circle. I clap my palm against my mouth as I understand that this isn't a headstone, but bloodless skin.

"Ines sent me this picture earlier." She reduces the image's size until the whole corpse can be seen, and gah, I'm going to be sick.

I scrutinize my white polished toenails until my stomach no longer feels like it's scaling my ribs. "Malachi said that rune only withdrew magic."

"We all wanted to believe this." She sniffles. "We were wrong. Tarian was right."

Her intake of air is long and gradual, like a swimmer about to dive deep. Is she crying for Symeon or for Barak?

"He's *never* going to forgive himself. He's probably never going to touch another person for the duration of his life, either. Can you imagine how lonely that's going to be? Not that he's the touchy-feely type, but still…" Electra sinks onto the bed beside me and cradles her head with her hands. "At least he has you."

"Um, what?"

She lowers her palms and flicks me a smile that makes her wet eyes sparkle. "You already wear one of his runes, so he can touch you without fear of killing you."

"That's not a given."

She gives me heavy side-eye.

"What? It's not. But more importantly, what makes you think I *want* to be touched by that man?"

Her smile intensifies, knocking the grief right off her features. Even though her amusement is at my expense, I'm glad it offers her respite. I let her enjoy it for a few heartbeats longer. I let *myself* enjoy it, too.

But then I sigh and refocus. "Did Tarian have the word *withdraw* twice on his body?"

She blinks. "What?"

"Were there two in his verse?" Since her dark eyebrows are still pitched toward her nose, I add, "After he stung his father, the word never returned, right?"

Her expression smooths. "Dorian thinks the word must've finally faded off Barak's skin and returned to Tarian's so that he could protect himself. Ines suggested exhuming the body to check." She shudders. "Saul thankfully shut that idea down."

I suddenly picture Barak standing on the threshold of Tarian's bedroom again. How odd that I met his ghost. Granted, he was a figment of his son's imagination, but still... He'd looked and sounded so real.

"*Protect himself,*" I murmur.

"What?"

"You said the rune returned so he could 'protect himself.'"

"Yeah. And?"

"Barak loved Tarian, didn't he?"

"His bond with Tarian was incredibly special."

"Then how come Tarian marked Barak for death?"

"It was an accident."

I coil one of my curls around my finger. "You surely know more than me about the way it all works, but what if it wasn't an accident? What if Tarian's magic peels off his skin to ward off danger that he, himself, didn't see coming? What if it marked me with the word *slumber* so that he had a way to communicate with the outside world, because it somehow sensed he was in danger and would need a magical channel? Does that make sense?"

She sweeps her palms over her thighs as though to invigorate the muscles. "I see what you're saying, but Barak adored his son, Callie. He would *never* have wished him ill."

"Maybe he wished Tarian's magic ill. Or, I don't know, talked smack about the mine?"

"*Talked smack?*" She smiles before pursing her lips. After a beat, she says, "I do remember Barak referring to our runes as *cursed* on more than one occasion."

"Just like Tarian." The look she shoots me prompts me to ask, "What?"

"It's just odd that you know him so well. Most people don't. Especially..." She sketches a circle in the air that encompasses me.

"Mere mortals?" I supply.

"Yes."

We smile at each other for a second, but then reality bites me in the ass. "Barak died a week after being stung." I have the timeline down pat since I expected—*expect*—a similar fate. God, I really hope Tarian's wrong about his magic ridding me of blood. "How come Symeon didn't get a week?"

"Maybe it works quicker now?"

"I'm still alive."

She rolls her eyes. "Your rune says *slumber*."

"I could die in my sleep."

She gives me another eyeroll.

"I broke my ankle, so I could."

Her eyeballs stay steady this time.

Why must I keep reeling this thought back in? Why can't I cast it away, once and for all?

I flop back on the bed and stare at the drum-shaped ceiling lamp. "I met Barak in the last dream we shared. I also met Amapola. It was heartbreaking."

Electra flattens her palms against the bedspread and twists her upper body to face me. Her spine pops as though her skeleton's as stiff as mine.

"I also met Malachi's mother. She looks—*looked*—a lot like him."

"Nora was a beauty."

"What happened to her?"

"She met another man when Malachi was young." Electra's eyes glaze over, not with tears or anger, but with reminiscence. "He was human. She tried to make him superhuman. She begged Barak to lend her Tarian, but Barak refused. Partly because no one had been converted into a new god since the week following the mine's discovery, and partly because he was angry with Nora for having forsaken his brother. To cut a long story short, she gave her new lover access to her blood. The council caught wind of this, and, well, she was punished."

I recall her saying that punishment was death. And then I recall something else: Bryn's version—a paparazzi chase that ended in a deadly crash. Either way, the outcome's so damn sad. Malachi lost his mom, and Nora lost her life.

"What do you think of Joslyn?" Electra's question catches me by surprise.

"I don't like her. She's a crap mom and crap human being. And yeah, she's beautiful, but I don't really get why Saul's marrying her."

"Because she's pregnant."

I sit up so suddenly that my head spins. "Joslyn? But she's... She's..." I perform quick math and realize that she's forty-three—her ovaries may not be the freshest, but they're hardly expired. "Is this widely known?"

Does Bryn know? Wouldn't she have told me if she did? We tell each other everything. Or, well, we used to.

"Dorian says she's been paying her gynecologist quite a lot of visits, so if it's not a baby, then it's a severe venereal infection."

I can't even smile at that. "Bryn might know. Or she could find out."

Electra shrugs. "She'll eventually start showing."

"Does Malachi know?"

"I haven't discussed it with him, and I probably won't. Family is a sensitive topic for him. All I know is that he's not happy about the wedding."

"I bet. I would hate it if my mother remarried." I realize the thought never even crossed my mind because of her condition.

Considering her age, if Tarian manages to repair her brain, my mother will surely date again. Dread scores my heart as I imagine her holding the hand of a man who isn't my father. Which is all sorts of selfish. However much I hate it, my mother deserves to love and be loved again.

A knock jerks me out of my head. I've never been so glad for the rap of knuckles against wood.

"Nurse Electra? Callie?" The edgy tonality of Mrs. Fiona's voice douses my relief.

I spring off the mattress and open the door. "What is it, Mrs. Fiona?"

"Thank the lord. I thought you'd all up and left."

"Nope. We're right here." I shoot her a reassuring smile as I glance past her at the TV that's now playing the karaoke version of "Flowers" by Miley Cyrus. "Is everything all right?"

She toys with her lanyard, and my nerves reverberate as loudly as the keys she doesn't even need since we're not home. The weight of them must reassure her. When I started preschool, I could never leave the house without bringing an object from home, be it one of the finger puppets Dad would use when he recounted bedtime stories, a flower I'd filched from the shop, or a neon sticky tab pinched from one of Mom's cookbooks.

"I was in the bathroom, and well"—she claps her keys, the veins on her hands straining against her sunspot-speckled skin—"my intestines have been givin' me trouble, so it took a while, and when I came out, Lisa was no longer singing, and the front door was ajar. Which is why I thought you'd all left."

"Shit," Electra whispers, causing all the fine hairs on my arms to rise. "Shit, shit, shit, I must've forgotten to reset the alarm."

"The alarm?"

"On the apartment door."

My heart halts midbeat. "Mrs. Fiona, where's Mom?"

"I was hopin' she was in here. With you."

# THIRTY-NINE

"Mom?" I yell.

I will my mother's voice to leap over Miley Cyrus's, but the only thing that wallops my eardrums is my thundering pulse.

"Lisa?!" I sprint past Mrs. Fiona and tear across the living room.

Electra must cast a net of magic, though, because I crash into nothing, and that nothing propels me into the sofa. I try to leap back to my feet, but Electra's magic doesn't let up.

I snarl, "Let go, Electra!" I don't care if Mrs. Fiona thinks I'm a couple pecans short of a pie for asking someone, who isn't even standing beside me, to free me from a sofa.

"No." She turns toward Mrs. Fiona, odd-hued eyes radiant, and tells her something I don't catch.

A second later, my neighbor pivots and plows toward her bedroom, her long lilac braid swinging like a clock pendulum.

As soon as her door shuts, I screech, "My mother's out there, Electra! Out on the street with no phone and no wallet! I need to go find her."

"You're not leaving this place."

"She's out there all by herself!" The second I say this, the blood deserts my face, because what if she isn't? What if someone took her?

I must give voice to the thought because Electra's suddenly crouched in front of me, phone screen propped in front of my face. "No one took her. Look."

Sure enough, it's footage of my mother walking out of the building by herself. I squint at the screen, my heart cramping when I notice her bare feet. How could she forget shoes?

I shut my eyes for a long second, focusing on the fact that no one kidnapped her and that it's midday. I still hate that she's alone and barefoot, but at least she wasn't forced to leave at gunpoint.

"I'm going to call a cop friend, all right?"

I shove my palms against the seat cushion but get no leverage. "Electra, please release me."

"Not until you swear you're not going to chase her down." Her tone brooks no argument.

I punch the sofa cushion. "Callie, I'm serious. You running out of here won't help your mother."

"Me staying here won't help her either," I snap back.

"But it'll help Tarian."

"I don't fucking care about Tarian right now."

"I know, but you will once the adrenaline wears off, because you're a good person with a good heart."

My fingers cramp, dimpling the luxe velvet beneath my ass. I rue myself for shutting the bedroom door. There was no rhyme or reason to it since Mom and Mrs. Fiona were singing so loudly, neither would've heard a word of our conversation.

Electra rubs the back of her neck, her phone already pressed to her ear. I catch her brother's name, then Symeon's amid her string of foreign words before she disappears inside the kitchen. I hear the snick of a door shutting and then the beep of the security system. I've never been claustrophobic in my life, but I suddenly feel like a prisoner instead of a sheltered witness.

"Your mother's description won't go out over the police radio in case..." Electra lets her sentence hang without tagging the obvious: *in case someone involved in Tarian's disappearance is listening.*

I'm too distraught to praise her presence of mind.

"I'm sorry, Callie. I was bringing in the groceries when Dorian called, and—" She rips out her hair tie before finger-combing her strands and wrangling them anew. "And I got sidetracked."

The pressure of her magic finally fades off my skin, and like a dam lifting, it releases a massive gush of gnawing worries and murky thoughts. "Why didn't they take me?"

"When? Who?"

"The night of the accident. Why didn't his abductors take me, too? Why didn't they kill me?" The chill that crawled under my skin when I realized my mother was gone spreads.

"Because you weren't a threat. If they'd known you wore one of Tarian's runes... If they'd known you two were connected..."

Again she lets her sentences hang there, unfinished, but again, I know how both end. "They'd have eliminated me."

"Or..." She tucks her tongue in the corner of her mouth like my father used to do when he was deep in thought.

"Or?"

"This is pure speculation, since all the cameras on the street were down—"

"Convenient."

"—but I assume you've met Bryn's father?"

My skin prickles, but this time, not with a chill, with an awareness. "You think Sergeant Lynch was the one who shot Tarian, then lifted him from the wreckage?" I sit up. "You think that's why I'm still alive?"

"No. You're still alive because Tarian shielded you."

Electra says this as though I could ever forget. I'm aware of his sacrifice. It's this awareness that keeps me from going after my mother, not Electra's human security system and inhuman powers.

"But yes, I do think that if Lynch is involved, then he didn't put a bullet in your head because you're his daughter's best friend."

My stomach lurches as I recall the crimson stain spreading over Tarian's white button-down. I gather my legs into my chest, press my clammy forehead against my kneecaps, and pray to the divinity that gave an entire nation magic to keep my mother safe.

And then I pray to that same divinity to keep Tarian safe as well.

ONE OF MY prayers is answered two hours later when the doorman calls Electra to announce the arrival of two women seeking access to the penthouse—a certain Lisa Bloom and a Bryn Fielding.

Relief wars with shock. "I thought you cleansed Bryn's memory of this place?"

"I did."

"Then how is she here?"

"I'm guessing your mother refreshed it," Electra says, right before telling the doorman to send them up.

As she deactivates the alarm with an app on her phone, I ask, "You don't think Delta sent Bryn here, do you?"

Electra rubs the back of her neck as though her runes were causing her discomfort. "If he did, it'll work in our favor."

"How?"

She smiles. "If he cared enough to spare his daughter's best friend, can you imagine the lengths he'll go to keep his daughter out of harm's way?"

My anxiety careens upward in time with the elevator carrying my mother to safety and my friend to hazard. "No harming her, physically or otherwise."

Gaze steady on the metal elevator doors, Electra murmurs, "I'm not a monster."

"You're an Atlantean with a plan and a grudge. That's more treacherous than any monster."

"I won't hurt your friend. I swear it."

I'd very much like to trust her, but our recent camaraderie has in no way made me forget that the ruthless killer beside me gave up her fellow Atlantean to find Tarian. The only thing that could stop Electra from sacrificing Bryn won't be a promise made in haste on the threshold of a safehouse; it will be a person.

*Me.*

# FORTY

"Holy Coco Chanel, this place..." Bryn twirls as she enters the penthouse, her armload of bangles scattering shards of midday sun across the modern kitchen. "I would *literally* set fire to my apartment if my insurance put me up in a place like this."

My mother frowns. "Arson's a felony, honey, so your insurance provider wouldn't even offer you a cushion to prop on the sidewalk if you deliberately set fire to your home. Why are we even discussing fires and insurances?"

Bryn stops spinning, her gaze vaulting to mine as she realizes the fire has slipped my mother's mind. I pray *I* don't slip Mom's mind next because I'm not ready to lose her again. I tighten my arm around her waist and pillow my head on her shoulder, my eyes still muggy with relief.

When she'd stepped out of the elevator, safe and sound and shod in a pair of designer espadrilles—courtesy of one of Bryn's many fashion sponsors—my rib cage had loosened as though the twine that held together all the curved bones had been snipped.

"No reason." Bryn licks her lip. "Nick really has amazing taste."

The smile that annexes my mother's lips is devastating. I wish she would smile more often. She used to when Dad was alive. Then again, he claimed his only job in life was to make his girls happy.

"I'm glad you found your way back here, Mom," I murmur.

She touches my chestnut curls that skim my waist. Once upon a time, she wore her hair just as long. Does she remember?

"Pretty hard to miss, sweetie. Like Bryn pointed out, it's the tallest building in Hadeztown."

My heart stumbles over a beat, and not because she called Boston Hadez*town*, but because Bryn couldn't have pointed it out. Unless…

The second my mother's attention drapes over the city, Bryn lifts a finger to her temple and taps, then grimaces. Thanks to years of friendship, I understand all the words she doesn't speak out loud: *my mother mentioned the building, then forgot.*

"Your father…" Mom gives her head a gentle shake. "I swear. He claims he has vertigo yet purchases a place like this."

Truth. During a family vacation through the Grand Canyon, my poor father broke out in hives any time Mom and I stood too near a ridge.

"Want something to drink, Miss Fielding?" Electra's tone crackles with dislike.

Bryn scrutinizes her from head to waist since the rest of Electra's hidden behind the island. "And you are?"

I understand Electra had to wipe my friend's mind, but did she really have to go so heavy on the compulsion?

"I'm the"—Electra flicks her eyes toward my mother, who's staring out the window at the white-capped surface of the Charles —"housekeeper."

"Gotcha." Bryn drops onto one of the kitchen barstools, propping her phone on the island in front of her. "I'd love some tea. It's deceptively chilly because of all the wind."

Even though my gaze roves to the window, to the brisk air I'd love to feel lick across my cheeks after days of being cooped up indoors, I don't miss how Electra's arrows straight toward Bryn's phone. The device suddenly skids off the island and hits the floor with a loud thwack that has Bryn hopping off her seat, swearing like a sailor.

"Lisa, I received some new cookbooks this morning." Electra nods to the living room as though she didn't just shatter my friend's thousand-dollar phone with her mind. "Calanthe said you were looking for new recipes to test out."

"She did, did she? Always so attentive, that one." Mom drops a kiss on my forehead.

I *had* mentioned them when I'd asked Electra for some arts and crafts books, but I'd assumed she'd forgotten since they weren't in the package.

"Shall we go read them together, Callie? You can help me plan meals for the week."

I let go of her waist. "Sure, but give me a second to catch up with Bryn, okay?"

"Take your time. And, Bryn, honey, thanks a million for the ride."

"Anytime, Lisa." Bryn plasters on a smile.

Once Electra guides my mother out of the kitchen, I pad over toward my friend. "Does it still work?"

"The screen's so shattered I have no idea. *Ugh*. To think I *just* got it."

"Was it a gift from one of your fashion sponsors?"

"I wish. The bedazzled case was, though." She pops the crackled phone free of the leather and gem-encrusted case which she chucks onto the island as though *it's* to blame. "I'll be taking that unboxing video down the second I have access to my account. What absolutely shitty quality. Handbag designers should stick to making handbags."

"Maybe your insurance will replace it?"

"My insurance sucks." She opens her quilted tote and dumps her shattered device atop a nondescript brown vial, probably a perfume sample she got gifted since she started advertising cosmetics. "Your mom's new nurse. She's intense."

"She was really stressed out about Mom."

"Also, she's Atlantean?"

I look away from her bag so fast my neck cracks. "What?"

She taps her nape. "She's got the tat."

I get up and head over to the electric kettle. "Loads of people have that tattoo." I fill up the kettle, then set it on its base and power it on.

"Orrr"—Bryn drags out—"she's from there. You did ask her, right?"

"She did." Electra's back, stealthy as always. "I'm a friend of Malachi's, actually. He's the one who recommended me. I hear you're well acquainted with his family."

Bryn watches her for a full minute before replying, "My mother's marrying Saul, but if you're a friend of Malachi's"—I don't miss the tight inflection she uses on the word *friend*—"then you must already know this."

Without missing a beat, Electra asks, "How do you feel about their union?"

"I'm happy for my mother. Saul's a really kind man."

I'm still not entirely sold on his kindness, but perhaps my impression of her future stepfather is colored by the fact that he's dying to use me as bait to lure Tarian's captors.

"Is your father happy for her?" Electra's bluntness makes Bryn sit up and cast me a look I interpret to mean, *The new nurse sure is nosy.*

"I assume he is. I don't know. Haven't spoken to him in months."

The Atlantean's eyes begin to gleam. "When was the last time you had contact with Delta Lynch, Bryn Fielding?"

"We video-chatted on Christmas." There's no hesitation. Then again, compulsion yanks the truth from people, so Bryn wouldn't have been able to hesitate even if she'd wanted to.

The exhale that flows out of me is as thick as the steam gushing from the kettle. I didn't honestly think my friend was complicit in her dad's evil machinations, but I'm nonetheless relieved to have confirmation of it.

"How did Calanthe's mother find you?" The beam of Electra's eyes keeps Bryn in a trance.

"She went to the bar across the street from Bloom's Blooms and asked Logan if he'd seen Callie. After noticing she was shoeless and agitated, Logan lied and said she was with me. He got her to sit down and then he called me. I rushed right over. I was really worried she'd hitchhiked her way back to Boston, since last I heard, Callie had taken her out of state to visit a neurologist. Lisa said they hadn't left Boston, but maybe she forgot?"

"Lisa is confused, Bryn. She was out of state with Calanthe, but they returned late last night. The neurologist couldn't help her."

God, I hate this so much. If only I could tell Bryn the truth. But if her father truly is involved…

"What sort of tea would you like, Miss Fielding?"

My friend blinks out of her daze. "Lapsang Souchong."

"And for you, Callie?"

I release a deep breath, glad the compulsion session is over. "The same."

As Electra forages through the drawer of tea tins, I round the island toward Bryn.

"Callie?" she hisses as I take a seat beside her.

"What?"

"Just surprised the new nurse is using your nickname, that's all."

"We've been spending a lot of time together since the fire."

She nods. "Didn't see a work crew at Blooms, but it doesn't look too battered. Do you know when you'll be able to go home?"

"No."

She waggles her brows. "You should call Tarian to find out."

"Um. Yeah."

"Have you heard from him?"

"He hasn't called, no."

She holds my stare as though she's not convinced I'm telling the truth.

"Why would he call me?"

"Because of Symeon."

"What's wrong with Symeon?" I can tell Electra's hanging on to our every word from how slowly and quietly she's spooning the loose-leaf tea in the strainer.

"What's wrong?" Bryn's head rears back. "He just died! I assumed you'd heard. It's all over the news." She misinterprets my surprise that the Hadezes haven't kept his death private for ignorance. "According to Mom, he OD'd and slipped off the deck of his yacht."

"And no one noticed? Isn't his yacht staffed? Where was Yasmin?" I realize I'm firing a lot of questions her way but I'm trying to gather all she's heard.

"He gave his staff the month off."

My heart ramps up as I realize that, not only was Symeon complicit, but the abduction was also premeditated. "A month off at the peak of summer?"

Electra's eyes twitch as hard as the vein at the base of her throat. I do believe that if Symeon hadn't already been dead, she'd have murdered him herself.

Bryn shrugs. "He probably planned to travel to Europe or something."

"So he gave his staff the month off and then took his boat out for a joyride and sank it?"

"Sank it?" Bryn repeats. "I thought you hadn't seen the news…"

*Crap.*

Before I can utter a plausible reason for my conclusion, Electra's irises flare nice and bright. "You told Calanthe that Symeon took his yacht out on his own and hit a reef, Bryn."

Bryn blinks, then lifts her hand and rubs her temple. "Saul's having the boat dredged. Not that I ever considered doing drugs, but after this, I definitely never will."

"Let's hope no one else was aboard," Electra says, even though her tone smacks of eagerness that someone else could be aboard. *Many* someones.

I suddenly picture Tarian shackled to the bottom of the ocean, lifeless. I chide my brain for summoning such an image and remind myself that Atlanteans can't die from drowning, especially Tarian. What if his kidnappers left him as bait for the sharks? There are so many Great Whites in those waters. If any attack, then what? Can animal teeth stab his Atlantean flesh? Could a shark swim him down into a trench too deep to access, even for an Atlantean?

I will my rune to flare, to transport me to him, but my brand stays cold. I sneak my hand beneath the fabric of my tank top and thumb the area of skin inscribed with his magic.

"What's up with your back?" Bryn asks.

"Oh. Um. It's feeling itchy."

"Could be some allergic reaction to the woo-woo ink. What did the guy use again? Henna?"

Before I can fabricate yet another lie, Electra says, "Tarian wasn't on the boat, Callie." I think she's trying to reassure me until I see her reading a message on her phone.

If Tarian isn't at the bottom of the ocean, then where is he?

# FORTY-ONE

If only I'd sent Malachi to the *Amapola* instead of to an aircraft carrier.

If only I'd understood the reason Tarian kept featuring *that* boat in his dreams.

Enraged with myself, I fist my fingers and tuck them into my lap. Tarian fed me all these clues, and what did I do with them? I misinterpreted every last one of them. I'm the absolute *worst* detective.

"Well, duh," Bryn says.

*Ouch.* Wait…I didn't say any of that out loud, did I?

Bryn narrows her eyes on Electra. "If Tarian had been there, he would've saved his brother."

"Was anyone, besides Symeon, aboard the *Amapola*?" I ask.

Bryn breathes out a sad, "No."

I side-eye Electra for validation. When she shakes her head, I can't decide whether to feel relieved or anxious.

Bryn swivels toward me, her crossed knees knocking into the side of my chair. "Um, how do you know the yacht's name?"

*Shoot.* I toy with a thread on the frayed hem of my shorts. "Tarian mentioned it."

"So you *have* been speaking with him?" Bryn smiles. "Of course you have. And let me guess. The insurance company didn't lend you this place, *he* did. Am I right?"

I roll the thread between my index finger and thumb. "You got me."

Bryn's grin is so wide I can see the fillings she had to get because of a childhood diet rich in candy and soda, and poor in homemade, balanced meals.

"Yasmin must be devastated." Electra's change of topic is so brutal it makes Bryn's mouth fold up and her chest lift with a melancholic sigh.

"I know, right? I tried calling her earlier, but she's shut off her phone. I tried calling Malachi too, but I got his voicemail. I'm guessing the funeral's keeping everyone busy."

As Electra pivots toward the cupboard over the sink and extracts two mugs, I ask, "You think Yasmin will be at the funeral?"

Bryn tucks a strawberry-blonde lock behind her ear. "Her boyfriend just died, Callie. Of course she'll be there. She's probably already there. It would be in super poor taste if she didn't show, don't you think?"

I think a lot of things about Yasmin, none of which I can share with Bryn.

"You should really come to the funeral with me. I'm sure Tarian would appreciate it."

Except Tarian won't be there. Unless…unless he managed to break free?

Electra props the mugs on the counter with *a lot* of gusto. They must be made of really strong stuff because they don't chip. "I'm still acclimating to Lisa, so it's best Callie stays here."

When she turns to grab two more mugs, Bryn murmurs, "Is it me, or is she totally incompetent?"

"She's young," I whisper back.

"So are you."

"Yes, but I've been taking care of Mom for a while. Electra just graduated from nursing school."

"Are you even sure she's a nurse?" Bryn hisses.

"That's what Malachi said."

That hushes her inquisition, since Malachi can say or do no wrong in Bryn's eyes.

"How are you getting to the Vineyard, Miss Fielding?" Although Electra's words are convivial, her tone sure isn't.

"By helicopter. Saul's." Bryn drops her elbow on the stone island and roosts her chin on her fist. "Come to think of it, if you're such a good friend of the family's, shouldn't *you* be attending the funeral?"

Electra pours tea into the mugs, then slides two across the island toward us. "I'm working."

"I'm sure Callie can handle her own mother for a couple of hours. After all, she's been handling her for two years on her own." Bryn palms her mug and carries it to her mouth, but she doesn't take a sip. She merely blows on it, ridding the water of a few degrees and giving her chin and cheeks a steam bath in the process.

"Symeon and I weren't very close. My brother's going, though. He should be coming around soon. He can drive you to the heliport."

"That would be great. Mackenzie and I were supposed to fly out tomorrow morning, but Saul's asked us to arrive tonight." Bryn blows on her tea again. "Mom's apparently bent out of shape over Sym's passing. It's absolutely horrible—don't get me wrong —but she barely knew him."

"Being pregnant heightens people's emotions." Electra slips that in with her usual, nonexistent tact.

Bryn sputters, then gags on her mouthful of tea. "What?" she croaks around harsh coughs. "Pregnant? *Mom*?"

"Why do you think Saul suggested marriage?" Electra continues.

Bryn smacks her mug down, sending hot water sloshing over the rim. It hits her skin, reddening it instantly. "Because she stroked his cock and ego just right." She wipes her hand on her frilly black shorts. "*Pregnant*? Are you sure?" Bryn looks from me to Electra. "Did Malachi tell you that?"

"No. I heard it through the Atlantean grapevine. I don't believe Malachi knows, so please don't mention it until Saul announces it." Electra nods to Bryn's hand. "Want some ice?"

"That must be the pregnancy Saul and Symeon were discussing!"

Electra's pupils turn almost slitted at the mention of the Atlantean traitor. "When?"

"About a month ago. I thought they were discussing *Yasmin*." She rearranges her overlapping bangles. "I can't believe they were talking about *Mom's* kid. I mean, it does work in my mother's favor to bear an heir or heiress, but wow. Didn't realize that was how she'd entrapped him."

"How did you find yourself part of Symeon and Saul's conversation?" Electra voices one of my *many* questions.

"Mackenzie was hogging the powder room, so I went and used the bathroom in Saul's office." Her cheek dimples as she bites the inside of it. "I didn't mean to eavesdrop."

My brain feels like an overheating computer with a bunch of new tabs bursting open. "I didn't realize Symeon and Saul were that close." I sound deceptively tranquil.

"They party together. Or used to. Mom actually met Symeon first. He was the one to introduce her to Saul."

The silence that ensues is so complete I can hear my mother hum as she thumbs through her cookbook in the other room.

Could Symeon and Saul be close enough to do more than

party? Could they have worked together to ensnare Tarian? "What were they saying about the pregnancy?"

"Symeon was telling Saul that it wasn't his." Bryn's brow puckers. "No, wait. Now that I think of it, I must've heard that wrong, because that would mean Sym slept with Mom...and—" Forget saucers, my friend's eyes go as round as dinner plates. "Oh my god, do you think Mom slept with Symeon?"

My heart bounces from rib to rib. "It would explain why she's so distraught."

"Doesn't explain why Saul would be marrying her though." Electra's reasoning sends my mind into another tailspin.

"Maybe he really cares about my mother?" Even Bryn doesn't sound convinced. "Maybe he really wants a baby, but his swimmers are no bueno?"

Neither of those two theories makes sense to me. In my book, the only reason a man like Saul would agree to a shotgun wedding is: A, the baby is genuinely his, or B, he's being blackmailed. If it's the latter, we'll know soon enough. After all, now that Symeon's dead, Saul has no need to uphold his promise.

Unless Symeon wasn't the one blackmailing him. What if it was Bryn's father? Or Yasmin?

Bryn suddenly goes ramrod straight. I assume Electra's compelling her to forget this whole conversation, but she's concentrated on her cell phone.

"Do you think that Saul was jealous so he had his own nephew murdered?" Bryn murmurs.

"No." Electra's lack of hesitation pulls a whoosh of relief from my friend.

"Can you imagine if the baby really is Symeon's?" Bryn palms her mug. "How messed up would that be?"

On a scale of one to *I'm meeting up with a man in my sleep*, I'd give it a two.

"I'll be right back." Electra strides out of the kitchen, phone in hand.

I assume she's going to call or message her brother. Or Ines, I suppose. The latter might know whose kid Joslyn is carrying since she works for Saul.

"Something smells fishy." Bryn's words create ripples in the brownish surface of her tea.

I give mine a sniff. "Smoky. Not fishy."

She snorts. "I was talking about the whole baby-daddy fiasco."

*Ah.*

"On second thought, I'm not going to the memorial."

"I think that's a good idea."

"Go call the elevator." She rises from her seat. "I'll go get Lisa."

"What?"

"You were right not to trust that family."

"Bryn, wait—"

But my friend doesn't wait. She marches right into the living room. However glad I am that she's finally seeing Saul for the dodgy being he is, her timing couldn't be more awful. I lurch off my stool and rush after her because I can't leave. Especially not now.

"How about some cake?" she's asking my mother.

Mom closes the cookbook slowly.

"Cake's not ready yet, Bryn!" I bellow.

"The cake should get ready." She shoots me an eloquent stare.

Mom shrinks back in the sofa, gaze skipping from Bryn to me before landing on Electra, who stands beside the bay window, speaking quietly on her phone. "Who are you? Where am I?"

"You're in your new home, Mrs. Bloom."

At the sound of the deep voice, Bryn whirls around while Electra tucks her phone back into her pocket.

# FORTY-TWO

"Mal?" Bryn's expression morphs from shock to dread to betrayal. "I thought you were in the Vineyard."

"Just flew back." He shoves both hands into the pockets of a crisp pair of pants. His white shirt, too, is wrinkle-free.

He's had time to shower and change, but clearly, not to sleep. I grimace because I feel like I'm to blame for this. If I hadn't sent him on a fool's errand, he may have been able to wind down.

"Did you come to pick me up?" Bryn asks.

"No. I came to visit my friend, Calanthe." I believe he says this hoping it'll quiet my mother. I don't think he's realized that she currently has no idea who I am.

"Your friend?"

I wish she wouldn't make such a big deal of this, because one, it's ridiculous, and two, it's agitating my mother. "Bryn, please."

Her mouth puckers.

*Stop*, I mouth, nodding to Mom.

I head over to the sofa and crouch in front of her, my hands itching to touch hers. She peers at me, her thin fingers toying with a woolen fringe on her sweater. Becoming a stranger in her eyes is one thing; becoming someone to be feared is another.

"Hi, Lisa. I'm Calanthe. I work at the flower shop with you and Nick."

My mother gapes and gapes, and then she opens her mouth and utters two syllables that mince my heart, "Who's Nick?"

I sink back onto my heels. She can't have forgotten my father. She just can't. He was her one constant. Her one true everything.

"Nick's your husband." *Your greatest love.* I suck in air and scrabble to my feet. "Her medication!" With all that's been happening with Tarian, I've forgotten to give it to her. "She needs her pills."

Even though nothing manmade can heal her, the prescription meds slow the rate of her cognitive decline.

"What pills, Callie?" Electra asks gently.

"Aren't you a fucking nurse?" Bryn snaps.

"Bryn. Not now." I scrub my hands down my face, my pulse trembling so hard it tosses my fingers. "The pill bottles are at home. On the shelf over the stovetop. Inside a box painted with flowers."

The palm-sized ceramic chest was a present from Mrs. Fiona to store my jewelry. For the last year and a half, instead of baubles, it's hidden prescription medication.

Where *is* Mrs. Fiona? Her closed bedroom door leads me to assume that she's asleep.

"I'll swing by the shop." Malachi runs a hand through his mussed blond hair. "Bryn, do you mind accompanying me?"

On every form she fills out that requires a physical description, Bryn jots down her eye color as amber. Never before has it applied so accurately. Bryn's stare has gone as firm and cold as fossilized tree resin.

"Sure." For the first time in her life, she doesn't sound enthusiastic to follow her crush. Then again, her blind adoration of the Hadez bunch just took a hit.

"What pills?" My mother's voice writhes with nerves. "Who are you people?"

"Electra, can you try to calm her?" I croak.

My mother burrows deeper into the sofa. "Calm *who*?"

"Bryn?" Malachi nods to the doorway, but my friend doesn't move as Electra crosses the room toward us.

"You're safe, Lisa." Electra's eyes become a lighthouse in my mother's storm, twin beams that guide her toward safe shores. "You were just about to watch a movie with Calanthe."

"Calanthe?" My mother no longer claws the couch. No. It's my heart she claws at now.

"The girl standing behind me." Electra nods to me. "That's Calanthe. You like Calanthe."

"I like Calanthe," my mother repeats robotically, eyes so wide her nutmeg irises float in a sea of white.

"Is she hypnotizing her?" I hear Bryn hiss at Malachi.

"Something like that. Come. Let's go fetch her medication."

Bryn must decide to trust him because the front door snicks shut a moment later.

Drained, I sink into the armchair.

As Electra clicks on the TV, she asks, "So what are you in the mood for, Lisa? A movie or the Food Net—"

Electra stops talking because she's landed on a channel, one that's showing aerial footage of Tarian's house in the Vineyard while two newscasters chat about the tragic death of the youngest Hadez.

"*…and only five months after his father passed away. I swear, Lillian, that family may just be cursed like the Kennedys.*" A male anchor with a sky-blue tie and a puff of black hair is drumming his fingers over a stack of papers.

"*Some people are saying Tarian Hadez has yet to arrive in the Vineyard, even though the rest of his family and many of their friends have already congregated there.*" The blonde, who must be Lillian, is seated across the V-shaped desk from the Elvis lookalike. *"There's talk he may not show at all."*

*"There's always talk surrounding that family, isn't there?"*

*"True, but according to sources close to the family, the brothers were not on the best of terms, especially after Tarian took over the conservatorship that their father had put in place."*

"That poor family," my mother whispers, watching the horde of sunglass-wearing mourners pouring onto Tarian's property.

Her voice startles Electra, who finally clicks on Netflix, putting an end to our dismal rubbernecking.

Once she's picked a movie and Mom gives it her full attention, I whisper, "Do you think Symeon abducted his brother to get out of having a guardian? Sym could've promised Lynch A-grade blood in exchange for help trapping Tarian."

Electra perches on the arm of the sofa, body coiled so tight she seems about ready to lurch off. "Possibly, but what about Yasmin? What would she have gotten out of this deal? Why would she have gotten involved?" I'm about to tell her about the wedding cake toppers when she murmurs, "*Shit.*"

"What?"

"Dorian told me she tried to get with Tarian before hooking up with Sym. What if she abducted him because he rejected her? Or worse, what if she abducted him in the hopes he'd develop Stockholm Syndrome?"

"What the fuck?" My exclamation startles Mom. "Sorry."

I lug Electra off the arm of the sofa and toward the window, out of earshot from Mom.

Trying to rein in my temper, I mutter, "Except unconscious people can't develop Stockholm Syndrome."

"Maybe he's no longer unconscious. Or maybe he is and she's planning on *saving him.*" Electra adds air quotes.

I saw red before; now I see pitch-black. "She was about to marry Lynch in Tarian's dream," I all but snarl.

"What?"

"Did I forget to relay that part?"

"Um, yes. And if it's factual, then it's a game changer since we assumed Symeon and Lynch were a team, but what if it was Yasmin and Lynch all along? Dorian said she was cheating on Sym. What if it was with Delta? What if she was using Symeon to get closer to Tarian?" Her eyes shimmer with excitement. "What if Symeon found out about their affair and decided to free his brother, and—I don't know—Yasmin shoved him into Tarian's body, and his magic misinterpreted Symeon's intent and marked him like it marked Barak?"

I try to picture this, and although it's not completely outrageous, something doesn't sit well. "That would imply that your goddess is a really poor judge of character if she withdrew the runes of not one but *two* innocent Atlanteans."

Electra hisses, probably worried that my little comment about Gaea's rashness will transform my rune into an "X." I'm not worried because my gut is telling me that Barak and Symeon weren't innocent.

Like a nail against a chalkboard, a thought grinds against the walls of my brain. "The guys mentioned a verse on Tarian's skin about the removal of runes if someone tried to steal his magic. What if Symeon and Barak both tried to collect Tarian's blood—Gaea only knows why—and *that's* why they lost their runes?"

That puts an end to Electra's hissing. Now she gasps. "And their blood..."

I wrinkle my nose. And that. Although I hope with all my heart it was only their magic. The same way I suddenly hope Tarian's not awake. Even if Symeon wasn't inherently good, they're still—*were* still brothers. I can't imagine how much his soul must ache.

Maybe that's why he hasn't resurfaced. Because he stayed away to grieve. My theory gains so much traction that it pulls me from the window and into my bedroom. I'm so wired that when I rest my head on the pillow, I don't think I'll sleep.

Sure enough, I don't. With a sigh, I return to the living room, except…except it's not a living room but a giant mall bustling with shoppers.

I spin on my heel, hunting the hordes for Tarian when Miley Cyrus sashays up to me, holding a pink rose. "Your boyfriend told me to give you this key."

I'm so shocked that she's referred to a flower as a key that I don't bother pointing out that Tarian isn't my boyfriend. Also, what does it matter? The popstar before me isn't even real; she's a figment of my—

Wait, that's actually worse. Tarian is *not* my boyfriend. He's not even my friend. He's a boy acquaintance. *Boyquaintance.* As I take the rose from Miley, I prick my finger on the stem, which works great at flinging my mind off my delusions and back on the reason for the rose's existence.

"So, um, what door does it open?" I suck on my bleeding fingertip.

"You've got to find him before the flower bleeds out."

Why? What happens then? Do I lose him forever? Does my rune vanish, and he stays lost? "Where is he?"

Miley backs up into the crowd, humming one of her hit songs.

I run after her. "Miley, wait! Where is he? What does the door look like?" It can't possibly resemble a regular door, can it?

Something cold splashes my bare toes. I shove the flower away, half-expecting to find blood speckling my white-polished nails, but the sap isn't red—it's gold. I hold the rose out just as another glob of liquid metal squeezes out of the stem and hits pale marble.

How long do I have to find Tarian?

Another droplet falls, robbing the rose of a petal, and me, of a heartbeat.

I can only pray that I have more time than this rose that's melting like a popsicle under the summer sun.

# FORTY-THREE

A new droplet of gold clings to the cut edge of the stem, trembling as it bloats. When it breaks free and collapses, my heart spikes and drenches my veins in adrenaline. *Shit, shit, shit.*

"TARIAN!" I scream at the top of my lungs, my neck cracking from the speed at which I propel my gaze off my bleeding rose key.

Faces swirl toward me. Faces that are missing lips. Well, this is next level. I'm not just descending into madness; I'm diving headfirst and kicking my way into the abyss.

"MILEY!" I scream, remembering that *she* had a mouth. "Where can I find Tarian?"

I receive zero answer because Miley is MIA, just like every dream-shopper's mouth.

I start to speed walk along the shop windows, peering into each one for a big man with ebony hair and a very intense stare, but instead, find only more mouthless people. Mostly women. Which is actually convenient since the god I seek is huge. I soon realize why most shoppers are female—because every shop I pass sells shoes, and not sneakers and slides, but designer heels.

Something brushes my knee, and I jump.

*A petal.*

"Tarian!" I shriek, since…why not? "TARIAN!"

I peer up, my stomach plummeting when I see that this isn't a regular mall but a skyscraper of shops. Dozens upon dozens of floors stretch toward an open sky crawling with squawking seagulls. Unlike the humans surrounding me, the birds aren't missing their beaks. Too bad they can't talk. Actually…what if they can?

Something cool and viscous slithers down my thigh, flinging my attention from the sea birds to my bare legs mottled with gilt sap.

*Think. Think. Think, Callie. This is your dream. Think!*

Wait, is it my dream? What if it's Tarian's?

I stare at my feet. A heartbeat later, the red patent stilettos in the nearby window materialize on my feet, propping me up a few inches. How did I ever doubt that this was my dream?

Although the heels are stunning, I switch them out for sneakers.

Another petal unfastens itself from the hemorrhaging stem and drops.

*FML. Or rather, FMI: Fuck my imagination.*

I sprint, on the lookout for a man with a mouth and a dark suit, almost tripping over my own feet when an idea pops into my brain. I picture Tarian wearing the outfit Macrazy had on the day we met. If his physique and lips don't help him stand out in the mouthless crowd of denim and basic tees, then a neon-pink pantsuit certainly will.

"Tarian!" My voice is hoarse, yet I keep screaming his name as I loop around the entire floor and find only shoe boutiques.

I lunge up the escalator, taking the motorized stairs two at a time. When I reach the top, I scan the shops—shoes as far as the eye can see. Is the rose supposed to unlock the door to one of these boutiques? Am I even looking for a door or should I be seeking a vase or a—

My gaze locks on a column of vegetation that shoots a gazillion stories high. The green leaves are dotted with pink blooms and… Are those glazed donuts? I squint. Yep, donuts. My father would have *a lot* to say about the combo of baked goods and ros—

I stare at the one in my hand, then stare back at the column. *Pink.* The rose I hold must've been snipped off the pylon. As the flower drips and loses another precious petal, I take a moment to think. This is my psychosomatic trip. *I'm* in control.

I study the belt of shops surrounding me. Shoes, shoes, and *more* shoes. I've never hated the sight of shoes before. Actually, that's not true. I was *not* pleased by the sight of the crystallized ones on Mackenzie's feet.

As I dawdle and fume, the rose bleeds and loses two more petals.

*Think, Callie, and not about Macrazy's feet. Think!*

The lights go out. Poof. I've never been afraid of the dark, but man, did my dream have to go dark? Thank god for the open sky tunneling light on the—

The pylon! My rose must go there. But where? Do I have to find the stalk from which it was snipped?

"Any chance I could get some glow-in-the-dark arrows to indicate where the rose hooks onto?"

No convenient cyphers light up the darkness. No birds swoop in from the heavens. No mouthless person points to a clipped stem.

I study the two-hundred-foot pole. Although wide, it's not wide enough to be accessed from any floor save for the lobby unless climbed, but to climb it, I'd need to head back downstairs.

I hesitate to clench my lids shut and will myself out of this phony world, but the symbol etched into Symeon's skin keeps my eyes wide. I need to find Tarian. I need to know if he's managed to free himself and is in hiding or if he's still in captivity. After all, the point of all these dreams isn't to render me mad; it's to save him.

Right?

"Tarian!" My shrill cry silences everyone in the mall and stops them in their tracks. "If you can't help," I growl, "then buzz the fuck off." Like faulty holograms, the humans all flicker out of existence.

*Huh.* Their disappearance empowers me. The rose may still bleed, nevertheless *I* call the shots.

I stare into the heavens and shout, feeling very much like a biblical prophet, "Show me the way!"

The escalator grinds to a stop. When it starts again, it changes direction. I take it without hesitation and then I walk up to the pylon, my rose ejecting petal after petal, sap droplet after sap droplet.

It's dying quicker. Why is it dying quicker? Because I'm going the wrong way? Because I'm going the right one?

I decide to see it like this: when Symeon got close, he died. That's why my rose is wilting. Because I'm getting warmer. Also, I staunchly refuse to lose at my own mind game.

I hold my flower up to the pylon. Gold drips, except…

Except this time, it doesn't detach itself from the stem. It lengthens like a spider thread until it reaches a vine before solidifying. I release the breath I've been holding since…I'm not even sure when.

When the stem begins to harden into gold, I jerk my fingers off Miley's key and watch, with bated breath, as the metal crawls up to the emaciated flower head and gilds it in turn.

"What now?"

The weight of the rose begins to make it list, and as it tips, a grinding resounds throughout the mall and spreads to my ribs.

My heart and head beat in tandem as stems snap and a crack appears in the pylon. I scramble backward, checking the stone floor for a fissure, but all I find are donuts. More glazed circles of dough drop from the rustling vines and roll around my sneakered feet like loose change, flavoring the air.

The pylon splits open with an ear-splitting whine, and a door swings out, gilded rose handle gleaming in the midday light.

I did it!

I found him!

*Hopefully.*

Before the door can slam shut, I lunge forward and yank it wide. I'm expecting stairs that lead into a gloomy basement, but of freaking course, it's not even close to what I find.

# FORTY-FOUR

A playground slide spirals out in front of me, descending not into darkness but into a sky smudged with cotton-candy clouds. *Ugh.* What now? Is this some second stage in my dream-Tarian hunt? Did I open the wrong door?

"Tarian?" My call is tentative, my voice raw with fatigue.

"Calamity?"

Tears prick my nose at the sound of his voice. Of that silly nickname he chose for me.

Inhaling deeply, I close my eyes and press my fingertips into my lids. "Are you awake?"

"I'm sharing your dream."

"I don't mean right this second. I meant...I meant before I carried you here?"

His answer comes so long after my question that I think he may not have heard it. "No."

I'm deeply conflicted, both relieved and saddened for him. Did it play out like Electra thought? Did Yasmin shove Symeon into Tarian? Or did Symeon touch his brother to hurt him? Will his other captors be found floating—

Holy Hades! I stagger back a step. Hundreds of feet beneath me, an ocean foams against a pale shore overrun by ants. I squint. Not ants, people.

"Can we continue this conversation face-to-face?" Tarian's voice claps my eardrums, snipping my attention from the humans milling about below.

"What are you standing on?"

"Isn't this *your* dream?"

"Because you know all that happens in *your* dreams, Hades?"

He mutters something I can't hear before muttering something I can. "A hammock."

"A *large* hammock?" I glance over my shoulder, huffing when I find only solid cement. I guess the only way out is down.

"I'll catch you."

Wonderful.

Just in case he misses, I conjure up a skydiving pack. I spiral once, twice, three times before the male's familiar scowling face appears, along with a familiar hot-pink suit.

His arms lock around me, and although my momentum bowls us over, we don't go flying off into the sunset. My relief combined with Tarian's outfit and the sheer vastness of the net we're sprawled out on propels a bubble of laughter from my lungs. He harrumphs, which only amplifies my amusement.

I lift my head off his chest, then swing my hair behind my shoulder to take another long look at him—priceless. "You should wear pink more often. It really brings out your—"

"Surliness?"

I banish my backpack but not my grin. "I was going to say complexion."

His mouth softens into a smile, but that's all that softens. If anything, his grip on me only hardens.

I press one palm against the slice of bare chest that peeks out from between the pink lapels of the jacket. "You can let go, you know?"

"I know." Yet he keeps holding on.

I imagine it's because he's glad to finally have company. "No longer worried about tattooing me with more of your runes?"

"I should worry, shouldn't I?" With a reluctant sigh, he guides my body off his.

I sit cross-legged on the taut rope. "When you said *hammock*, I was picturing the sort stretched between two palm trees. Not"—I gesture to the giant net strewn with pink and red velvet pillows—"*this*. I mean, we even have fancy throw pillows."

Smirking, he snatches one and props it behind his head. "Any chance I could get another outfit? I've officially lost all sensation in the groin area."

My gaze skips there, to the seam that visibly digs into his nether regions. "Should've taken your pants off."

"And stood in your sky playground buck naked, ignorant of what you had in store for me?"

Feeling merciful, I dismiss the pantsuit and replace it with an item of clothing that makes my dimples dig deep. "Better?"

Tarian lifts his head to take stock of his new accoutrement, then cocks one eyebrow my way. "Interesting."

His bicep bulges as he bends one arm and slots it between velvet pillow and tousled hair before releasing a blissful sigh that I feel glide down the side of my neck.

His lashes sweep low. "Remind me to acquire some Speedos, but in a solid color. I'm not really a leopard print kind of man."

What was intended to irritate the Atlantean and amuse me, backfires. He's amused and I'm...I'm... Is his cock swelling and pulsing? Oh shit, it totally is. Thankfully, his eyes are still shut, so he doesn't catch my transfixed perusal.

I swallow, but it does little to douse the heat spreading through me. "I'll tell Electra to add them to her shopping cart."

Tarian cracks open one lid. "Electra?"

I shrug, but it comes off like a shoulder spasm. "I guess I can remind you at Joslyn and Saul's wedding. I expect we'll both be in attendance, what with Saul being your uncle and Bryn being my best friend and all."

Tarian's lips go rigid at the mention of the wedding. "Planning on avoiding me until then?"

I frown. "Isn't that—" I lick my lower lip. "We'll have no reason to hang out."

"As long as you carry my magic, you and I have plenty of reasons to hang out." It sounds like a warning.

"I won't talk. I already told you." The line of his mouth quirks upward, thrusting my pulse out of alignment. "You better not be planning on locking me up inside one of your manors."

Smile firming, he closes his eye.

"I'm serious, Tarian."

"You sound it."

Teeth gritted, I fling my gaze off his smug face. Instead of landing somewhere safe like the mall or the setting sun, my attention snags on the ridiculous prominence between his thighs.

*Stop looking*, my brain commands, but do my eyes listen? Nope. They rebel. The spandex stretches and stretches, and then the waistband begins to lift, and…is that…?

He hums. "On second thought, I may stock a few animal prints."

I shoot my attention to his face, praying that his lids are still shut, but they're at half-mast, and his lips, at half-smirk.

I capture my windblown locks and snap them back over my shoulder, then plait them to keep them off my heating skin.

"You have a little drool"—Tarian taps the corner of his mouth—"right…here."

I'm about to knuckle my mouth when the man's smirk recasts itself as a devilish grin that makes me realize he's borrowing my sanity for a joyride.

As my body temperature plateaus at a toasty two hundred-plus degrees, I grumble, "How old are you?"

"Thirty-three."

"It's an expression."

"I'm aware. Merely reminding myself."

"Because you often forget your age?"

"I do." A sad smile gusts across his face. "Symeon says the mine messed with more than my blood. He claims it transformed me into a 'veritable fossil.'"

The verb tense Tarian uses rattles me so deeply that my fingers slip off my hair. I swallow, relocating my attention to my sneakered feet, worried my corneas might display the truth that Symeon's dead.

"Even though you didn't choose this connection, Calamity, even though our meetups aren't all fun and games, spending time with you has reminded me that fun can still be had in this pitiless world."

I wonder what sort of fun he means: hanging out in a sky lounge, or watching me blush like a hormonal tween?

When blunt nails brush against my ankle, I gasp, "You shouldn't touch me."

"I know." Yet he keeps touching. Keeps caressing. "My magic doesn't work in this dimension."

"Your point?"

"My runes aren't going anywhere."

I should crawl toward the side of the net. Put some distance between us. And not because I'm worried about getting stung with another one of his runes, because I'm not—after all, I don't wish the man or his magic harm.

Even so, I don't crawl. I stay planted beside him, relishing the feel of a man's hand on my body. Of Tarian's hand.

*He called you a mistake.* The thought, like always, is sobering.

"Your hand isn't going anywhere either." I pin him with a glare which I pray will distract him from noting how affected I am by his touch, by his presence, by his very essence. "After all, it would be a *mistake.*"

His eyes glitter darkly as he wheels onto his side to reach more of me. Even though it should really be the least of my concerns when his fingers spiral up my calf, I try to remember when I last waxed my legs.

I shake away the absurd contemplation and shift my legs to the side. "Fun can still be had, but not with my feelings, Tarian. You may be lonely and bored, but that's not a reason to play with me."

As he hinges back, every rune surges and sinks atop the violent swells of his muscles. The second I wake up, I'm going to rub my clit raw, because I need a clear head around Tarian. And no, I will not picture his fingers while I make myself whimper. I will not picture his face. I will absolutely *not* picture his mouth.

My underwear dampens. I swap it out for a dry thong. While I'm at it, I also replace my denim cutoffs and white tank top with extra roomy and extra unattractive potato-brown flannel pjs dotted with mini pizzas.

I inspect Tarian's Speedo to observe the effect of my new outfit. I scoff when I note that his swollen tip is still wedged between his waistband and stomach, leaking precum onto his happy trail. How can the man still be hard? It's completely aberrant.

I shove up my baggy sleeves, but the material is so heavy, it collapses right back around my fingers. I consider unfastening a few buttons to allow the night air to lick across my overheated chest, but that would defy the purpose of my flannel armor.

"The word on my back, where was it before?" My tone is brusque and dry, unlike the crotch of my newest garment.

"Cute nightwear."

I squeeze my thighs together, willing my core to stop reacting to a man who will only use and discard me. Or imprison me. Or kill me.

He rotates his right arm, vein side up, and nods to a blank space. "On my forearm."

"And your dad's?"

He rotates his right shoulder to display the empty space, and although I see it, I also see another break. Another missing word.

Right where the spell winds around his bicep to spill down the inside of his arm.

Is that where Symeon's mark used to be?

# FORTY-FIVE

I chew on the inside of my cheek as I contemplate the words preceding the first blank space. "What does *maktos da* mean?"

"*Yours to.*"

"And the word after that?"

"You'll have to be more precise. *Maktos da* is inscribed five times in my awakening enchantment. The first sequence leads to the word that killed my father—*itfir.*" Slowly, he murmurs, "*Yours to withdraw.*"

His solemn tone pebbles my skin. "And *yamtelok*?"

"*Possess.*"

I keep reading, my gaze skipping over *maktos da* to the word following it. "*Amalar*?"

"*Carry.*"

"And the next?" *The one that's missing.* Maybe, just maybe, it'll be a palindrome of *itfir*?

*"Samntalik—wield."*

There goes my hypothesis. I chew on the inside of my cheek as I piece together all I've gathered: unconscious Tarian stung his brother with a rune that morphed into a symbol. Unless he gave someone else the rune *wield* and the word on his brother's skin was forged by his captors to make us all believe Tarian killed his own brother?

"Calanthe?"

"Yeah?" I keep staring at the blank piece of skin, keep dwelling on my theory, keep braiding leads in the hope of a lightbulb moment.

"What's caught your attention?" When he peruses his bicep, the blood drains from his face. "Where? Where did I sting you?"

Before I can reassure him that my body wasn't on the receiving end of his rune, he sits up, jostling the net.

"Where?" he barks.

I latch on to the ropes. "Nowhere."

"The rune didn't just evaporate into thin air!"

If only I could penetrate Tarian's subconscious and pick through everything that his dormant mind might have recorded. "It didn't sting me."

"Prove it."

"How?"

"Take off your clothes."

"No."

"Calanthe, this isn't some sleazy way of getting you naked. I just—"

"I understand. My answer is still no."

"Calanthe," he growls.

"Trust. Me."

His eye twitches. "If I didn't sting you, then who the fuck did I give the rune *wield* to?"

*Symeon. Possibly.* "Maybe to one of your captors."

Tarian rams his hand through his hair that glows umber in the sunset. "If I did, then I've doomed us all."

"Not necessarily."

He snorts. "Do you know the meaning of the word *wield*, Miss Bloom?"

I reply with a raised middle finger. After a beat of wrought silence, I say, "I understand you're angry, but that doesn't give you the right to be a condescending jerk. As for your missing rune, maybe it transformed into a symbol or into another word like mine."

"So either I fucking killed someone, or I'm about to share dreams with one of my captors? Here's to hoping it's Yasmin and not Bryn's daddy."

His comment dropkicks my heart. "Why? So you can *seduce* your way to freedom?"

The ghost of a smirk plays on his mouth. "Would that bother you?"

I attempt to flatten my temper, but it comes soaring out. "That might bother your brother." It's low to use the dead as a shield. "Then again, from what I deduced in your train dream, he shares her with Sergeant Lynch, so maybe he wouldn't fucking care." I swipe my tongue over my teeth and suck in my cheeks, trying to relax my mandible before I end up cracking enamel.

"What about you? Do you care?"

"Nope. Like I said the day we met, 'You do you, Hades.'" My tone is as prickly as nettle.

Although it does nothing to claw the amusement off the male's face, it deflates some of the tension thickening the air. At least, the air around him. I'm still too riled up to relax. Also, what if he does start dreaming of Yasmin?

"Calamity Darling, there's not a single woman I'd rather dream about than you."

I side-eye him. "An easy statement to make when you don't have an actual choice in the matter. Also, *darling*?"

The smile he gifts me is dazzlingly white. "It's catchy."

"Let's hope it doesn't catch," I grumble.

He sighs. "Do I get to know why you're mad at me?"

"I'm not mad. You're just giving me emotional whiplash. One second, you're licking whiskey off my mouth, the next you're sticking Mackenzie in the crystallized heels you gave me, and then you're touching me while screaming *mistake*, and now you're trying to get a rise out of me by flinging Yasmin into the mix."

My rant demolishes his smile. "Touching you was the mistake, but it was *my* mistake, not yours. The only sentiment I harbor toward Yasmin is profound abhorrence. As for the shoes, I have no fucking clue what you're talking about."

"In the circus dream, Mackenzie was wearing those sandals that wrap—"

A dent appears between his eyebrows.

"Never mind. Doesn't matter."

"It matters to you, so it matters to me. Tell me about this offensive footwear."

Am I misremembering them? What if she was wearing glittery tights and crystal-embellished shoes, and my mind saw what it wanted to see? Or rather, what it *didn't* want to see?

"Talk to me."

I scrub my hands up my face, then through my hair. "So you don't like Yasmin because she may be holding you hostage, or you never liked her?"

"Talk to me about Mackenzie and the shoes."

"No."

"Calanthe."

"She's everything I'm not, all right? She has everything I don't. I didn't want her to have"—*you*—"my shoes."

He releases a protracted exhale. "Once I break free, I will hire a designer whose sole purpose in life will be creating footwear for you. He will never produce more than a single pair, and that pair will only ever grace your feet, and once you're done with them, we'll burn them so they can never find their way into someone else's closet."

My chest stings. My lids, too. "It would be a crime to burn shoes."

He releases a melodramatic sigh. "Then I'll just have to add shelves inside my dungeon to store all the pairs that cease to bring you joy."

A strange ache seizes my heart, a combination of ardent melancholy and improbable affection. How can a man who has nothing in common with my father, besides an appreciation for travertine, make me think so acutely of him?

I knead my breastbone. "You're ridiculous."

His expression is soft. So soft, it makes me want to cry. I must be PMSing. That's the only explanation I can find. Why else would I feel like weeping over a conversation about dungeons and shoes? Then again, I'm monumentally tired and hungry, a mix that could very well be to blame for my pathetic state. On a side note, this would explain the pizzas flecking my pjs and the donuts on the pylon.

"You'll want display cases, not shelves." I keep massaging the skin over my heart, trying to ease the messy beats. "You know, because of blood splatter."

Tarian's gentle smile strengthens into a dazzling curve. "Solid point, Miss Bloom."

The wind ruffles his dark hair, catapulting the scent of spice and brine toward me. Does he smell like the ocean because we sit above it or because that's the location of his real body?

Since he hasn't woken up, asking about his whereabouts would be futile, so I ask instead, "Do you really have an in-house dungeon?"

He arches a provocative eyebrow. "You'll just have to explore my home to find out."

"Explore, huh? Here I thought I'd be locked up in some tower until the rune took me."

His molars grind. "The rune won't take you."

I regret pressing my finger against this raw nerve. For once, I hadn't meant to bring up my uncertain future.

"Yasmin," I end up saying. "You said you weren't a fan of hers. Is there a particular reason?"

"The woman came to Boston with an agenda, a design on my family."

*On you,* I think, but bite my tongue. One jealous outburst was enough.

"She's not with Symeon for the right reasons."

*She's not with Symeon at all.*

"I believe she funnels money into his account. I'm not quite certain what he gives her in return, though." He narrows his eyes on the line of liquid gold that demarcates sky and sea. "Possibly his blood?"

*Or yours.*

"I've put off dealing with this for months. As soon as I wake up, I'll get to the bottom of their rapport."

"He gave her access to you," I murmur.

Tarian's gaze hurtles off the horizon.

I shrug. "Obviously, spur-of-the-moment kidnappings happen, but an abduction of this magnitude—capturing *you*—that takes planning."

"Are you saying that my brother and Yasmin have pretended to date for months to trap me?"

I hold his stare, communicating my answer wordlessly.

"How did they know I'd use my power to keep you alive?"

"Luck?"

"I don't believe in luck."

"Maybe they'd planned for it to go down that night, and I was just conveniently *there.*"

"My brother was in the car with me the night you threw a rose at my windshield. He commented on your tits and I fucking jumped down his throat. I usually never react." Tarian kneads his temples. "And then he looked up the name of your shop and made the connection with Bryn. *Fuck.* He must've compelled Mackenzie to hire you."

"If I'd arrived on time, our paths wouldn't have crossed."

"They would've. I was supposed to get home earlier, but he wanted to sit down with Vic to discuss patenting his lab-grown

Atlantean diamonds. He kept dragging the meeting out. And then at some point, he just stood up, grabbed his baubles, and reminded me that I was hosting a party so I should get home."

His eyes glaze over, and I wonder if he's back at that meeting with his lawyer and brother, or if something's happening to his body in the real world. When he doesn't flicker out of existence, when his lips don't warp into a grimace, the pressure in my lungs eases.

"I didn't just walk into his trap, I ran head-fucking-first."

"Technically, I'm the one who did the running head-first." When my quip doesn't blow away his somber mood, I sigh. "Tarian, if your brother truly is the brains behind all of this, could he have dosed you with something that made your magic volatile?"

A vein snaps at his temple. "It's possible."

However awful, I'm suddenly glad Symeon is dead.

"During our last dream, you said Symeon phoned Electra." Why must Tarian's memory be so crisp? "Why did he call?"

I toy with the idea of confessing the truth, but he already feels such guilt toward his father. Even if Symeon was deserving of his fate, Tarian's heart will inevitably take a beating at the news.

*What if he didn't end Sym's life, though?* I refuse to discard that option. It's this persistent doubt that beats the confession off my tongue.

"What did my brother have to say, Calanthe?"

"The call was to inform us that his boat sank." *There. Not a lie.* "The *Amapola* hit a reef—"

"Why the fuck are you dreaming about my brother naked?" Tarian's growl makes my heartbeats clatter against one another.

"What?"

He sweeps his arm toward the inky surf below and the nude body edged in foam.

"How do you even know what he looks like without his clothes? Has he disrobed in front of you?"

My forehead slickens before creasing, because... Hasn't he noticed the dead part?

"So help me, Gaea, if he has," he snarls. "I will murder him."

As though to echo his mood, the sky rumbles, then lights up, but not with a storm—with fireworks. Pink and green and yellow embers swirl over our heads, a bouquet of colored tinsel. Did my mind conjure up this show to distract Tarian from—

My spine snaps into alignment. "Where's the mall? And the slide?"

When Tarian's expression slackens, I take it he's only just noted their disappearance, too.

Oddly enough, we stay afloat, the untethered sides of our net snapping in the wind. That's what I get for watching *Aladdin* a few too many Sunday mornings with my father. Is a big blue genie about to appear to grant me three wishes? How convenient would that be? I know exactly what I'd request. For my mother's brain to heal. For my father to be alive. For Tarian to be free.

Another burst flashes across the sky. It's so bright that it paints the beach in full color.

The beach that's surging toward us. Or are we gliding toward it? Whatever's happening, it's not good, because the nearer we get, the more discernible Symeon's rigor mortis becomes.

I realize that I can't hide the youngest Hadez's fate from Tarian forever, but I *can* hide it a while longer. *Please, please, don't let me be the one to break the news*, I implore the Atlantean goddess. *Let me preserve the man from heartache and guilt until he wakes up. Please.*

"Calanthe!" Tarian pushes to his feet, the writing on his skin as incandescent as the glittery sprays overhead, as incandescent as his wild stare. "Wake up! You've got to wake up!"

His face is bone-white and glazed with so much perspiration that I assume he suffers from motion sickness or vertigo like my father, but I'm wrong. It isn't our vertical velocity that's spurring his anguish.

No, he's agitated because our collapsing ride is on fire.

# FORTY-SIX

I call upon Gaea who poured Her magic into my veins, imploring Her to buffer our fall with a forcefield, or at the very least to keep our bones from splintering upon impact.

Malachi may be able to heal Calanthe in the real world, but the mere idea of her aching bludgeons my soul, and the mere idea of his hands on her body fills me with aggression.

"Come—the bloody hell—on," I mutter. Though my runes grow increasingly hot and bright, I cannot harness their magic to shape an airflow. "Calanthe!" Her name tears from my throat as painfully as the runes ripped off my skin.

Well, two of them.

I didn't feel the third one lift.

I can't believe I fucking lost a third.

Another pyrotechnic device booms, spitting sparks that slap our hammock and ignite new fires. Calanthe's knuckles pale around the ropes, and her lids clench, rucking the delicate skin at her temples.

As fire shrinks our floating pallet, I fall to my knees in front of her and grip either side of her face. "It's only a dream, darling. We're not dying. It's only a dream."

Her lashes rise, revealing pupils barely larger than the freckles that dust her nose. Does she fear the fall? Does she fear my touch? I attempt to let go, but can't, and not because of any magic, but because her anguish rids me of both common sense and willpower.

I trace the edge of her sharp jaw with the pad of my thumb as I repeat, "Wake up."

A shiver distresses her body, distressing mine in turn. Heart storming, I pull back to assess the nearness of the ground and the fire's progress. Both are too close.

I try, once more, to bargain for a divine intervention, but Gaea is deafeningly quiet. She's abandoned me. She's abandoned *us*. What malice to have placed Calanthe inside my bleak world, to have embroiled her in my rotten reality. Is her suffering my punishment for snuffing out Father's life, or is this some wicked trial to assess whether the *Blessed Son* is still worthy?

Unless…

Unless this has nothing to do with me and everything to do with the mine? Could something have happened to it? Could someone have toyed with it? Tried to destroy it? Squeezed magic from its stones?

As I twist that last contemplation over in my mind, the rancid, muggy air shrivels my lungs and elicits a wet cough, which I muffle against my shoulder. If someone has meddled with the mine, it would explain my inability to break out of my catatonic state. It would also explain why my runes are leaking out of me left and right. The newest gap in my verse itches as we plummet, reminding me that I may have given one of my attackers the power to wield, but to wield what, though? My blood? *Fuck.* That better not be it.

"Spare us, and I'll tell him. Please, Gaea." Calanthe's tremulous appeal whips me out of my head.

The ground is getting close, the people on it large enough for me to make out a few familiar faces. My gaze lingers on two—Saul's and Joslyn's. They observe our fiery plunge with a mixture of pity and complacency, as though our fall is both inevitable and enjoyable. I realize that this is Calanthe's dream, and thus, a projection of her views, yet chills incise my spine, exacerbated by Joslyn's dark satin gown that snaps against Saul's black suit and the floral wreath they carry.

I tip Calanthe's face up. "We're not dying."

Her eyes are still closed, and everyone around us, still garbed for a wake.

"Did you hear me? This isn't our funeral."

Her throat moves over a shallow swallow. "I know." She inhales a shaky breath and finally opens her eyes. They glisten like the ocean. Blaze like the flames. "I'm so sorry, Tarian."

"You've nothing to feel sorry about."

"I do. This is happening because...because—" She licks her mouth.

"Tell me once we land, all right?"

"What if we—"

"Calamity." I sink my fingers deeper into her hair, drive my thumbs harder against her skin. "We. Are not. Dying."

"But I can't conjure a chute. I've tried. The same way I can't wake up."

"You don't need a chute. You've got me." Praying I won't transfer any more runes, I get to my feet and hold out my hand. "Let go of the net now."

The hesitation and fear that dilate her pupils are a jab to the heart. Why would she trust the architect of her nightmares to save her? Yet her fingers tear free, and she rises, eyes lambent and hair untamed. Gone is the trepidation that kept her down. In its place is a determination to survive, to fight this fate, to endure this hell.

I waste a heartbeat admiring her and another desiring her. And then I snap into action and scoop her up. She tangles her arms around my neck and curls her head into my chest.

I crush her to me, feeling the panic rattling her heart, the dent of her fisted hands, the point of each knuckle. "Remember that this world isn't real."

"But we are." Her croaked murmur fans across my throat, tightening my Adam's apple and angering its relentless jostle.

I suddenly picture her body being ripped from my arms. Her neck breaking. Her skin tearing. Her blood gushing. What if this is the end I feared the night I caught my rune glowing on her skin? What if this is the moment my magic kills her?

*No.* She will not die in my arms. Not tonight. Not any night.

I focus on the sand, on the distance remaining between us and it. When I estimate we're close enough, I lurch through the fire, curling myself around her as we drop. My feet burn—I imagine they picked up a few flames along the way. I can't bother to care, especially when the beachscape brightens, then darkens into a whole new dreamscape.

One without sand and without fire, without mourners clutching sympathy wreaths, and without naked brothers splashing about in the waves.

# FORTY-SEVEN

Tarian curses a blue streak as he wobbles and flails forward, sending us hurtling into—

Into…

I peel my face off his chest to peek past his shoulder, because never has sand been this springy. Maybe dream-sand is though?

*Ah.* Although his runes burn with the light of a thousand moons, so does the color-changing bulb in the floral fabric lampshade dangling over us.

I let my head fall back on a groan. Not only are we alive, but we're also no longer on the beach. I have never, *ever* been so glad to be enclosed by four solid walls—even if these walls are papered with pink roses and boy-band posters.

It's probably a matter of minutes before my mind throws something unpleasant my way. After all, I haven't had a nice, peaceful, boring sleep since I met Tarian. Regardless, I'm still thankful for our newest whereabouts.

Muttering a string of Atlantean curses beneath his breath, Tarian slides his arms out from behind my back, pries his muscled body off mine, and flops back onto the perfect replica of the orchid-patterned comforter which has graced my mattress since I graduated from crib to big-girl bed.

Granted, it doesn't seem fit for an adult, what with such an impressive male specimen stretched across it, feet dangling off the side, even though half of him is propped against the powder-purple headboard.

Tarian inspects the perfect reproduction of my childhood haven with the meticulousness of a crime scene investigator. "Old bedroom?"

"Current bedroom." I've toyed with the idea of tearing off the wallpaper and painting my walls a sensible, adult shade, but I was worried change would perplex my mother.

"One Direction. A fan?"

"Diehard." A smile creeps over my mouth at his slight grimace. "They didn't make it onto your playlists?"

He slides me a look that kindles a laugh followed by a cough from my aching lungs—damn dream-fumes. Although he doesn't return my grin, his eyes are soft on my face. Soft and sobering.

The man seems at his wit's end, and here I am poking fun at him. I'm about to apologize when he lifts a framed picture off my nightstand. It's a shot of my parents standing against the glass facade of Bloom's Blooms on the day of its inauguration. My mother has her arms crossed in front of her chest and wears the most dazzling grin. My father also smiles, but unlike Mom, he isn't staring into the camera; he's staring at her.

"You look like your father."

I arch an eyebrow.

"What?"

"My dad looks like a Viking."

"And?"

"And I took after my mom."

"You may not be as tall and flaxen-haired, but let me reassure you, you're just as terrifying and fierce as any Viking."

"You're so full of crap, Hades. I am the absolute *least* terrifying person on planet Earth *and* a total coward to boot." Symeon's corpse flashes before my eyes. I blink him away, which just serves to prove my point.

"A coward wouldn't stand up to me, yet you do." He sits up in bed, which makes his stomach flex, and holy wow. I have to cross my legs to keep my ovaries from racing out and shrieking that they volunteer as tribute to save him from a life of physical isolation.

"Because our interactions aren't real."

He returns the frame to my nightstand. "The scenery and people may not be real, but every word we exchange, every look" —his gaze scrolls over what little skin I have on display, creating a trail of heat that spills far and wide—"every touch"—he hovers his palm over my stomach, hesitating a heartbeat before letting it land—"those are *all* real."

My ovaries sigh, elbowing one another to get nearer to his palm. I truly, deeply hate how weak I am to resist Tarian. Also, how can a simple, localized touch make so much of me tingle? Because he's a magical being? Because the ties that bind us are? Or do I self-combust in his presence because of my prolonged dry spell?

I try to picture another man's hands on my body. The sheer contemplation curdles my stomach. "I know why we landed in my bed."

"Do tell," he all but hums.

"We're here to work our mutual attraction out of our systems."

Tarian grows eerily still.

"Because this thing between us is screwing with our focus." Since Tarian has yet to speak, I add, "We don't even have to bother with preliminaries."

The air turns ripe with the electricity of an impending storm. I'm half expecting lightning to fork across my ceiling, thunder to howl at my window, and rain to crack the plaster and flood my room, but no freak tempest hits.

"I can transfer runes in my sleep, Calanthe." Tarian's words are as measured as his tone. "For all we know, they can leak from my blood in this realm, too."

Ah, yes. I sensed he wouldn't throw caution to the torrid wind of our communal yearning. "Your runes can reshape themselves. Since I already wear one, I don't see why your magic would waste another on me when it can just tweak the one on my spine at will."

He lapses back into silence.

"If you're not convinced—"

"Tell me something about yourself that no one else knows."

"What? Why?"

"Because I want to get to know you."

"I've just given you a free pass to skip over all that first-date tedium and head directly to fourth base."

"I don't want to *skip* over anything with you." His pinkie begins to graze the fabric of my pjs, sketching tiny arcs over the brown flannel. "Especially not the preliminaries. Now, give me one of your secrets."

My cheeks heat. "Any sane, *unattached* man would jump on my offer."

"When did I ever claim to be sane?"

His steady caress sparks a shallow blaze over my skin. One that spreads both high and low. That seeps into my core and beneath my ribs. That engorges my heart, making it strike harder, faster, brighter.

"I don't have secrets from Bryn." Well, one, but I doubt Tarian would enjoy hearing about the time her hockey player ex cornered me after social studies to tell me how hard I made him before proceeding to show me by steering my hand to his crotch.

After freezing up from revulsion, I'd relocated my hand to his testicles and crushed them through the fabric of his sweatpants, hissing that if he ever laid a finger on me or Bryn, I'd phone up Daddy Lynch, who was a decorated sniper. He must've heard about the sergeant's proficiency with rifles because he broke things off that very night with her and never again approached me.

Tarian sighs. "Fine." His pinkie nail bumps into one of my pizza-shaped buttons. "Then tell me whatever it was that you wanted to say when you thought we were dying."

Secret it is.

I dig through my memories until I locate the perfect story to tell someone who won't be sharing my life for much longer. *And not because I die*, my mind rushes to add, *but because I save him, and we go our separate ways*. My spine prickles as though to remind me that this may not be possible, but mind over rune, and all that. I forge ahead with my self-deprecating tale before I can further dwell on our inopportune magical connection.

"Back in college, I decided to give myself a Brazilian wax." I imagine he knows what that is. If he doesn't, the rest of my story will fill in the blanks. "I was trying to save money, but also, believe it or not, spreading my legs in front of strangers made me crazy uncomfortable. Anyway, I misread the instructions on the label and zapped the wax too long in the microwave. When I smeared it on, I screamed and passed out."

I grimace as I recall how my foot had slipped off my table and hit my desk chair, which had shot away.

"Anyway, when I woke up spread-eagled on my dorm room rug, the wax had hardened. Took me almost an hour to peel the damn thing off. I sweat through the whole process and almost passed out a second time. Long story short, I lost a layer of skin, my ability to sit for almost a month, and a pretty impressive amount of dignity when I had to walk the cute on-call doctor through the events that led to a bump on the head and a burn on the labia. To add insult to injury, he insisted on taking a look at the damage before prescribing ointments. Cherry on top of the cake? I now have a patch of permanently discolored skin I've been passing off as a birthmark."

I expect Tarian to snort, possibly even laugh, but he's gone all stone-faced and lugubriously silent.

As the bulb lacquers his stiff features green, then pink, then orange, my brow furrows. "Was that too much for your masculine sensibilities?"

His jaw strikes a perfect perpendicular angle. "You've been passing it off as a birthmark to whom?"

I start at his gruffness. Here I thought I'd disgusted him, but that isn't the emotion zinging off the big guy. No, the man sounds pissed off.

"My gynecologist, my ex-boyfriends, and the lady who now lasers the area." No way in hell will hot wax ever be slathered there again. Not even by a professional.

His pinkie sneaks under the placket of my shirt. Where it meets skin, goosebumps erupt. He slides another finger beneath the flannel and then a third and a fourth. Only his thumb remains atop.

"That's a fuck lot of people." His timbre is as stern as the look he gives me.

I rear back. "That's like, six people! Not that my number is *any* of your concern." I shake my head. "If I'd known you'd react like a total creep, I would've told you the story of my aversion to artificial grapes. Actually, I wouldn't have told you *any* story. Seriously"—another headshake—"who are *you* to judge *me*?"

His nostrils flare.

I bat his hand away. When that fails, I grip his wrist and tug. "I've changed my mind about sleeping with you."

I manage to extricate his fingers from underneath my shirt, mostly because he doesn't put up any resistance. When I try to fling his arm away though, he flattens his hand against my stomach and glides it down to the intersection of my thighs.

My breath catches in my lungs when the heel of his palm hits my pubic bone and his middle finger unspools against the seam of my pajama bottoms.

"I know I've no right to mentally pick off every person who's so much as glanced at your scarred cunt"—he clamps his hand over me, eliciting a startled gasp from my mouth—"but Gaea preserve their mind and eyes if our paths ever cross."

His aggression should *not* be sexy. But damn, it hits me right in the girly bits.

"And let's clear up a few more things. I'd never judge you for the number of men you've slept with, but I'll always hate it. Hate *them*"—he curls his upper body over mine—"because it feels like they took something that's *mine*."

I hum. Yeah, *hum*. I'm so easily manipulated. "It's the rune that makes you feel this way."

"No." Tarian drives his middle finger against my pj bottoms, wedging the seam into my folds. "I wanted you the instant you tossed that rose at my car."

The combination of rough timbre and marvelous pressure makes me mewl.

"Does that scare you?"

The only thing that scares me is him coming to his senses and remembering that I'm a trifling human.

"Tell me to stop, and I'll obey, Calamity. And I'll never touch you again, even if it kills me."

In spite of multiple deep swallows, my voice comes out all scratchy. "I'm not scared."

*Lie.* I'm terrified that he's going to chew me up and spit me out. That once I've had him, I'll be unsatisfied with any future lover. That the word on my back will end up transforming once I've served my purpose.

I lock away these confessions and toss away the key, because I'd prefer to die with Tarian's hands on my body than to exist without ever knowing his touch.

"Should I fuck off"—he curls his middle finger and drags the tip up to my clit, then back down—"or fuck you?"

New fireworks explode, this time in my head. They brighten the neon air and haze my ability for rational thought.

"What'll it be, Calanthe darling?"

"Fuck me," I breathe out.

# FORTY-EIGHT

The roguish gleam that ignites Tarian's eyes makes my heart hurdle over a thousand beats before puddling at his feet.

"Good," he rasps, "because I'd have been extraordinarily disappointed not to see your scar."

A sharp breath saws into my lungs.

"How about you make these clothes disappear?"

That's right. I forgot I had that power. Instead of making them vanish, however, I replace them with something I sense the Atlantean will enjoy more than bare skin.

Sure enough, the man's finger stills its assault on my wanton flesh, and his eyes blacken with lust. Not even the light from my color-changing bulb manages to penetrate.

"Are you trying to finish me off before I even get started?" Tarian's heavy breathing whooshes across my lids, driving my lashes low.

I smile as his gaze devours the lace and velvet underthing I've magicked on—a thong bodysuit that ties up my front with strategically placed bands of velvet. The flat ribbon crisscrosses over my ribcage, then over my nipples before tying around my neck with a bow. I saw it in a lingerie shop eons ago and had every intention of buying it, but the price tag had me bolting from the boutique as though it were infested with furry spiders.

Tarian caresses the lace before smoothing his palm over my bare hip and then higher, over the latticework of ribbons that mold to my palpitating stomach. When he reaches my breasts, he flicks a lock of my hair away, then traces the skin that, for once, isn't corralled by any band or wire. His slow, thorough quest ripples upward, tightening my nipples into points that threaten to carve up the taut ribbon.

While he knuckles my pebbled areolas, he presses his nose to my temple, then runs its tip down my cheek until his mouth aligns with my ear. "If anyone wakes you up any time soon, I will murder them."

I'd murder them first.

Slowly, he props himself up on his magnificent forearms, then drapes one leg over mine and rolls. His knees land on either side of my thighs, jostling both the mattress and my pulse. I survey him with my eyes first, then with my hands. I fan my fingertips over every jagged bone, every rounded muscle, every strained tendon. I circumvent his navel to follow the thickening trail of hair toward the shiny, swollen tip peeking from the leopard spandex.

When I skim the small, tight slit, his large body shudders and a bead of moisture dampens my skin. I hunt his gaze as I carry my wet finger to my lips to taste him.

Like spilled ink, his pupils dilate, absorbing into his irises. "A word of warning"—the runes on his biceps glitter as he brushes a kiss to the hollow of my collarbone—"you've awakened the beast, Calamity Darling, and beasts aren't always gentle when they devour."

"Devour away, Beast."

Tarian's mouth curves as it crests my left breast, lingering on a tiny freckle before plucking the velvet and lace off my nipple with his teeth. Once free, he takes the bud into his mouth and sucks.

My spine arches off the mattress and my lashes flutter closed. It's been a *really* long time since anyone has had their mouth on my body. Not to mention that Tarian isn't just anyone. He's… He's…

He lashes my wet nipple with his tongue before swirling it and suckling anew.

"*My* beast." Stars ignite on the backs of my lids, and a slow, tortured moan floats past my teeth.

He releases me with a shallow pop, then rises to his knees. "That's right, darling. *Yours.* Now be a good girl and hook the fabric between those plump lips of yours and pull it aside for me." When all I do is blink at him, he smirks and maneuvers my hand south. "Your thong, please."

I tremble as I draw the soaked fabric aside for him.

He smooths his palms over my thighs, which he parts farther.

His throat dips once, twice before he brings one finger to my scar and traces its kinked edges. "Who would've thought the devil would one day kneel before the pearly gates"—he ghosts his callused fingertip back up the patch of paler skin—"and demand entry?"

Even though the state of my sanity is touch and go at the moment, his words patter against my ears and elicit heart palpitations, followed by an eyeroll. One he fails to notice, concentrated as he is on my body's holy gateway. Though my pussy and I are both extremely flattered, I'm neither an angel nor the keeper of—

Oh.

*Oh…*

Tarian's finger has traipsed off my scar and landed on that tiny, magical bud, the one that can empty a mind of thoughts and the body of liquid heat when flicked right and long enough. Irrationally, I think long enough in Tarian's case might be, like, five seconds.

I groan when after only two—*two!*—targeted strokes, he forsakes my clit. Mischief glosses his expression as his finger travels down my folds. He knows how desperate I am for an orgasm, which is why he's withholding it from me. *Ass.* When he spears his digit inside my center, I rescind my name-calling and bask in the acute, blinding jolt of pleasure.

"My, my, how tight you are, Calamity Darling."

"It's been a really long," I choke out. "Time."

He leisurely pumps his finger, then adds a second one, and…

Oh.

My.

God.

*Gah.*

I whimper, but not from pain. Okay, there's a tiny, teeny bit of discomfort, but there's a significantly larger portion of utter delight.

One that rises to a crescendo when he says, "I cannot wait to get you on my dick."

"I cannot wait"—I moan—"to get on your dick."

A look of raw, masculine satisfaction drapes across his features.

Panting like I've sprinted around the Common, I wheeze out, "I'm ready."

"No. You're a long, *long* way from ready for me."

"Because you have a pornstar dick?"

He snorts. "Because you haven't come multiple times on my face."

I gape, struck mute by his reply. I know some men enjoy giving oral sex—my very sexually active best friend confirmed this—but I never imagined I'd find one of these unicorns.

As he works me, he scoots his body low on the bed, then drops a forearm along my thigh and grips my hip. I pick my head off the mattress to watch him. It's silly, but I want visual confirmation that he's eager to do this.

"Why have you gone all tense on me?"

I bite my lip. "Are you sure?"

"That I want to do *this*?" He licks me from entrance to clit before resuming fingering me.

"Yes?"

"Didn't we already establish that your ex was a selfish prick who didn't deserve you?" He sweeps the flat of his tongue over me again, and I swear I hear a choir of baby angels sing.

Adult ones, too.

There's *a lot* of singing. A little off-key, but the melody is still enchanting.

"I said no interruptions, Calamity," Tarian snarls against my wet flesh. "Tell them to fuck off."

"Hmm. What? The angels?"

"*Angels*?" He hooks his finger inside of me, which springs a choked scream from my lungs. "Angels are banging on your door?"

"What?"

"Your door. Banish whoever's there." After a slow lick, he adds a low, "Please," that does nothing to restore my lucidity. If anything, my mind frays a little more.

"Stop. I can't concentrate. What—"

Three rapid knocks sound on my door, dispelling the haze clouding my mind. When another insistent knock echoes through the bedroom, Tarian growls.

I purse my lips because this is so freaking typical of my sexy dreams. I get all hot and bothered, and then *poof*, my alarm blares, or my mind screeches, "*Cut*," and plunges into a segment where I have a plane to catch but forgot to pack my suitcase and need to ride a turtle to get to the airport, which is, naturally, a thousand miles away.

"Callie, baby?" my mother calls out.

The scrap of red lace skids off my crooked finger. I swallow, my pulse ramping up, even though I know this isn't real and that my mother isn't actually there. Someone laughs; someone else sings. A chorus of someones.

Tarian settles back on his heels, ebony locks gliding over his strong brow.

"Your father got the carolers to come inside the shop. Hopefully, it'll attract customers. We really need them, or it'll be handmade gifts again this year. Anyway, it's so lovely. Come. You're missing out."

My breath stops dead against my ribs. I'm aware this is make-believe, yet I sit up so brusquely that I almost topple off the bed.

Tarian watches me from beneath bunched brows. "How bad is your family's financial situation?"

I blink at him. "It's—it doesn't matter. My father's here."

"How bad?"

"Not now, Tarian."

I think he may pursue his line of questioning, but surprisingly, he says, "We better get dressed, or your parents will think me a pool boy with paltry taste in swimwear."

"We don't have a pool." I'm not sure why *this* is what I choose to say instead of, *Sorry I didn't send them away*, or *Thank you for understanding.*

He leans over me and spears his fingers through my hair until he reaches the back of my skull. Cupping it, he brings our foreheads together. "If at any point it becomes too much, just let me know, and I'll find a way to dismiss them, all right?" And then he brushes the sweetest, softest kiss along my cheekbone, liquefying the stone between my ribs until it floods my veins.

Tarian asserts we have agency in these dreams, but what if he's wrong? What if I control all he does and says?

He tucks a piece of hair behind my ear. "Are you okay?"

I'm falling for a stranger, a man who haunts my dreams, and I'm about to see my dead father, so no, I'm not okay. I'm the furthest thing from okay.

"Yep. Fine." My fake smile must lack verve, because Tarian's eyes glint with concern.

The jagged ball in my throat expands as I add up all his quali-ties—empathetic, protective, jealous, muscled, huge dick, hung up on making me come—and arrive at the conclusion that he's not real.

Yes, I'm aware he exists since I've met him, but real-Tarian cannot possibly match dream-Tarian. Which is why we haven't found him! Because the man kneeling between my legs, the one whose forehead is still pressed to mine, is some magical trick of the mind. Some character I've erected in real-Tarian's image, but who's not actually him, because dream-sharing isn't an Atlantean power. It's just *my* power.

I shove back my surging disillusionment before conjuring us some clothes, then I untangle myself from Tarian and stand.

Magical torture, that's what these dreams are. They may not end up withdrawing my blood, but they'll end up withdrawing my sanity. It's only a matter of time until that happens.

Tarian extends his hand. I stare at it for so long that his eyebrows bend.

"We don't have to leave this room if you don't want to."

Except I want to see my father. I want to hug him, even if he's not real.

I feed my fingers through Tarian's and let him pull me toward the door. When it sweeps open onto the shop instead of the living room, I don't bat an eyelash. *Make-believe. All of it, make-believe.*

"Who's this?" my mother's dream-clone asks, the bulb at the tip of Rudolph's nose reddening the surrounding yarn.

As I stare at the sweater my father gave her during their first Christmas together, I say, "He's the man of my dreams."

I stare up into Tarian's beautiful face, wishing he existed in more than these fantasies, but odds are, this version that I've crafted is nothing like the true version of the Atlantean mob boss.

Odds are the true version won't remember the girl with the slumber rune.

"My Nick."

# FORTY-NINE

"Is that a Yuletide expression?" I whisper into Calanthe's ear as she leads me into a shop filled with red and white flowers, fairy lights shaped like snowflakes, a tree that glitters with tinsel, raucous caroling, and a very tall man dressed like a Christmas elf.

"Is what a Yuletide expression?"

"The *your Nick* comment?"

"Nick's my father's name. He's the perfect man. He was my mother's everything."

I stop walking, bringing Calanthe to such an abrupt halt that her body twirls toward mine. "Are you calling me perfect, Miss Bloom?"

Her hazel eyes brush across my face. "Unfortunately."

"Unfortunately? Why Unfortunately?"

"Because you aren't real."

"I'm real."

Her dimples tuck into her cheeks as she slides her lips together.

I lift her hand to my face and force her to touch me. "I'm real."

"I meant—"

Before she can tell me what she meant, a voice that could only be described as boomingly chipper rings out beside us, "I hear I have someone important to meet?"

The elf man stands beside us, his cheeks as high in color as the turtleneck sweaterdress Calanthe has donned. Her hand slips from my face, and she spins.

"Daddy," she breathes, her batting lashes clumping with emotion.

Where there's no mistaking that Calanthe is her mother's daughter, her resemblance to the tall, grinning blond is even more pronounced than in the picture. It's in the almond shape of their eyes and razor-sharp jawlines, in their identical dimples and the proud tilt of their heads, in their squared shoulders and lithe figures.

He stares at her with so much fondness, so much adoration, that I ball my fingers at my sides, wishing he still had blood in his veins that I could call upon to resurrect him, because without blood, there's no reviving the dead.

"What's with the tears, sweet pea?" One of Nick's light brown eyebrows spikes.

Having dreamed of my own father recently, I'm aware that this version of the man is a fabrication of Calanthe's imagination, but I'm also aware that the love he projects is genuine. It's the love that Calanthe will carry in her heart, always.

"I'm just happy to see you," she croaks.

"You look it." Nick snorts and shakes his head, which agitates the bell on his slouchy elf hat. "Doesn't she?"

I stroke her waist with my thumb, hoping it will help ground her. "It's so nice to finally meet Calanthe's benchmark for masculine excellence."

Nick's dimples dig deeper. "You've briefed this one, I see."

*This one?*

Calanthe mumbles, "My exes weren't *all* bad."

Nick harrumphs. "They were passably friendly and didn't appreciate my baby girl the way she deserved to be appreciated."

"No one would ever have been good enough in your opinion, Daddy." Her red-slicked lips barely shift over the words, yet I somehow hear them over the caroler's rendition of "Killing Me Softly," an odd choice for a holiday jam.

They must reach her father's ears as well, because he asks, "What's with the past tense?"

The breath Calanthe inhales is both brisk and tremulous. "I was distracted by the music. Sorry."

Nick scrutinizes his daughter for a long while, as though waiting for her to repeat the sentence in the present tense. When she doesn't, he finally breaks the silence. "Do I get to know the name of your boyfriend?"

"He's not—" Calanthe bites her lip.

Nick tips his head. "Not...?"

She keeps torturing her beautiful mouth. I believe she's loath to call me her boyfriend, but when she glances up at me, her expression isn't veiled with distress but with sorrow.

"Not..." she tries again, but again, holds off on finishing her sentence.

My gut churns as my mind fires off endings, all that displease me. "What Calanthe's trying to say is that I'm not her boyfriend, Mr. Bloom. I'm her fiancé. And my name is Tarian Hadez. Pleasure to make your acquaintance."

Calanthe's mouth pops open.

"Didn't you two just meet?" Nick narrows his grass-green eyes on me, then on his daughter.

Her lids spasm. Her entire face, for that matter. Her manic twitching sends her tiny candy cane earrings frolicking against the dark mass of her unbound hair.

"When one finds one's soulmate, one doesn't wait. Isn't that right, Mr. Bloom?"

The word soulmate clears his gaze of suspicion as effectively as compulsion. "I suppose you're right."

"You suppose?" Although her eyelids are still twitchy, Calanthe's tone is smooth. "You didn't even wait a full month before you asked Mom to marry you."

"But *she*, sweet pea, made me wait on her answer for *two* years." Although he doesn't question his daughter's decision to marry me out loud, it infuses the air.

"Life's too short to wait for certain things, Dad." She stares up at me, her jewel eyes drawing me so deep into their depths that the line between reality and charade begins to waver and fade.

How dangerous.

"Well, then." Nick holds out his hand. "Welcome to the family, Tarian."

Although firm, his skin exudes the cloying chill of death. The second the handshake ends, I surreptitiously scrape my palm against the leg of my black trousers and pull Calanthe closer, craving her warmth and her vigor.

Nick rubs his palms together, and I think he's getting rid of the feel of *my* skin, until he says, "One step closer to grandpadom."

The quietest, most heartrending whimper rises out of Calanthe.

I tug her even closer. Her red and white-striped heels click against the tiled green floor as she lists toward me and pillows her wet cheek on my shoulder. Have I completely stopped fearing another rune will lift off my skin and sting her? No. But I'm so selfish, so beguiled, so fucking needy that I've convinced myself that my magic won't harm her any more than it already has.

"What's with the tears, sweet pea?"

"It's just been an emotional day, Daddy."

"I bet." He shoots me a kind smile before returning his tender gaze to his daughter. "Did you tell your mother yet?"

Calanthe shakes her head, which prompts him to scan the

shop, on the lookout for his wife, who's wandered over to a drink fountain manned by a purple-haired senior citizen.

"He used to tease me that I was merely a means to an end." Calanthe's words are soft yet sink into my chest like bullets. "And that end was becoming a grandfather."

Keeping one hand pinned to her waist, I raise the other to brush the tears off her cheeks. Though I understand her sadness, it's oddly easier for me since I never contemplated starting a family—to my father's great regret—so I never pictured him surrounded by grandkids.

She sighs. "I better conjure a ring to sell our engagement now."

I pinch her side. "Contain your enthusiasm, Mrs. Hadez."

"I'm going to need my head examined when I wake up. *Mrs. Hadez? Wow.* Bryn would have a field day if I told her. Which I won't."

As Nick waves his wife over, I murmur, "Let's see the ring."

She holds out her left hand that glitters with a tiny heart-shaped diamond.

"Cute, but you do realize that the diamond I'd give you would be significantly larger?"

"I bet." She gives her head a brusque shake. "No, I don't bet. I need to *stop* betting, or I'll end up monumentally disappointed the day I get engaged for real."

"Why?"

"Because, Tarian, my future fiancé will be a *real* man with a *real*-size bank account, not some gazillionaire with superpowers and a ridiculous penis."

I realize that my only claim on this woman is a magical one and that marriage isn't something I've ever aspired to, but I deeply dislike picturing her with another man.

"You find my penis ridiculous?" I ask, choosing to focus on *that*, rather than on my irrational jealousy.

She hitches up an eyebrow as though my question is just as ridiculous as my dick.

"Ridiculously good or bad?"

"Bad. *Obviously.* Do you realize what sort of expectations it gives a girl? Do you realize how unimpressed I'll be when my future boyfriends whip off their boxers?"

My fingers dig into her ribs a little harder than necessary. "Lucky for you, you won't have to go looking for other dicks as long as mine's around for the riding."

She cranes her neck, emotion scoring her smooth brow and disquieting her pupils. "Oh, Tarian. If only you were—"

"Before I give you two lovebirds my blessing," Nick says, cutting in before she can finish her sentence. A sentence I'm hell-bent on hearing the end of. "I have a *very* important question to ask."

If only I was *what*? *Romantic*? *Serious*?

"Does Tarian have a sense of humor, sweet pea?"

Calanthe's wet eyes twinkle green and gold like the dazzling conifer in the corner. "He has anything I give him, Daddy."

Her cryptic answer makes my gut churn.

Nick seems as befuddled as I am, with his quirked eyebrows and pursed lips. "Sweetheart, have you been hitting the eggnog with Fiona?"

Calanthe stiffens. "What?"

"What you just said makes no sense. Right, Tarian?"

She sighs. "I don't expect it to make sense to either of you."

"*Eggnog,*" Nick coughs into his fist, just as his wife walks over, nursing a mug brimming with the custardy beverage. "Speak of the drink, and the drink doth appear."

"I'm a drink now?" Lisa titters as she hands her husband the mug.

He waggles his eyebrows. "A tall drink of delicious goodness."

She retracts her offering. "On second thought, I'm keeping this. You've clearly had your fair share for the evening."

Nick grins. "Elves don't drink, honey."

"This elf does." She crooks her thumb toward her husband, her smile crinkling the skin ringing her warm, chestnut eyes. "Especially eggnog. It's his favorite."

Calanthe sniffs, the illusion messing with her mind and perplexing her heart.

Lisa takes a sip of her eggnog, her gaze jumping from me to her daughter. "So what was so important I had to rush over?"

"Our little girl's getting married."

Lisa chokes on her mouthful, then proceeds to cough for a solid ten seconds. "Married?" she finally wheezes. "Absolutely not. Our daughter can't marry a murderer."

"Mom!" Calanthe gasps.

Nick reels back. "Murderer?"

"Mr. Hadez is an Atlantean. From *Atlantis*. Those people have magic. Everyone knows it. Well, everyone except for our daughter." Lisa sips her beverage, then licks the white foam off her upper lip. "Not sure why you refuse to believe it though, Callie."

At least talk of my murderous ways has dried Calanthe's tears.

"I know who Tarian is, Mom. I know what he can do."

"Then that makes bringing him here, into our home, all the more shameful."

"Now, now, Lisa. He's not going to slaughter us."

"He might not slaughter you, since you're already dead, but—"

"I'm *what*?"

"Dead, honey. You're dead." She pats his chest, her red nails drumming against the green velvet of his costume.

"How?"

"You gave up on life. You gave up on us."

"That's not true! Dad fought." Under her breath, Calanthe mutters, "Why do I even bother? You're not real. This conversation isn't real."

"Our demons come out in our sleep," I murmur against the shell of her ear. "All of them. Not just the one standing at your side." My attempt to lighten her mood falls flat.

"I suppose it's better this way." Nick's eyes are losing their vibrancy, as though the illusion is fading. "One diseased parent is enough for our daughter."

"Diseased?" Lisa's tone is so shrill, the carolers miss a beat. "You're calling *me* diseased?"

"You have Alzheimer's, sweetheart. The aggressive type. At the rate it's progressing, you'll be just as dead as me in no time."

Calanthe's attention swerves toward her father, her jaw going slack.

"Your mother will live, Calamity. And she'll recover. I swear it." I press my mouth to her pillow-tossed hair that smells like ocean wind, wildflowers, and me. "This conversation is merely a trick of your mind. A trick of my perverted magic."

Nick's irises have veered from green to gray, a tint that's spreading to his skin. "I love you, sweet pea. Unconditionally and for always."

Calanthe's ribs rattle with a choked sob when he puffs out of existence and his elf costume falls in a heap on the floor, jingling the little bells hooked onto the toes of his shoes. As she stacks her palms over her mouth to stifle her scream, I curl her into my arms.

"Just an illusion," I murmur.

Lisa scrutinizes the heaped green fabric. "Oh please. Like you care." She upends her mug, and although some of the viscous drink must end up in her mouth, most of it spills down her pointy chin and onto her reindeer jumper. "A man capable of killing his own father and brother cannot possibly have qualms about a stranger's death."

Calanthe's sobs come to an abrupt halt.

"Is this really the sort of man you want in your life, Callie?" She slides her mug onto a table laden with vases, then scrubs the bulb on her sweater that glows like hazard lights against the green and brown yarn.

We may not control the actions or speech of the people we place in our dreams, but they nonetheless reflect overheard conversations or our innermost qualms. Either Lisa Bloom isn't a fan of my person, or Calanthe, for all her promises to the contrary, truly does fear me.

I cradle Calanthe's face and raise it. I want her to *see* my honesty, to *feel* it. "I'd never kill Symeon. Not even if he did aid and abet my captors."

Her throat bobs with a swallow.

Lisa snorts. "Don't be fooled by the good-looking ones. They're always the cruelest. And most dangerous. Next thing you know, I'll be burying you."

A frisson shoots up Calanthe's spine.

"I may be cruel, but I'd *never* hurt you, Calamity. I swear it."

"I know," she murmurs.

The carolers assemble in an arc around Mrs. Bloom and begin on a new number, one I've never heard but that has the word "liar" on repeat.

"Do you really?" I nod to the singers. When Calanthe frowns, I say, "The lyrics. Are they in my honor?"

"No." Another swallow. "It's just a random tune." She steps away from me, contradicting her assertion.

I cross my arms. "So your mother's loathing has nothing to do with your wariness of me?"

"My mother doesn't loathe you, Tarian." The little candy canes in her earlobes quiver as she shakes her head. "Whenever your family came up in conversations, she'd change the subject. Still does when she's...when she's all there." She squeezes the bridge of her nose. "Why am I even justifying myself to you? You're not even real."

"Can you *please* quit saying that?"

Her pupils distend before shrinking, much like her cheeks, which puff with air before hollowing. "Don't growl at me."

"Then stop fucking cancelling me."

She snorts. "Like real-Tarian would ever use the word 'cancel.'"

"That's it! Kick everyone out of the shop, and I'll prove to you that I'm real, right here, right now."

"Let me guess...by screwing me against a wall? By tonguing my clit for the next hour, since you're just *dying* to do that?"

"I am, actually. How did you guess?"

"How did I guess?" She raises her eyes toward the ceiling and counts to five. "I *guessed* because I control everything you say and do."

Huh.

All the odd comments she's uttered since we stepped out of her bedroom join together, painting a picture I finally understand: Calanthe Bloom sincerely believes me to be a figment of her imagination.

My smirk matures into a grin. "Is that right? Then tell me, Miss Bloom, what's my next move? Are you picturing me on my knees?"

Her freckles darken, and that sultry sweet scent of hers deepens.

"You are, aren't you?" I step back into her body and mold my palms to her glorious ass. "Can you feel how hard I am for you, Calamity Darling?"

Her breathing hitches. "Of course you're hard. If my imaginary lover didn't get hard, then that would make me the most incompetent dreamer of all time."

"Don't insult my fiancée," I rasp against her neck, delighting in how violently she trembles.

"Can't believe my fantasy is to be engaged to a man I don't even know," she mumbles. "And who'd probably scare the shit out of me in real life."

Her admission dampens my desire to play with her. With a sigh, I ease my body away from hers and tuck a long strand of her chestnut hair behind her ear.

I'm about to confess that I'm not some marionette when she says, "Oh, fuck it. I really need to get laid. Considering my lack of options in the real world, may as well make the most of this dream."

The little growl that just erupted from her red, red mouth tightens my balls.

She spins on her heel and starts toward a wooden lattice screen that partitions the shop. "Come."

"You, first."

She freezes.

When I reach her, the green and gold and gray are eddying around her engorged pupils. She blinks, shakes her head, then resumes her brisk march. As soon as we're out of sight, she whirls, seizes the hem of her dress, and rolls it off her body.

This time, I'm the one who freezes, because not only is she still wearing her getup of ruby velvet and lace, but she's also added a garter belt and thigh-high white stockings. My dick swells up so hard and fast that the trousers, which actually fit this time, begin to feel as maladjusted as that godawful neon suit.

"Pull your zipper down," she commands.

It takes her words a second to make their way from my dick to my brain. Once they land, I cock an eyebrow. I've never been one for authoritative partners, but feisty, sweet Calanthe could just incite me to change my ways.

I seize the slider but don't tug. "Say please, darling."

She releases an exasperated sigh. "*Please*, Mr. Hadez."

I'm tempted to prolong this little game but can't bring myself to exploit her vulnerability. Sensing that the only way to convince her that I'm real is to regain control of the narrative, I say, "Actually. Stick a finger inside your pussy, and I'll unzip myself."

She chokes on air. "Wh-what?"

"Finger yourself." With a dark smile, I add her favorite word, "Please."

Brow furrowed, she shunts her thong aside and plunges a digit into her tight, gorgeous body. "Fine. Done." As she pulls her finger out, she nods to my crotch. "Your turn."

"Not yet." I gently circle her wrist, lift her finger to my mouth, and suck.

Her eyelashes flap as though she cannot believe what I've just done.

Once I've cleaned her thoroughly, I lower her hand to my trousers. "Slide me out."

"I...I..."

"Is that not one of the lines you've scripted for my character?"

Her pupils throb like her pulse.

"What is it?"

She lets out a short huff. "It doesn't make sense."

"What doesn't? That I'm not being a good sub?"

She reels her hand off my waistband, her fingers shaking as they curl into her palm.

"Submitting isn't in my nature, Calamity."

"Well, sticking my finger inside my pussy isn't in *my* nature, so I don't get why I would've made you ask me to do that."

I sigh. "You didn't *make* me ask you anything."

After shock, comes anger. "You're in *my* dream."

"Yes, but I'm not some mindless performer like the rest of them."

"That's not possible."

Great Gaea, the woman can be stubborn. "Why does my realness seem so improbable?"

Her eyes flash. "Because only men in cheesy romances would spout out the lines you use on me. Lines which are usually written *by* women. No *real* man would ever say any of them. No real man would want to spend hours licking a woman, the same way no real man would ever look—correction, *has* ever looked at my scarred labia and thought, *Destination pearly gates, unlocked.*"

"I'm uncertain whether to be offended or amused."

"See? Even your reaction is not manly."

I watch her fume, because yes, my girl is fuming. "All right. Think of my next move but don't say it out loud."

"Why?"

"So I can show you that you don't control me."

Her heart beats so fast, it jostles her breathtaking breasts.

"Ready?"

She stares me squarely in the eyes. "Ready."

I crouch.

She sighs. "I knew it."

I pick up her dress and rise, then turn it right side out. The shallow furrow between her brows tells me that she didn't anticipate *that*.

"Arms up." Even though the last thing I want is to wrap her back up, not only is her mother still part of this dream, but also, the tears on her cheeks have barely dried.

Her soft skin pebbles as she slowly unknots and raises her arms.

I don't rush cloaking her curves, sensing this may be the last time I get to touch her in this dream. "I never thought dressing a woman could prove as arousing as undressing one."

Her breath is thready and nips at my jaw.

"Fuck. I really do sound short of testicles, don't I?"

"Can't believe you're real." Her cheeks burn the same shade as her dress.

I crook my knuckle beneath her flushed jaw. "This perfect man of yours is no figment of your imagination."

She grimaces. "All those things I said…"

"Will live rent-free in my heart and dick for the rest of time." My terrible line does nothing to suppress her blush, so I tip her chin higher. "I bloody loved your confidence and honesty, and can only hope you won't shy away from showing me both in the real world."

She swallows.

"I don't want any falsities or pretenses between us." I caress her blazing jawline, wishing my touch could quell her anxiety. "Understood?"

"Yes," she gasps, as though the word was bottled up deep inside and had to be shaken loose.

I expel a tired breath. "How about we get out of here?"

"How? The door to my bedroom is gone."

"The shop entrance. Perhaps it'll lead us somewh—" I grit my teeth and bounce away from Calanthe.

"What's happening?" She reaches out for me, but I back up, panicked that my toxic magic is about to harm her.

"My runes." Sweat souses my brow as I shore up my body against the wooden screen. "Something's wrong."

My right bicep feels as though it's being carved with a knife. I grip the collar of my dress shirt and wrench it open. As the white buttons plink against the green tiles, I shove the fabric off my shoulder.

Something is *supremely* wrong.

# FIFTY

**M**y heart hurtles over several beats as I stare at the blood dripping down Tarian's arm. *Blue* blood. "Did you cut yourself?"

"No." Tarian's mouth flattens.

"But… Am I imagining the blood?"

"No." His dark eyes finally alight on mine. "I *am* bleeding, but I'm bleeding from the area of skin where a rune used to be. The one I lost." His teeth are so gritted they seem cemented shut, yet the words, "In my sleep," find their way out.

*Shit.*

*Shit. Shit. Shit.*

I grip the edge of the scarred table to keep my hands from shaking. "Do you think"—I lick my lips—"that you're bleeding in real life?"

"I don't fucking know," he grits out. "And why the hell is my blood blue?"

"Because the mine has blue diamonds, so it's symbolic?" Guilt wafts off me like fury pours off him. I scan the shop for a way out. Anything to escape the emotion gnawing on my conscience.

To think I just promised him complete honesty. To think he's real.

"We have Band-Aids under the register." My throat feels like someone's stuffed it with broken Christmas ornaments. "I can—"

"A plaster won't fix my missing rune." He shrugs his shirt back on. "Can you give me a jacket?"

"You think extra fabric will help?"

"It'll hide the disturbing stain, which will save you from swooning. I'd catch you, because I wouldn't want to deviate too far off my maudlin-hero narrative, but I'd prefer not to touch you."

His last words clang against my eardrums, brasher than my guilt. "Why?"

"Why what?"

"Why don't you want to touch me anymore?"

His brow furrows. "Because I don't want to risk another rune getting into your skin."

*Oh.*

"That's not where your mind went, is it?" He offers me a smile that is equal parts grievous and gentle. "Calamity, once I've figured out what's wrong with my magic, you can bet your stunning ass my hands will be all over *it* and the rest of you."

Heat doesn't just envelop me; it sears me from the inside out.

He pulls his shoulders back as he readjusts his shirt and does up a few buttons. "You'll be begging me to stop."

"Never."

Tarian seems to grow a foot taller. I wonder how many more feet he'd shoot up if I confessed how my underwear never stays dry around him. How the mere sight of him excites my blood.

"Do you think it'll feel the same in the real world?" I ask.

"If what will feel the same?"

"This attraction."

"No."

"Oh." My hands slip off the table's edge, and I avert my gaze, choosing to concentrate on a dent in the wood.

The one I made the day of Dad's funeral when I took my anger and pain out on the shop, stabbing the tabletop with my stem cutters over and over. It was Bryn who'd pried them out of my fingers; Bryn who'd sat me down on the floor; Bryn who'd dug tiny bottles of vodka out of her giant purse. At my cocked brow, she'd said, *"Swiped them from the hotel room I shared with that sexy French pilot I told you about."*

Out of all the details to pour into this false shop, I wonder, *Why this dent?* Actually, I know why it's here. To remind me what's worth grieving and what's not, and that I have a friend in the real world who'll heal my squished heart. I suddenly wish she were here. Oddly enough, I think I hear her voice.

"I think it'll feel a hundred times more potent."

My gaze bounces back to Tarian. More potent? I'm going through underwear like Bryn goes through shoes. Honestly, I don't see how my body can be any more receptive to Tarian's. The man hasn't even made me come, yet I wouldn't hesitate to crown him the best lay I've ever had.

A thought suddenly percolates through the fog of my lust. "As long as I wear your magic…"

He stares back, his eyes unfathomably dark beneath his lashes. I want him to contest this, but he doesn't, because he knows as well as I do that even if this attraction budded before he stung me, it bloomed after. Then again, our *before* lasted mere minutes.

A loud honk followed by insistent banging jolts me out of my head. Tarian lurches away from the wooden lattice screen and wheels around, parking his massive frame in front of me. I taste copper, but I also smell it. It takes me a second to connect the scent to the bloodstain on Tarian's shirt, the one that's mere inches from my nose.

"Callie, baby, Bryn's here," my mother calls out over the caroler's version of Patti Smith's "Because the Night."

As my heartrate decelerates, I slide out from behind Tarian. "Do you think car honks will always set us off?"

The tendons roil in his corded neck. "For a time, yes."

"I almost wish you could compel me to forget."

"I wish that as well, Calamity." He offers me a tight smile as he runs a hand over his forehead that glistens with sweat beneath his tousled locks.

"Oh look, Bryn brought us a shopper!" My mother's eager tone makes me step around Tarian and the lattice screen. "We haven't had many of those lately."

Who else did I transport into—

I stop dead in my tracks at the sight of Bryn and "the shopper" beyond the frosted glass door that my mother is desperately trying to open. I whirl on my heel to tell Tarian to stay put, only to find him standing right behind me.

"You need to let the customer in, baby," Mom says, as she hunts the door for a handle that doesn't exist. "We need his money, or we'll have to shut down."

My ears begin ringing so incessantly that I can't hear the carolers anymore.

Somehow, though, I hear Tarian. "That's twice now that this has come up. Is your family business on the brink of bankruptcy in the real world?"

I blink at him, shocked that he's focusing on that instead of on Bryn's customer.

"Ask Malachi to wire you a hundred K, or however much you need to stay afloat until I'm back."

I stare and stare. And then fresh tears sprout on my lash line. The second his gaze wanders off mine, he'll rescind his offer.

Before that happens, before his generosity warps into disgust, I grip his face between my palms, push onto my toes, and press my mouth to his. He's not expecting the kiss. I can tell by how rigid his lips stay. Nevertheless, I persevere, sliding my tongue over their seam in an attempt to break his decorous seal.

I will Bryn away.

I will the banging to stop.

I will myself to wake up and leave Tarian with the memory of my kiss, rather than with the one of the man at my best friend's side.

Tarian's hands close around my elbows, and then he's stepping back, holding me at arm's length.

Because he saw.

Because he knows.

"Don't." His breath is coming out in rough spurts. "My runes."

He didn't see.

He doesn't know.

"Your runes won't hurt me, Tarian." I consider magicking my dress off to distract him, but I'd only be delaying the inevitable. After one last failed attempt at waking up, I close my eyes and drop my chin into my neck.

The banging transforms into a crunch.

Of course it does. The truth always finds a way in.

The air thrums.

"Why the fuck," Tarian bites out, "do you keep dreaming of my brother naked? Seriously, Calanthe, why?"

"I'm so sorry, Tarian."

"Did you sleep with him?"

"*Eww.* No!" My neck snaps back, and I meet his cold stare. "Some women may be into that, but I'm not. Even if you didn't want anything to do with me after tonight, I would never go after anyone from your family. *Never.*"

"So what the fuck are you sorry about?"

"I'm sorry about trying to hide who you stung with your missing rune!" I shout over the sound of Symeon pummeling the crackled glass, Bryn chanting my name, and Mom imploring me to let our customers in.

Everything goes still, but not as still as Tarian, who becomes one with the tiles. "My brother?" The bleakness of his tone chills me. "I stung my brother?"

I cross my arms at the elbows and squeeze them into my chest. "Apparently."

"What do you mean, *apparently*?" he snarls. "He wears the fucking word on his fucking chest!"

He snaps his arm out toward the store window. Even though I'm very much done with this psychosomatic guilt trip, I glance over my shoulder at the smoldering rune cut into Symeon's white flesh. The word flickers, shrinks—not in height, but in width. The letters shift, melding into one another to form the abominable circled "X." Is this how it morphed in reality, or was this little show courtesy of my boundless imagination?

The zombie raises his fist. I assume he's about to resume bashing the window but I'm wrong. Symeon contemplates his split knuckles that bleed black, then dips one finger into the wound and begins to paint letters in the frost: "Y," "O," "U," "A," "R."

As he sketches an "E," Tarian growls, "Tell me everything. And I fucking mean, *everything*, Calanthe." His anger, combined with the use of my real name, is a punch to the heart.

"Fishermen recovered his exsanguinated body off the coast of Nantucket, not far from where the *Amapola* sank." The pointy toes of my candy cane stilettos come in and out of focus. "Electra showed me a picture of him laid out on the coroner's table." Come to think of it, he was probably not brought to any coroner. "The rune had already mutated into a symbol."

"Don't ever try to conceal the truth from me again." Tarian barely powers his entreaty, yet I hear it loud and clear.

It's all I hear. "I was trying to protect you."

"You can't protect me from *me*!" He stabs a hand through his hair, his chest pumping with escalating breaths. "No one can!"

More tears pop along my lash line. Not because he's angry at me—he has every right to be—but because he really believes he's somehow doomed to hurt forever.

"And never fucking use your body to distract me from the truth again."

The tears trundle down. "I'm so sorry."

Tarian mashes his lips. Will he ever forgive me, or is this it for us?

"Please stop crying," he rasps.

Which just makes me weep harder. I drive the heels of my palms into my aching eyes.

"Callie, the door!" Bryn shouts.

*Please, please let me out of this nightmare. Please.*

"Fuck," Tarian murmurs.

The rune on my spine burns. It's the only spot of heat on my body. The rest of me is ice.

"Who?" Tarian yells. "Who's next, Sym?"

I wipe my face on my sleeve just as Symeon finishes and underlines his dripping threat with blood: YOU ARE NEXT.

Does he mean me? His mouth opens and white air plumes out. But not only air—a name. He yells it over and over.

"Why is he calling out to Malachi?"

I frown. "I don't know."

"It's your dream!"

"I'm aware, but I don't fucking know why he's shouting your cousin's name!" I go back to clutching my biceps. If I don't relax my grip, my nails will end up slicing right through the cashmere.

Does he mean Malachi's next? Fear stabs my lungs.

Tarian must've reached the same conclusion because his skin has become as bloodless as Symeon's. "Go back!"

If only I— The shop fades. I hold my breath. Are we changing dreamscapes, or am I waking?

"Callie?" Bryn's eyes flash in the obscurity of my bedroom back at the high-rise. "We have to go," she hisses. "Now."

I sit up, fisting the sheets tangled around my legs. "What? Where?" I made it back. I managed to make it back! "Why?"

"Because it isn't safe for you here," she whispers. "Come on."

Even though the room is steeped in darkness, I don't miss the bruise that purples her temple and puffs up her eyelid. "Oh my god, what happened?"

She raises a finger to her lips. "Shh." When she lowers it, she leaves behind a carmine stripe. "Atlanteans are hard to kill. It might not have worked."

"Kill? That's impossible. Only Tarian—"

She shakes the little brown vial I'd spotted in her purse. "It's possible, thanks to Tarian's blood."

My heart is beating so wildly I feel like I'm choking. "Who did you kill?"

"Electra."

I can't breathe. I can't—

"She was in on everything, Callie."

My throat narrows to the width of a straw. No, of a toothpick.

"Her brother killed my father."

A thread of oxygen returns, and I wheeze. "Dorian found them? He found Tarian?"

Bryn's head rears back, and her upper lip hitches up. "Dorian. Killed. My. Father. Callie. He killed one of *us*."

"Your father kidnapped Tarian, Bryn."

She straightens, her eyes alight with hurt and disappointment. "Whose fucking side are you on?"

"I'm on the side of justice. Your father and Yasmin abducted Tarian." Even though the only proof I have of their duplicity emanates from my dreams, it rings true.

"Since when do you care about Atlanteans? About *Tarian*?"

"Since you introduced me to them."

"So, it's my fault now?" She laughs, a sinister cackle that's so at odds with the girl I grew up with that I begin to suspect this might be another dream. "It probably fills you with some sort of sick joy that I'm fatherless. You don't have a dad, so no one else gets to have one."

I gape at her for a solid minute before pinching the inside of my wrist. *This isn't real. Not real.*

Bryn snorts. "Oh, it's real."

My heart misses a beat because I didn't speak my theory out loud. I start to sigh when her arms come up in front of her. Moonlight dusts across the room, catching on a gun barrel. One that's pointed at me.

I scramble out of bed, my feet knotting in the sheets. I slam down so hard that my teeth click. "Lower the gun, Bee!"

"My sister told me you'd pick them over me."

"Mackenzie?"

"Not that sister."

"You have another sister?"

"I'm sorry, Callie. I really hoped she was wrong. I hoped you'd pick us."

I tear the pillow off the bed and fling it at dream-Bryn just as she fires. I don't know where the bullet ends up, but it's not in me.

As I lurch to my feet, Bryn growls and straightens her arms.

"Please, Bryn. Don't." She might be make-believe, but the injuries I carry back to the real world aren't. "*Please!*"

She shoots, and although I pitch my body sideways, the bullet bites into my skull.

# FIFTY-ONE

Pain bleaches my vision.

My skull burns. My spine, too. But the rest of me is ice.

I listen for sounds but hear only my blood trounce my eardrums.

Is fake-Bryn still here? Is her gun still pointed at me?

My face is sticky and wet. My lids, heavy like anvils. My heart and scalp, tender and throbbing.

I try to stay alert but fail and drift, weaving in and out of consciousness.

"CALLIE?"

Air burns my lungs, blisters my skull.

"Where did all this blood come from?" *Electra.*

My nails catch in the tufted rug as I try to lift myself onto all fours.

"Don't move." Her palms bracket my head to keep it still. "Seriously, Callie, no moving. I need to locate your wound." My eyes water as Electra's fingers brush a tender spot. "What did you hit your head on?"

"Bullet," I murmur.

"What?"

"Bullet," I repeat, powering my voice so that it doesn't vanish in the plush rug that smells like a basement filled with musty pennies.

"What was a bullet doing in your bed?"

"It wasn't in her bed." Knees click. "It was in her dream. Who shot you, Callie?"

I suddenly don't want to tell them. Even if the altercation was a figment of my imagination, it'll color their view of Bryn. "They wore a mask, so I don't know."

Electra and Malachi are quiet. Too quiet.

"Will I need magical stitches, doc?" I inject my voice with false cheer.

Electra sighs. "Malachi, hold her steady." As large hands settle on either side of my head, Electra murmurs, "It may sting."

"No magical numbing cream for me?"

"I'm afraid I'm all out," she chirrups at the same time Malachi says, "It'll be quick."

Electra tugs on strands of my hair, probably to clear the wound, then propels what feels like a fireball at my injury.

"Are you…welding my skull…with a blow torch?"

"I fell from a bridge once." Electra's tone is so conversational that it momentarily distracts me from her mending. "Broke every bone in my body. *And* drowned. Remember, Malachi?"

"Not exactly the sort of thing one forgets." His voice is gravelly and edged with a dark sentiment that makes me think the memory isn't only raw but also thoroughly despised.

"Anyway, Dorian fished me out, and then he and Malachi got to work setting my bones because my magic wasn't healing me fast enough to their liking. It was horrible. I'll take another month of training with Ines over those two's 'healing method' any day."

"You trained…with Ines?" I wheeze.

"Dorian made me. Said she was the best."

"Is she?"

"The best torturer."

"Elle," Malachi sighs.

"What? Ines is tough."

"What Dorian and I couldn't be with you." Malachi's touch gentles when I wince. "That's what makes her such a good teacher. *I* trained with her."

"You were the boss's kid. If she damaged you, she'd have lost her job."

"So you think she went easy on me?"

"No, but she never broke *your* neck."

There's a long pause before Malachi asks, "She broke yours?"

Another long pause. "Forget it."

Their conversation is so enthralling that I've completely forgotten about my bullet wound. The second my mind goes there, though, pain webs my skull. "Is that why you…handed her over to the…Holy Hunters?"

"Electra, here, can hold grudges like no other. Avoid incensing her."

I swallow. "Noted."

"By the way, how does one fall"—I grind my teeth as Electra's curative magic spreads—"from a bridge?"

"When one finds herself on the wrong bridge at the wrong time with the wrong crowd."

I want to hear more about this story, but the pain grows so bright, I lose my ability to speak.

"Do you know any self-defense, Callie?" she asks.

"I have pepper spray." A welcome coolness slicks over my sweltering skin.

"Unless you decide to cut ties with us, you'll need to be trained."

I'd never cut ties with them. Not willingly, anyway. "Are you offering, or warning me I'm about to get to know Ines really well?"

"If Calanthe hangs out with us, Elle, then she'll have *us*. She'll have Tarian."

After thudding with pain, my heart thuds with something else —hope.

"True. He'll probably sic Dorian on your ass." Electra snickers, getting to her feet. "Which would be completely awesome as it will get him off *my* ass."

With Malachi's help, I press myself onto my knees. "You guys are a lot."

Electra grins, which makes her look her age. It also makes her look happy. I catch Malachi eyeing her on the sly, his brows heavy against his lash line as though he were solving an equation.

"I'm sorry for ruining your rug, Electra."

"Forget about the rug. Sheesh." She vanishes into my ensuite to wash her hands. "It's so *blah* anyway."

It's not. Although I've only ever seen Dorian's sister sporting black, I feel like she's a repressed palette of pastels.

"Did you learn anything new?" The subdued beam of light streaming out of the bathroom exposes the burst vessels surrounding Malachi's irises.

*That you're next.* Could he mean that Malachi will bump into Tarian, and it'll rob him of his magic? Malachi is so good that it doesn't make sense. Oh, shit... Could he mean that Tarian's captors are about to go after Malachi?

"What? He told you something, didn't he? Please tell us. Please." Malachi's desperation crimps my heart.

"He still hasn't woken up." I try to push my hair back, but it's as stiff as cardboard. "Which means you were right, Electra." I say this a little louder, although it's unnecessary as she plods out of the bathroom, patting her hands on a gray towel. "They must've pushed Symeon onto Tarian's body. Or maybe Symeon touched him by mistake."

"Rewind." Malachi's brow ruffles like a hibiscus petal. "Who pushed who?"

"Lynch and Yasmin. Callie and I are convinced they're behind the whole thing. Along with Symeon. All three have motive. Symeon was always jealous of his brother. Yasmin wanted Tarian but he rejected her. And possibly, Lynch and Yasmin are a couple." Electra nods to me. "Callie saw a wedding cake in one of her dreams. Although we're not entirely sure who's at the origin of the abduction, we do believe all three are involved. The same way we believe Tarian's magic protects him when it senses ill intent, and that's why Sym lost his magic." I like that Electra and I are a *we*. "Because he made Tarian bleed."

The beat of silence that ensues is disturbed only by the gush of water in the bathroom. Is Electra aware the tap's still running?

I'm about to point it out when Malachi says, "That's impossible."

I forget all about the tap and sit back on my heels. "Why?"

"Because if his magic *were* protecting him, it wouldn't have killed my uncle."

"What if Barak extracted some of Tarian's blood, Mal?" I suggest.

"He would never—"

"By mistake." Electra tosses the hand towel at him so he can wipe down his palms.

"Do you hear how nuts that sounds, Elle?" As he works the towel between his fingers, he balances his elbows on his bent legs.

"If you have a better idea as to why Tarian's leaking runes," she says, "then by all means, we're all ears."

His gaze narrows on Electra, who glares right back.

Before they can resort to magical warfare to settle their differences, I point out, "Tarian's magic is acting independently from him. He wasn't even aware that he'd killed Symeon." I snare my lip but release it swiftly because it tastes like blood. "I tried to hide it from him, but my conscience just wouldn't stop plopping Symeon inside our dreamscape."

I picture how disappointed and angry Tarian was with me right before I faded out of the shop. Maybe getting shot by Bryn was his way of punishing me for trying to hide the truth.

"So he *unintentionally* gave Sym one of his runes?" Malachi's lips are so tense, they're a slash of pale pink on his wan face.

I grimace. "Yes." As I stand, I add, "Also, the word that lifted off Tarian's skin is *wield*."

Malachi frowns. "*Wield*?"

"His runes can reshape themselves."

"Like the one on your back…" As he gets to his feet, he cracks his neck, but it does nothing to relax his rigid posture. If anything, his body seems stiffer than it was before. Even more so when he crosses his arms.

"The word on her back changed?" Electra asks.

Heat prickles my collarbone. "Not exactly. It just reads differently to Tarian than it does to the rest of you."

"What does it read to Tarian?"

"You forgot to turn off the tap, Electra."

"I'm running you a bath because—" She scrunches her nose and gestures to the whole of me. "So you were saying…the rune on your back?"

"I wasn't saying anything."

"Now I *need* to know what it reads to Tarian."

A crooked smile seizes Malachi's lips.

"Don't you dare," I breathe out, shaking my eyeballs from side to side.

If Electra gets wind of the word, she'll *never* let me live it down. She already thinks I'm enjoying my dreams, which I'm not. I suddenly picture Tarian kneeling between my thighs and my body temperature escalates a dozen or so degrees. Okay, fine. I'm enjoying *some* parts, but considering how our latest fantasy ended, I'm thinking there won't be any more sexy times in my near—or distant—future.

Electra speaks to Malachi in Atlantean. Even though she could potentially be discussing a whole other topic, her sparkly expression tells me I'm the subject of her conversation. I mimic zipping my lips as I stride toward the bathroom.

"I'll drag it out of one of you soon enough!" Electra calls out.

I have no doubt she'll try her darndest. I stop on the bathroom threshold to ask, "Is Bryn back at her place or here?"

"She's here," Malachi says.

The atmosphere in the room goes from warm to chilly so fast, my skin breaks out in goosebumps.

"What's going on?"

Electra waves her hands through the air. "Sound shield," she explains when she catches my cocked eyebrows. How…*neat*. "Just reapplying it in case it had faded."

My gut begins to churn, and although it isn't connected to my brain, it makes the last segment of my dream scurry back to the forefront of my mind. I hear the bullet's zing. I feel the heat of it streaking across my skull.

"She tried to place a call from your landline. When Malachi walked into the kitchen, she tossed the phone, then pretended like she'd elbowed it off its base."

"Who did she try to call?"

Malachi's still rubbing his hands against the towel, even though they're probably clean at this point. "Not sure. I told her she could use my cell phone if she wanted to. She insisted she hadn't tried to call anyone."

My knees lock up as my heart delivers so much blood to my extremities that every inch of me begins to tingle. "Didn't you compel her to tell you the truth?"

"I did. Her story didn't change."

This should iron out my pulse, but it doesn't. "Then why is this bothering you?"

He shrugs. "It just felt like she was lying."

"I thought people couldn't lie when compelled?"

Electra eyes the door as though expecting Bryn to burst into this bedroom at any second. "If they have some of our blood running through their system, they can. It wears off, though. Which is why Malachi brought her back here."

"You said there were side effects. In case she did get her hands on"—I can't help the wrinkle that seizes my nose—"*blood,* what sort of side effects will she get?"

"Bloody nose is the most common. Sometimes, it'll create bruising. If it was given freely, though, she shouldn't have any side effects."

My lids light up with the shine of Bryn's gun barrel. Was it premonitory? What if Tarian's rune is adding another magical layer to our dreaming? I shake my head, dispelling the insane thought. Bryn's my best friend. I may have woken up freaked out, but the shootout, Bryn's *other* sister…those things weren't real.

The bedroom fades, and I'm suddenly back in the train wagon with Bryn, Yasmin, and Lynch, sitting in front of that monstrous wedding cake. And then I'm standing in the penthouse's kitchen with my mother, and she says, *Like Bryn pointed out, it's the tallest building in Hadeztown.* Bryn had been compelled to forget, yet she'd remembered. What if Tarian added her to the train wagon because she's complicit?

*Not that sister.*

"Callie?" Electra flaps her hand in front of my face.

My blood thunders against my eardrums and my vision pixelates. I fling my arm out, smacking my nails against the door frame before managing to seize it.

"Are you about to pass out?" Electra's voice sounds like it's emerging from a metal pipe.

I shake my head.

"How about you lie down?" She snakes a hand around my waist. "Just in case…"

"It's not the rune," I croak.

"Then what is it?"

Although the sergeant is now bald, his hair used to be flame-red. Where the gene only tinted Bryn's locks, it soaked into

Yasmin's. I tighten my fingers around the dark wood, yet feel like I'm falling.

"What is it, Callie?" Malachi towers over Electra, and Electra isn't petite.

Not sure why I'm noticing their height difference now. Why it's even holding my attention. Because my feverish brain is seeking something solid to cling to? That must be it.

I swallow. "I think Yasmin is Delta Lynch's daughter." I also think, *My best friend is involved,* but I keep that to myself.

# FIFTY-TWO

I flip the tea tag over and over as I stare out the living room window at the horizon that's graying with a new dawn. I hope I'm wrong about Bryn and Yasmin's kinship, the same way I hope my best friend hasn't been aiding her father this whole time.

But the more I think about it, the more I become convinced that Yasmin wasn't cheating on Symeon with Delta, and that Bryn isn't an innocent bystander.

Electra joins me by the floor-to-ceiling window, her gaze darting to her bedroom, which she lent to Bryn.

I circle the mug with both hands. "What did Yasmin's mother say?"

"Malachi decided not to call her."

"Why not?" I twist my neck, which in turn twists my body and jostles the tea from the mug.

It sloshes onto my shiny black leggings. Although I typically favor matte ones, my clothing choice is a tad limited in this realm. At least until the washer beeps, announcing my load of laundry is done.

"Because"—Electra's gaze darts to the door—"he worries she's involved."

I clutch the mug that's gone as cold as my insides. "What do you think?"

"I think you're on to something." Milky sunlight punctures the heavy cloud cover, highlighting the unsettled waters of the Charles and the sleepy Boston streets. "Malachi drove over to Symeon's place to try and locate something of Yasmin's so we can run a DNA test." Her brown iris burns gold in the muted dawn while her blue one sparkles like glass.

"Would Saul know?"

"He may. He's part of the council. Then again, Nora died around the time Yasmin was born. From what my parents and Dorian told me, he kind of checked out for a while after her death, so he may be as clueless as the rest of us."

"I could be completely off the mark."

"Or you could be smack in the bull's eye."

Although Electra healed me, a phantom ache remains, and it reminds me of the illusory bullet that tore through my flesh. It reminds me that I may not know my best friend as well as I thought I did.

"I want you to get my mother and Mrs. Fiona away from here. From us."

Without glancing away from the sky, she says, "I know someone. Someone I trust with my life. Someone I'd trust with your mother's. My brother might kill me for contacting him, since it ended sort of tragically between them, but Diego's the best."

"I thought Ines was the best?" I taunt her.

A grimace reshapes Electra's face.

"So Diego, why did it end?" I ask this to put her out of her misery, but also because this feels like an important detail to learn before I entrust my mother to a jilted ex.

"Diego wanted Dorian to relocate to Texas with him, but my brother didn't want to quit his job."

"And Diego couldn't move up here?"

"He was here for three years."

"Is he from Atlantis?"

"If you want to keep them safe, it's best if—"

"I was just asking to make sure he was."

As Electra dials Dorian's ex, I head over to the couch and sink onto it. My body feels like it weighs six tons, my heart alone, four. I settle my lukewarm tea on the coffee table, then slide my legs underneath me and burrow into the plush back pillows.

I must bump the remote because the TV screen brightens with a picture of Tarian. I stare at my dream lover's scowling mouth and chilling stare. No wonder I thought the worst of him. The vibes he gives off are terrifying. And alluring. But mostly terrifying.

Too soon, his picture fades, replaced by another—*Yasmin*. I startle at the sight of her, then drop my gaze to the banner on the bottom of the screen: *Hadez girlfriend missing*. My fingers jerk against the mute button, deactivating the setting, and the reporter's voice blares from the speakers. I smash the volume button to dim the noise, hoping I didn't rouse the entire building.

The reporter replaces Yasmin's portrait with a shot of her and Symeon during a circus-themed birthday celebration that apparently cost Yasmin over a million dollars. Explains why *that* colored one of Tarian's dreams. Not only did he attend the party, but it's also in direct correlation to Yasmin.

*"Sources close to the family worry that the pharmaceutical heiress was on the yacht when it sank."* The picture is replaced by an aerial recording of the white-capped, boat-infested ocean surrounding Martha's Vineyard. *"Last night, the head of the Fablez family posted a video on every social media outlet, offering a reward for information pertaining to her granddaughter's case."*

I sit up straighter. So Saul didn't divulge that Tarian was

missing but he revealed that Yasmin was? Was this his idea? Catalina's?

Just as her name crops up in my mind, the screen fills with a reel of Catalina Fablez, the raven-haired, seventy-year-old matriarch who doesn't look a day over forty. She also doesn't look an iota like the granddaughter whose safe homecoming she's praying for.

*"Since this video went viral, hundreds have taken to the ocean. Now let's go over to the Vineyard. Jacob, what can you tell us about the ambient mood? Are people hopeful to find Yasmin Hassek alive?"*

Catalina's recorded entreaty is replaced by live feed of a man in a heavy-duty rain slicker. *"I'm afraid to report that the mood is unenthusiastic over here, and that's not taking into account the weather that's rolling in. This isn't a good time to be lost at sea. Not for an Atlantean. Not for anyone."*

"Holy Coco Chanel, Yasmin's missing?"

I jump a whole foot off the couch as Bryn plops onto the couch beside me.

"That explains why she hasn't been responding to my texts."

I stare at my friend's profile, then past her, at Electra, whose attention is on us even though the phone is still pinned to her ear. Does that mean she's still trying to convince Diego, or is she refining the details of his task?

"I need to call Mom." She pats the pockets of the terry robe she added over her blush-colored camisole and lacey boy shorts. "Ugh. I keep forgetting that my phone's broken." She spins on the couch, the robe parting around her bare legs, revealing a large bruise on her hip and outer thigh. "You think your mother's nurse will let me borrow her phone?"

"Unlikely. What happened to your leg?"

She prods the bruise with a chipped fingernail. "I must've banged it during the night. Maybe in your apartment when I went to grab your mother's medications?" Her forehead grooves. "I did do that, right? I didn't dream it?"

"You did."

"Good. I thought I was losing it." She wrinkles her nose. "With everything going on—the wedding, your move here after the fire, Symeon's death—I feel like the days have been ticking by extra weirdly. I mustn't be getting enough sleep, because half the time, I walk around dazed and confused."

My stomach contracts from guilt as she describes the side effects of compulsion. Unless she's faking her stupefied state?

"Did you give Lisa her medication yet?"

"Not yet." My ribs clench. What if Bryn tampered with Mom's pills?

I give my head a small shake. Bryn might've helped godnap Tarian, but there's no reason why she'd want to hurt my mother. Unless she's trying to hurt me?

I press my palm against my stomach. It's as hard as those cookies Bryn and I once baked in the oven for an hour instead of ten minutes, because we got sidetracked by our favorite TV show. "Any chance you found my EpiPen when you were at my house?"

"Your EpiPen? Didn't Dorian buy you one?"

My skin prickles as I remember discussing this with her over takeout three nights ago. How come she remembers? When Electra emptied her mind of the visit, didn't it rid Bryn of all conversations had during her time here?

"Callie, why are you looking at me like that?" Bryn tugs on the lapels of her robe.

"Why would Dorian buy me an EpiPen?"

She fusses with her robe until she's managed to pull it snugger around her chest. "Because he's Tarian's right-hand man and you're Tarian's...*friend*."

"I'm not."

"Hun, look at where you are."

"Where am I?"

She drops her voice as though about to impart a secret. "In Tarian Hadez's high-rise, that's where." Her gaze goes to the screen that's back to displaying coverage of the Hadez funeral.

*"Memorial postponed. Because of the weather or because brother has yet to arrive?"* she reads. "Tarian's not in the Vineyard yet?"

"Apparently not."

Her gaze revs back my way. "*Apparently*? Hasn't he called you?"

Does she really think he can call me or is this part of her act? "I know you're convinced that there's something going on between us, but I haven't seen or talked to him since your mom's engagement party."

Although her eyes aren't shovels, I can almost feel them prodding, digging. "I really wish I had my phone. Mom might know something these reporters don't."

"About Yasmin?"

"Well, yeah. Oh my god, do you think there was foul play involved?"

This time I'm the one who stares long and deep, and the longer I stare, the more my conviction that Bryn is hiding something strengthens.

"Can I borrow your phone, Callie?"

"I don't have it."

"Is it in your room?"

"It got destroyed in the fire."

"It did? But that was like, last week. You haven't replaced it yet?"

"That was three days ago, and no, I haven't had time."

"Why don't you send the nurse to get you a new one?"

"She needs my ID, which got incinerated."

"She could lend you a phone though, right? Or maybe Dorian could get you a burner?"

"Dorian works for Tarian. Not for me."

Her stare darkens with annoyance. "Maybe Mal can get you one?"

"Mal? Why would he?" My heart thuds so hard, it vibrates the white Bloom's Blooms logo on the forest green hoodie Dad designed and sold at the shop one year. "I barely know him. Not to mention, he's probably in Martha's Vineyard for the memorial service."

Her pupils tighten. "Right. And let me guess. There's no land-line in this place?"

"They haven't had time to plug one in."

The silence that ensues lasts a beat too long for comfort. "Only one reason someone would be cut off from the world."

Is this when she pulls a gun on me and calls me a liar? I check her bathrobe for pistol-shaped bulges but find none. Maybe she stashed her weapon in the back of her boy shorts. Electra must have the same thought because, when Bryn leans in, the Atlantean raises her palm. She must create some sort of air shield around me because the strands framing my face begin to lift and snap.

"I think you're hiding something from me, Callie. Something that involves Tarian." Bryn's words penetrate, loud and clear and perplexing. "I think that fire you all claim ravaged the shop didn't happen."

Goosebumps ridge my forearms, brushing against the extra soft fleece lining of my sleeves.

"I think that nurse isn't a nurse at all." She side-eyes Electra, who's still on the phone—or pretending to be.

"Why"—I clear my throat—"do you say that?"

"She's speaking in Atlantean." Bryn's tone is so hushed now that it barely reaches my ears.

"Since when can Atlanteans *not* be nurses?"

Bryn's pupils spread out like water on paper. "Why in the world would a supernatural *choose* to be a nurse?"

"Supernatural?" The word startles a cough from me.

"I know you refuse to believe supes exist, hun, but Atlanteans can do stuff."

I lean over and grab my mug, then take small sips to hydrate my throat.

"I once went clubbing with Yasmin"—Bryn reaches under her robe to snap one of her camisole straps back into place—"and she tossed a girl off the VIP podium with a flick of her fingers."

I gag on my mouthful of tea, which irritates my throat anew. "Was the girl"—I wheeze—"all right?"

"Unfortunately. She landed on someone's table." Bryn shrugs as though she were describing just another night out. "Cops arrived and arrested her."

"Yasmin?"

"No, the girl. Keep up. It turns out she was one of those crazy Holy Hunters."

"I can't believe you never told me that."

"Really?" She wriggles her index finger around the penthouse. "How about you tell me what you're *really* doing here?"

"The accident wasn't an accident." I'm trying to decide how best to impart truths without revealing *the* truth. "Tarian's car was targeted."

Her irises grow as large and shiny as pennies.

"Even though I wasn't their mark, Tarian and Malachi decided it was best to keep me in a safehouse until the guilty party was caught."

I watch my confession trickle through Bryn.

"I'm sorry for not telling you, but I was sworn to secrecy."

Bryn mindlessly pushes up her bathrobe sleeve and reorders her bangles. "Who?"

"Who what?"

"Who's after—" She blinks, her fingers freezing against her bracelets. "It's the Holy Hunters!" She claps her palm against her lips as she realizes she may have used too much volume.

I check my mother and Mrs. Fiona's bedroom doors, finding both thankfully closed. As I return my attention to my friend, I meet Electra's narrowed stare. Is she wondering what game I'm playing?

"Sorry for telling her, Elle. I know I wasn't supposed to, but Bryn and I have no secrets from each other. Right, Bee?"

"I find the fact that you're asking a little hurtful." Bryn shakes her head. "At least, everything's starting to make—" Her attention has drifted back to the TV. "Do you think it's connected to Symeon's death and Yasmin's disappearance?"

"We do." Electra's the one who answers.

Bryn gives another slow shake of her head. "Wow. This is insane."

Beeping erupts. I startle until I realize it's just the washing machine. I get up to throw my clothes into the dryer. When I come back into the living room, Bryn's no longer on the couch and the TV is off.

Electra's frowning at the dark screen. "She's making you breakfast."

Sure enough, cupboards clap and cutlery clangs in the kitchen. "What do you think?"

"Of breakfast? Most important meal of the day."

I arch a brow.

"I think we shouldn't divulge too much"—Electra picks up the remote and presses a few buttons—"but I also don't think she's involved."

Hearing Electra confirm my belief is comforting. "Can you let her keep the knowledge?"

She nods, distracted by the remote.

"Is Diego coming?"

"Yes. He's on his way."

"Thank you." My eyelids prick with gratitude, relief, and fatigue. "Hey"—I drop my voice to a mere whisper—"the other day I noticed a small brown vial in her bag. Check if it's still there?"

Her gaze swings off the remote and bangs into my face at the same time a peal of thunder rocks Boston and does away with the lights.

"I heard the word hurricane before the damn TV went dead." She starts punching the buttons. "Ugh."

Lightning forks across the sky, gilding the clouds and the phone which Electra has extracted from the back of her black cargo pants.

"No cell service." She stuffs her phone back into her pants pocket, then nods to her bedroom. "I'll go dig around. You keep her in the kitchen."

As rain begins to pummel the bay windows with the force of a car wash, I pad into the kitchen.

"I'm glad they're postponing the memorial, because there's no way I could've made it to the Vineyard today." Bryn heaps Lucky Charms into two bowls. "Remember the time we downed a family-sized box on a school night?"

Her armload of jewelry tinkles as she splashes milk over the colorful cereal. I don't know how she can stand so many bracelets. I can barely tolerate a watch.

"I remember." I smile as I fish two spoons from the cutlery drawer.

We'd been so high on sugar that it had taken us hours to fall asleep. Mom wasn't happy; Dad, on the other hand, had found our hyperactivity hysterical, especially the following morning when he'd woken our groggy asses up for school an hour earlier than necessary.

"So Electra, she's not a nurse, is she?"

I'm about to say no when the front door swings open on a bolt of thunder. I'm not sure if it's the weather or the fact that there's no electricity, but I squeak, drop the spoons, and smack a palm against my palpitating chest.

The second I spy a blond mane gone brown with rain, I calm an iota. After closing the door, Malachi probes the modern alarm panel beside the door that's as obscure as the rest of the apartment.

"No electricity." My tongue still wobbles from my unsettled pulse.

Furrows reshape Malachi's brow. "The house alarm should still work. It's connected to—"

"Cellular is down." Electra trundles into the kitchen, eyes alight with anxiety.

Maybe storms frighten her? Unless she found the vial, and—

She catches my stare and shakes her head. No vial, or nothing suspect to report inside the vial?

I crouch to pick up the spoons. "The elevator worked?"

"The building's equipped with a backup generator." Malachi flicks a switch, and the kitchen floods with light.

Even though I love storms, my ribs loosen and my breathing quiets. Electra and Malachi, too, seem to shed a layer of tension.

Bryn sets the milk carton down. "Wait…did you all think this" —she twirls her finger around the kitchen—"was the Holy Hunters' doing?"

Malachi's chin dips. "Holy Hunters?"

"I told Bryn that Tarian and I were targeted the night of the accident, and she believes it could've been by that sect that hates your people." I try to communicate by subtle eyelid shifting that this is the extent of what I shared.

"We actually unmasked the perpetrators, Bryn." As he ambles toward the square marble dining table, I frown.

"And?" she prompts him. "Who are they?"

He pulls out a chair, its legs shredding the quiet like chalk on slate. "Your father and your sister are the ones who attacked my cousin."

*Your sister.*

My fingers tighten around the spoons while my gaze tightens on Bryn's. If I was right about Yasmin being Bryn's sister, then does that mean I'm wrong about Bryn being harmless?

# FIFTY-THREE

The cap Bryn was screwing onto the milk carton slips from her fingers and tumbles, bumping into Electra's combat boots. "My father? What does Calanthe have to do with my dad and Mackenzie?"

My eyes meet Malachi's for a fraction of a second before he moves his attention to the sliding door that separates the living room from the kitchen.

"Not Mackenzie." With a flick of his pointer finger, he slides it shut.

Bryn gasps, but is it from his use of magic or from the news that she has another sister?

"You should sit." Malachi drops into the dining room chair as though he weighs a ton, then pulls out the chair next to his for Bryn.

She remains stock-still. "I have another sister?"

Malachi unzips the navy suede bomber he layered over a basic white tee, *à la* James Dean, then slides his fingers inside the breast pocket and extracts a folded sheet of paper, which he smooths on the table. The top right corner is emblazoned with the logo of a lab, and beneath it, a familiar abbreviation.

Bryn finally shuffles toward him. She doesn't sit though. She merely snatches the paper off the table and carries it to her face. After a quick read-through, she smacks it back down. "What does this all mean?"

"They're DNA results," Malachi replies.

"Whose?" she bites out.

"Yours."

"*Mine*?" Bryn squawks. "Why were you testing *my* DNA?"

"Because it's come to my attention that Delta Lynch may have fathered another child before he had you, and I wanted to verify this. It turns out that he did—Yasmin."

"Yasmin's my sister? Yasmin Hassek Fablez?" The last time her eyes went so wide was the day my parents took us on an outing to a candy factory to observe how sugar was spun into colorful sweets. "*The* Yasmin, who's now missing?"

"Technically, she's not missing. She's at large with your father and Tarian." Malachi rolls his neck. "We merely dropped the 'missing' storyline into the police's lap to foil her plans of leaving the country. The more people looking for her, the better."

*Leaving the country…* I'm suddenly back in that train wagon with Bryn, Yasmin, and Delta, the one heading to Atlantis. Tarian misconstrued the ties that bound Delta and Yasmin, but not their destination.

"There's more." Malachi drums his fingers against the marble tabletop.

Bryn's complexion is a mottled shade of white and scarlet glossed by perspiration. I'm not sure my friend can take more.

"When I was retrieving Yasmin's DNA from Symeon's apartment earlier, I saw a picture from my aunt and uncle's wedding. My parents were standing on either side of the bride and groom. The reason I mention it is because, when I walked past it, I did a double take. I thought I was seeing someone else." His fingers stop moving, and a slow breath coils from his lungs, adding to the tense anticipation. "I thought I was seeing Yasmin."

A chill races up my spine and spreads to my farthest extremities. Holy cherubs, is he saying that…that…?

Malachi thumbs his mouth a few times before flattening his hand to the table. "I had my DNA tested as well. The human my mother ran off with twenty-five years ago was your father, Bryn." His glazed eyes roam over the printout before going to the spectacle beyond the kitchen window.

Electra's mouth gapes but no sound emerges. Just air.

All she told me yesterday reels through my mind: Nora begging Barak to lend her Tarian in order to give her lover superhuman powers; Barak refusing; the council voting for Nora to be put to death for giving her blood to a mortal.

"They *are* headed to Atlantis." My voice is so breathy from shock that I'm not a hundred percent certain it pricks anyone's ears besides my own. "That's why Yasmin abducted Tarian."

Bryn's pallor rivals her bathrobe. "Yasmin abducted— But I thought the Holy Hunters…I-I don't—I thought Tarian was keeping you safe?"

I snare my lip. "Tarian was with me in the car the night of the accident."

"He was taken that night. By your father and Yasmin." Electra's gaze is locked on the back of Malachi's head. "We believe Symeon played an integral part, although we're not a hundred percent certain what that part was yet."

Bryn's throat bobs with swallow after swallow. "Yasmin was at the engagement party. So was Symeon."

"We know, but they were still in on everything, Bee." I lay the spoons on the kitchen countertop before I drop them again. "By the way, did you ask your sister to hire me for the floral decorations?"

"No. Why?"

I swallow. "Because that's what Mackenzie said." Although

both Electra and Bryn are frowning, I don't tell them about Tarian's theory. *Symeon, Symeon, Symeon, you absolute asshole.*

"Can someone please *fucking* explain why my father would *fucking* kidnap Tarian Hadez?" Bryn white-knuckles the back of Malachi's previously offered chair, her chest rising and falling at dizzying speed.

"Because my cousin's the conduit through which the mine can transfer supernatural abilities to the common mortal." Malachi's voice seems to emerge from an abyss. From the mine itself.

She blinks at him, then blinks at Electra, then finally at me. "You knew! All this time you knew that Atlanteans had powers, Callie?"

I grimace.

Electra squares her shoulders. "Humans aren't allowed to know our secrets, Miss Fielding."

Bryn's mouth warps into a nasty expression. "Isn't *Calanthe* human?" She hasn't used my full name since the day we met at that concert almost two decades ago, so it stings.

"Calanthe was told because Tarian transferred one of his runes to her." Malachi's lids finally rise. "It's made her immune to our compulsion."

Bryn stays quiet.

Even though she didn't ask for any clarifications, Malachi feeds her one. "Compulsion is the ability to place or eliminate thoughts from a human's mind."

Her throat clenches. "And runes?" Is she asking to appear curious or because she truly doesn't know?

Electra raises two fingers to her nape and taps the skin. "The thing you call an 'Atlantean tat.' Not ink."

"And Calanthe has one of those?" Again with the third person.

"Yes." Electra makes the fallen carton cap levitate toward her hands.

To know that magic is real is something, but to observe it, that's truly something else.

"The strange word on her back." Bryn doesn't look at me as she puts two and two together. "That's the rune?"

"Yes." Electra screws the cap onto the milk carton.

"Does Tarian have to be conscious to enter the mine and transfer magic?" I ask.

"That scenario's never presented itself."

While Bryn keeps murdering the small of my back with her gaze, I ask the other question that's been titillating my brain. "If Yasmin and Delta were planning on sailing to Atlantis, how come the boat was still hanging around the North American coastline?"

"Either they heard of our trip to the aircraft carrier and knew we'd be checking for boats crossing the Atlantic, or they were waiting out the storm." Malachi nods to the kitchen window that's getting hosed with rain. "The *Amapola* may have been a sturdy yacht, but she wouldn't have fared too well over the swells we saw when we visited the aircraft carrier."

"Couldn't they have flattened the ocean with their magic?" I ask.

"Not hurricane swells. *Even* if Sym and Yasmin worked together. Actually…" Malachi's voice peters out.

"Actually, what?" I'm on tenterhooks.

"They could've magicked the boat to endure the harsh crossing."

"Symeon stayed in Boston an extra day. That's why they didn't cross immediately!" Electra's eyes flash with the thrill of locking all the puzzle pieces together. "Because they were waiting for Sym to board."

I visualize how it must all have played out. "So, he gets on board. Bumps into Tarian or *is* bumped into him. Why did the boat sink?"

"Maybe he developed scruples and sunk his own ship?" Electra offers.

His bloated flesh scores my lids in time with a burst of lightning. "How long does it take to exsanguinate a body?"

"A few minutes. If you're an Atlantean." Malachi drums his fingers.

Our conversation has robbed Bryn of color. She's become as white as Symeon in death, as white as the sheet of DNA results.

Yet I forge ahead. "They must've boarded another ship."

"Or a plane." Electra slides her cell phone out of her black pants. "I'll get Dorian to check all flights that left the region in the last two days."

Malachi says something to her in Atlantean. The only word I grasp is "Atlantis." Is he warning her that they could already be there? Wouldn't they have been alerted?

"Cell service is back?" I ask.

"Fuck. I forgot about that." One glance at her phone has her head shaking.

Malachi nods to the alarm panel, then says something in Atlantean that makes her stride over to it. She jams her finger against the little touchscreen that remains dark even though the ceiling lights glare.

Malachi studies Bryn, who's still clutching the back of the chair as though her balance depended on it.

When Electra speaks to Malachi in Atlantean again, a chill scampers up my spine and raises the fine hair on my nape. "What's going on?"

Malachi stashes the paper back into his jacket pocket and rises, then walks toward Electra. After another hushed exchange in their native tongue, they open the door. Electra disappears onto the landing. A moment later, she comes back inside and bolts the door.

"What?" My voice writhes with nerves that only intensify when a black chopper punches through the purple clouds and rises out of sight.

Bryn gasps. "Did you all see that?"

"One of ours." A rapid swallow jostles Electra's narrow throat.

Does she mean the chopper? She must mean the chopper. And if it is *ours*, then why does she look and sound panicked?

# FIFTY-FOUR

**E**lectra carves a hand through the air, ramming the big kitchen door open. "Callie, let's go wake your mom and Mrs. Murphy."

My breath catches, teeters before falling out in the form of a brisk exhale. "Was Diego in the chopper?"

"No. Dorian."

"Dorian?" Dread fuses my joints and stiffens my muscles. "Why is Dorian here?"

"To fly us out of the building." Electra nods to the living room, but I can't get my legs to move.

"Us?" Bryn asks.

"Yes." I'm not sure when Malachi wandered away from the door, but he's now standing beside the window, scanning the storm-washed street below. "We're all leaving."

My heart clobbers my ribs. The only reason we'd *all* be leaving a safehouse is because it's no longer safe.

"In this storm?" Bryn shrills.

"We can use magic to shield the chopper from the worst of the weather." Malachi's jaw ticks. Because he's spied something worrying below?

Bryn sucks in air, expels it, then draws in another lengthy inhale before finally unhooking her fingers from the chair and locking them around her elbows. "Are we under attack?"

"I was tailed on my way back from the lab, so I called Dorian to run the plates. Either he wasn't reassured by the owner's identity, or he was worried because he couldn't reach us." I must look as nauseous as I feel, because he adds, "I'm certain it's the latter, Callie. Dorian's a mother hen."

Even though I don't know Malachi well, I know him well enough to know that he's not certain of anything at the moment.

Apparently, Bryn's of the same mindset because she says, "You think it's my father, don't you?"

His deep-set eyes gleam like chiseled aquamarines.

She must somehow realize he's about to compel her to drop the conversation and forget everything, because she slaps her palms over her lids. "Before you screw with my mind, tell me one thing. Why do you assume my father's involved?"

Is he about to reveal my psychosomatic connection? As much as I want to confide in my best friend, it's our ace. One I pray we'll be able to play soon.

"I don't assume, I *know* since I have footage of him at a marina in Martha's Vineyard," he bluffs. "That same marina where the *Amapola* was docked."

Lightning slashes the sky. It must hit the building because it blows the backup generator and vibrates the floor. Unless it's my body that's shaking.

Bryn's hands skid off her face. "How come Tarian's still missing if you have footage of my father with him?"

"I was given the footage too late to intervene," Malachi lies.

*Mom and Mrs. Fiona. Mom and Mrs. Fiona.* I work to haul my stiff body away from the countertop and out of the kitchen.

"Show me." Bryn crosses her arms, grip so taut her pointy nails look about ready to gouge the terry fabric of her bathrobe.

"It's on Dorian's phone."

"How fucking convenient."

Malachi cocks an eyebrow at her venomous tone. "Excuse me?"

"For all I know, you could be making all this shit up to discredit my family so that your father dumps my mother."

Shock solders my feet to the threshold.

"What exactly would I gain from my father dumping your mother, Bryn?"

"You'd ensure the Fieldings didn't become part of your precious little clan, since you all think we're garbage."

"You have no clue what I think." Malachi's voice is low but not soft.

She gives a humorless laugh. "Oh, please. It's written all over your face. The only one who didn't think that way was Symeon."

"Stop it, Bryn," I snap. "Being vindictive won't help anyone. Not Tarian and not your mother."

She hikes her chin up. "You've clearly picked your camp, Callie. Then again, you've always thought the very worst of my mother."

I understand she feels cheated and deceived, and not just by the Atlanteans, but by me. Regardless, Malachi doesn't deserve her spite.

"Just tell me one thing, why is it that you were so quick to accept *her*?" She gestures to where I stand, evidently incapable of tearing myself away from the train wreck taking place before me. "Because she's so broke and desperate, and the Hadezes are such magnanimous beings?"

She holds no gun, yet it feels like she's just shot me with her words. It feels like there's a great big hole in my chest that no amount of Atlantean magic will ever be able to fix.

"Bryn?" Malachi shifts his jaw from side to side.

She snaps her attention his way. This time, she's not quick enough to shield herself from his compulsion.

His eyes become the only source of light in the kitchen. "You'll forget all about Atlantean powers and that Calanthe wears one of Tarian's runes. You'll also forget that Tarian was abducted. You believe we're getting on the helicopter for Symeon's memorial and that Calanthe's coming because Tarian wants her there. Now go get dressed."

I wait for him to add more items to that list—like Bryn's kinship—but the inhuman glow of his eyes snuffs out. Did he forget to erase this from her mind or is he letting her hold on to the knowledge because he plans on making it public?

Banging rattles the front door.

I jump a foot in the air, calming only once I hear Dorian's voice boom, "Mal! Elle! Let me in."

Malachi rubs his palms down his jeans, then sidesteps Bryn, who charges past me without so much as a glance in my direction. "Your mom, Callie. Go get her." Although Malachi's tone doesn't wobble and the line of his shoulders doesn't bend, a nerve feathers his jaw.

"Will you be okay?"

I catch a flash of white between his lips. "I'm an Atlantean."

"So was Tarian. *Is.* So *is* Tarian."

"I'll be fine."

Still I linger.

Malachi calls out something in Atlantean, and Dorian answers. I take it he was verifying the identity of the man behind the door. I wouldn't put it past Atlanteans to have the ability to modulate their voice in order to impersonate one another.

Malachi opens the door. When my gaze clocks Dorian's, the air trapped in my lungs sneaks out and I finally march off. Mom's stepping out of her room, followed by Electra.

"Sorry." I go toward my mother, trying to catch her attention, but her eyes are glazed.

Electra nods to my socks. "Shoes, Callie."

I run to my bedroom, then toe on my sneakers at record speed.

"Mrs. Murphy," I hear Electra call out. "Time to go."

Keys jangle. "Coming." Our neighbor pulls her braid out from underneath her lanyard, then finishes doing up the buttons on her cotton candy cardigan.

"Ladies." Malachi stands in the doorway. "Please follow Dorian."

Like zombies, they shuffle past him, then out of the apartment.

"I hypnotized them so they'll stay calm. Here." She tosses me a nylon bag. "I dumped all your clothes from the dryer inside. Everything else, we'll replace." She's carrying another bag. Probably with her things, unless it's my mother's and Mrs. Fiona's?

She's so calm whereas I'm racked with tremors. "I can't believe you took the time to pack."

"I manually shut down the elevator," Electra says. "We're on the eighty-fifth floor."

"So you think someone's after us?"

"Don't worry."

Obviously, her words spark just that. And panic. One that makes my dream of falling feel like an enjoyable carnival ride.

Malachi cants his head to the gaping front door. "Go up with Callie, Elle. I'll get Bryn."

Adrenaline fuels my strides, and I all but fly up to the rooftop where the gleaming black chopper sits, rotors spinning. Dorian's helping Mrs. Fiona inside as I rush across the slick rooftop, the wet wind lashing my cheeks and drenching my hair.

Dorian snares my waist and hoists me inside a huge cabin with two rows of seats that face one another. And then he's boosting his sister up. "Get their harnesses on!"

Electra shoves the duffel under a seat, then crouches beside Mrs. Fiona. I watch how she straps her in before gripping my mother's halter and lap belt and clicking them together. Electra brackets Mrs. Fiona's face and says something that's got my neighbor's lids collapsing. And then she grabs a headset dangling from a small hook on the ceiling and places it over Mrs. Fiona's ears.

Electra then swivels toward my mother and, eyes glowing, repeats whatever she told Mrs. Fiona. Mom's lids slip shut as Electra places a second headset over her ears.

As she straps herself in, she explains, "They'll rest until we reach our destination."

I suddenly wish her magic would knock me out, because I'd give anything to feel a fraction more chill.

With trembling fingers, I snag my own harness and drop it around my neck, then secure the lap belt to it.

As I look back up, I catch sight of a mocha-skinned woman with a plaited crown of platinum hair, golden aviators, and sleeves of tattoos—not the magical kind—sitting in one of the two pilot chairs at the front of the aircraft.

"Ines," Electra huffs, as she drops into the seat beside Mrs. Fiona's, the one that places her back to her fellow Atlantean's.

For some reason, I was expecting a more matronly woman instead of a tatted-up warrior princess from an exotic land.

"Where's Mal?" Dorian yells over the slapping wind.

"He was getting Bryn," Electra barks back.

Brother and sister exchange a look that makes my insides go as cold and damp as my hoodie. Electra unfastens her halter.

"Don't you dare move!" He jabs his finger in her direction, then jogs across the blustery rooftop.

The backs of my lids spark with Symeon's ominous warning: YOU ARE NEXT. I clutch my thighs, trying to stop their feverish drumming. What if Lynch compelled people to collect Malachi to use him as leverage to get out of the country? What if we were wrong to trust Bryn? What if she faked being affected by the compulsion? What if this is unrelated to Lynch? What if the Holy Hunters are out for Atlantean blood?

The door swings open just as Dorian reaches it. When Malachi bursts out, carrying Bryn in a fireman's hold, I gasp. He runs to the chopper while Dorian shuts the door with a slap of his wrist and sketches its metal frame with his pointer finger. Is he welding it shut with magic? Boobytrapping it? Whatever he's doing, it's taking too long.

Malachi lays Bryn down across the two seats beside Electra's before hopping into the seat beside mine. Even though my friend's lids are shut, her chest rises and falls.

"What happened?" I yell, scouring her body for injuries.

Aside from the bruise peeking out of her frilly black shorts, she seems unharmed.

"I found her unconscious on the bathroom floor," Malachi yells. "She must've slipped and passed out."

Wouldn't she have a bruise on her head if that were the case? Or I don't know…something? Just as I think this, a trickle of blood runs out of her nose. My heart stops, and I gape at Electra, but she's staring at her brother, shouting at him to haul ass while distractedly shoving Bryn upright and clipping her inside a harness.

Dorian whirls and sprints just as Ines guns the helicopter upward. What the fuck! My lungs crumple like a water bottle during an altitude change, crushing my thready stock of air. Why is she taking off?

"Wait!" My harness feels like it's cutting into my torso. "Dorian!"

Ines keeps pulling on some lever.

The chopper keeps rising.

Dorian lunges, vaulting inhumanly high. He claps Malachi's outstretched arm, then rolls inside the giant chopper just as a cloud of smoke mushrooms off the rooftop.

I think it may be Dorian's doing until I spot people in tactical gear stepping from the smoke as though crafted of the very substance.

# FIFTY-FIVE

Even though I couldn't have heard the explosion over the snarling sky and drone of the helicopter engine, it somehow zings between my temples in time with the realization that we were ambushed.

My stomach tightens, then lifts and wags like a dog's tail—left, right, left, right. I simultaneously smack my palm over my mouth and crush my fist into my abdomen to appease the knot of motion sickness bunching my insides.

Dorian straightens enough to walk around the cabin, weaves himself through the rows of seats and drops into the co-pilot's chair, his black T-shirt glued to his broad, pumping chest. He runs his hands down his face, plonks on a pair of headphones, then waves his palms in a circular motion like he's wiping down a bar top.

Even though the storm outside rages, the helicopter steadies.

I've never loved magic so hard in my entire life. My head lolls back as the swaying comes to a complete halt.

Electra must've finally noticed Bryn's nosebleed, because she's got a tissue wadded against her face while Malachi looks on, expression rife with so much anger he seems about ready to slide the door open and pitch my friend from the chopper.

Did Bryn lead those people to our doorstep? "Who was after us?"

Electra leans forward, unhooks a headset from the ceiling, and tosses it at me, then grabs another pair for herself. Her voice suddenly crackles against my eardrums. "I think you were right about Bryn using Atlantean blood."

I position the mic in front of my mouth. "She fell in the bathroom. Maybe she hit her nose?" While I suggest this, I realize how unlikely that scenario is without a bruise swelling her face.

"After what she said to you"—Malachi's grim stare scrapes across my face—"I'm surprised you're still jumping to her defense."

Electra sits back. "What did she say to you?"

With a sigh, I murmur, "Nothing that wasn't true." I *am* broke, just like I *am* desperate, and not only to find a solution to our shop's slow demise, but also, and especially, to my mother's worsening— "Mom's pills!"

"Got them in here." Electra taps the bag under her seat with her boot.

Relief douses my rush of anguish. "So who were those people?"

Dorian's voice jazzes up my headset. "Holy Hunters."

*Not fellow Atlanteans.* That's good. Right? I contemplate the tissue filling up with blood. Is all of it Bryn's or is it tinged with someone else's?

I reach under my hoodie sleeve for the hair tie I snapped around my wrist this morning, then attempt to wrangle the springy mass. "Who were they after?"

"Malachi." The unfamiliar voice jerks my gaze to the braided, tattooed woman flying the helicopter. "We caught some encrypted chatter about a big payday for whichever faction managed to apprehend Tarian's cousin." After a beat, she adds, "At least my stay among those crazies wasn't all for nothing, Elle."

"Anytime, Ines," Electra chirps. "Anytime."

I'd have smiled had Electra's eyes not been radiating unease. "Why do you think they targeted you, Mal?"

He shrugs. "Perhaps it was Yasmin's way of getting back at me for that missing-person APB."

Symeon's warning echoes once more between my temples, ridding me of what little warmth my fleece hoodie is lending me. "You need to be careful."

A smile warps his lips. "I'm an Atlantean," he repeats, as though it'd slipped my mind during our mad dash out of the apartment.

"Doesn't make you immune to getting kidnapped and tortured," Electra grumbles. "Or to idiocy."

Malachi's eyebrows jolt in surprise.

"Electra Serran," Dorian hisses.

She rolls her eyes, then sneaks a hand into her leather jacket and extracts her phone.

As she types, I ask, "Is it working again?"

"Yep. Jammers were localized." She stashes the thing back into her pocket. "Ines, land atop Marion Tower."

"Why?" Ines's voice crackles through the headset.

"'Cause I've made other arrangements for Callie's mother and neighbor."

"They'll be safe in the Vineyard," Malachi says.

"They'll be safer away from us, Mal." Especially since I don't trust his father.

His cheek dimples as though he were biting the inside of it. "What's in Marion Tower?"

"Diego's apartment." Electra stashes away her phone. "And in a few hours, Diego."

The speed at which Dorian turns in his seat is dizzying. The helicopter swerves and rocks. Malachi snaps his palms skyward, steadying the hovering deathtrap.

"You know how much I trust him and how little I trust most people." She says this so conversationally, one would think she was unaware of how the veins along Dorian's temple bulge.

Her lips twitch. Dorian's, too. But where Electra's biting a smile off her lips, Dorian does *not* look amused.

I glance toward Malachi, who's thumbing away the curve of his lips. Dorian shoots him a short scowl before returning his attention to Electra, whom he glares at until we touchdown on another rooftop. The lightning lacerating the sky reflects in the lenses of his sunglasses and the thunder reflects in the angle of his jaw.

"The worst of the hurricane is supposed to hit in about two hours," Ines announces through the headset intercom. "I want to be on the ground in Martha's Vineyard before then."

I blink at the dense clouds and ropes of rain, wondering how exactly it could get worse.

Electra's already unfastened. Malachi, too. As they work on Mrs. Fiona and my mother's gear, I remove my own.

Dorian shoulders through the aisle, then lifts my mother with the utmost care. "I got her. You stay here with Ines and Bryn, Elle."

Electra cranes her neck to meet his fiery stare. "I told Diego I'd wait for him with—"

"*You* are going to the Vineyard," he snaps.

She shoots him a smile that makes him grumble something in Atlantean as he drops out of the chopper. Malachi hoists a sleeping Mrs. Fiona into his arms and carries her out. I hop out after them, my ponytail flogging my cheeks.

"Callie?" Electra calls out.

I glance over my shoulder. "I just want to say goodbye."

"Take this." She dangles the black nylon duffel stashed beneath her seat. "Pills are in the zippered pocket. I've texted Dorian to look for them."

"Thank you for remembering."

She nods. "Hurry."

I start to jog but pause. And then I cup my hands around my mouth and shout, "Ines and Bryn will still be here when we get back, right?"

"They better be." Malachi must've stopped to wait for me because he slides Electra a meaningful look.

DORIAN PRESSES his thumb against a biometric lock. He seems almost surprised when the door unlatches.

His relationship with Diego might've ended, but there evidently weren't too many hard feelings if his ex didn't rescind his access to the home they'd shared. Then again, Diego doesn't live in Boston anymore, so maybe he didn't think to delete Dorian's fingerprint?

We enter through a wide foyer that leads to a kitchen on the left and a living room on the right. Although quainter than the penthouse, Diego's tenth-floor apartment is still breathtaking. Malachi and Dorian deposit both women on the sofa, and then Malachi murmurs something in their ears that makes their lids reel up.

He straightens and gestures around him. "So this is the apartment we discussed you could relocate to while the construction company finishes fixing the shop."

My heart aches for Dorian, who swallows a great many times as he takes in the navy walls covered in monochrome cityscapes. I can only imagine he's picturing the last time he was here.

"Beautiful." My mother blinks. "And it's got great vibes. What do you think, baby?"

I squeeze a smile on my lips as I drop the bag on the silver rug. "I really like it, Mom."

"Cor blimey, this storm." Mrs. Fiona toddles over to the window that overlooks the Old Harbor. "Street below's flooded."

"It's a category three hurricane," Malachi tells her.

"A hurricane?" Mrs. Fiona whirls, her keys bouncing against her ample bosom. "In Boston?"

Malachi shoots her a kindly smile. "Not the first one, Mrs. Murphy."

She looks him up and down. "What did you say your name was, Son?"

"Malachi Hadez."

"Hadez? From *the* Hadez bunch?"

"Yes."

"I'm sorry for your loss. It's so sad when people die before their time." Her eyes flick to my mother.

The tragic topic makes Mom scoot to the edge of the sofa and toy with the fringes on her favorite belted sweater.

"I need to go see my family, but Dorian here will be staying with you to help you get settled. Anything you need, he'll get for you." Malachi smiles gently as he backs up toward me and murmurs, "We should get going."

My mother's forehead creases. "Where's your dad, Callie?"

I say the first thing that pops into my mind: "Fulfilling an order."

Mom grimaces. "In this weather?"

"It's for a wedding."

Her expression softens. "Ah. That makes more sense."

When Malachi's eyebrows scrunch, Mom explains, "A huge storm hit Boston the day Nick and I got married. I wanted to cancel everything, but my husband convinced me it was a great omen. He said—"

"'A wet knot can never be untied,'" I murmur.

He had the saying engraved inside my mother's wedding band.

She must remember this as well because she frowns at her left hand. "What did I do with my rings?"

"Dad took them to be polished." I blurt this out so she doesn't dwell on their actual whereabouts—the little safe bolted to the wall inside her closet.

She massages her chest. "Can you call Lucas to check if they're ready? I'd really like them back."

I keep hoping she'll scrap my ex from her mind, but not only does she remember him, she also remembers that his father is a jeweler.

"I'll call him." I force myself not to grimace.

Lucas replaced me so fast I'm half convinced the other girl was his side piece. I didn't dig around, though. Between my dad passing away and my bastard ex dumping me, my heart was too battered to withstand more pain. And then as the weeks bled into months, I simply stopped caring.

"Anyway, Mom, I gotta go."

"*Go*? Where?"

"On a weekend trip with Bryn and Malachi." Shit. Is it even the weekend?

She frowns. "In this weather?"

"We're driving to Newport." I lick my lips, hating the bitter taste of lying.

"I don't think you should be taking a car anywhere."

"Dad said it was okay."

She blinks. Once. Twice. And then she knuckles her lash line. "That's not funny, Callie." Her voice catches. "Why would you say such a thing?"

When tears drip, horror seizes me. She's back in the here and now where Dad doesn't exist.

"I don't know why I said that." A lump forms in my throat. "I'm so sorry."

Mrs. Fiona's kind eyes gleam with pity. "Hey, Lisa, let's go check out the kitchen. I'm in the mood for something to eat." She starts toward the foyer, but stops and lingers, waiting for my mother to follow.

Even though Mom's mind has been messed with too many

times today, I don't want to leave her with tears in her eyes. Tears brought on by me.

"Malachi?" I croak.

He understands what I'm asking without me having to add any extra words. Making sure his back is to Mrs. Fiona, he murmurs, "Lisa Bloom, you'll forget that your husband is dead." Malachi stands so close that the heat of his body blasts my frozen skin. "You also won't worry about our trip, because I'm a good friend of Calanthe's and I would never let anything bad happen to your daughter."

Mom's hands fall away from her face and anchor themselves to mine. "Drive safely and call me as soon as you reach the hotel."

"I will." I crush my mother in a hug and whisper a quick, "I love you so much."

"Love you more. Always more."

As we climb back into the elevator, Malachi says, "They won't come after her, Callie. She'll be safe."

"I know. Just don't like saying goodbye when you don't know how long it'll be before you see a person again."

Malachi leans back against the mirrored panel. "What else did Tarian mention in your last dream, besides Yasmin and Bryn's kinship?"

"It started out in a mall…" As the elevator rises, I rehash how Miley Cyrus handed me a bleeding rose to unlock the door behind which I would find— "Saul and Joslyn are in the Vineyard."

It's not a question, yet Malachi nods.

My heart begins to accelerate because I suddenly think that, even though it was *my* dream, Tarian was showing me where he was being kept. "He's still there, Mal!"

"Still where?"

"In the vicinity of Martha's Vineyard." Like a brush soaked in silver paint, my conclusion adds luster to Malachi's eyes, brightening the blue and glossing the white.

I pray with all my might that I'm not peddling false hope. "Do you trust Ines?"

"I do."

"Do you trust your father?"

Silence.

Interesting that he'd trust someone who works for the man but not the man himself. Then again, the man's marrying Joslyn. I've no doubt that created some tension between father and son.

"Did you tell Ines what my rune allows me to do?"

"No. But I told her that you wear one so that she understands why you're so important to Tarian, and thus, to us."

"Did you tell anyone else?" This seems important to know before heading onto an island filled with Atlanteans.

"No."

"So your dad—"

"Doesn't know."

"And you're sure Ines didn't say anything to him?"

He sighs. "I know Electra probably built Ines into a monster, since that's the way she sees her, but she's not, Callie. Ines has saved my ass more times than I care to remember. She is as loyal to me as Dorian is to Tarian."

"She's also loyal to your father."

"She is. Which is why I didn't tell her what your rune allows you to do."

The elevator dings, sweeping open onto the rooftop floor.

"Ready?" Malachi asks.

To fly into a hurricane? As Logan would say, *I'm as geared up as a trout on a bike.* But to rescue Tarian? I am so fucking ready.

His question must've been rhetorical, though, because he blows the rooftop door open with a burst of magic. Rain dives through the opening and lashes at our bodies. Malachi swiftly shields us from the elements, yet the bite and chill of the storm lingers on my face. Penetrates.

I suddenly stop our mad dash toward the helicopter and crane my neck, squinting at the raging sky. "Mal?"

He pauses.

"Do you think the mine could've created this storm to keep the *Amapola* from sailing across the ocean?"

His eyes flash, lightning-bright. "Either the mine or Tarian, but yes. Both have that power." He must've dropped his magical shield because the storm snatches my ponytail and soaks through my clothes.

I don't shiver though, the same way I don't jump when thunder cracks and vibrates the rooftop, because this gorgeous, powerful weather system isn't going to hurt me, it's going to carry me to *him*.

As I think of Tarian, my rune begins to prickle. I could fight his pull, but why in the world would I? It doesn't matter how our last dream ended, the only thing that matters is how this new one will begin.

# FIFTY-SIX

W hen my lids open, I'm standing in an oblong boardroom, empty save for the male sitting at one end of an oval table that can comfortably fit twenty. I glance down and find I'm wearing a skirt suit that's very unlike anything I own, with patent stilettos which are, on the other hand, very much like something I do own.

"How's Malachi?" Tarian's voice is so clipped that I look up brusquely. He's thumbing through a thick binder.

"He's fine." I'm tempted to tell him about the ambush, but why worry him with a situation that was resolved? With my luck, anyway, the Holy Hunters will storm this dream and attempt to capture Malachi in front of our eyes.

Tarian flips to another page, then another. I wonder if he's searching for a specific file or if he's actively avoiding my stare. He can't still be angry at me if he conjured me into his dream, can he?

*Flip. Flip. Flip.* "Have I killed anyone else with my magic?"

"Not that I know of. What I do know…well, strongly assume" —I turn on my heel, scanning the elongated room for a window, but the walls are entirely padded in black silk—"is that you're in Martha's Vineyard." When I spin back around, his fingers are creasing a page. "Anything useful in that binder?"

"No." He goes back to flicking through it.

I sigh. "If there's nothing useful in there, will you at least look at me?"

He doesn't.

I understand I deceived him, but it wasn't with ill intent. "I'd wake up, but we both know that won't help me find you."

"*We*? Last I checked, there is no *we*. There is a *you* and there is a *me*." He reclines in his leather office seat, sets his elbows on the armrests, and curls one big hand over the other in front of his chest. The crack of his knuckles resonates through the oddly shaped room. "After all, team players don't keep secrets from one another. For a venture to succeed, *all* must be laid bare."

"I was trying to spare you guilt and heartache." I blow air out the corner of my mouth. For someone who seems about as thrilled to see me as Macrazy was the day I arrived with my load of cacti, he took a great deal of care crafting my appearance.

Unless this is what his secretaries wear? I don't have a reason to be jealous, yet the transparency of my blouse combined with the sheerness of my thigh-highs suddenly pisses me off. Porn stars wear classier outfits in their office skits.

"Problem?" He wheels himself away from the giant table and hooks one leg over the other.

"Do the women who work for you choose their outfits or do you dress them?"

"They're mistresses of their own wardrobes."

I pinch my skirt's hem and lift it to reveal the silicone bands that hold my stockings up. "Do they all come dressed like high-class hookers?" When I catch his dark eyes licking up my legs, I release my skirt. "I suppose it fetches them better bonuses."

"How do you like the shoes?" His timbre's as rough as his ocular caress is gentle.

When he reaches my peaked nipples, I cross my arms over my chest. "They're fine."

"How can I make them better?"

"By not being a mercurial asshole."

A smirk fractures the hard line of his mouth.

"How many workplace-affair lawsuits have you compelled out of existence?"

"Zero."

"Right. The women who work here are probably throwing themselves on their knees to service you."

The curl of his lips harshens. "The reason no one's filed a lawsuit against me has everything to do with my hands and eyes never straying over bodies I don't intend to kill."

My heart misses a beat. "You fuck them, then kill them?"

He snorts. "I don't shit where I eat, Calanthe, and I don't make a habit of touching people, except to inflict harm. As for office wear, if any of my employees showed up wearing anything remotely like your outfit, they'd be fired on the spot. I don't tolerate lack of professionalism."

"Yet here I am, wearing…*this*."

"You don't work for me, Calanthe."

"I also apparently don't work *with* you."

The reminder washes away the lust glossing his features.

"Which is a shame, really. I bet you would've enjoyed hearing all I've learned."

He inclines his chin, which darkens the hollows beneath his cheekbones. "Tell me."

"Why? We're not a team, Hades."

He growls and lurches out of his chair, and then he prowls toward me.

I stand my ground, boosting my chin as he stalks closer. "I know what you're doing, and it won't work."

"What am I doing?"

"Trying to intimidate me into spilling my terrific secret."

His smile is back, except this time, it's all teeth. He unfastens the button holding his suit jacket closed. "I do plan on learning your *terrific secret*, but not through intimidation. I plan on coaxing it very gently from your lips."

My heart vaults so high I feel it beat inside my throat. "My lips aren't a genie lamp, Mr. Hadez." However hard I try to power my voice, it comes out ridiculously airy.

"Which set of lips are we talking about?" His palm rises to my nape before smoothing down my spine.

I should step back. Put the boardroom table between our bodies.

"Because I clearly remember these"—he palms one of my ass cheeks through the skirt, his fingertips stealing into my crease—"releasing many secrets when stroked."

"You're a real bastard. You snarl at me for using my body, yet that's exactly what you're doing."

"Except I'm not using your body to hide a truth. I'm using it to divulge one."

"So that makes it acceptable?" I reach around me and clasp his wrist, then fling it away. "I'll tell you what I learned, but don't touch me."

His lips flatten.

"Yasmin and Delta aren't dating."

Their names are like a bucket of ice water, cooling the heat crackling between us.

"They're related—father and daughter."

His pupils shrink. "What?"

"There's more. Yasmin is also related to Malachi. She's his half-sister. The man Nora Hadez ran off with was Bryn's father. We believe that's why they took you. To finish what Nora tried to accomplish before dying—giving Lynch sigils." I count to ten to allow all my words to settle before continuing. "Apparently, she wanted to use you two decades ago, but Barak blew her off and then he turned her in to the council for supplying Lynch with her blood."

Although Tarian's gaze is still affixed to mine, he's suddenly miles away.

"Maybe you should sit?" When he doesn't react, I twirl one of the chairs and lead him to it.

He sinks down heavily. A short squeal leaves my lips as he hooks my waist and drags me onto his lap. I try to press up, but his arm tightens like a vise. I stop trying to lever my body off his at the look of utter desperation that crimps his brow. I'm guessing he doesn't even realize he's holding me.

With a sigh, I say, "At least we know the *who* and the *why*. Now to pinpoint the *where exactly*. Any chance you've heard anything?"

His absent look makes me graze his cheek.

"Tarian?" When he blinks out of his daze, I repeat my question.

"It's been quiet." He splays his fingers on my hip, anchoring me to him—or rather, anchoring himself to me. "Are you certain Yasmin is Nora and Lynch's daughter?"

"Yes. Malachi ran a DNA test."

He leans back in the chair. "That must've been a shock."

"You can say that."

"Does Saul know?"

"We're not sure. Maybe your dad told him? Maybe Catalina did? She must know, right? After all, her daughter raised Yasmin as her own."

He inhales slowly, then exhales even slower. "Actually, he mustn't know or he would've hated the very sight of her."

"She looks like Nora, and he loved Nora."

"He loved her until she left him. And then he reviled her. He didn't even attend her funeral."

I grab the hem of my skirt that's ridden so far up, the silicone band of my thigh-highs is on full display. "It probably hurt too much."

His hand cruises past mine, settling on the band of bare skin between skirt and stocking.

"Tarian," I sigh.

"What?"

"You shouldn't touch me."

He grips my chin. "I apologize for lashing out at you." His nostrils flare, and he blinks.

Although no tears trundle down the steep cliffs of his cheeks, I can feel them welling inside his broad chest and slickening his bobbing throat.

"When I was a kid, I told my father—" His voice breaks, and his lashes sweep low. "I told him that Symeon was my favorite toy. I used to cuddle him like a stuffed animal. I used to carry him everywhere because I was scared he'd bruise his knees crawling around." He takes a deep breath. "I had this tricycle with a basket in the back. I would put him inside and pedal around our garden, making sure to go over all the tree roots so he'd get to bounce. How he'd laugh."

Although I barely knew Symeon, grief strikes me square in the ribs. It only gets worse when one of the fabric panels brightens like a screen and begins to display a reel of heartbreakingly tender home videos. Symeon and Tarian may have fallen out as adults, but as children, they were thick as thieves.

When a sweet giggle erupts and bounces around the room, Tarian's fingers tremble against my thigh. I curl up against him, nestling my head in the crook of his taut neck and snaking my arm between his shirt and blazer. To think the world perceives Tarian as a frightening beast. All I see when I stare at him is a beautiful, bleeding heart.

Even though the images of his youth are still beaming over us, he's no longer watching the screen; he's watching me. "I'm a monster."

"Monsters are soulless and heartless, but you, Tarian Hadez, are in possession of both a soul and a heart."

His pupils shrink before swelling. "I killed my father and brother."

Anger spikes my chest. "You withdrew their magic. We don't know that you killed them."

"Their magic kept them immortal." His eyes drop to my navel.

Is he thinking of my rune? He must be because it starts to burn like when he summons me.

"Perhaps you should stop looking for me, Calanthe. Perhaps I'm better off locked away from the world."

I smack his pec. "Don't be selfish."

He startles. "How does my desire to stop massacring innocents make me selfish?"

"People care about you, you big oaf. *I* care, lord only knows why. And don't say it's because of the brand, because your magic is *always* there, and you don't *always* inspire love."

Shock ripples over the taut planes of his face.

*Crap.* "I mean, *affection*." I avert my gaze as my cheeks warm.

His fingers begin to caress the skin ringing the silicone band of my thigh-highs. "What else do I inspire? Besides"—he pauses—"affection?"

"Lust. Mostly."

That sponges the temper from his handsome face.

"Irritation. Often. Violence. Sometimes." I forbid the word *pity* from trespassing and dulling the male's haunting sparkle.

"Anything else?"

I shake my head. He tilts his.

"What do I inspire?" I ask.

He raises his hand to my jaw and cups it with such reverence that my pulse threatens to derail. "You inspire my heart to beat, Calamity Darling." He traces the outline of my mouth. "To keep beating."

To trap all those precious beats, I press my palm against his chest, my cheek into his long fingers, and my mouth to his.

# FIFTY-SEVEN

I curl my fingers around Calanthe's delicate jaw, wondering what on Earth I could've done to deserve this woman's affection and forgiveness. I deserve neither. I deserve nothing. Yet I take and I take, siphoning the wild momentum of her pulse until it seeps beneath my skin and pools inside my blood.

As she fists my shirt, I work on memorizing the shape of her lips, teeth, and tongue. I've never hungered for anyone like I hunger for Calanthe Bloom. It's debilitating, enthralling, terrifying, all-consuming. I gather her closer, yet she still isn't close enough.

My dick swells, craving her soft skin and sweet warmth just as violently as the rest of me. I scrape my fingers across the velvet of her skin, slip them into the silk of her hair, then draw her lips wide and sweep my tongue against hers. I expect her to come to her senses, to shy away from me, to retreat, but the intrepid woman fists my jacket lapels and matches me stroke for stroke, fanning my thirst, fueling my hunger.

I nip her lip, then spread my fingers wide against her skull and tow her head nearer until every breath in my lungs cycles through hers. When she gasps, I take pity on her abused mouth and scrape my teeth down her throat, to the pulse point at the base of her neck. She seizes my shoulders when I press my lips to the palpitating skin that smells like spun sunshine.

Her throat works around deep swallows as I mar her skin with a bruising kiss, which the possessive male in me hopes she carries back to reality. I want the fucking world to see that Calanthe Bloom belongs to me. She shivers, and her hair tickles my flaring nostrils, propelling her bright scent into the darkest recesses of my being.

I lick the spot I've wronged, then drag my nose back up her neck toward her ear, warming her lobe with my gruff admonition, "You shouldn't have done that, Calamity."

Her heart misses a beat, and her eyes dart around my boardroom. Doesn't she realize that her only escape from me is waking up? Not that it will be much of an escape, because the second she vanishes, I'll bring her right back.

"Shouldn't have done what? Kissed you? We're both consenting adults, aren't we?" Her husky pitch coupled with her cute insolence curves my mouth.

As I straighten, I fist her hair. Uncertainty widens her pupils and vibrates her wet lips. Oh, to drive my tongue back through them. To hear them stretch around my name. To watch them glide down my chest and wrap around my weeping cock. To slicken them, not with my kisses but with my cum.

I trace the crease of her ear with my thumb, eliciting another shiver. "Have you never heard of the myth of Pandora?"

Her uneasy gaze slams back into mine—steady and unwavering. "Who hasn't?"

"What happened when she opened that legendary box?"

"All hell broke loose."

"Correct."

Her head rears back, or attempts to. My grip on her locks is too punitive to allow her much leeway. "Are you saying you're about to unleash hell because I kissed you, Hades?"

"I'm saying that you just pried open a box that was safer left sealed."

Calanthe Bloom quirks a brow, evidently impervious to the rot lurking beneath my flesh. Ironic, considering she's experienced my brand of evil firsthand. "Is the box a euphemism for your mouth?"

I ferry over a dark smile. "You shouldn't have let me taste your lips."

"Which ones?"

My delight deepens. My thirst, too. I trace her collarbone, first with my eyes, then with my fingers. My knuckles come to rest in that marvelous hollow before traveling up the center of her throat, soaking up each brisk swallow. I want to spread her on the boardroom table and feast on every inch of her but settle on licking her mouth before bruising it with another kiss.

When I feel her gasping for breath, I pull back. "I didn't think I'd enjoy this so much."

"Toying with my soul? Here I thought that was the god of the Underworld's favorite pastime."

"The act of kissing." I knuckle the dainty edge of her collarbone before tracing the swells of her heaving breasts.

"How inexperienced were your past partners?"

"The only part of my anatomy my past partners were allowed to kiss was my cock, sweetheart."

She wrinkles her nose.

"Kissing leads to expectations." I catch a piece of her hair that has escaped from her ponytail and run it between my fingers. Unlike most women I've been with, Calanthe's locks aren't brittle from chemicals—they're supple and bouncy. I visualize her curls slipping across my stomach, getting tangled in the coarse hair beneath my navel, gliding across my thigh. "Unlike fucking."

Calanthe inhales a bladed breath as I release her hair, admiring its mahogany gleam. "*Promises* lead to expectations. Kissing only leads to sex."

My pinkie bumps against the erect nipple punching against lace and silk. "Is that why you kissed me, Calamity?"

When my smile sharpens, her breathing slows, simmers. "Well, you did leave me high and dry last time."

"A veritable crime." I glide my hand higher on her thigh, tracing the scalloped edge of her lace panties, which I know are pale pink like her bra since I picked them. "Only soaked and satisfied from now on."

She shivers, then shivers again as I tease the edges of the triangle on my way to its lowest…warmest…moistest point.

"Actually." She claps my wrist. "I need—"

"To come. Profusely."

"No. I mean"—a rasping exhale leaves her lungs—"yes."

I strike gold, and her pupils flood her autumn irises, leaving behind only slender rings of color.

"Tarian." She chokes on my name. "Not now."

I stop circling her clit but keep my finger in place. "Why the fuck not?"

"Because I'd rather not start moaning in Malachi's ear."

His name percolates into my skin, heating my venomous runes. "What is your mouth doing next to his fucking ear?"

"My mouth's not next to his ear. I think. I just assume I'm sitting beside him in the helicopter that's taking us to your house in the Vineyard." Her eyes gleam as though she were about to compel her proximity to Malachi out of my mind, except she's incapable of compulsion.

I soon realize they're reflecting the screen I've stopped paying attention to. "Even though there's no one I trust more than Malachi, I hate that you're with him. I hate that you're sharing the same fucking air." Jealousy drives my finger beneath the lace and deep into her heat.

She gasps.

I kiss the underside of her jaw. "Moan, darling. I want him to know just who you belong to."

"Tarian—"

I realize she probably means to add a directive after my name, but I nonetheless quip, "That's right. *Me.*" I kiss the bobbing column of her neck "Now tell me, why are you going to my house in the Vineyard?"

"Your hand. Can't think."

I drop another kiss on her satiny skin. "You don't need to think. Only to talk…and feel." I swirl my middle finger around her tight canal. "Why are you going to my house?"

Her walls clench. Her throat, too. Yet she manages to wheeze, "Because the Serrans' penthouse in the city was made. Dorian thought we'd be safer—on the island."

Fury tightens my muscles and stills my finger. "Made? By whom?"

"By the Holy Hunters. I can't believe we're chatting about this while you're fingering me."

"Did anyone hurt you?"

"They were after Malachi. Not me." She touches my cheek. "No one's hurt me, Tarian. I'm safe."

She's the furthest thing from safe.

I close my eyes and pull my hand away, then lean back in the chair and tug at my hair.

"You know what you need?" she asks.

"To get you the fuck away from my world?"

"Too late for that."

"Is it?"

She frames my face with her palms. "Open your eyes."

I obey fucking no one, yet she has me cracking my lids open.

"Don't look away."

I narrow my eyes.

She slides off my thighs and kneels, then presses my legs wide. "Magick away your trousers."

I snort. "Fuck no."

She sits back on her heels, pouting. "Are you really turning down a blowjob?"

I lean forward and scoop her back up. "You come on my hand, and I'll let you suck me off."

"You're not sitting on a helicopter with an audience."

"Maybe I am." I crack my knuckles. "I'm not going to let that stop me from doing what I want. They've already taken enough away from me."

A sigh softens her pout. "Fine. Make me come."

I cock up a single eyebrow and snort. "Ask me again. With enthusiasm this time."

She clasps my hand and guides it beneath her skirt. "How's that for enthusiasm?"

"Better. Now, spread your legs."

She obeys, and I slide my whole hand beneath the wet lace.

"Thank you," I murmur as I cup her. I realize it isn't her heart I'm holding, but it's equally precious.

"For what?"

"For brightening my darkness. For trusting me with your body." I grip her hip with one hand and strum her folds with the other.

A moan vibrates her throat. I lean over and press my mouth to hers to apprehend the sound. And then, in perfect synchronicity, I thrust my tongue past one set of lips and my finger past the other. Her thighs clench around my forearm. I ease them back apart, half wishing I could replace my finger with my dick.

Someday, I will.

Someday, I will lay her bare and fill her up, but not today.

She grinds herself against my palm, seeking friction for her greedy little clit. I curl my finger and drive the heel of my hand lower, right where she wants it.

Her hand flops onto my crotch. I believe by mistake, until she molds me over the fabric and massages my ridged length. My nostrils flare as I try to catch my breath, but she strokes me again, and my lungs empty.

Fucking hell. I feel like I've just hit puberty and discovered my fist.

Her hips roll faster, harder, and then she stills, sucks in a breath, and breaks apart against my hand, choking on my tongue and milking my finger.

Or rather, I milk her. Her orgasm drenches my skin, her pleasure thick and sticky like honey.

I bite her lips that tremble with uneven breaths. "That's a good girl."

She shivers.

"Should we see how many more orgasms I can wring out of your beautiful body?"

Her lashes sweep high, and she pins me with an almost brutal stare. "We had a deal. One orgasm for me, one for you."

I start playing with her. "Just one more."

"Tarian…"

"A quick one." I trail my finger up her slit to her clit and circle it. Thrice around, and she detonates. I gather her wetness and paint her swollen pussy. I start on her clit again, running my nose down the slope of her throat, inhaling her sweet, sweet scent.

"You don't play fair."

"Never have. Never will."

She shatters once more against my palm.

I stroke her hipbone and suckle her pulse point, wheedling as much pleasure from her as she'll allow me, because every time she gasps my name, every time she souses my palm, I win back the control I've been stripped of.

"Pants. Off," she gasps, struggling with the hook-and-bar fastening on my trousers. "Now."

I magick my clothes away. Hers, too, while I'm at it. Save for her underwear, tights, and shoes. I keep her in those. She glances down at her body and tilts one eyebrow. I tilt mine right back as I relax in my chair and splay my thighs wide.

She sinks to her knees, then spirals her fingers up my thighs. She eyes my stiff length as though trying to figure out how best to handle me. As I watch her watching me, my dick leaks. Her tongue darts out and scoops the salty droplets before they make contact with my balls.

My lungs squeeze as she flattens her tongue against me and licks up my length. "Fuuuck." I rub my chest, my slick fingers painting the dark hairs over my heart with her scent.

The fragrance drifts upward, and I think I'll blow my load before she's even reached my engorged tip. But then her mouth's right there, her lips stretching over me, hot and soft, her palm cradling my sack, and her jeweled eyes gazing up at me as though I'm worth something.

She swirls her tongue over me from tip to root, kindling heat along my spine. With a groan, I stoop lower, spread my legs wider. I'm aware that my magic didn't soak into her flesh because her mouth was custom-made to fit my dick, but fuck if it doesn't feel that way when she feeds herself my length.

Calanthe takes me to the end of her throat, managing to submerge half of me. When she gags, I thread my fingers through her hair and tug gently. However exquisite the sensation, I don't want her to choke.

With a sweet little snarl, she sucks back the inch I freed her from, her throat clamping so hard around me that my balls tense and my spine grows as hot as the runes along my arms. Understood. Although I keep my fingers twined through her hair, I don't intercede again. I merely caress the long strands as she establishes her rhythm.

When her hands throttle the inches of me she can't fit, sparks shoot into my blood stream.

"Calamity," I rasp. "I'm going to come." The buildup is so intense that my vision goes white. "Calamity." I growl her name as a final warning to pop her lips off my dick, but they just clamp tighter, and she swallows.

And swallows.

And swallows.

I have never, *ever* come so profusely.

After a full minute, threads of pleasure are still jetting out of me. Since she's disconnected her mouth, they catch on her chin and drip, and fuck if that doesn't make my dick weep some more.

I thumb away what she doesn't manage to swipe with her tongue. "I don't think you realize what you've just done."

"Cracked open Pandora's box a little wider? Drank my weight in sperm?"

Spent dick finally flagging, I lean forward and cradle her cheeks. "You've just branded me as yours."

"Please. The second you come out of your coma, you'll find another good Samaritan to dip your wick in, and—"

"Shut the fuck up, darling."

Her eyes go wide with shock.

I scoop her onto my lap, then fan my fingers over her ass to hold her against me. "There will never be anyone else for me. I sensed it before, but now it's far more than a feeling—it's a conviction. You've burrowed yourself so fucking deep inside me that pieces of your soul have merged with mine." I trace every letter on her spine, reminding her of their presence, of their meaning. "I'm not saying that you have to stay with me—I may be an asshole, but I would never take that choice away from you—but I am saying that I am irrevocably and entirely yours."

Her pulse gallops. "One day, you'll wake up—"

"And speak this vow out loud."

Her lashes fall, dusting her freckled cheeks. "Please, don't."

"Don't what?"

"Don't make me promises. Not until you're conscious."

I tuck a long curl behind her ear. "All right. Can *you* make me a promise, though? Can you promise to wait for me?"

When her pupils contract inside their forest-fire backdrop, I realize the unfairness of my ask. What if I never rouse?

I stare off in the direction of the lit screen and clear my throat. "For a reasonable amount of time, that is. I'd never ask you to suspend your life—"

Her palms connect with either side of my face and peel my

gaze off my worst fear. Well, my second worst—something happening to the girl on my lap has become what haunts me first and foremost. Getting sealed inside a coffin and buried inside the bowels of the earth, the runner-up.

"Tarian Hadez"—her slender thumbs sculpt my cheekbones—"I'll wait for you."

Hope beats back my sudden attack of morosity, and I turn my face. Not to avoid her stare this time but to kiss the center of her palm. "Say it again. I need to hear it again."

"I'll wait for—" Like the weight of her body, her voice evaporates.

Punching back in my chair, I growl and bellow at the mine to bring her back. When Gaea doesn't indulge me, I call on the rune that binds us to activate our bond, but the inch of skin that used to bear the magical inscription doesn't itch like it did in the past.

*Fuck!*

I scrub my hands down my face, catapulting her scent deep. Instead of quieting me, it heightens my distress because it's laced with another fragrance—varnished oak and metallic adhesive. I take a second whiff, forehead grooving when I'm hit by the same woodsy, chemical aroma.

Frost swarms my veins. I slam my gaze back on the fabric movie screen just in time to catch a scripted name slashed by a flying dove—*Madar's*—and beneath it, two little words that bolt my ribs to all the soft tissue they cage.

I jerk my arms in front of me, but the bulbs go out, and I'm plunged into a darkness so complete not even my runes manage to shine through. How is that possible? Have I lost control of my magic entirely? Have I—

That last image on the boardroom's screen imprints itself against my lids. Have I lost my immortality?

# FIFTY-EIGHT

**M**y body jostles against something relatively soft. An arm. A thick, masculine one that smells like... Not like Tarian. I jerk away.

"Are you all right?" Malachi's rough timbre chafes the rumbling air. "Is he?"

My surroundings come back into soft focus. The helicopter. The bruised, flashing sky. The Atlanteans flying the vessel. The human glowering my way, one hand toying manically with the buttons on the embellished denim jacket she wears over a blood-speckled white cami.

"Anything?" Malachi asks, carrying my attention back to his worried face.

I bite my lip. At the salty taste of Tarian's cum, I lean farther back and scrape a hand over my chin and mouth. A tiny splotch of white dampens the navy suede of Malachi's jacket. Is that—

"Callie, did he say anything?" Malachi's headset sits around his neck like an airplane pillow. When he catches my gaze straying to it, he leans close. "I disconnected it when you started panting and choking." His sunglass-shaded gaze drops to my legs. "Anything broken? You sounded in a lot of pain."

Heat blazes inside my cheeks. "Nothing broken."

"Were you being chased?"

If I don't come up with an excuse for my earlier panting, Malachi's going to connect the dots, and I will perish from embarrassment. Already the white stain on his jacket is making me die a little on the inside. Not only because of what it is, but also because of what it represents—my epic investigative failure.

Instead of interrogating Tarian and forcing his mind to cough up any stray word it may have registered, I was blowing his massive cock. Granted, I don't regret the act, but I do regret that the only thing I carried back to reality was the taste of his semen and—I shift my legs—supremely drenched underwear.

Since Malachi is still staring expectantly at me, I say, "We were in a windowless boardroom and there was a screen playing memories of Symeon from birth to…to now." I wrinkle my nose as I recall the shiny ebony coffin. Thank God it was closed because I don't think I could've stomached another glimpse of his bloodless, bloated body.

"In a boardroom?"

"Yeah."

"Sitting on chairs?"

I'm about to say yes when I remember his panting comment. "No. On elliptical bikes. We had to pedal or the TV turned off."

Malachi, bless his naive soul, doesn't question my brand of insanity. He merely cracks his neck to relieve it of the tension he's been carrying around for days on end. "We're about to land."

I've been out for less than a half hour? Incredible. Even though it pains me to have left Tarian behind, I'm glad I abandoned him in a state of bliss. Sure, it was quickly overshadowed by worry, but for a moment back there, he'd let go.

Through the slashing rain, I detect a sprawling lawn, and

beyond it, Tarian's white mansion. It's so odd to arrive in a place I've visited in my dreams. My heart twinges at the idea of walking across the floorboards of his home without him.

Ines must have many hours of flying under her belt because she lands the aircraft with expert precision. I suppose Electra's waving palms must help. I find it almost surprising to see her sitting beside Ines, working with her.

The second the wheels kiss the grass, Malachi hangs up his headset and unhooks his harness, then he unlatches the door and hops out. As I'm unclicking my belt, Bryn flings me a look that freezes my fingers.

Over the still churning rotor blades and the gusting wind, she says, "Who are you?"

Are the repeated bouts of compulsion or her use of Atlantean blood to blame for her absent memories? "I'm Calanthe. Your oldest friend. We met—"

"What the fuck are you on?" Her nose crinkles as Electra rises from her pilot's chair and exits the aircraft, throwing me a raised eyebrow.

My dirty power nap must've rusted the wheels in my head because it takes them a couple seconds to grind back into motion. Bryn wasn't asking about my identity. No, it was a snide remark, but *why*? What did I do to deserve such rancor?

She grips the top edge of the helicopter cabin. "I won't tell Tarian because that's not the sort of person *I* am"—her gaze ventures to my neck, to the hickey Tarian imprinted into my skin —"but the truth has a way of coming out. Especially when you don't even try to hide it."

Malachi holds out his hand to help her out.

She hikes up her chin. "Not touching that now that I know where it's been."

Although she huffs this under her breath, the wind blows her words into my ear. They must blow into Malachi and Electra's ears, too, because they both frown. As Bryn storms past him, his forehead smooths and then he *grins*. Electra, though, keeps frowning as she walks off.

I shoulder my duffel bag, then duck beneath the metal hood and slap my palm into his. "Why are you smiling? She thinks you and I were—" I grimace, unable to utter the rest out loud.

His grin only deepens. "Were you riding an elliptical or my cousin?"

Heat rushes into my cheeks. I'm tempted to insist it was a stationary bike but instead, I squeeze his fingers tight. "I'd definitely wash your hands."

His attention jerks to our linked palms, then to my face. For a second, his amusement falters, but then it transforms into peals of laughter that rival the booming thunder.

Too soon, Malachi's chuckling wanes into a crooked smile. "No wonder we're not getting any closer to finding him."

That scrubs the brazen grin right off my face. He's right. Tarian and I shouldn't be playing sex games. We shouldn't be playing *any* games. Not until he's found. Once he's safe and sound, we can revisit the matter. Especially if this dream-sharing ability endures.

Especially if he and I endure.

After my feet touch the ground, Malachi releases my hand. He must sense my spiraling mood, because the empath that he is slings his arm around my hunched shoulders and lassoes me close.

"They won't succeed." His voice is barely louder than the angry sky and angrier waves slapping the wooden pier. "*We* will."

I cant my face toward his. "Thank you, Mal."

"For?"

"For protecting me. For not getting angry with me. For helping my mother. The list of reasons I'm grateful is long."

He squeezes me a little harder. "Electra doesn't trust or like many people, yet she trusts and likes you."

"What does Electra's opinion of me have to do with anything?"

Malachi must've tossed a forcefield around us because the

hurricane doesn't touch us even though it's snapping leaves off branches and branches off trunks.

"It may sound odd, but I'm not true to my gut like she is. I sometimes warm up to people who don't deserve my regard or friendship. Something she always calls me out on." He slides his lips together. "I used to think her childhood made her overly wary, and perhaps it did, but it also made her incredibly perceptive. Anyway, that's why I trust you without reserve."

"So not because I wear your cousin's rune?"

"Symeon and Barak each wore one of his runes."

The parallel makes me cringe. I want to remind him that the use of our runes is different, but out of the corner of my eye, I see Ines traipsing toward us, and something else takes precedence. "Your father and Catalina…what are they aware of?"

"That Tarian's been abducted by Yasmin and Lynch. I imagine Catalina knows who Lynch is to Yasmin and who Yasmin is to me since her daughter raised her. I'm uncertain whether my father knows, but I intend to find out. They're also aware that the Holy Hunters are after me."

In the doorway of the seaside mansion, I spy a blonde I haven't seen in a long while—Joslyn Fielding.

I slow down so I can finish this conversation without her eavesdropping. "Any lead on who offered the Holy Hunters money to find you?"

He shakes his head just as an umbrella pops open over us.

I catch my reflection in Ines's gold lenses. "It'll look less suspicious when Calanthe walks in with dry hair." She begins to turn on her heavy-duty boots but stops to pin Malachi with an eloquent look. "Electra mentioned the DNA results. Perhaps wait to deliver the news until we find your sister. Your father's not in a good headspace."

Malachi doesn't nod. "He might already know, Ines."

"He doesn't." She presses the umbrella into Malachi's hand and takes off in the opposite direction than the one we're going.

"Is Ines married?" I ask, studying the leggy female from head to toe. I suddenly wonder whether Electra's dislike stems more from the woman's appearance than from her refusal to adopt her.

"No."

"How long has she worked for your father, again?"

"Barak hired her the day my mother left. Sometimes I think he did so in the hopes she'd become a mother figure to me."

"And? Is that what she became?"

"No."

"How old is she?"

"Thirty-eight."

I blink. "She does *not* look thirty-eight."

He starts up again, towing me along. "We age well."

"Did anything ever happen between your dad and her?"

"No."

"And between you and her?"

"When I was a kid, I had a crush on her, which contributed to me not being able to see her as a mother figure. Every straight guy I knew has had a crush on that woman at some point."

"Even Tarian?" I ask, chiding myself for asking a question I fear the answer to.

"Except for him." Malachi's still beaming while I feel like I've swallowed a rock.

The relief I expect to feel doesn't come, because my chest aches for Electra. "Did it ever become more between you and Ines?"

That snuffs out his amusement.

"Forget I asked. It's none of my business." I still will him to tell me.

His jaw flexes.

I wait.

Another flex, but still his mandible remains soldered shut. As I plod toward the yawning front door, I decide to ask Tarian during our next dream, since I imagine he knows all when it comes to Malachi.

Joslyn's no longer alone in the foyer. Her eldest daughter has taken root beside her. The resemblance between mother and daughter is even more striking than I remembered—frosty blue eyes, ice-blonde hair, sickly skinny, and excessively pouty.

"Hello, Mackenzie." I nod to the taller Fielding, whose fluffy, skintight sweater is the same baby pink as her manicured nails. "Ms. Fielding."

Joslyn's lids twitch. Because I referred to her by her maiden name? Does she already pass herself off as Mrs. Hadez?

I suddenly remember Tarian teasingly calling me that, and my heart fires off a bunch of extra beats. Not for the first time, I wish he was at my side in this outsized foyer. I wish he was the one about to show me around his island home.

I swing my bag in front of me, clasping the handles with all ten of my fingers as I gaze at the framed pictures that run the length of the staircase. Most of the shots are of Tarian, Symeon, and Malachi, but a select few feature Saul and Barak. Although none contain a woman, the many paler squares on the wall speak of pictures that were taken down.

"Bryn said you two won't be sharing a room," Mackenzie proclaims, "which is a problem since there are no other free bedrooms. Mom and I called some of the neighboring hotels and managed to find you accommodations. You're welcome."

Although I have no claim to Tarian's house, her territorial bitchiness chafes.

"Cancel it." Malachi's voice rings across the giant foyer. "Calanthe will be staying in Tarian's room."

"It's occupied." Joslyn's shoulders square, which makes them look extra narrow and spiky beneath her belted, cream cashmere sweater dress. If the woman's pregnant, she's hiding it awfully well. "Mackenzie moved into it when we heard you were flying in more people."

More people? Does she mean her daughter and me?

But mostly, *what the fuck?* My fingers choke my bag strap. I am *not okay* with Mackenzie sleeping in Tarian's bed. Not okay at all. "What if Tarian shows up?"

"*When* he shows up"—Joslyn shoots me a plastic smile—"he'll have a pleasant surprise."

Mackenzie's chin hikes up in arrogance while mine dips in fury.

"This isn't your home, Jos." Malachi tucks his sunglasses inside his breast pocket extremely slowly.

"Neither is it yours. Besides, it was your father's idea. If you have a problem, I'll let you take it up with him."

Malachi drums his thigh, as though it's taking everything in him not to use his magic on the two smug blondes. "Marsha will help Mackenzie transfer her things to my bedroom."

Mackenzie's dewy complexion goes waxen. "What? I'm not sharing a room with you. How presumptuous that you'd even—"

"Relax, Mackenzie." With a sigh, he says, "I'll be moving into the gatehouse with Ines."

Of course he says this the second Electra trundles down the stairs. It slows her footfalls and hardens every line in her body. He must sense her presence because his gaze zeroes in on her. Does he see the pain that bleeds beneath the brown and the blue, because I suddenly see only that. Also, where will she sleep? In my room?

Joslyn grins, which stretches the Botoxed planes of her face without creating a single wrinkle. "How accommodating you are to shack up with the staff, Son."

Malachi stiffens at the moniker.

The idea of being enclosed by four walls with women who deeply dislike me becomes suddenly very unappealing. "On second thought, *I'll* take the gatehouse with Ines. And Electra?"

Either she doesn't grasp that it's a question, or she didn't hear me over her rush of jealousy? I know firsthand how loud that feeling can be.

"No," he murmurs.

"I really don't mind, Mal."

"*I* fucking mind, Calanthe."

I wonder why he cares where I sleep. Or is it that he cares where Mackenzie sleeps?

The she-bitch in question chirrups, "Since you'll be in the gate-house, Calla Lily will take *your* room."

My middle fingers itch, yet I keep them curled around my bag strap. I won't give Macrazy the satisfaction of getting under my skin.

"Elle, get Marsha, please," Malachi grits out.

She descends the remaining stairs before disappearing down a hallway.

Mackenzie folds her arms in front of her perky boobs. "I already slept in Tarian's bed, so it would make more sense if Bryn's friend took your room. One less set of sheets to change. Besides, I'm sure your cousin will much prefer hearing that his personal space wasn't bummed by a stranger." She uncrosses her arms. "I'll call him." She pats down her dress as though expecting to find a pocket. "Shoot, where did I put my phone?"

The look Malachi ferries her way could single-handedly stop the polar ice caps from melting. "He's working, Mackenzie. He doesn't appreciate being disturbed."

"I still think—"

"I don't give a fuck what you think." Affable Malachi is clearly done being pleasant.

That shuts her up. It also increases the force of her scowl, which she directs at me. I try to remember if there was a lock on Tarian's door.

"Callie," Malachi snaps.

I jump.

"Here." Malachi digs a cell phone out of his pocket. "I programmed our numbers into it."

I gawp at the phone, then at the man tendering it to me, my heart twinging at the mark of his trust.

"Good morning, Mr. Malachi." A bright-eyed elderly woman with white hair piled in coils atop her head bustles into the foyer. "I'll get started on Mr. Tarian's bedroom immediately." She takes my measure, her expression remaining impeccably neutral.

He smiles at her. "Thank you, Marsha."

As she heads toward the stairs, I scan her nape for runes but find only bare skin.

Marsha pauses halfway up. "Would you like me to pack your things, Miss Mackenzie, or would you prefer packing them yourself?"

"I'll do it myself," she grumbles, silver stilettos clacking on the shiny hardwood floors.

"Oh, Ms. Joslyn, Mrs. Catalina and Mr. Saul request your presence in Mr. Tarian's office. The police have a few questions for you."

"Oh for fuck's sake, what do they want now?" Joslyn begins to back up, but before leaving, she says, "A word of warning, Malachi. Your father's very displeased with you."

"Isn't he always these days?"

"If you acted in the best interest of our family—"

"*Our* family?" I startle at the intensity of his voice. "You may be marrying my father, Jos, but that doesn't make my family yours. That only makes my father yours."

Her palm drifts to her stomach. "I take it your father hasn't yet shared the happy news. You're going to be an older brother. Isn't that just wonderful?"

Malachi goes as white as the tall shiplap walls enclosing us. "That's impossible. He can't—"

"He can. He did. I carry the proof." She leaves, leaching more color from his face.

I jam my phone inside my hoodie pocket, then slide my hand beneath Malachi's elbow to keep him from—keeling over? Repainting Tarian's foyer with Joslyn's brain matter?

I attempt to catch his stare, but it's pinned to the air, which Joslyn's just soiled with her pungent perfume and noxious personality. "What did you mean by *he can't*?"

"He tried to have another child after my mother left. Tried with a whole bunch of women. He was dead set on growing our family, to give me a sibling, to prove to her—to *himself*—that he'd moved on."

"That explains why the baby might not be his." I keep my voice soft, in part so that my confession only percolates into his ears, and in part because I worry that speaking any louder will rattle him further.

He blinks out of his daze. "What?"

"Apparently, Jos was close with Symeon. He's the one who introduced her to Saul."

"You knew?"

"That Symeon introduced her—"

"No. Not that part."

I bite my lip. "I heard rumors."

"From?"

Deciding not to toss Electra under the bus, I say, "Bryn."

He growls a deep *fuck*, then jams his fingers through his locks, shoving them off his low-slung eyebrows; the ones he got from Nora; the ones he shares with Yasmin.

"If it's not your father's, then—"

"It doesn't fucking matter if it's his or Symeon's. *Shit*."

"Why doesn't it matter?"

"Because, Callie, once pregnant with an Atlantean's child, a human becomes immune to our magic."

Oh. *Oh.*

So Joslyn knows things... What if that's the reason Saul's marrying her? To keep her quiet? I hope so, for Malachi's sake. Having one parent make poor choices is— A realization fires across my skull: Nora met Delta first. What if Delta never gave Joslyn more than one night because he wasn't over Nora? What if that's the reason Joslyn preyed on Nora's ex—to win some sort of justice for her bruised ego? Could Saul be that unwittingly impressionable?

What Malachi just said about his father's desperation to grow his family returns front and center. This pregnancy is a dream come true for Saul. Of course he'd want to keep the mother of his unborn child close. But what if it's not his child?

# FIFTY-NINE

A s we wait for Marsha to announce that my room is ready, Malachi shows me around the house. The living room and bar are the same as in Tarian's dream, but not the dining room, thank goodness. I don't think I could've stomached a meal at a table made of black glass set with gold plates and individual candles.

Their tragic glow pricks my lids. I close them, then shake my head to drive the nightmarish meal away. When I open them, I find Malachi parked behind the bar, a bottle of gin in hand. He tosses the cap off, then drinks straight from the bottle.

"I'm really sorry, Mal."

His lashes flutter as he chugs down more gin. The bottle's opaque, so I can't tell how much he slugs down, but his Adam's apple bobs without pause for a full minute.

I slide my phone out of my pocket and click on the contacts icon. It holds three numbers—Dorian, Electra, and Malachi. The diminutive list makes me realize how few people I can trust. As Malachi guzzles liquor like it's milk, I message Electra.

ME: Joslyn just revealed her pregnancy to Malachi. He's drinking his weight in gin. Advice?

ELECTRA: Fuck. He never drinks.

ME: Come?

The dots dance, then vanish, then dance again. I picture the pain that ripped across her face when Malachi suggested sharing the gatehouse with Ines. I think she might tell me to deal with it when three little words finally appear.

ELECTRA: On my way

I'm about to put away my phone but the temptation to check on my mother wins me over.

ME: Hey Dorian. Malachi gave me this phone. It's Callie. Everything ok?

I start to peek up at Malachi when a reply materializes on my screen. I scan Dorian's words, my heart lifting and swelling.

DORIAN: I gave your mom her medication. Diego has arrived safely. He's won over the women with his love for cooking and word games.

He sends me a picture of my mother stirring something at the stovetop, sandwiched between Mrs. Fiona and, objectively, the prettiest man I've ever seen. Diego's all tanned skin, sparkling dark eyes, and dimples.

DORIAN: I'll stay the night to help with the transition. Don't worry.

My ribs constrict in gratitude, but then Malachi slaps the bottle down on the bar, jerking me out of my feels, and I tuck my phone back inside my kangaroo pocket.

"I hear congratulations are in order!" His tone is gruff, stained by liquor and anger. "How about a drink, Father?"

"I think you've had one already." Saul's clear blue gaze surfs over his son and me.

"But I didn't have one *with* you." He grabs another bottle by the neck. "Oh, fuck. I forgot." He looks at me, then flips open one of his hands and splashes whiskey onto it. "Beats soap." With a wink, he takes a swig, then proffers the bottle to his father. "Another half-sibling. How fun!"

I'm guessing dirty laundry is about to get aired.

Saul takes the bottle from his son but doesn't bring it to his lips. "What do you mean by *another* half-sibling?"

"Huh...Ines wasn't kidding when she said you didn't know." Malachi leans against the stone bar, then gestures toward the woman who appears behind Saul in a bouclé dress that looks sewn onto her hourglass curves. I recognize her from the news channel I watched mere hours ago with Bryn, even though it feels like it's been an entire month since we were in Boston. "Cat didn't tell you? Yasmin's my sister."

"I may have slept with my fair share of women after your mother's passing, Malachi, but I remember them all, and Paloma wasn't one of them."

I deduce that Paloma must be Catalina's daughter.

Malachi guffaws. "Oh, Father, Yasmin's not *yours*. She's *Mother's*. Mother and Sergeant Asshole's. You know, Bryn's daddy? The ex of the woman you've decided on a fucking whim to fucking marry."

Thankfully, Electra bursts into the living room and arrows straight for us. "How much?" she asks me quietly.

"Has he said or drunk?" I murmur.

"Second thing."

"Bottle of gin and a swig of whiskey."

"Yasmin's your sister?" Joslyn trills.

*Great.* Bridezilla's back. I assume she's asking Malachi until I spot Bryn standing at her side.

"Apparently." My friend—ex-friend?—crosses her arms over a blousy top that must be Macrazy's, considering its hue. "According to Malachi and my stolen DNA."

As Joslyn makes a huge fuss about how stealing DNA is reprehensible, Electra grabs a glass and fills it with water from the built-in tap, then shoves it in Malachi's hands. "Drink."

"Not thirsty." He snaps his index finger off the glass to direct it at Joslyn. "Let's discuss repressible...reprens...reprehissable...*you.* You and your million-dollar monthly expenses. A million fucking dollars." He snorts.

She purses her lips. "That's between your father and me."

"Wrong." He wags his finger, splashing water from the glass that soaks into his suede sleeve. "It's *my* inheritance."

"You've got billions in the bank, Mal," Joslyn crows. "You're all set."

Electra steps in front of Malachi to capture his attention and murmurs something in Atlantean that she accompanies with a chin nod at the glass in his hand.

Without tearing his gaze off Joslyn, he grunts and finally takes a sip.

"The whole thing, Mal." Electra sticks a finger on the bottom of the glass to coax it back up to his mouth. He indulges her with another sip.

"So, Saul, did you get with my mother to get back at my father for stealing your wife?" Although Bryn's nostrils are a little pink, all signs of her nosebleed are gone.

It takes me a minute to unravel all the clauses she's strung together. Once her theory registers, I swing my attention to Saul, who's pursing his lips so hard, little wrinkles bracket his mouth.

"Not that I owe you an explanation, Miss Fielding, but I'd appreciate you curbing your tone. But I *will* answer your question to prevent false rumors from proliferating. The day Nora left, she became dead to me. I didn't look into what became of her or who she'd taken off with." He shifts his gaze to Joslyn. "Did *you* know, Jos?"

"Symeon mentioned one of my exes had dated one of your exes, but I didn't dig to find out which ones." She says this with perfect aplomb, but the rosy hue of her cheeks betrays the legitimacy of her answer.

Sure, her complexion gained color when Malachi mentioned her lifestyle expenses, but Joslyn's the type of woman to research her next catches with extreme thoroughness. Where I don't think jealousy was the motivating factor behind her decision to hook herself a Hadez, there's no way she wasn't aware which of their exes had been together.

"What's going on?" Mackenzie travels toward us, heels clicking, hips swaying. Once a pageant contestant, always a pageant contestant.

"Your sister is related to Yasmin, who's related to Malachi," Joslyn explains.

The tendons in Saul's neck strain so hard I worry they'll tear.

Mackenzie frowns at her sister. "You're Saul's daughter?"

"No. Yasmin's my half-sister," Bryn grits out. "She's also Malachi's."

Her forehead remains rucked.

Catalina, who hasn't made a single noise this entire time, snorts, then says something in her language to god-knows-who, since Electra's watching Malachi, Malachi's watching his father, and his father's watching Joslyn. "Malachi's mother, Nora, had a child with Bryn's father. That child was Yasmin."

Mackenzie glances around the room. "I can't believe we're, like, all related already. What a crazy coincidence."

"Crazy, indeed," Saul murmurs.

Joslyn's palm skips over her flat abdomen. Since she doesn't have a maternal bone in her body, I imagine it's to remind Saul of the baby she carries. I have little doubt she got pregnant extra fast to insure she couldn't be dumped.

Bryn catches my disgusted expression and glowers. Even though I'm not an advocate of compulsion, I may just beg Malachi to bleach her mind of this whole day once the Atlantean blood is out of her system. Maybe the nosebleed already rid her of her immunity?

"Malachi," Electra snaps. "Water. Now."

He slams down the contents, then smacks the pretty etched cup against the bar top, breaking both glass and skin. "Hey, Jos?"

She jerks her attention off the crimson rivulets oozing out of Malachi's palm.

"Can't wait for that paternity test." He plucks a shard of glass from his palm and flicks it in the general direction of the sink. His shot goes wide.

The silence that ensues is as deafening as the crush of rain-drops on the windows.

"That's enough, Son." Saul's mouth is so flat and tight, it looks drawn with a fine-tipped marker.

"I'd hold off on your *I do*s until you get those lab results, Dad. Unless you *want* to raise Sym's kid."

"The child's mine, Malachi. Not Symeon's. He's mine!"

"*He*?" Malachi's pupils expand, consuming his irises.

Electra snatches Malachi's wrist and lifts his hand vertically, then grabs fistfuls of cocktail napkins from a silver holder on the bar and squashes the black paper against the wound. Atlanteans may heal fast, but they don't heal instantly. Also, and this is really neither here nor there, but I'm a little glad I'm not the only reason his jacket is soiled.

"You already know the gender?" His head swivels toward Joslyn. "How fucking far along are you?"

"Three months." Saul's gaze sweeps almost reverentially over Joslyn's abdomen. "Your brother will be born before the end of the year."

I can tell he's already in love with this unborn child, but I just don't get how he can be in love with the mother. Also, if she's three months along, then according to the timeline of their relationship, they basically conceived this kid the night they met.

"Electra, please go bandage my son's hand before he bleeds out."

Malachi's liquor-induced volatility and volubility strike again. "Is that a threat, Father?"

Saul grinds his jaw, threads of his magic braiding with the air and thickening it. "Do I need to call Ines or are you apt enough to take care of my son, Electra?"

Although she doesn't talk back, not even to answer his question, her livid stare speaks volumes.

"C'mon, Callie," Malachi slurs, digging his navy suede loafers into the hardwood. "Let's blow this popsicle."

"Calanthe will stay with us." Although Saul doesn't use compulsion, I realize that objecting is probably not an option.

Could I feign needing a nap?

"I'll be back as soon as I get him settled," Electra murmurs through taut lips as she brushes past me, dragging along the very inebriated blond god. Although her strides are steady, her arms vibrate with barely contained indignation.

On the inside, I am screaming at her not to leave me. On the outside, I am stoic.

"Lunch is ready," someone announces. I assume it's Marsha, but the woman in the doorway wears her brown hair in a long braid and looks about Joslyn's age. Since she sports a uniform, I take it she's another member of Tarian's staff.

"Thank you, Severine. We'll be in in a minute." As she vanishes in the direction of the dining room, Saul returns the whiskey bottle to the bar that's still reddened by his son's blood. "I told you that *I* wished to break the news to my son, Jos." His tone is as tight as his fiancée's dress.

She tucks a white-blonde strand behind her ear that winks with a giant heart-shaped blue diamond. "Sorry, but Mal accused me of not being part of the family, and it just…slipped out."

"I bet." Catalina gives Joslyn a chilling smile.

"Speaking of family," Mackenzie whines. "Malachi kicked me out of Tarian's room, Saul."

"Why were you in Tarian's bedroom to begin with?"

She purses her glossy lips. "Because last night, Mom said—"

"It was the only free bedroom in the house. That's why I suggested it." Is it me, or are Joslyn's ears reddening like her cheeks?

"Lunch." Saul nods to me, then to the Fieldings. "Start without us. I need a word with Cat."

"Go," Joslyn tells her daughters.

"You, too, Jos."

She plants a hand on her hip, clearly not appreciating that he's not including her in this chat. I think she's about to complain, but in the end, she huffs and hoofs it out of the room.

I follow, not too close behind, but close enough to hear Joslyn mutter, "We're having your favorite, Bryn. Lobster."

"Shame it's not scallops," Mackenzie says.

I assume it's because she prefers scallops to lobster until I catch the cruel look she flings my way, and I understand that it wasn't her stomach talking but her spite. "What the actual fuck, Mackenzie?"

"What?" She simulates surprise, but she's as bad an actress as she is a human.

I wait for Bryn to tell her sister that her comment was uncalled for, but Bryn says nothing.

"Glad you're here, Sis." Mackenzie slides an arm around Bryn's waist.

Although Bryn doesn't reciprocate her sister's sentiment, she also doesn't pull away.

As they recede from my line of sight, I hear Catalina murmur, "I thought the sisters didn't get along."

"Calanthe, please head to the dining room," Saul bites out.

I do as I'm told, but once I reach the dining area, I fake a pressing urge to pee, book it across the foyer toward the pool room that's adjacent to the bar, and flatten myself against the wall, throwing my hearing as far as it can go.

Unfortunately, Saul and Catalina don't speak in English. I punch the camera app on my phone, then scroll to the video option and hit record, and then I slide the device on the shelf that holds Tarian's rowing trophies. According to my laconic tour guide—poor Malachi was still digesting the news of the pregnancy—Tarian had been a big-time rower back in college.

I tiptoe past the sapphire felt pool table and bluster into the bathroom across the hall, then pace the white tiled space decorated with watercolor paintings of seashells. Once I sense my absence will be noticed, I flush and wash my hands.

When I exit, my heart vaults into my throat, because Joslyn's standing on the threshold of the bathroom.

"I thought you might've gotten lost, Callie."

"Nope. Mal gave me a tour of the house earlier."

"He's giving you a lot of things, isn't he?" Her attention sweeps over my hickey.

"Do you want something, Joslyn?"

"Why are you here?"

"Because my bladder was about to explode."

"I obviously meant in Martha's Vineyard. Why did Malachi fly you out here?"

"Because Tarian wanted me at the memorial."

The corners of her downturned mouth twitch. She's dying to call me a liar, but that would mean revealing that Tarian is MIA, and although she's a bitch, she's a careful one.

"We should get back to lunch," I say. "I'm starving."

"*I* should get back. *You* should find a hole to crawl into until I can convince Saul to toss you out of this house."

"Why don't you tell me how you really feel?" I flash her an impertinent grin.

Her arm swings up. I manage to shackle her wrist before her palm can land on my cheek.

Digging my fingers into her skin, I hiss, "Don't. Ever. Touch me." And then I toss her hand away.

"I'll ruin you."

"You can't ruin someone who has nothing to lose."

"You still have that flower hovel you call a shop. You still have your degenerate mother. You've got things to lose."

My heart holds still before banging back into motion. "If you touch a hair on her head, I will—"

"Ms. Joslyn." Someone clears their throat—Ines. "Saul's asked me to come and fetch you."

I glare at Bryn's mother, making sure my intent trundles into her skull. I may not be able to compel, and I've never actually murdered anyone, but as I hold her soulless gaze, I realize that I absolutely would go through with it.

"Can't you see I'm in the middle of something, Ines?" Joslyn snaps.

"Mackenzie's up in arms about melted butter all over her lobster. She's fired the chef. Saul's most unhappy."

Joslyn snaps her attention toward the tattooed Atlantean. "We'll hire—"

"He's on Tarian's payroll, not ours. I'm afraid Saul's insisting, and I quote, 'that you remedy the situation and teach Mackenzie to rein in her adult tantrums.'"

*Adult tantrums.* I snort as Joslyn shoots off, muttering under her breath. Saul may not be such a guileless man, after all.

Since mother and daughter—I almost make that word plural but refuse to let today color my impression of Bryn—have identical personalities, I do wonder why he's so intent on marrying Joslyn. Because of an old-school upbringing? Surely, he could string her along until she gave birth, then trade an exorbitant amount of money in exchange for full custody of the child.

"He cannot possibly love her, can he?" I blink at Ines's unshaded gaze. Her eyes are huge, black, and heavy-lidded. No wonder every boy and his best friend had crushes on this woman. How is Joslyn not fiercely insecure about having a woman like

Ines around? Sure, Bryn's mom is model-gorgeous, but Ines's beauty is otherworldly.

"What's not to love about that woman?" Her question carries my attention off her startling stare.

I can't tell if she's serious or also under Joslyn's "charm." "For one, she has the personality of a rabid poodle."

"And for two?"

"For two, she's clearly with your boss for his money."

Ines neither nods nor challenges my opinion.

I grimace. "Don't tell me you like her?"

"My boss deserves happiness."

My head rears back. "And you think he'll be happy with her?"

"He's wanted a child since I entered his service."

"That's not what I asked."

"Your lobster will be cold."

I want to stop by the pool room, but that would raise Ines's eyebrows. Her loyalties may lie with Malachi, but they also lie with Saul.

"Your bedroom's ready, Miss." I jump at the sound of Marsha's voice. "I've taken the liberty to dry and press your clothes. I hope you don't mind."

I muster a smile as I pivot toward the woman descending the stairs, toting a basket of rumpled linens. "That was very thoughtful of you. Thank you."

"Would you like me to show you—"

"I'll take her upstairs after lunch, Marsha." Ines gestures toward the dining room.

Great. Can't wait. So thoughtful.

As we make our way to the dining room, I ask, "How's Mal?"

"Electra's at his bedside. If you want news, I'd suggest you text her with your new phone."

I trip on my own two feet but manage to catch myself on the doorframe of the dining room.

"Everything all right?" She probes my face with her black eyes.

A chorus of, *she knows, she knows*, detonates between my temples. "Low sugar."

There's no reason she'd know, I reason. Unless Saul felt me in the adjacent room and asked her to check?

No, no. I'm reading too much into her stare.

I order myself to take a breath, a step, another breath, another step. Odds are her suggestion to text Electra was just that, a suggestion. Right?

# SIXTY

There are two free seats at the lunch table: one beside Mackenzie, who's ogling her empty placemat as though attempting to coax a green salad out of it; the other, between Catalina and Bryn. Grim pickings.

"Sorry for my tardiness. Where should I sit, Mr. Hadez?" I ask, as Ines parks herself along the wall, taking her guard duty very seriously. Does she always hang around while he eats or is she sticking around because she doesn't trust me?

"Since Malachi won't be joining us." Saul sweeps his hand in a wide arc. "Sit anywhere your heart desires."

My heart desires a table not crowded by gods and women bearing the last name Fielding.

Mackenzie's chair legs scratch the hardwood floor. "She can have my—"

"No. Stay." Saul's tone is so bladed that it jabs the air and pins her to her seat. "The chef's preparing a new dish especially for you."

She purses her lips, cheeks puffing with many, many annoyed breaths. "He'll probably slather it in butter."

Her earlier scallop threat makes me say, "Or arsenic. Sorry. Wishful thinking."

The silence that blankets the dining room is thicker than triple-ply cashmere.

I think I'm about to get booted out of the dining room, which would be ideal, but Catalina—of all people—bursts out laughing.

The horror and hatred that ooze from mother and daughter is so tangible that it only heightens Catalina's delight. I don't check Bryn's face for a reaction, because I fear where her loyalties lie.

"Sit beside me." Catalina blots the corners of her eyes on her napkin. "Thank you. I needed that."

As I sink into the seat that faces my archenemies, I don't delude myself into thinking that Catalina's on my side. After all, her granddaughter abducted Tarian. Considering the preexistent rivalry between the Fablezes and the Hadezes, she could've encouraged Yasmin. She could be aiding and abetting her.

"Your choice of friends is deplorable, Bryn." Mackenzie's mismatched pearl earrings jiggle as she tucks her chair back in.

Bryn doesn't say anything. She just keeps raking her nails across the sleek black box beside her placemat, picking at the shrink-wrapped packaging. It takes me a second to recognize what it contains. When I do, my gaze jolts to hers, which is affixed to the blustery panorama that stretches behind her sister and mother.

Like me, she got a new phone. Unlike me, her allegiance doesn't lie with the Hadezes. I'm tempted to ask who gave it to her? Her mother? Saul?

Are they aware that she may use it to call her father? Maybe that's what they want... Unless her mind was wiped, and she doesn't remember that he's taken Tarian hostage?

My fingers itch to tap out a text to Electra but faking a need to visit the restroom again won't fly, so I flatten my fingers on my lap and bounce my leg. The waitress circles the table with a plate topped with an artistic white roll—an egg-white omelet maybe? As she places the plate in front of Mackenzie, I try to recall her name. It was something that sounded French and started with an "S." Sophie? Sylvie?

*Severine.*

"Why does it smell like bacon?" Mackenzie's nose is all but planted on her omelet. "I bet he cooked it in bacon fat!" She shakes her head so wildly that the dangling charms on her earrings smack her puffing cheeks. "He's doing it on purpose, isn't he?"

"My dear, you're intolerant to almost everything." Saul snaps his lobster claw with his bare fingers. "Poor man's probably running out of ideas of what to serve you."

"*Poor man?*" Mackenzie chokes out. "With all due respect, Saul, the second I landed yesterday, I gave him a laminated sheet that details everything I can and cannot eat. Unless he's illiterate, he should've been able to cook something that won't make me sick." After a beat, she adds, "You should fly your chef in from Boston. He cares—"

"This isn't my house, Mackenzie." Saul slices into his lobster meat.

She huffs. "Can't wait for Tarian to get here."

Saul finishes chewing, then pats his mouth. "Because you think he'll give his chef leave to suit you?"

"Yes, Saul. I do." The haughty tilt of her chin draws my gaze away from the sky, but then lightning lacerates the dark clouds, and my full attention returns there.

"It's quite the spectacle, isn't it?" Catalina murmurs into my ear.

Does she mean the storm or Mackenzie's latest tantrum? Either way, I reply with a nod since both are entertaining in their own way.

A large plate holding two lobster tails enthroned on a mound of corn salad appears before me. I thank Severine and unfold my napkin onto my lap.

My stomach growls at the mouth-watering aroma of melted butter. Even intolerant to dairy, I'd still sneak butter into my diet. "This smells delicious."

Mackenzie's eye twitches. Probably because she believes I'm sucking up to Saul.

I fork some corn into my mouth, and. Oh. My. God. It's the single, best thing I've eaten in my life.

"By the way, Calla Lily"—Mackenzie plops her pointy elbows on her placemat—"I know you wanted to recoup your cacti, but Tarian asked me to toss them after Mom and Saul's party. Couldn't stand how cheap they looked in his house in spite of how nicely I showcased them."

I keep chewing on my wonderful corn, not allowing her nastiness, and consequent financial loss, to affect the flavor. Not to mention that Tarian couldn't have asked her to toss them, since Tarian was already in Yasmin and Delta's clutches.

"They were so tawdry," Joslyn says. "Thank god, my daughter is talented. She really managed to make the most out of them. Didn't she, Saul?"

"I'm sorry, but I don't recall the décor. It was a rather eventful evening."

"That's right. Callie crashed Tarian's car." Mackenzie twirls a large diamond and pearl ring around her bony finger. "Did your insurance company drop you?"

"Tarian took care of everything." I flash her a cruel smile, then shove more corn into my mouth. After I swallow, I add, "He told me not to worry. Oh, and he also wired me the amount you're withholding for the cacti." I take a minute to appreciate how wide Mackenzie's eyes have gone before refocusing on Saul. "You have a very generous nephew."

Will he agree, or does he actually dislike Tarian and couldn't be happier that he's gone?

"Mom, I forgot to tell you. Fleur-de-Lys accepted our request to do your wedding." Mackenzie proclaims this as though it had been a feat to snag our competitors.

Obviously, she's decided to bring this up only to annoy me. Oddly enough, though, I'm not annoyed. Maybe once this is all over, once Tarian's home, I'll worry about the shop again, but at the moment, it's the farthest thing from my mind.

"Hope you weren't counting on our business, Calla Lily?"

I'm wondering whether to respond or to just let this conversation wither.

Catalina takes the choice away from me. "Mackenzie, I'd like another serving of lobster. Be a dear and fetch me some more from the kitchen."

Mackenzie stops fiddling with her ring and jams her shoulders back. "I would, but that's not my job."

"Well, Severine isn't here, and I'm positively famished."

Mackenzie's arm shoots out toward the Atlantean leaning against the wall. "Have Ines do it. She's just standing there."

Saul cracks his neck. "Mackenzie, I'm running low on patience today. If you don't want to end up on a ferry back to Boston, please pull your weight around here."

Mackenzie glowers, but an encouraging forearm squeeze from her mother sends her stalking toward the kitchen.

As the door flaps behind her, Joslyn seizes her wine glass but doesn't drink immediately. She merely holds it, swirling the yellow liquid inside. "Catalina, I'd appreciate it if you treated my daughter with a little more respect. She's here to support me—"

"Respect's a two-way street, Ms. Fielding. If she begins to show some to the staff and to Tarian's guest, then she'll earn mine. And as your elder, I'd prefer if you addressed me as Mrs. Fablez."

"Cat..." Saul sighs.

"I have three decades on your future bride, Saul."

My knife skids over the broiled white flesh, and not because it's as flaky as cod but because of the reminder of Catalina's age. Even though a part of her youthfulness is surely due to her Atlantean genes, another part is probably due to her miracle serums since Saul appears distinctly older.

As Mackenzie pounds back in like a chuffing bull, I picture

my mother's turquoise pot of Fablez-manufactured cream and briefly wonder if it's the same one Catalina uses or a commercially watered-down version with potentially harmful side-effects for humans. I'm about to ask when my palate is hit with the full flavor of the lobster, and I moan. The chef must use magic in his cooking because everything on my plate is perfection.

"And now I'm thinking of the helicopter ride again." Bryn jams her knife through the tines of her fork and parks both on the side of her plate.

Heat bursts inside my cheeks, but quickly recedes when another wave of heat hits me elsewhere.

*Crap.* I seize my glass of water and down it. *Not a good time, Tarian.*

"What happened in the helicopter, Bryn?" Mackenzie grins at me like the blonde embodiment of Chucky. I bet she already knows the story, or senses it'll paint me in a poor light.

"Um, could I—" My rune flares so hot that my jaw slams shut. I focus on the shiny, sunshine-yellow kernels on my plate, begging Tarian to release his hold on me, but the heat only grows fiercer. I lean forward in my seat and try once more to be excused. "Could I please—" I suck in air as the pieces of corn smudge into a blob.

"Bryn, whatever happened on that helicopter ride is between you and Calanthe." Saul's voice drills my buzzing eardrums. "Let it stay that way."

She snorts, tearing the shrink-wrap clean off her new cell phone box. "More like between your son and Calanthe, but sure, I wouldn't want to ruin anyone else's appetite."

Her spite lashes at my heart, mincing the soft, thudding flesh and converting the beats into drips that bleed down my ribs. As I stare into her astringent gaze, Tarian's fiery call cools. I hate that I resisted him.

Although my appetite has vanished, I force myself to consume the rest of my meal while Catalina discusses plans for the memorial and the ensuing repast at her daughter's home.

Bryn balls up the plastic with a frown. "I thought the memorial had been pushed back?"

"We decided to go ahead with it." Catalina side-eyes Saul. "The sooner we bury the body, the better."

"You're burying him here?" I ask.

"No. I have business in Atlantis tomorrow. Since Tarian has yet to show, I offered to fly Symeon home to spare Saul."

"How kind." Joslyn takes a sip of her wine. "Remind me… Why aren't you staying at your daughter's house again, *Catalina*?"

Is it wrong of me to hope that the Atlantean matriarch will throttle her with magic?

Joslyn flicks her hand in my direction. How she can even keep it lifted with the knuckle-sized diamond gracing her finger is a feat that defies gravity. "Especially now that we have so many guests."

Even though I don't want to react, her comment is the acrylic nail that breaks my back. "*We*? This house belongs to Tarian, not to Saul. So unless you're after Tarian now, *you* have no guests. You *are* one. Just like the rest of us."

She reclines in her seat, smiling. "I see our little conversation didn't bear any fruit. Not that I'm surprised. You are rather dense."

"Mom," Bryn gasps, and although she doesn't say anything more, it's enough to alter the way my heart had begun to beat for her.

"What?" Joslyn lifts her wine glass to her lips.

I will her to choke on her sip. Might not kill her, but oh, how satisfying it would be.

She sucks in air, wheezes, reddens, then proceeds to cough.

*Whoa.* Did I just—

I catch Ines scratching her throat, a smile tucked deep into her cheek. When she feels my eyes on her, she drops her arms into a loose fold in front of her and banishes her smile. But I saw it, the same way I saw her finger crook. Could she have made Joslyn's sip go down the wrong hole? She certainly enjoyed the show.

From the stretch of Catalina's lips, I suspect that she also enjoyed the show. Saul, on the other hand, doesn't look like he enjoyed it one bit. But he's also not leaping out of his chair to smack his fiancée's back. Then again, it's wine; it won't kill her.

When Joslyn finally manages to catch her breath, she slits her eyes and glares around the room.

"Pardon me for interrupting"—Severine shifts from one foot to the other—"but the chef would like to know whether you'd like the cake you flew in yesterday to be brought out, Miss Mackenzie? Or would you prefer he toss it?"

"Toss it?" she squawks. "Why in the world would he think I'd like to throw away my mother's wedding cake? I brought it here so she could sample it!"

As Severine enumerates all the ingredients it contains—all of which Mackenzie can't digest—my pulse ramps up, and my ears begin to ring. If this wedding cake looks anything like the one in Tarian's dream, I'm going to barricade myself in the gatehouse and ask Malachi to scour the house for guns.

Meaningful dreams are one thing, premonitory ones, another.

"It's honey vanilla," Mackenzie says. "A combination of your favorite flavors."

The cake is brought out in plated slices. One look at the ombré frosting and snowdrop-white dough makes my glass of water slip from my fingers. It hits my placemat without breaking, splashing my napkin-covered lap with whatever remained inside.

A dishtowel appears in front of me and sponges up my mess, and then a fresh napkin is extended my way. I'm too stunned to thank Severine.

"I would think sampling a wedding cake during such a tragic time would bring bad luck." Catalina runs her fork tines over the frosting, then sucks them clean. She wrinkles her nose. "Why does it taste like rotten oysters?"

"Rotten oysters?" Mackenzie stabs her fork into the cake, then into her mouth. And then she gags, grabs her glass of water, downs the contents, but still she retches, drenching her cake in vomit. After belching and expelling another dollop of bile, she shoots to her feet and streaks into the kitchen, yelling, "What did you fucking do to my cake?"

I push my plate away, stomach swishing at the sight of Mackenzie's slice and the reek that's embalming the dining room.

Bryn tosses her napkin onto the table and scrapes her chair back. "I'm sorry, Saul, but puke makes me want to—" She slaps her palm over her mouth, grabs her new phone, and dashes off just as Mackenzie bursts back into the dining room, quivering with anger.

"He kept my fucking cake in the walk-in fridge beside Symeon's corpse!" Tears trundle down her cheeks. For half a second, I think it's because of Symeon, but then she mutters, "I bet the asshole did it on purpose. Disgusting!" She spins on her heel and pounds out of the dining room.

As the dessert plates are cleared, Joslyn casts an accusatory look Saul's way. "I thought we'd agreed Symeon would stay at the funeral home until you were ready to repatriate his body."

"It felt wrong to leave him there alone."

"Why? He's dead, Saul! *Dead.*"

"Watch your tone, Jos."

"Or what? You'll cancel the wedding?" The grin she shoots him is so manic that I do wonder if being pregnant with a magical baby takes a toll on a human's mind. "You have more to lose than I do."

Even though I don't think she'd go through with ending her pregnancy, I do think she'd be nuts enough to blackmail and extort Saul until she's popped the baby out of her loins.

I'm so disgusted that it takes poor Severine six reiterations of, "Tea or coffee?" before I finally blink up at her and reply, "Coffee. Black. Please."

"At least put him in a pine box!" she calls out over her shoulder.

"We don't bury our dead in coffins, Jos," he calls back.

The coffin I saw on the screen in my last dream floats back before my eyes. Was it some macabre symbolism for death or—

The boardroom's oblong shape.

The windowless walls upholstered in silk.

Holy shit. I need to tell Electra.

I shoot to my feet so fast that my chair skids backward. "Sorry, I'm feeling a little unwell too."

I race out of the dining room, then tear across the foyer and into the pool room. I sneak my hand behind the largest trophy, hunting for the device I stashed there. My fingers meet only wood.

My heart stops. I take the trophy down. The space behind it is empty. My insides go cold, then hot, then cold again.

Was it the squatter trophy I hid it behind?

I pull down every trophy, ramming them back on the shelf helter-skelter.

Nothing.

"Looking for this?"

I spin around, my battering heart dumping adrenaline inside my veins as I take in the outstretched phone pinched between Ines's thumb and index finger.

# SIXTY-ONE

That comment Ines made about texting Electra… She said it because she knew I didn't have my phone on me.

"It is yours, isn't it, Miss Bloom?"

Could I pass it off as someone else's and ask Malachi to retrieve it for me later? Just as I have that thought, the thing lights up with a message.

ELECTRA: Did you survive lunch?

ELECTRA: Sorry for abandoning you.

I chew on the inside of my cheek, wondering if I could still pretend I've never seen this phone before. Technically, Electra could be texting anybody.

ELECTRA: Callie?

Well, fuck. "You found it!" My exclamation squeaks past my heart, which, at present, is lodged in the vicinity of my collarbone.

"I did. Care to explain why it was on a shelf?"

Even though I want to fire back, *Care to explain how the hell you knew where to look?* I choose a much less aggressive approach. One that will hopefully keep me alert and breathing a while longer.

"I challenged Malachi to a game of pool, but he got sidetracked by—"

"The gin bottle?" She unmoors herself from the doorway and drifts toward me.

"I was going to say the pregnancy, but there was definitely some gin involved." I rake one hand through my hair, snagging more strands out of my elastic. "Look, grill me all you want in a minute. Just let me text him."

"He's sleeping."

"Then I'll message Electra." The speed my pulse is averaging cannot be healthy.

"Why not just tell me?"

*Because I don't fucking trust you.*

She flips my phone end over end as though it were a fidget spinner. Maybe it's de-stressing her, but it's having the opposite effect on me. "Dictate the message. I'll type it out."

I'd rather lick Mackenzie's dessert plate clean. My stomach shrivels, sending a burst of bile upward. Fine. Maybe not.

I end up saying, "It's private."

"So was my boss's conversation."

My ribs ache from how fiercely my heart beats. If it wasn't for the rune stamped into my spine, I'd worry that cardiac arrest was in the cards for me, but Tarian's magic keeps me safe from death. Right? Shit, does it?

"Fine. Don't hand it over; but press dial and put Electra on speakerphone." I may be about to reveal my ace, but I'm also about to play it.

Unless I'm wrong?

I picture the windowless, doorless boardroom again. The

padded fabric walls. The odd shape of it. The movie reel of Tarian and Symeon. What if the dream was all about Symeon and has nothing to do with Tarian's current location?

If I tell Electra to look into funeral homes and I'm wrong, then I'll have played my ace in the wrong game. But if I tell her and I'm right, then we get Tarian back tonight. Especially if the funeral parlor is located in the Vineyard. For interminable seconds, those huge eyes of Ines's gulp down every minute twitch of my expression.

"I'll make you a deal. I'll go see Saul and Catalina and confess that I eavesdropped on their conversation—"

"Eavesdrop is a bit of a euphemism for what you did, wouldn't you think?"

"—if you phone Electra and let me tell her one thing."

She flips the slender device once more, then finally fucking stops. "You do realize I could just show them your phone?"

"You care about Tarian, right?"

She tilts her head, studying the mark my possessive lover left on my neck.

"*Right?*" Every word feels too large for my mouth, too wide for my lips.

She finally lifts her stare back to mine. "I care about every member of this family."

"Then for the love of Gaea, I beg you, Ines, press dial."

Since the phone isn't passcode protected, she clicks right onto my call app and hits Electra's name.

The phone rings twice before she picks up. "I was starting to worry you hadn't survived lunch."

"Elle, funeral home. Coffin."

"For which Fielding?"

"What?" I croak.

Is it me or are the corners of Ines's mouth twitching?

"Which body needs burying?" Electra's tone is springy.

Does she really think I murdered someone during lunch?

"While I appreciate the fact that you'd help me bury a body, I didn't kill anyone, Elle. I remembered something."

Silence.

I worry Ines has hung up until I hear Electra breathe out, "Fuck. You think they buried him alive?"

Horror strikes me so hard that my lungs empty of air. "No—I mean, I don't—" I shudder. "Shit. Did they?"

Ines sighs. "I assume you two are discussing Tarian."

Although I can't see Electra's face, I can imagine her mouth contorting. And then I can hear it when she says, "Oh, hey, Ines. How awesome to have you on the line."

"Their goal is to bring him to Atlantis"—Ines's attention drifts over the jumbled trophies—"so they wouldn't have buried him, but they could be preparing him for transport. Easier to hide a body in a coffin."

Although Electra's suggestion stretched my heart on my rib rack, Ines's theory makes its edges snap off the bone and retract.

"Whatever made you think of coffins, Miss Bloom?"

"Just a hunch."

"There's only one funeral home on the island. I just looked it up." Electra sounds breathless. "I'll go check it out."

"Not alone, Elle!" I snap.

"I'll be fine."

"I'll go with you."

A snort. Then, "Dream on, human. Actually, yes. Go do that while I swing by Madar's Prestigious Home for the Departed."

"Electra, I'm all for being brave, but charging criminals without backup is beyond reckless."

"I won't charge them. I'll do a little recon."

"Elle, no!"

She hangs up.

On the tail end of a growl, I hiss, "You can't let her go alone, Ines."

"I won't. Let's go."

I trail her into the foyer but pause when I catch a shadow in the door gap of the foyer bathroom. Is someone in there or is the lighting creating illusions?

"Calanthe?" Ines opens the door and nods to the storm-soaked land.

Even though I'm still planted in the middle of the foyer, I feel the sting of raindrops and the bite of humid air against my cheeks. She raises one palm, and the elements stop hurtling into the house.

I check the door gap. The *shadow-free* door gap. I shake my head. Nerves. It's only nerves.

"I hear a car," Ines grumbles, while I hear only thunder and the hectic thud of my heart.

I'm about to ask her if she senses someone in the bathroom, but I find the doorway empty. Shit, shit, shit. I race out after her, then sprint down the gravel driveway. By some miracle, I catch up to her. It's probably not a miracle.

She must decide on a shortcut, because we veer off the path and onto the lawn, where mud sucks so hard at my sneakers that I feel like I'm lifting the very earth with each footfall. I skid, only managing not to faceplant thanks to Ines gripping my arm. And then she's propelling me forward just as an SUV shoots out from behind a diminutive version of Tarian's manor—the gatehouse, I presume.

The car stops. She saw us! When its wheels spin, kicking up clumps of mud, I realize that Electra didn't spot us. She's getting bogged down. Ines's doing?

Once we reach her, Ines releases me and snaps the passenger side door open. "You. Wait."

Electra squeezes the gearshift with so much gusto that her knuckles are pale. "Callie stays here."

"*Obviously.* I'm going to drop her off with Malachi because I don't fucking trust the Fielding women. You move, and I sink this car in mud, and then we'll have to walk to the funeral home. Oh, and Elle? I expect a lot of fucking explaining."

Electra's jaw ticks at her impending cross-examination.

Ines and I hurry toward the gatehouse, shielded by magic. Once there, she unlocks the door, and I bolt inside.

Right before snapping the door shut, she shoves a cell phone into my chest. "If you *remember* anything else, call me immediately. And lock the door."

I'm too rattled to nod.

She whirls and sprints back toward the SUV. I start to push the door closed when thunder cracks over the land and lightning strikes the sky. A gust of wet wind slams into my body as I stand there, staring at the furious heavens. *They're coming, Tarian.*

Once the SUV shoots out of the driveway, I close the door and lock it, and then I kick off my shoes. The gatehouse is so quiet, so still. Like me. I feel suspended in an odd, silent bubble. Adrift. Clutching my phone, I wander. The living room boasts an open kitchen, a wall of windows that overlook Tarian's house, and four doors that all lead to bedrooms.

I find Malachi in one of them, sprawled on top of a comforter, his head buried in a pillow. The snores that escape his parted lips rival the thunder growling outside. My lips want to bend into a smile, but they're frozen, like the rest of me. I plod back to the sofa and stare first at the spectacle beyond the window, and then at the digital clock on my phone—2:16 pm.

A shiver makes me drop my phone and peel off my soaked hoodie. I lay it on the back of the sofa, then pick my phone back up. Although I don't expect to find any trace of my earlier recording, I still browse my photos app.

The storm blurs.

The walls of the gatehouse fade.

And not because I'm about to fall asleep, but because shock tightens my vision to a single point, a single square, casting the rest of the world out of focus.

Ines didn't erase the footage I recorded of Catalina and Saul.

# SIXTY-TWO

I must forget to breathe because I'm suddenly wheezing. And then I jump, because the house shudders and every bulb in the house flickers. Did lightning just strike the house? Another question takes precedence over that one: how is the recording still on my phone?

Did Ines forget to erase the video? She doesn't strike me as someone who forgets to do anything. She must've left it on my phone because it's not actually anything all that exciting or incriminating.

I press play and hike up the volume. The conversation is faint but decipherable. Well, decipherable if one spoke Atlantean, which isn't my case. I watch the three minutes and ten seconds four times. The only words I recognize are names: Nora, Yasmin, Barak, Paloma, Symeon, Lynch, and Tarian.

I am *dying* to wake Malachi up, but the poor guy hasn't slept in days and just drank his weight in gin. Still, I gaze at the entrance to his bedroom for *long* minutes. When I can no longer sit still, I pace the living room, gnawing on a hangnail beside my pinkie. I check the time on the phone again.

Ten minutes go by.

I text Electra, then Dorian, eating away another two minutes.

I browse the news for thirteen minutes.

Impatience has me creeping into his room and whispering, "Mal, are you awake?"

He stirs, but his eyes remain sealed.

I tiptoe a little closer, then, keeping my voice extra low, I ask, "Mal?" Did I crouch a little? Maybe. But honestly, it's a super small crouch. "Okay, fine, I'll let you sleep."

The Atlantean grumbles some unintelligible words followed by three intelligible ones. "Better be important."

"It is." I plop down on the bed beside him. The mattress is so buoyant that it manages to make him bounce a little.

He scrubs his hands down his haggard face, then back up and through his hair. "Did you dream of Tarian's location?"

"I may have."

He bolts upright.

The ripple effect almost topples me off the bed. "What is up with this mattress?"

"It's filled with water."

"Seriously?"

"Mrs. Serran is a fan, and since she and her husband were the caretakers under Barak, that's what they bought. Why are we discussing bedding?"

"Because it's very bouncy."

He scoots up until his back rests against the wooden headboard. "Tarian. You know where he is?"

"I'm not a hundred percent certain, but during lunch, Joslyn mentioned coffins, and Saul said you didn't bury your dead in wooden boxes."

He rubs his eyes, as though that might help him see more clearly where I'm going with this.

"I told you that we were in a boardroom in my last dream. It was windowless and oddly shaped and padded in black silk. The more I think about it, the more I'm convinced that Yasmin and Delta put Tarian in a coffin."

"Fucking hell." He vaults off the bed.

I grip the edge of the mattress as it jounces.

He stares around the room, blinks. "My shoes. I need my shoes."

"Electra and Ines went to check it out."

"What?" he exclaims, almost blowing out one of my eardrums.

"There's only one funeral home on the island. They went to check it out."

"Without waking me up?"

"They were letting you sleep off your ginfest."

"I hate gin."

"Well, you didn't two hours ago." I throw my legs over the edge of the mattress and walk over to him.

He pats his pants before glancing at the nightstand and swiping his phone off the charging base.

"Mal, wait. There's something I need to show you." I decide to just hit play on the recording and jack up the volume to the max.

As the seconds tick by, the divide between his lips widens and widens until I can count his molars.

Malachi lifts the phone from my fingers and plays the whole thing again. "How did you get this?"

"I eavesdropped on your father." I add a quick but not heartfelt, "Sorry," because I'm not sorry. Especially if it can help us locate Tarian.

Although if it could, then Ines wouldn't have bothered confronting me. She would've sprang into action. Except...

Oh my god. What if Saul's behind the kidnapping and Ines knows it, and she accompanied Electra to get rid of her and warn the others that they've been made? I feel like I've just downed a pack of frozen peas and the icy spheres are pinballing against the walls of my stomach.

My hands tremble. My molars chatter. "Do they know where Tarian is? Is that what they're talking about?" My tone is half pant, half wheeze.

Malachi slants his eyebrows, breaking their perfect line. "No."

I expel so much air that my body goes limp, and I drop onto the foot of the bed, sinking a little lower than anticipated. "If it doesn't have to do with Tarian's abduction, what does it have to do with?"

"How Yasmin became a Fablez." Malachi slumps down beside me, the wavelets he creates lifting my ass before sliding it closer to his.

I have to clutch the sheets to avoid toppling into his lap. "How?"

"Barak." He squeezes the bridge of his nose. "Symeon."

I wait for him to expand. When he doesn't, I ask, "Can you translate it for me?"

And so he does.

He tells me that Barak brought Yasmin to Catalina all those years ago, passing her off as an orphaned preemie. Since the baby had the runes, and Catalina trusted Barak, she didn't ask questions and only uncovered the child's lineage about a decade ago because of Yasmin's striking resemblance to Nora.

I learn that Symeon overheard his father and Catalina discussing Yasmin a few weeks before Barak's death, which led Tarian's brother to track down a clueless Lynch and collect a sample of his DNA. And when I say clueless, I'm talking completely so. Not only did the sergeant have no recollection of the pregnancy, but he also didn't remember Nora.

I never thought my heart would beat with anything other than loathing for the man, but as I realize what Barak did, what he stripped the man of, my heart breaks for Lynch, because the loss of certain memories is as tragic as the loss of a loved one. Also, for all his flaws, the man does care for his children.

"Anything else?" I ask as the last minute of the recording fritters in the space between us with no translation.

Malachi says that's all, yet I sense there's more since his lips are wedged so tight they're white. I don't press him for the rest, though. I'm already damn grateful he translated any of it for me.

Empathy and guilt scatter chills along my spine. "I'm sorry for having snooped on your family, Mal."

He nods. Does that mean he accepts my apology or merely acknowledges it? I try to catch his attention, but he keeps it planted on the white-washed wooden dresser in front of the bed. Why is he refusing to look at me? Is he worried I'll decipher the part of the conversation he's keeping secret?

His phone screen suddenly brightens with an incoming call—*Ines*.

He stares and stares.

"Mal, pick up!" I snap.

He jumps and jabs his thumb against the screen. "Hello?"

"Hi, Brother."

# SIXTY-THREE

y heart, which flatlined at the sound of Yasmin's voice, leaps back into action.

"I heard you finally figured it out. Symeon was worried you'd spot the resemblance before we could get our act together, but you didn't."

If she'd called from any other number, I might've felt excitement.

Malachi gives voice to my trepidation. "Why the fuck do you have Ines's phone?"

"Why do you think?"

"I don't want to think. I want to know."

The chills that have seized my spine rush over the rest of me.

"Daddy spotted her creeping around the woods and shot a little lead into her head. He's really good with guns. Like, really good."

Perhaps I should be horrified by her confession, but the only emotion I feel is dread because *where is Electra?*

Malachi stares at me, and although I can't read minds, I think he's asking himself the same question.

"She's alive, but we'll be removing her runes if you keep interfering." It takes my addled brain a second to realize Yasmin's still talking about Ines.

The disappointment I experience fills me with shame. I should be relieved they haven't irreparably harmed Ines, but I'm far too worried about Electra.

Malachi opens up my text message thread with Electra and taps out a message.

"If anyone else comes looking for us, not only will we murder your family's watchdog, but we'll hide Tarian's body so well, no one will ever be able to find him."

Malachi springs to his feet. I think he's about to tear out the door, but he just stands there, his gaze riveted to the unbridled sky. "Only Tarian can extract an Atlantean's runes."

"How convenient that we have him, no?"

"Take me instead."

"Oh, we will, Mal." Yasmin must be vaping because a rush of air sounds through the receiver. "We'll be taking you *and* Bryn to Atlantis with us. My sister's already idling in the car outside the gatehouse, ready when you are. Chop, chop."

"How?" he gasps.

I stand and walk over to him, then press mute so she can't hear me. "Someone gave her a phone. She probably used it to get in touch with her father to warn him."

I picture the shadows dancing beneath the door of the guest bathroom. I knew there was someone in there. I should've checked. I hate Bryn so much right now. I hate her for choosing a father who never raised her and a sister she barely knows over *me*, her oldest friend.

Malachi unmutes the call. "You'll free Tarian after the visit to the mine?"

"Tell Bryn's little friend that the next time she wants to impart secrets to you, she shouldn't bother pressing mute. We have eyes and ears everywhere."

Malachi and I both spin toward the window.

"And yes, Brother. We'll free the great and fearsome Tarian after he gives us—" She stops talking so suddenly that I think the call dropped, but then she says, "After he gives my father and Bryn runes."

Malachi steps nearer to the window. "You do realize the council will punish you?"

"They're not in favor of Tarian's body going missing."

"What's that supposed to mean?" he snaps.

"We have a long journey ahead. I'll explain everything then."

Malachi's jaw flexes. "Tarian will come after you."

"Your concern is so fucking sweet." The lilt to her voice confuses me.

How is she not terrified of Tarian's vengeance? Even if they found a hideout in the most far-off land, Tarian will hunt them down.

"You have thirty seconds to walk out of that house, or Callie gets a bullet through the heart."

Malachi's eyes clock mine. Actually, they clock my chest and the red dot shining like fresh blood over the Bloom's Blooms logo.

"Twenty-three. Twenty-two."

He grabs my arm to spin me away from the window. Glass breaks, and something punches my shoulder with such strength that it rips my body from Malachi's and slams me onto the ground. Malachi drops onto his knees beside me, his shaking palms skimming the back of my head before gripping my sweater and towing it up.

"My dear brother, always trying to play hero." Yasmin's delight scratches through the phone. "That was a really stupid move."

His knuckles are pale but the rest of him is flushed. For several long seconds, all we do is stare at each other and breathe.

"Walk out the door, or she gets another bullet. And this time, my father will put it in a part of her body that has no chance of healing."

"Shit, shit, shit," he mutters.

"Once you get here with Bryn, Daddy will phone his ex to let her know Callie's been shot and needs healing."

I feel myself fading. "Not Joslyn. She'll let me bleed out."

"I'm so sorry, Callie." Malachi's raw timbre claws at my aching chest. "I'm so fucking sorry."

"Toss out her phone and walk out."

He jumps to his feet, tremors making his body judder harder than the azalea shrub shivering outside the window.

"No, not beside Callie. Out the broken pane." After a beat, Yasmin says, "That's it. Now walk out."

"Not Joslyn," I croak as he shuffles toward the door.

"Not Joslyn," he whispers around a gulp of emotion.

And then he pounds away, and a door claps shut.

I try to keep my lids lifted, to stay conscious, but my lashes feel caked in mud. A gust of wet air ribbons into the room and strokes my cheek. I imagine it's Tarian caressing me. Tarian reminding me that he's there, that everything will be all right because his magic runs in my veins.

I hold on to that shred of hope as the room darkens and the rug beneath me softens, and I slip.

Right through the floor.

Right through the earth.

I drift like a snowflake caught on a breeze. Like down shaken from a pillow.

My body is weightless, but my heart is heavy, an anchor that drives me down, down, down.

I finally land with a thump. When I reel my lids, I'm no longer in the gatehouse.

# SIXTY-FOUR

**M**y eyelids twitch as I stare at the shelf of trophies in my billiard room. The ones that injected my father with such pride, as though an Atlantean beating a human at anything was an achievement.

When I'd mentioned boxing them up during one of our last games of pool, he'd set his stick down and said, *"I don't keep them because you won, Son. I keep them because you competed. Because you went out on that ocean and allowed yourself to feel something other than responsibility for the world. You allowed yourself to have fun. To be selfish for an instant."*

I slide the largest one back into alignment. "I called you."

"I know." Her answer is a sigh. "I'm here."

"I meant before, Calanthe. I called you, and you didn't come."

A beat of silence echoes between us.

I stare at her reflection in one of my polished trophies.

Although it distorts her body, I don't miss how she rubs her shoulder.

My posture is so rigid that my bones grind as I twist to face her. "What's wrong with your shoulder?"

"Nothing." She says this too quickly for my liking.

"Turn."

"Seriously, I'm fine."

"Turn."

With a sweet huff, she indulges me, spinning on herself. "See. I'm fine."

I'm not entirely convinced and have every intention of examining her body for myself later. "So why did you shun me earlier?"

"I didn't shun you. I was just in the middle of lunch with your uncle and Catalina Fablez, so psychosomatic tripping was tricky."

"I called you because I believe I know where I am. Or where I've been."

"*Madarsfuneralhome*. I figured it out after our last dream."

Surprise jostles my Adam's apple. "You caught the logo on the screen?"

"No, I—" She bites her lip, and even though I'm unconscious and enclosed in a space that reeks of death, the sight of those plush lips rouses everything within me. "The boardroom's shape. The silk-padded walls. It reminded me of a coffin."

*Smart girl.* Of course she would see something I needed spelled out. "Come here."

I worry that reality will have broken the spell of our last dream, but she steps around the pool table and into my open arms with no hesitation. I cart her into my body, breathing easier when her arms wrap around my middle and she clutches me with the same desperation with which I hold her.

"I thought I'd died," I rasp into her hair. "I thought my runes were gone."

She presses her cheek against my thudding chest and lets out a muffled cry.

"They're still there." I run my mouth over her head, replacing the reek of death with the scent of life. "Still there."

"What if they bump your body against tons of Atlanteans so you lose them all?"

My heart should beat with unadulterated joy that I've been found, but only caution agitates the muscle. "They?"

"It was Yasmin and Lynch all along. You were right."

"You're certain of this?"

She cranes her neck to meet my probing stare. "Yes. They called to explain they want safe passage to Atlantis, otherwise they hide your body somewhere no one will ever be able to find it."

"Except you."

She doesn't nod. I don't press the issue. She found me once; she'd find me again. She may doubt it, but I don't.

Her teeth dent her lip. "Yasmin wants to give her father and sister runes, after which they'll release you."

"Considering the mine's volatility, they'll either perish or be cursed." I briefly wonder what it might do to my body but sweep the thought away. "Let them take me. Let them use me. They won't come out of this alive." Either I'll murder them, or the mine will.

She slides her lips together. "What if the mine punishes more people than just them? What if it punishes all of your people?"

"It will prove that our species wasn't worthy of magic."

"Collective punishment would be unfair."

"We didn't make the world a better place."

"It's only been thirty years."

I coast one of my hands beneath the layers of her hoodie and T-shirt until I reach smooth warmth. "It'll rid you of your rune."

Her breath hitches. "I don't want to be rid of it!"

Even though the words flew out of her, I hunt her stare.

She brackets my jaw with her palms, pressing her thumbs into the hollows beneath my cheekbones to angle my face to hers.

"I don't want to be rid of you." Her murmur skates over my

lips. "Not anymore and not ever. But I need to get back. Send me back so I can stop them, Tarian."

As much as I want Yasmin and Lynch to be stopped, I don't want *her* to do it. "Did you tell anyone about your suspicions of where they're keeping me?"

She nods, the end of her high ponytail swishing against my forearm.

Perfect. I'll be keeping her right here with me then, locked inside this dream until my people retrieve me.

*Almost free.* "Good girl," I murmur before eliminating the thin divide between our mouths.

The tension in her body loosens instantly, and she sinks into me with a soft moan that seeps straight down into my cock. Gently, I part my lips and stroke her tongue. Heat builds inside of me, billowing out, warming all those spaces that go dead when she's out of my arms and out of my sight. To think that soon, I'll be able to hold and cherish her in the real world. To feel her against me in slumber and in wakefulness.

I visualize a body chain made up of linked diamonds. I picture them coiling around her thin neck, cresting over her collarbone, and dripping between her heavy breasts before clinching around her waist. When I feel her clothes vanish and her breath catch, I pull away. The effect of the jewels is even more mesmerizing than it was against my lids—like droplets of sea spray gilded by a rising sun.

She glances down with a swallow that flutters the bruise along her throat. "Tarian, I need to get back."

I sculpt her body with my palms, dropping onto one knee and then the other to follow the toned curves of her thighs and calves.

Vivid hazel trails my descent. "Tarian..."

Before she can entreat me to let her go, I flatten my tongue against her, then curl the tip between her scarred folds, leisurely licking up to that pulsing bud. The next time she says my name, it's accompanied by a marrow-deep moan.

I spiral my hands around the backs of her legs to the curve of her ass cheeks and ease her legs apart. Her ponytail slips over her shoulder as she gazes down at me, her forest-fire eyes glittering as wildly as the diamond chain.

As I lash at her clit, my balls grow tight and my dick long. I vanquish my clothes to give myself more room to expand. Her fingers tangle with my hair, alternately caressing my scalp and tugging at my roots. I suck her in, then release her with a pop and go back to laving that magical spot on her body that makes her body go liquid for me.

She whimpers, the sound so fucking sweet that I quicken my assault only to hear it again. Sure enough, she fills my ears with more heady moans before her body goes still and she bastes my tongue with her pleasure. I lick her clean before dirtying her anew.

When the tautness ravaging my balls becomes too painful, I stand up, pick her up, then walk her to the pool table and sit her down on the wooden frame.

"Tarian, you need to—send me—"

"Over the edge again?"

"What?" she croaks, lids at half-mast.

I know what she really wants, but it's not something I'm willing to offer. "I'll give your greedy little cunt as many orgasms as it can stand."

She blinks shiny, unfocused eyes at me. "That's not—"

"It's what your body needs."

Another stunned blink.

Before she can attempt to argue, I take my dick in my hand and press the swollen head against her slick pussy. She blinks at it, eyes pitched wide now, as though to fit as much of where we connect into the lens of her vision.

I squeeze her hip with one hand, squeeze my dick with the other. "I won't penetrate you, Calamity Darling."

I rub myself against her, making sure to linger a little longer on her clit before sailing down her glorious sex to the hole it's taking every fucking fiber of my being not to enter. "You feel so good, baby. So warm. So soft."

Whatever resistance she'd started to put up melts on another moan.

The sultry essence of her mixes with my musk and salt, punching up my nose, driving my pulse wild. She's so wet, I slip and slide. Her hips buck just as my dick is cresting back down her folds and an inch of me glides right into her.

I'm about to apologize when she grips my ass and cries out, "More."

I smirk and pull out. "You'll get more—*all of me*—soon."

"Now."

"No, baby. Not now."

She pouts. "Why not now?"

"Because the first time I make love to you, I want it to be in the real world." It's not the only reason. Chiefly, I want her mind—our minds—to be unencumbered by anything other than *us* and that won't happen until I'm free.

"This is real," she complains.

Still rubbing my cock against her, I catch her mouth with mine and kiss away her sexy pout. Her nails dig into my skin every time my dick goes low. The little vixen is trying to test my resolve, but I won't break.

On my dick's tenth trip, she impels my body forward and succeeds in sheathing my head into her heat.

"Calamity," I growl, pulling back out.

She draws me back in.

I plant my heels firmly into the ground to stop myself from falling into her. "Fine. But only the tip."

"Yes!" she pants.

Fuck, what did I just agree to? So I'm not tempted to dive deeper, I seize my dick right where it mushrooms and run it up her slit, massaging her needy clit before slamming that swollen, weeping inch of flesh into her. Her walls contract, coaxing a string of precum with which I paint her clit. Her throat tautens around a whimper that develops into a gasp when I nudge myself back inside.

My spine begins to burn, my balls to lift. I don't want to blow until she comes on me, so I pull out and grind myself against her clit until her hands spring off my ass and slam onto the sapphire felt. One of them lands on the eight-ball, sending the rest skidding across the table.

I jerk my hand off her hip and onto her spine to keep her from collapsing, all the while working myself up and down, in and out. She throws her head back and shouts my name. My chest broadens with masculine pride and my heart bangs with thunderous beats.

I pepper her clenching throat with kisses, letting her ride out her orgasm before I allow myself to seek out my own. I slam back inside, and although so little of me pierces her, it feels like my entire body has sunk into hers.

An electric jolt makes my ass clench and heat bursts up my spine. I flip my thumb up and bear down on her clit. When she chokes on another orgasm, I pull out and spray her from navel to puffed pussy.

I watch her skin glow with my cum, sparkle with my diamonds, and shine with my saliva. A primal part of me feels such possession and pride at seeing her drip with me. "You wear my rune and my cum to perfection, Calamity Darling."

I release my dick, sweep the pool balls away, and ease her onto her back. Her arms flop over her head, and she sighs. I bend over her and kiss one nipple and then the other. And then I kiss the hollow of her collarbone before trailing my lips up her neck.

She threads her fingers through my hair. "Tarian, you need to send me back now."

I don't tell her that she's not going anywhere. Instead, I keep kissing her, lingering on one corner of her mouth before pressing my lips to the other.

"Tar…"

I silence her entreaty by sucking her bottom lip into my mouth. Although she sighs, she slants her mouth over mine to deepen the kiss. I think she's given up trying to escape when my body lists forward and my mouth grazes felt instead of flesh.

"Calanthe," I growl, punching off the pool table. I concentrate on the rune she wears until my skin burns with its phantom presence. "Calanthe, come back!"

She resists my call. I hate that she's learned to do that.

My fingers close around the eight-ball, and I lob it at the wall. A chunk of plaster falls to the ground. I'm about to pitch another ball when a loud gasp rises from the next room. I lunge toward the wall and stick my eye to the hole to find a hotel room steeped in sunlight, and in the middle of it, my uncle and father sitting around a laden breakfast table.

I'm about to call out to my father when I hear him say, "Who told you, Saul?"

"It doesn't matter who told me." Saul butters his toast before drizzling it with honey. "What matters is if it's true. Barak Hadez, have you been drugging me to prevent me from having more children?"

My father's jaw ticks. "Yes."

"Why?"

"Because since Nora, you've fucked everything with a pulse."

Saul flings the honey dipper back into the glass pot. "And how is my sex life any of your concern, Brother?"

"Malachi doesn't deserve to split his heritage with a thousand bastards."

Saul works his jaw from side to side.

"I care about you."

"Fuck you, Barak." Saul's eyes sharpen on his brother's neck. "Fuck. You."

Suddenly my father begins to choke. He clutches at his throat and wheezes out a "stop" as thin and brittle as those Atlantean crispbreads he ate every morning of his life.

"No wonder Gaea eradicated your runes. You didn't deserve them."

Even though I know this scene isn't real, I find myself clawing at the tiny hole to widen it and shouting at Saul to stop. But he doesn't hear me, and the plaster doesn't give.

My father's face flushes a deep crimson.

"Saul!" I yell.

"Never fucking mess with me again, Barak, or else…" He lets his threat hang there as he flicks his wrist, toppling my father's chair. He must release his magical chokehold, because my father gasps in a breath a second before his head clouts the stone floor with such force that I hear something crack.

I assume it's the wall between us finally giving way, but the plaster isn't even webbed. I jerk my gaze back toward my father.

My fingers slip from the hole and smack my thighs, which have gone as numb as the rest of me.

A crimson pool slickens the stone beneath his head and spreads.

Saul grips his toast and takes a bite out of it. "Now get out of here and let me finish my breakfast in peace."

But my father doesn't get out. The same way he doesn't get up.

"Barak?" When he's met with silence, Saul shoves his chair back and gets up, and then he's lunging around the table and kneeling. "Fuck."

He grips my father's face, which has become as white as our sun-bleached home back in Atlantis, and his veins, the blue of the Mediterranean that cradles our island.

"Barak?" My father's name is a broken whisper on my uncle's lips. "Symeon!"

He looks in the direction of a gaping door. Although the person standing behind it is hidden from Saul's line of sight, I see her, like I see the phone she's sliding into her robe pocket as she backs up.

"Symeon!"

My brother suddenly bursts out of the room, a towel wrapped around his middle, black curls wet from a shower. "What is it?"

"Call Tarian."

Symeon pads over. "Is he—dead?" His voice is flat, emotionless.

"Call Tarian, Sym. Call him so he can bring him back."

But my brother doesn't retreat into his bedroom to grab a phone. He merely stares. "Drain him."

"What?" Saul cranes his neck to look up at Symeon, wan cheeks crosshatched with tears.

"The original rune Tarian gave him said *withdraw*."

"I don't—"

"Withdraw his blood, Saul. One stone, two Atlanteans."

Saul sits back on his heels and runs a shaky hand through his hair, reddening the silver strands. "I-I-I—he was my… What did I do?"

"You didn't do anything."

"I made the chair—"

"You were at home. You didn't spend the night here."

"Ines—"

"She's on a trip with Malachi, remember?"

"But our guards… They saw him come inside. And someone surely drove him over. What if it's Dorian? That one never lets anything go."

"Dorian's with Tarian. As for the guards outside, a drop of Tarian's blood on the tongue will do the trick to compel my father's visit from their minds."

My uncle rubs at his temples, smearing crimson there. "*Your* brother, *your* tongue."

"Oh, come now, Saul. We're a team."

"I'll take care of the whore. You take care of everyone else." Saul gets to his feet and starts in the direction of the bedroom.

"You may want to shower first, Uncle." Symeon nods to Saul's bathrobe that's drenched in Father's blood while I raise my fist and bite down so hard I break skin. "And, Saul, once every-thing's done, I'll have the hotel concierge call you, and you'll hurry on over. And then you'll phone Tarian to announce the tragic news."

My uncle's throat bobs, and he shuts his lids, fresh tears pitch-forking down his damp cheeks, striping his face red and white.

When a sob lurches from his throat, Symeon says, "Remember what he did to you. To me. To Nora. *Remember*."

Symeon crouches beside my father. "Send Mother my love." And then he shuts our father's lids and splays his fingers over his deadened heart.

As he forces the organ to pump out every last ounce of blood, I stare at the monster who convinced me that my rune was to blame. He must feel he has an audience because he cranes his neck.

I capture his soulless stare, hold it, throttle it.

My skin crawls. No wonder my magic killed—

My magic only rid him of his runes.

*I* didn't kill my brother, the same way that *I* didn't kill my father.

Unless my fucked-up brain has just made all this up? But all of it makes such disgusting sense that I believe it's real. That someone—Symeon, perhaps—took great pleasure in spilling this tale next to my paralyzed body.

I simmer with so much rage and sorrow that blisters form on my heart. They will eventually tear and weep, but for now, they only expand. Had my brother called me, Father could still be part of this world.

I'm glad Yasmin, or whoever the fuck else was on that boat with them, drained him of blood, for if he'd still possessed even an ounce, I'd have brought him back to life and murdered him again. And again. And again. I'd have become the monster that he spent his adult years accusing me of being.

I've no real need to calm down, nevertheless, I focus on the fact that my girl isn't destined to perish. Even though the perspective doesn't rid me of rage, it does soothe the parts of my afflicted heart that aren't bubbling with constrained fury.

An explosion rattles the floor beneath my feet. I rip my fist from my mouth and smack the wall to keep from buckling. The tremor echoes up my legs and around my kneecaps before racing up my torso.

The balls on the pool table jounce around the blue felt.

My rowing trophies topple like dominoes.

The art deco lamp my father bought at auction for an exorbitant sum swings my way.

I duck and it smashes against the wall, crumbling the plaster until only timber and aluminum remain. I clutch one of the beams as the earth gives another violent shudder.

And then all goes still and quiet, save for a single distinct wail, one I would recognize anywhere because it vibrated my eardrums and shoulders for days on end two decades ago.

"Malachi?" I call out.

"She's dead, Tarian."

My lungs collapse like the wall.

"They killed her." He emits that wretched sound again.

"That's impossible. She wears my runes. She can't—That's—" I shake my head and scrutinize the words that glow diamond-blue beneath my skin. Fucking *blue*. Why must everything in this bloody dimension be so off?

"Do you know what I learned today? That my father paid her to seduce me. How fucked up is that?"

My neck cracks from how fast I look up. "Saul did *what*?"

Malachi squeezes the bridge of his nose. "He paid her to screw me because he was worried I'd fuck a kid."

What the hell is he talking about? "What *kid*?"

Either this version of my cousin doesn't hear me, or he's trying my patience, because he says, "I would never have screwed her back then." His pale eyes darken like ink. "I still wouldn't screw her. She's like a sister to me."

"Drop the bloody pronouns and use names, Malachi! I don't understand who the fuck you're talking about."

"Ines. Electra."

As I compute what he's saying—that Saul paid Ines to distract him from Electra—I rub my chest. "I thought you were talking about Calanthe."

"He paid Ines, Tar!"

"I know."

"You—" He chokes, then guffaws. "Of course you know. Was it your idea?"

"The fuck. I'd never do that to you."

"Wouldn't you?"

"No. I wouldn't. I found out when I went over the family finances with Vic after Father passed away. I don't know that it was entirely Saul's idea since the funds came from our account." My lungs must've reconstructed because I'm breathing easier. "Ines is dead?"

"Yes. Good fucking riddance."

"Don't say that, Mal. She wasn't all bad."

"She seduced me for money! Has anyone seduced you for money?"

"Everyone. Until Calanthe."

"Calanthe? What the hell are you on?"

"We meet here. In this limbo world."

He snorts. "Are you serious right now?"

"Deadly."

He streaks toward me, his eyes incandescent. "And she seduces you?"

"It's mutual. And we've gone a few steps past seduction."

His fist comes at my face so fast that he lands the hit.

I palm my throbbing nose. "What the hell, Mal?"

"She's the best thing that's ever happened to me, so fucking stay away."

I gnash my molars and close my eyes.

*Not real.*

*Not real.*

"She's *mine*." His breath slithers over my face—icy and stale. Unlike a real breath.

Because Malachi isn't real, the same way Ines mustn't be dead, and my brother and uncle didn't join forces to murder my father. How messed up is it that I prefer being the only monster in this story if it means Calanthe remains mine and mine alone?

# SIXTY-FIVE

With a groan, I reach around myself and palm the area that Lynch shot. My hoodie is dry and hole-free. Did I imagine getting shot or did Tarian heal me in the in-between? Actually, my shoulder wasn't bleeding there. My body mustn't export the wounds I get in the real world into Tarian's dream world.

I push myself to a sitting position, then stay there a full minute, waiting for my vision to firm and the ground to stop bobbing. Everything I did with Tarian clings to my mind like it clings to my skin. If I had any doubt as to whether it truly happened, my sticky T-shirt dispels it. Although I don't regret anything, I'm a little peeved at him for having deliberately distracted me to keep me from going after Malachi.

The rune on my spine prickles and heats. I clench my molars until I've sawed through the tether. I need to stay in this world.

When I feel steady, I climb to my feet. How long was I out for?

I stumble out of the bedroom and into the open kitchen. My eyes lock on the digital microwave clock that blinks, flashing 00:47 am. The one on the oven as well. Since it's still light out, I assume it's not midnight but a glitch due to a power shortage.

I spy Malachi's suede jacket draped over the back of the kitchen chair and go through his pockets until my fingers close around his phone. Hallelujah. Before I can even make out the time, I'm struck by the twelve missed calls from Dorian. I can only imagine that he's tried Ines and Electra's phones, perhaps even mine, and he's getting voicemails left and right.

I'm tempted to call him back, but Yasmin has Tarian's blood. Surely lots of it. All of it lethal. Even if Dorian has no ill intent toward Tarian, my lover's stolen blood will hurt him. What if it kills him? I've never been gladder that he stayed behind in Boston, for if he'd been here, he would've charged into the funeral home.

*Focus.* I read the time: 3:35 pm. What time was it when I reached the gatehouse? Two-something? Or was it still one-something? No, I remember a two. I'm relieved to learn I haven't been out long, but what if it's still too long? What if they've already packed up and—

A white Adirondack sails across the lawn outside, trailed by a log the width of Dorian's thigh. My breathing eases. They're not going to attempt an Atlantic crossing until the storm calms. Or are they?

I snap into planning mode. First things first, a car. I start toward the front door when its hinges groan and it flaps open with a fierce thwack. I jump so high, my head almost grazes the ceiling. I half expect to find someone on the threshold, but it's all steel air and lashing rain.

Did Tarian's magic unlock the door?

I grab a knife from the butcher block and slink toward the entrance with extreme caution. Adrenaline courses through me so dizzyingly fast that I shake like the leaves of the honeysuckle that races up the walls of the gatehouse.

The crunch of gravel snaps my head toward the drive where a

riderless quad rolls toward me. In reverse. Is Gaea sending me a ride, or is the storm blowing the four-wheeler toward me? Does it matter how the bike got here? It has wheels and a motor. I jam my feet into my mud-caked sneakers, then, fingers of one hand crushing the knife handle and fingers of the other clutching Malachi's phone, I run to the quad and throw my leg over the large seat. I press the ignition button and the engine rumbles to life.

I haven't ridden an ATV since a long-ago Thanksgiving trip to the Hamptons with Bryn. We'd gotten into so much trouble because neither of us had a driver's license back then, not even a permit. I shake my head. Now isn't the time to reminisce about the past.

I peer down at Malachi's phone and swipe up. It prompts me for a passcode. My thumb hovers over the keypad before moving like the planchette on a Ouija board, grazing six numbers—6-4-1-9-0-1. My breath stutters past my lips when the screen unlocks.

I believed in a supernatural being before—how could I not after witnessing Tarian stopping Bryn's car with a raised palm and getting stung with an enchanted word?—yet I'm admittedly stunned. I'm even more stunned when the screen lights up with a map. I'm about to enter my destination when a path appears, and a feminine voice instructs me to take a right in five-hundred feet.

Gaea wants me to find Tarian.

Even though it's not the smartest place to put it, I stash the knife in my hoodie's kangaroo pocket and stick Malachi's cell in the phone mount clipped onto the handle. Sending a prayer of thanks to the growling sky, I follow the highlighted path toward the god Fate has picked *me*—a measly, powerless florist—to save.

As my bike and heart rev, I wonder whether the rest of my rescue mission will be as easy. I also wonder, *why now*? Did I have to earn Gaea's trust, or is this all Tarian's doing somehow? I dismiss the latter theory. Tarian doesn't want me anywhere near his captors so he wouldn't be leading me straight into the serpent's nest. It has to be Gaea.

As I splash down deserted roads framed with shuddering vegetation and swinging electrical cables, the roiling clouds overhead split, creating a runnel of blue sky through which fans sunlight. The beams lick up a wooden pole graffitied with the letters "T" and "C" enclosed in a heart.

Obviously, this heart wasn't painted by Tarian, but it nonetheless sparks my pulse. Soon, though, that little twinge of delight is replaced by a twang of dread.

Could this be Yasmin's doing? And I don't mean the romantic engraving, but the map that appeared out of nowhere and the sky that split in half? Could she know about my connection to Tarian and be piloting me to come to her? Is that the sort of power which an average Atlantean wields?

I go over a pothole, and the knife bumps against my squirming belly. It feels like such a small weapon to bring to a supernatural fight. May there not be a fight. At the very least, not until I've managed to free Tarian.

I imagine waking him. I imagine his real stare burrowing into mine. His real hands and real breath grazing my skin. His real throat rasping my name, or the one he's given me, or any word, really.

The ATV stalls and sputters, tearing me out of my reverie. Did my magical ride run out of magical fuel? I tap on Malachi's phone, which has decided to go dark. It must've happened at the same time as the quad.

I try to recall the map. I think I had to get off the main road somewhere but—

Something clicks right beside my ear. My heart misses a beat, then jostles to make up for it by pouring a thousand new ones into my bloodstream.

I creep my hand into my kangaroo pocket and palm the knife handle. Then, pulse thundering like the hurricane-ridden sky, I turn my head to meet my fate.

# SIXTY-SIX

There is no gun barrel aimed at my temple.

There is no Lynch, no Yasmin, no Bryn.

There is only me, a thousand trees, and a diamond-shaped yellow sign nailed into a utility pole.

A thousand trees that are bending and creaking, leaning away from each other as though to free the trapped mist. White wisps coil and tear, curling around my legs. Although it's no more substantial than a cloud, it coaxes me off the ATV.

I heed its call, propping the knife in front of me like some ancient huntress. Chills race up and down my spine as I inch toward the tree line, squinting into the brightness. I must stay motionless for too long for Gaea's liking, because a gust of wind charges into my back, propelling me forward.

"Okay, okay. I get it. I'm going." I slink past one tree, then another. Perhaps I should be sprinting, but considering how hard my thighs rattle and how tight my lungs have become, it's a miracle I'm even standing upright.

As I carve through the mist, branches creak and wind howls, adding a certain *je ne sais quoi* to my trek. Actually, I know exactly what: a slasher film atmosphere. It rarely works out well for lone girls venturing into the woods, but I try not to focus on that.

*This is not one of your true crime podcasts, Calanthe. You're not about to get chopped into pieces. You're about to free the god of gods.*

The gusty silence is so oppressive that I start to hum but swiftly stop that nonsense. Humming? May as well start hollering Yasmin's name. Then again, the mist probably stifles the sound I make. Still, I grow quiet and contemplative as I amble forward, shiny blade slicing through these earthen clouds.

I start to count in my head. When I get to sixty, I start over. By my fourth time around the dial, the tip of my knife bites into something solid. Wood. And not a tree trunk, but white siding.

I hold my breath as though a mere exhale could float through the slats and alert Tarian's abductors of my presence. The mist presses against my right arm. I pivot right. I must've misunderstood Gaea's silent command because when I try to take a step in that direction, I'm shoved backward.

Okay, left it is.

I twirl. This time, when I take a step, the mist offers no resistance. A bush tickles the side of my calves. I try to step away from it, but the mist slams back into me and clears just enough for me to spot what looks like a flattened grenade. Is that a…*landmine*?

The blood drains out of me, and I drop my knife, just missing my big toe. *Get ahold of yourself, Callie.*

As I bend over to retrieve it, my pulse clouts my lungs, beating the air out of me. I suck in a deep inhale. Instead of revitalizing, however, the dampness is stifling. My vision dots. I grab onto the nearest rubbery shrub, waiting for the spots to subside and my vision to fill.

Gaea must sense I'm not enduring this stress all too well because She rubs a gentle path between my shoulder blades. I think of my father then, picture him by my side, soothing me, encouraging me like he used to do every time he'd come out to one of my cross-country meets the year I decided running might be my thing. It wasn't.

My rune tingles and heats. I snap upright so fast that I spring off both the phantom fingers kneading my vertebrae and the damp chill that's permeated my bones. I grind my molars and push back against Tarian's call until the burn subsides.

Visualizing his mounting annoyance spurs me back into motion. Three strides later, spongy grass morphs into firm asphalt. For some reason, the feel of solid ground solidifies me further. My marrow thrums but no longer shakes, and my gait grows fluid. I don't even care if the mist is escorting me to the front door. I feel disposed to take on the—

A faint groan interrupts my thoughts, mincing my confidence. Even though I'm enveloped in a white shield, I hold still. The mist tears, offering me a direct line of sight to a door. A door that's ajar.

I scramble sideways, flattening my back against the siding. I clench my trembling fingers around the knife handle and prop it up once more, side-eyeing the entrance for movement. When nothing stirs in the obscurity, I flick the door wider with the edge of the knife.

The wood groans just as a loud boom—which doesn't sound like thunder—resounds through the haze.

I crane my neck. After a full minute of stillness, I sneak inside. The reek that assaults me is eye-watering. I tug my sweater over my nose and breathe in the damp cotton that smells like Tarian and his storm. Although it doesn't cancel the scent of rot, it keeps my stomach from turning inside out.

Insipid light trickles through windows embedded at the top of the tall walls. It glosses metal shelving units stacked high with slats, long worktables, and machinery that looks nothing like the sort stocked in morgues. Not that I've ever seen a morgue, other than in movies. Perhaps this is a new addition that's still under construction? It would explain the goggles and hardhats on the tables.

I spy an architectural drawing beneath one of the bright orange helmets. Mud padding my footfalls, I tiptoe toward it, hunting the paper's corners for a logo. My breath jams when I spot one—Smith & Son Timber. This isn't a morgue; it's a fucking lumber company! Did Yasmin and Lynch relocate Tarian's body after Ines sprung up on them, or is this where they've been hiding him since the boat sank? Perhaps this warehouse abuts the funeral home.

Lightning strikes, offering me a clearer view of this impossibly vast room with its grid of shelving aisles. I'll take needles in haystacks any day. At least, they're not made of the same material. How am I supposed to fucking locate a pine box in a timber warehouse?

A narrow light beam spills from the ceiling.

I suck in air.

Even though I'm super thankful for Gaea's help, Yasmin and Lynch are bound to spot the single beam. I toss out my human senses as far as they can go. Save for the whir of an AC unit, the warehouse is quiet.

Shit. Of course. They're not hiding in the same place they put Tarian. Even though they're merciless and hateful, they're far from idiots. I throw caution to the wind and sprint toward the light, booking a sharp left turn down Aisle C. The beam souses the lowest shelf that's cluttered by stacked window frames.

I heave them out, then almost weep when I spy the familiar shape of a varnished pine coffin behind the frames. I stick my knife on the shelf above, then pull down the piles, my biceps tautened by the adrenaline coursing through my veins. Once I've cleared a path for the coffin, I grab onto its handles, ask Gaea for strength, and heave. I don't expect to slide Tarian out in one go, but that's what happens. The coffin all but skates off the shelf.

When we were kids, Bryn told me the story of a man who managed to lift a car off a body trapped underneath it. Apparently, adrenaline lent him superhuman strength. After digging through the internet, I discovered that this was an urban legend. Now I think that there must be truth to it, because, even though I didn't lift the coffin, I slid it toward me. A box that must weigh close to two hundred pounds by itself, not counting the god inside.

My throat stings with emotion as I graze the lid—relief but also grief. I'm suddenly two years in the past, negotiating coffin prices while my mother stares blankly at a potted mound of succulents teetering on the corner of the funeral director's desk.

I'm not here to bury; I'm here to liberate.

The mist must've trailed me inside because it stripes my cheeks and dances against my clumped lashes. I swipe my sleeve over my face to scrub away my tears. I don't know how long I have before they come to retrieve his coffin for transportation.

The pale wisp rushes past me and circles the coffin like a stroke of highlighter.

"I know, I know. I'm hurrying," I murmur. "I found you, Tarian."

As I flex my biceps and heave, excitement coalesces with dread, but then frustration overwhelms both feelings because the damn thing is locked. Of course they wouldn't make it easy. I grab the knife and shove the blade between the cap lid and ebony body. Even though I lean all my weight into it, all I accomplish is bending the blade.

I suddenly remember the funeral director explaining how the coffin locked with a key, one that was wedged inside a tiny hole and rotated. I remember thinking how it resembled those L-shaped tools supplied in building kits, but on steroids. Could there be one here?

I spin and scan the shelves when a thud makes me drop into a crouch. I'm still in plain sight, just closer to the ground. The mist thickens, filling the entire aisle as though someone had flicked on a concert hazer.

I try to smother my hectic panting against my sweater as my pulse undulates through me, making me shake all over.

Something clangs at my feet. My knife. Except...the blade has become long and thin, like a metal skewer. Like a…like a coffin key! Without rising from my crouch, I jam the tool inside the hole and whirl until I hear the latch click. *Holy fucking gods and monsters, it worked.*

I palm the wood and rise slowly, slowly, slowly. The mist stays dense around me but begins to disperse around my hands.

I gape. And then I let the lid slam into place and bounce backward.

And I vomit.

# SIXTY-SEVEN

I'm not sure when I collapsed but I'm lying on my side, vomiting up everything inside my stomach, every beat inside my heart, every sob inside my throat. Tears stream down my cheeks as my lids glow with Tarian's bloated, bloodless, *rune*less remains.

He's dead.

They drained him of magic. They drained him of blood.

That's why they weren't there. That's why no one tried to stop me. Because Tarian's dead.

I've been fantasizing about a dead man. Or maybe he was alive, but someone tried to intervene. Maybe Malachi tried to take out Bryn, and it pissed off Yasmin and Lynch. Maybe the council finally intervened, and Yasmin drained Tarian to punish the rest of her people.

I picture her peeling off his runes with her magic, which sends a new wave of bile lurching out of me. The acrid burn lingers on my lips. Those same lips I had pressed to Tarian's only a few hours ago.

*He's dead.*

*Bang. Thud.* They're coming for me now. I keep my lids sealed, suddenly not caring whether Lynch finally puts a bullet through my skull. I want the image of Tarian's corpse wiped from my mind, and only death is capable of bestowing this mercy now that Atlanteans no longer have powers.

Besides, I don't want to live in a world without him.

I suddenly understand my mother's heartbreak when Dad passed away and left her behind. My poor, sweet mother. How will she survive once I'm gone? Will Mrs. Fiona take care of her? Will she be put in a home? Is that where she'll finish her days? Surrounded by ghosts and strangers?

"Calanthe!" Dorian's voice blooms against my throbbing skull.

I stay quiet because I don't want him to find me. I just want to sleep. Sleep and dream of Tarian. Stay forever with him in this parallel universe where magic still exists. Where *he* still exists.

Big hands scour my body, roll me over, then grip my neck and hoist me into sitting. "Fuck. What happened to you? Where's Malachi? And why isn't Electra answering her damn phone? Or Ines? Where the hell is everyone?"

"I didn't—I couldn't—" Grief gusts against my chest, dispersing my heartbeats like florets until all that remains is a naked stalk. "He's gone."

I want Dorian to uproot what's left of me so the pain stops. I need it to stop. I feel damp cotton slick over my mouth, my cheeks, my eyes.

He hitches my sweater up, hissing at the sight of my bare back. "Where? Where did he go?"

*To heaven.* Do Atlanteans believe in such a place?

I gesture in the general direction of the coffin. "Look inside."

"Inside what? The dresser?"

"What?" I croak, prizing my swollen lids apart. Can't he see the—

The bedroom with the water bed swims into focus. I blink, then swing my gaze left to right. I move too fast, and my stomach lurches. I clamp my teeth against the rising bile until it recedes, singeing off yet another layer of my throat.

"You carried me back here?"

Dorian looks like he's aged decades. "I think you were dreaming."

"So Tarian's not…he's not dead?"

"He can't—" His eyes go wide, and then he's twisting around. "Do I still have my runes?"

New tears slide down my cheeks when I see that scrawled, foreign script. "Y-You do." I hiccup a sob, then raise one hand to my heart and rub the sore muscle. "Do I still have mine?"

He removes my T-shirt, leaving me in an exercise bra. "You do."

*Tarian's alive!* Like the tide, my relief retreats as I recall that some of my dreams have been premonitory.

"Where is everyone, Callie?" Dorian asks as he warms my shoulder blade with his magic.

When I feel something wriggle beneath my skin, my vision goes gray, then black, then white.

"Bullet's out. You're okay." His voice scratches my eardrums like a gramophone needle. "You're okay. Now tell me, where did everyone go?"

If Malachi's gone, then that means the phone call happened. That means Ines has been taken hostage, and Electra… I don't know what happened to her, but if Dorian hasn't gotten in touch with her, then it can't be good.

"Callie? Where are they?" Dorian's bloodshot eyes are stone-gray, like the sky beyond the cracked window.

I've never been gladder for a hurricane, because it means Yasmin and Lynch are still stuck on this island, instead of cruising toward the one across the Atlantic.

Even though I sense the truth will rob him of several decades of life, I remind myself that he's Atlantean. He's immortal. As long as he doesn't rub up against Tarian—and even then, I can't imagine Tarian's magic harming him. So, I tell him. About Electra and Ines driving to the funeral home. About Yasmin's call. About Ines's capture. About Bryn getting in contact with her father, before driving Malachi out to Lynch and Yasmin. About Yasmin's threat to push Ines into Tarian to rid her of her runes.

By the end, the poor guy's running his palm manically over his buzzcut. "I should've left Electra in Boston. I should've been here."

"She's still alive, Dorian."

"How do you figure that?" he snaps. "How do we know they didn't push my sister into Tarian?"

He has every right to be angry with me. I'm the reason she's missing.

"Because you trust Ines. Right?"

His nod is slow to come, but it comes.

"Yasmin didn't mention Electra, so my guess is they don't have her. My guess is she and Ines split up. Can you track her phone?"

"I tried but signals are jammed."

"What about the SUV? Modern ones have satellite trackers, no?" That's how they found a missing child in an episode I listened to a year back. "Maybe they stopped on the way to the funeral home?"

His expression brightens, and he jumps to his feet. "Which car did they take?"

"You have more than one?" I ask before realizing how utterly silly my question is.

"We have three Yukons and two G-classes."

I have no idea what either of those models look like. "Which one is the biggest?"

"Yukons. G-classes are boxier."

"They took a Yukon then."

"Actually, Saul and Catalina took one of the Yukons to Paloma's house. And a Mercedes was located in Oak Bluffs."

"So maybe they took the Mercedes?"

As he dials a number, probably to ask one of the house staff to check the garage, I pad into the bathroom to glimpse the damage done to my shoulder.

Although my bra is black, I can tell it's caked in dried blood, just like my shoulder. I run the sink, drench a hand towel, then pump soap onto it and rub my skin. As the blood lifts, it reveals bruising that ripples off the puckered entry wound from my nape all the way to my rune. I wring out the towel, then saturate it with fresh water and sponge away more blood before scouring my abdomen to clean up some other residue, the kind that would've made me blush had I not been so distressed.

Dorian knuckles the doorframe. "One of the Yukons is missing. I was able to access its GPS." He taps on his screen. "It stopped by a motel before heading toward that funeral home. I'm going to go check it out."

"I'm coming with you."

"There should be some clothes that'll fit in the closet!" He's already pounding out the door. "I'll call you if I find Electra. Keep your phone close."

My phone is currently planted in the azalea shrubs, but that's the least of my worries. "Wait!" Even though muscles I didn't even know I had are aching, I jog after him. "Dorian!" When he keeps walking, I yell, "You don't know where he is!" I clasp his massive forearm and dig my heels into the doormat. "Wait."

"I *can't* wait. They might have my sister! They have Mal and Tarian, Callie." Heartbreak fractures his voice.

"We're going to get them all back."

"You're not Atlantean. I can't risk—"

"I was shot, and I healed. I may not have gotten power from the mine, but Tarian obviously gave me *some* power."

"I'll go get a car." Rain forks down his haggard cheeks.

"And you'll come back for me?"

"I'll come back for you."

"Promise?"

"Promise."

Even though his lips shape the word, he's not coming back for me. I can tell. And not because I've learned to read him all that well, but because this week has worn him down to the marrow, leaving him jittery and unguarded.

"Good, because like I said, I know where Tarian is, and you don't."

He stops halfway down the porch steps. "You said he was at the funeral home!"

"They moved his body."

"To where?"

"I'll tell you after the motel stop."

"Callie—"

"Honk when you're out front."

If he yells anything more at me, I don't hear him because I'm halfway across the living room, on the hunt for something to wear that isn't bullet-ridden and bloodstained.

# SIXTY-EIGHT

Dorian pulls up in a vintage Jeep. We don't speak during the trip to the motel, both of us simmering with too many thoughts. After throwing the car in park, he orders me to stay put, then hands me a gun, which I don't know how to use. I regret not having grabbed the kitchen knife or a tool to unlock the coffin in case my dream was a little premonitory.

Dorian jogs from the reception area toward one of the rooms, shoulders the door open, then rushes inside. Seconds later, he's pounding back out, his sister cradled in his arms. Her limbs flop around, but her cheeks are high in color.

Did Ines knock her out and drop her here? I hop out of the Jeep and rip open the backseat door. A gust of wind snatches the handle from my grasp. When metal groans, I worry the hinges are about to snap, but it's not the hinges, it's a garbage can that's sailing straight at my head. I duck just as the can is propelled several feet into the air before crashing farther away.

"Get back inside the car!" Dorian hollers.

I scramble into my seat and grip my door handle. It takes every last ounce of strength I have to yank it shut.

Dorian lays Electra out gently, then slams her door and races around the bumper before diving into the driver's seat. "Ines drugged her."

"To keep her safe?"

"Looks that way. We'll know once she wakes up."

Or once we find Ines…

"Gun?" He holds out his palm.

I hand it back.

"So, where are we headed?"

"Smith & Son Timber."

He stares at me a long while before he pulls out of the lot and puts the car in drive, apparently knowing the way. Considering his parents were Barak's groundskeepers, I imagine he's spent a lot of time here. He probably has the island memorized.

"Once we get there, you stay in the car with Electra." He must not be able to perform magic and drive at the same time because the windshield wipers are whisking the pounding rain at full throttle, and still it's a miracle he can see a foot in front of him. "I don't get why the fucking council isn't intervening. Everyone's on the fucking island."

I toy with the zip pull on the leather jacket I grabbed back at the gatehouse, wishing it would slide all the way up, but the jacket's cut too narrow. "Yasmin threatened to hide Tarian's body. They must fear she'll bury him somewhere he can never be found. Or they're scared of getting shot with Tarian's blood? I imagine Lynch and Yasmin have a large supply of it." When he doesn't say anything, I ask, "Unless you think the council members are complicit?"

"If they're not, then they're fucking cowards. All of them." Dorian hooks a right turn, and the wheels skid. "I'm taking a detour in case someone's monitoring the roads."

My fingers whiten on the door handle and perspiration dots

my forehead. My stomach feels like the power lines outside my window that swing like jump ropes. How the poles aren't tipping over is frankly a marvel of verticality. Lightning strikes, gilding the drenched wood and highlighting—

I spin around in my seat and blink, even though the "T" and "C" enclosed in a heart are long gone.

"What is it?" Dorian's voice skips with nerves.

"This is the road I took in my dream!" When a diamond-shaped bicycle sign appears, I cry out, "Stop!"

"We're a mile away."

"This is the place."

"Callie, I've been to that lumberyard. It's—"

"Through those trees." I nod to the forest, wishing an arrow of mist would materialize to confirm my conviction. "I must've walked five or ten minutes. Just follow—"

"No. You're staying right—"

"There were landmines. I saw them in my dream." Well, I saw *one*. Maybe that was just Tarian's overactive imagination. "They might not kill you, Dorian, but they'll slow you down, which will give Lynch and Yasmin time to—"

"All right! Fine." After scrawling a message on a movie ticket stub and sliding it inside his sister's clamped fingers, Dorian and I set out, trekking through the sodden woods in complete silence.

What will await us there? The same empty warehouse? Will Malachi and Ines be there, or are they being kept somewhere else? Will Yasmin be patrolling inside, and Lynch sniping from the rooftop? Did they give Bryn a job? I have so many questions, yet even more arise as we trudge ahead.

"Fuck," my companion whispers.

My gaze drills the mud around his boots for the shape of a landmine. When I don't see any suspect device, I crane my neck to look up into his face and murmur, "What?"

He juts his chin. "Your shortcut beat my shortcut."

However hard I squint, I can't make out a thing through the rain.

"Warehouse is right ahead of us."

Since my directions were accurate, does that mean that everything I foresaw will come to pass?

"Show me your neck," I say urgently, almost passing out from relief when I spy the whorls of ink peeking out of his upturned jacket collar.

Dorian's magic is intact which means Tarian still has his runes.

Tarian is alive.

# SIXTY-NINE

I touch Dorian's bicep. "Follow in my footsteps. And I mean that literally."

"I've got a better idea." He slashes the air with his hand.

I'm about to ask him what he just did when an explosion resounds over the growling thunder and blows my eardrums. Reflexively, I drop into a crouch and raise both my arms to shield my face. Something damp sloshes against my leather sleeves. I'm praying it's mud because the alternative... If it's brain matter...

I slowly uncrook my arms and crack my lids, a shriek clawing up my throat at the sight of Dorian's blood-splattered face and white tee. Air presses against my lips, stifling my scream.

"It's not mine," he murmurs. "Shh."

"It might not be yours but it's evidently someone's!" I hiss. "Not to mention you've just fucking alerted them that they have company!"

Dorian either doesn't hear me over the air he's blowing into my face, or he's not interested in what I have to say.

He sniffs his hand. "Atlantean."

My heart derails, because Yasmin wouldn't step on her own trap, and Bryn and her father are human. Which leaves—

"Tarian's," he murmurs.

"Tarian's?" I squeak, trying to catch another glimpse of Dorian's nape, but I'm crouching and he's ridiculously tall.

"Stay down." He chops the air again.

Are they coming at us? Are they firing at us? I squeeze my lids shut when another explosion goes off, and another, and another. I count eight, one of which reverberates so near, it makes the shield he's erected around us wobble.

"What the fuck?" Yasmin's voice both echoes and trills through the whipping rain. "Did one of the hostages wake up?"

She's close. Too close.

I squint into the wind-soaked mist and think I spy her shadow until her voice sounds again nowhere near the blight.

"Branches." Lynch's answer crackles through a walkie-talkie or her phone, or whatever it is they're using to communicate.

"That fell on nine different landmines at the very same time? Are you sure?"

"I just thermal-screened the area."

I peer up at Dorian who's waving his palms around frantically, performing some serious magic.

"I'll go set up new ones," Lynch says. "Go be with your sister. She's still pretty rattled."

Rattled by what? The explosions?

A shadow blunts the cottony whiteness. There one second, gone the next. And then a door bangs.

*Now,* Dorian mouths.

I stand.

He grips my arm. I don't know if it's to keep my body temperature from registering or to prevent me from dashing forward. My tongue is too swollen with adrenaline to ask. Besides, I prefer not to make any sound.

In perfect synchronicity, we slink around the building. When we reach the bush, I jerk to a stop, then shove him hard. He scowls, but the emotion quickly dissipates when I nod to the undetonated device sitting an inch away from the toecap of his boots.

My breaths feel serrated, as though someone's sawing through my ribcage, desperate to reach my lungs. After too many seconds of standing still, recovering from what could've been, we start moving again.

Like in my dream, the door to the building is ajar. He knocks it wider with his shoulder, eyes glowing just as brightly indoors as they glowed outdoors. Slowly, slowly, slowly, he edges inside. Since his fingers are still clamped around my bicep, I slot right in after him. The second we're through, he shuts the door, sinking us into an obscurity it takes my human eyes a full minute to adjust to.

Dorian eases me forward. Although his grip is firm, I don't miss the frenzied thumps of his pulse, which match my own. He closes his eyes.

After a second, he flips them open and murmurs, "They're upstairs."

I crane my neck but all I see is a grid of metal pipes.

"Where is he?"

"Aisle C."

As we slink forward, I rise to my toes to murmur, "We're leaving footprints."

He flutters the fingers not gripping me, and our muddy tracks disperse as though made of dry dirt. We advance swiftly but carefully, pausing between shelving units to peer down aisles. When we reach Tarian's aisle, Dorian picks up speed. It takes everything in me to keep up.

"Here." I nod to the teetering window frames.

My sidekick blows the piles aside as though they were no more substantial than the pages of a book. Tarian's coffin gleams as vividly as Dorian's eyes. The big man blinks hard, then, with more magic, rakes the death box off the shelf and into the aisle.

I press my trembling fingers against the lid that seems to vibrate, as though the wood can barely contain the power within. *I'm here, my love.*

Dorian tugs on the lid.

When a grunt falls from his lips, I murmur, "Coffin key."

Wood splinters. Silly me. Who needs human tools when one possesses magic? I inhale a raspy breath, exhale a raspier one, my pulse ratcheting as I imagine Tarian rising from his prolonged slumber like Lazarus.

Dorian cracks the lid up an inch, two, three. And then it's open.

And there Tarian is, his bare torso gleaming white in the obscurity. I blink when my vision goes soft with tears.

*I found you.*

The man before me is a stranger.

He's also the other half of my soul.

I admire his willful jaw shaded by overgrown stubble, his ebony locks curling around his pale forehead like smoke, the cut of his broad chest and trim waist that feeds into legs so long they barely fit inside this disgusting coffin.

I start to reach inside when Dorian hisses.

"What is it?" My heart bangs.

"Wake him." He sweeps his hands, sending everything flying off the shelves and piling into the aisle. "Quick, Callie. Someone's coming."

A bang shreds the air and buckles Dorian's knees. He slams into me, and I go down hard. Right onto my bruised shoulder.

*Shit. Shit. Shit.* I pat Dorian down until my fingers close over his gun. I pray it's an automatic. And then I pray automatics automatically spit out bullets, because unlike Bryn, I don't know the first freaking thing about firearms.

Even though I'm ringed by a mountain of debris, I speed-crawl around the coffin. I expect Yasmin to sweep away the mess with her own magic, but a peek past my wooden shield shows she hasn't. Must be Lynch.

But then I glimpse flame-red hair beyond the debris. "Before I put a bullet through your skull, I'm dying to know how you found Tarian." *Yasmin.*

I grab Dorian's ankle and shake him hard. *Come on, Dorian. Come on. Wake up.*

"Oh, Dorian Serran is out for the count, thanks to my Tarian-enhanced miracle mine sleeping aid. A bit of a tongue-twister. I need to work on branding. What do you think of Magitonin? Or Atlantitonin?"

"What I think is that you're a fucking lunatic." How come craziness is such a common trait among villains? Does one have to be crazy to be a villain or does one become crazy? More importantly though, why am I pondering this chicken-and-egg question at a time like this?

"An entrepreneur, Calanthe. These enhanced bullets will stop a human heart in under three seconds. And they don't even need to be fired anywhere close to the person's chest. I put a bullet in the funeral director's foot, and he keeled right over. Same thing happened to the fisherman who tried to rescue us. Daddy's already gotten a shitload of orders for our state-of-the-art ammunition from his old pals in the military. We're just trying to decide on pricing, since our stock will sadly be limited. Anyway, should we see how it affects you?"

"Hard pass."

For a moment, she's quiet. Too quiet. But then her voice rings anew. Oddly enough, it sounds like it's coming from farther down the aisle. Is adrenaline distorting my hearing or did she back up?

"So, what's your deal, Calanthe? Why did you get involved in something that doesn't concern you?"

I lick the sweat off my upper lip. "You concerned me when you involved me in a traffic accident."

"Yes, but my father let you live. Why didn't you just mind your own business? Especially considering how sordid a man Tarian Hadez is. We did the world a favor, you know?"

Fucking delusional psychopath. "So…Symeon?"

"What about him?"

For the life of me, I can't figure out where her voice is coming from. Is she using magic to distort it? The temptation to peep over the edge of the coffin is strong, but my desire to keep my head hole-free is stronger. "You must've been devastated when he died."

"The traitor got the end he deserved."

"Traitor? Wasn't he aiding you and your father?"

"He had his own agenda when it came to Tarian. He wanted to sink his body inside a trench. That's why he suggested crossing the Atlantic by boat. Imagine his surprise when my father figured out his plan and beat him at his own game. You should've seen his face when we pushed him into Tarian, and the asshole lost his runes. Priceless. Dad and I took such pleasure in draining the two-timing rat."

*Dad and I?* So Tarian's magic wasn't to blame.

Thunder growls as heavy clouds scurry over the warehouse, blackening the dank air impairing my weak human sight. I think I hear the rustle of fabric nearby, but I must be imagining it since that would mean Yasmin managed to vault over the pile. What if she did? She has magic, after all.

I crane my neck and squint. *A divine beam would be mighty practical, Gaea.* Just as I think it, blue light spills over the coffin's edge and drenches me. *On Yasmin. Not on me.*

Something squeaks behind me. I twirl just as a human-shaped shadow appears at the other end of the aisle.

The one not encumbered by detritus.

"Boo." Yasmin grins, takes aim, and fires.

# SEVENTY

As I throw myself sideways, I jerk the trigger of Dorian's gun. I must land a bullet because Yasmin howls. Unless she's howling because she didn't succeed at striking me down?

Probably the latter.

Fighting the tremors racking my arms, I take aim. Lightning flashes, highlighting her body. I joggle the trigger. The gun clicks. Nothing comes out.

A crescent of white slashes the darkness. "Aw. Are you all out of bullets?" She limps out from behind the shelves just as the sky rumbles and the ground shakes.

I toss the gun at her face. It strikes her temple. She blinks. I do, too, because holy hell, that was a good throw.

She puts an end to my smugness by popping out bullet after bullet. I speed-crawl around the coffin as they fissure the air, plinking against cement, metal, and wood. Not a single one breaches my skin.

*Someone needs a little target practice.* Actually, no. It would be preferable that Yasmin never learns to wield a weapon.

"You're dead," she snarls and discharges more bullets.

I reach out and grab a slat from the pile that clogged the aisle, then pop out and hurl it at her head just as she flicks her trigger. The wood deflects the shot. She snarls and, before I have time to duck or find a buffer, her rifle sparks.

The blue light already limning my trembling body thickens, then ripples as the bullet touches it, springs off, and drops. Just drops. I blink back the heat gathering behind my lids as I realize what Tarian's glowing runes have done. The man built a shield around me. *Oh, Tarian…*

"Sweetheart?" Lynch's voice crackles off the watch on Yasmin's wrist. "I hear gunshots. Talk to me."

An ounce of solace surges behind my breastbone as I realize that Lynch isn't in the warehouse. Even though Tarian is here with me, I much prefer facing one monster at a time.

Yasmin grazes her watch with her chin. "I have a situation. Aisle C, Daddy."

"Copy."

If only I could shove her onto Tarian's body so his runes could neutralize her magic. As I plot a manner to achieve this, the warehouse flashes with lightning. *Is that a yes, push her on top of me,* or a *no, keep her the fuck away, my love?*

"You want to know how this ends, little human?" The diamonds on her earlobes shine as blue as Tarian's runes.

"I already know how it ends." I back up, making sure his light follows me. "Tarian wakes up and murders you all." Without looking away from Yasmin, I crouch and snatch another piece of wood off the mound.

She snorts. "Cute, but no. I may hate Symeon for trying to fuck us over, but Great Gaea, the kid was brilliant."

A chill trips down my spine, making my fingers clench around the wood.

"Tarian Hadez is *never* waking up."

"He's immortal."

She grins. "Of course he is. So is the goddess of our mine. If you come closer, I'll tell you what we did."

"I can hear you just fine from here."

Her red hair rushes around her face, obscuring the faceted shine of her earrings. "No deal, Calanthe. Either you come here, or —" Her body sails into the nearby shelves.

My lashes sweep high, low, high, low. Did Tarian's magic just—

"So, what did I miss?"

I snap my head up and meet a gleaming set of eyes. "Electra?"

"Is that my jacket?" She bobs her chin to the leather encasing my torso like clingwrap.

"Thought it was Dorian's," I deadpan.

She snorts. "Makes you look badass."

Yeah. Like a badass sausage link.

Yasmin growls as she attempts to stand.

Electra clicks her fingers, and a piece of splintered wood rises from the pile behind me and whizzes past my body.

My friend catches it. "Move one more inch, Yas, and this goes through your abdomen."

Yasmin doesn't listen. The stick soars through the air and plunges into her flesh with a sickening wet *snap*.

I press my palm against my spasming stomach, wondering how I ever contemplated becoming a homicide detective. "Remind me never to get on your bad side."

Electra snorts as she crouches beside Dorian and frames his face. "That would imply I have a good side."

"Yasmin shot him with a mine-dust bullet." I don't add that the dust is laced with Tarian's blood because that will only freak her out. "He still has his runes, right?" *Please let him still have his runes.*

"Mine dust only neutralizes—"

"Just check." My throat tightens. "Please."

She frowns but indulges me. "He still has his runes."

My relief is so fierce that it rids my lungs of every molecule of air.

"Can't wait for that fucking bitch to rise from the dead so I can stake her again."

Even though Yasmin deserves it, I grimace.

"Actually…" She traipses back over to Yasmin's corpse, swipes the semi off the floor, then plants the barrel against the redhead's unmoving chest. "This is for my brother." *Bang.* "This is for Tarian." *Bang.* "This is for Malachi." *Bang.* "And this is for my first female friend, Callie." *Bang.*

"I'm"—a bead of icy perspiration trundles down my nape—"touched." And also about to hurl. I fling the back of my hand against my mouth as blood spurts from the mess Electra has made of Yasmin's chest.

"I can't believe she's related to Malachi."

*And to Bryn.* Shit. Bryn. Is she aiding them or is she a victim of her family tree?

Rifle in hand, Electra approaches the coffin. "Why the hell is he glowing blue?" Although her eyes refract Tarian's light, his radiance doesn't envelop her like it envelops me.

I step over Dorian's body and park myself next to her. "I don't—I don't know…"

Thunder lashes at the warehouse, shooting a tremor that threatens to sweep the floor from underneath my feet. I grip the edge of the coffin just as something hot sprays my chin and mouth.

Is that—is that blood?

Electra's eyes roll to the back of her head as she flops sideways, taking me down with her.

My lungs contract around a scream just as I hear the distinct pop of a rifle. Tarian's blue light rushes over my face like a wave, shielding me, smothering me. My lungs rattle as my skull collides into Dorian's harshly muscled thigh, and my forehead, into Electra's.

Tarian's shield doesn't soften the blow of bone against bone, nor does it buffet the slap of the rifle against my rib cage. As my eyes dampen with shock, Electra's head lolls off mine, her short hair painting blood across my lashes, nose, and mouth.

*She's not dead.* I have to repeat this to myself a great many times. I swallow but instantly regret it because I taste her blood. My tongue, my palate, my veins tingle with it. What will it do to me since it isn't freely given? But more importantly, how did Yasmin already rise when Dorian's still out?

My answer comes in the shape of large, black boots—men's boots. They land right beside where I lay, sandwiched between brother and sister. I snap my lids shut, praying that Lynch didn't notice my alertness.

"Yasmin?" His voice resonates through the chilling silence. "No! No, no, no, no…"

When I hear his knees click, I prize open my eyes. He's prodding her neck, her chest, the skin around the wooden stake. Is he hunting for a pulse? Whatever he's doing, he has his back to me, and I have a rifle.

I also have a body atop mine.

Heart hammering my ribs and lungs like a nail gun, I slowly, *slowly* coax the rifle up, sliding it between Electra's body and mine. What I wouldn't give for a lungful of air that neither reeks of blood nor rings with marrow-shredding wails.

"Daddy?"

I startle at the sound of Bryn's voice.

"Your sister…your sister—" His voice breaks on a sob. "Malachi's little whore…she—she—she—" He howls his anger and grief as though Yasmin was dead-dead and not temporarily out for the count.

My rune begins to prickle. I think it's Tarian's way of

reminding me that he's here. Unless he's calling to me to find out what's happening around him? Whatever his reasons, I resist. I don't want to risk passing out and waking to an empty coffin. If only I could rouse him. If only I could unhook him from whatever is siphoning out his magical blood so that he can start healing.

Yasmin's words clang between my temples: *Tarian Hadez is* never *waking up.* I don't know why she said that other than to piss me off. I decide not to believe her. There's no reason he won't heal.

Fueled by my rage, I dock my index finger on the trigger, swipe the rifle out from underneath Electra's body, and aim at Lynch.

Bryn's eyes snap to mine. Before she can shout a warning, I squeeze the trigger.

The sergeant picks that exact moment to rest Yasmin's limp body back onto the cement, so my bullet sails over his hunched spine. Before I can squeeze out another bullet, he swings around with inhuman speed and snatches the weapon from my clammy fingers. He tosses it at Bryn as he jumps to his feet, kicks Electra's body off mine with enough force to fracture her ribs, and levels his sniper rifle at my clenching throat.

"You little cunt." His finger begins to flex. "What a fucking mistake it was to let you live."

Tarian's blue light swarms my neck, bending Lynch's tawny eyebrows.

"Daddy, wait! She ruined my life, too, so the least you can do is let me end hers."

I gape at her. And gape. Never in a million years would I have thought my best friend would desire my death.

"Fine." He steps aside, his boot catching on Electra's outstretched fingers.

When he purposely grinds his heel into them, anger like I've rarely known overwhelms me. I will feed his corpse to the Great Whites swarming these waters.

Bryn raises a handgun—not Yasmin's rifle. "I loved you so fucking much."

Even though I have faith that Tarian will keep me alive, her farewell shatters what was left of our wrecked friendship.

Her lids twitch. And then her arms swing, and she fires.

Not at me.

Did Tarian's magic redirect her bullet, or was that all her?

# SEVENTY-ONE

Lynch wheezes as Bryn's bullet punches his shoulder.

"I'm sorry, Daddy. I know they hurt you. I know they took away the woman you loved and hid a child from you, but that was Barak's doing, not Tarian's."

He bangs into the shelves but doesn't crumple.

"It wasn't Malachi's fault. Or Ines's. Or Electra's. Or that school bus driver's. Or the countless others who lost their lives because they got in the middle of your vendetta." Bryn squeezes out another shot.

Lynch howls in pain and drops to his knees, his rifle clanking between his body and Electra's. I dart my hand out to grasp it. Just as my fingers close around the grip, he sticks his knee on my hand and drives the full force of his body down. Tarian's magic desperately nips at my skin, trying to insert itself between us, but fails to keep the sergeant from grinding my wrist bone.

*Bang.*

Blood suddenly spurts out of his cheek. "Bryn." He gurgles, lashes reeling so high that his eyes bulge. "What...have you...done?"

How is he still talking?

I try to scrabble away, but he hooks my broken wrist and jerks me to him.

How is he still fighting?

Bryn's shadow drapes over us. "I would've done anything for you, if you'd only asked, Daddy."

He bands his arm around my throat and squeezes, shredding my breath. "You shoot me again, and I break her fucking neck."

I curl my neck forward, then snap it back. Something sharp and hot scrapes across my scalp and drenches my hair. Is that Lynch's blood? Mine?

"Callie?" Bryn's complexion is as pale as snow, but her eyes are pink and watery with tears. "Oh my god, Callie. Did I—Is any—"

I rip Lynch's arm off my throat, then grab his rifle with my good hand, and although the weapon fucking weighs a ton, I prop it against my shoulder, climb to my feet, and shoot him. In the chest, in the head, in the neck, in the groin.

"No!" Bryn tries to wrest the rifle from my grip. "Callie, stop!"

I elbow her so hard it knocks her onto her ass, then resume firing at the monster until the fatal bangs transform into empty clicks. Only then do I stop and toss the rifle.

"Oh my god, what have you done?" she screeches as she drops to her knees beside his corpse, spilling something from a small vial into the holes I drilled into his evil flesh. "What have you done?"

I frown until I realize what she's doing. What she means. Why she switched guns. "That was all an act. You meant to keep your father alive."

She rips a second vial from her pocket and pours, both growling and sobbing because the Atlantean blood isn't knitting the sergeant's flesh.

My bruised forehead, rib cage, and wrist tingle. Is Electra's magic healing me? Is Tarian's? "You realize he would've been hunted down?"

She glares up at me. "He wouldn't. Saul promised that if I managed to subdue my father"—her voice snaps with anger—"he'd scrub his memory and help him start a new life."

"That's why he gave you a phone, isn't it? So you could get in contact with him?"

"Yes."

"How benevolent of you to have called ahead to warn your family about Ines and Electra's arrival."

Bryn's lips flatten into a harsh line.

"Give me your gun, Bee."

"I'm not going to shoot you, you bitch." Her lids twitch. "How could you even think that?"

The debris clogging the aisle creaks, making both Bryn and I jump. "She thinks *that*, because you tried to save your odious genitor." Ines hobbles through the narrow space she's cleared, her gaze arching over the four motionless bodies. "Your gun, please."

Bryn's fingers contract around the little weapon, but a flutter of Ines's fingers makes it clatter onto the floor and skid toward the Atlantean who hinges at the waist to scoop it up. As she tucks it into the waistband of her pants, she limps past Electra and Dorian, stopping only to collect the rifles, which she bends before flinging aside.

"Might want to tie up Yasmin in case the mine dust wears off, Ines." Even though it hurts to move, I go to Tarian.

"She's not waking."

I gasp. "Because of the Tarian-blood additive?"

"The blood only made the effect of their damn little bullets last longer." Ines's platinum crown of hair shines scarlet around her right temple. "Yasmin's not waking because she lost her runes moving Tarian's body."

That explains why she wasn't using magic! *And* Lynch's unrelenting bawling!

"Don't try to run, Miss Fielding."

Bryn crosses her arms. "I'm on a fucking island, in the middle of a fucking storm, with a fucklot of supernaturals, Ines. Can't exactly swim back to Boston, now, can I? Besides, I have nothing to reproach myself for. I was only trying to help. You can ask Saul once he gets here."

"I will." Ines flashes her a smile that makes Bryn sway on her high-heeled booties. "Now, why don't you tell us why my boss's nephew is shining blue like a Smurf? What the fuck did they do to him?"

# SEVENTY-TWO

The luster of Tarian's runes coils around my chilled body, strokes my grimy cheeks, and slicks across my blood-clumped lashes. I reach a tentative hand into the coffin and graze his cheekbone. His skin is ice. I trail my fingers down his neck, which is oddly smooth, oddly firm. His bare torso is even more rigid. His arms and legs, stone.

I glance away from Tarian and into the reddened eyes of the girl I would've done anything for once upon a time. "What the fuck did they do?"

She stares at my neck, at the bruise Tarian's kiss left behind. "Why do you care so much about him, Calanthe?" The use of my full name widens the distance between us. "You barely know him. Unless you lied about having met before?"

"No. Tarian and I met the night of the accident." Sweat glues my bra and tank top to my spine, icing my clammy skin.

Her forehead grooves. "Then—"

I cut her off. "Tell me what they did, and I'll explain why he means so much to me."

Ines's gaze sears the side of my face, making me wonder if Electra ended up unveiling my secret. Knowing the girl and her relationship with Ines, she probably didn't.

"You first, Callie." Bryn spits out my nickname as though it tastes disgusting.

"I dream of Tarian, and he dreams of me. Now talk, or Ines shoves you against him."

Bryn pales, clearly aware of what my dream lover's body is capable of, even in slumber. "How can I trust that you won't push me into him if I tell you the truth? How can I trust that Ines or your bitchy new bestie won't hunt me down?"

"Because I have better things to do with my time. As for Electra, I can't vouch for what she does. She is rather…rancorous." Oddly enough, Ines's tone is light, almost as though Electra's grudge-holding amuses her.

"I give you my word that she'll leave you be, Bryn," I promise.

The knot of her arms tightens. "Your word doesn't mean much anymore."

The precipice between us broadens. "You do realize that if you don't tell us now, Mal or Ines will compel it out of you later? The Atlantean blood you ingested will eventually wear off."

She wrinkles her nose. "I didn't drink any blood."

I frown.

"Pop any pills lately?" Ines asks.

Bryn swings her stare toward her.

"Those contain Atlantean blood, Miss Fielding."

"Aha. That's what you were carrying around in that vial inside your bag."

"You went through my stuff, Calanthe?"

Ines drums her fingers against her thigh. "Who gave them to you?"

"Some girl in a club. She said that if I ever wanted to 'see clearly,' I should take one."

"And you trusted a total rando?" I shake my head. "Those pills could've killed you."

"Like you fucking care. Besides, after the accident, everyone was acting so off. So I tried one. And guess what? It did clear a hell of a lot of things up."

"Calanthe's correct, though, Bryn." The deep voice has me spinning around. "Long-term use of those pills will make your organs fail." Malachi walks slowly through the path Ines cleared earlier, a hand digging into his waist.

"I only took two, Mal."

"Then you should be fine." As he approaches the coffin, jagged swallows agitate his throat. "Why are Tarian's runes blue?"

"That's what we were waiting to find out," Ines grumbles. "Miss Fielding, would you be so kind as to elucidate what"—she mutters a word in Atlantean before reverting back to English—"was done to Mr. Hadez?"

"If I tell you, no one fucking messes with me, right?"

"You have my word," Malachi promises.

She tucks a lock of hair behind her ear, her hand rattling so hard that her bangles clank. "Symeon crystallized his brother's blood."

"I'm sorry." Ines sounds as though something's stuck in her throat. "What?"

"He put Tarian in one of those machines he bought to create diamonds. Since his brother's blood was so carbon-rich, he knew exactly how much pressure, how much heat, and what gasses to…"

My pulse rushes against my eardrums, its clamor so loud Bryn's voice weakens to white noise. I clasp the edge of the coffin with both hands until the ground stops trying to trip me. My crushed wrist screams, but the pain is nothing compared to the one shredding my heart.

"Symeon solidified Tarian's blood?" Malachi's shout snaps me out of my stupor.

My throat is so dry and tight that I have to swallow a great many times before I can get it to work. And even then, my words come out brittle. "How do we reverse the damage?"

Bryn's lips twist. "It can't be reversed."

I press my knuckles to the base of Tarian's neck. His skin doesn't dimple. It doesn't pulsate, either.

"There has to be a way." I skate my juddering palm toward Tarian's lips and hover it there, waiting for his breaths to strafe my cold skin. "His heart! We need to make it beat. Malachi, how do we make it beat?"

Malachi starts to circumvent Dorian and Electra's bodies but freezes beside Electra's bruised and swollen hand. He crouches, then tucks between his glowing palms the fingers Lynch took such vile pleasure in injuring. When he sets her hand back down, her skin is pink, and her phalanxes narrow.

As he marches up to me, his stare sharpens. "If they weren't already dead..." he grits out, lowering his hand to Tarian's marbled chest.

I snatch his sleeve. "Mal, wait! You can't touch him."

"He won't hurt me, Callie."

"If his magic stung you, he'd never forgive himself." My rune flares so hot it momentarily steals my breath. I clinch Malachi's arm to keep myself from tipping out of this world and into the dimension where Tarian's heart still beats.

"And I'd never forgive myself if I didn't even try." He gently tugs his arm out of my grip and touches Tarian.

My wild stare skips from the black scribble partially hidden behind Malachi's dark-blond mane to where his palm connects with Tarian's bare skin. After what feels like an eternity, Malachi extinguishes his curative glow with a hard fist.

The ink on his nape is still there. Still there.

"You didn't lose your runes." My breathing harshens as Tarian's call becomes more insistent. Did he sense his cousin's touch? Can he hear our voices?

Malachi's lashes fall, fanning across his wan cheeks. "I also didn't jumpstart his heart."

"Mal, he's calling me." My vertebrae are scalding now. I consider climbing into the coffin and curling myself around Tarian, but what if my flesh absorbs his runes? "Make sure no one touches him, all right?"

"Don't worry. Go to him." Malachi's eyes flash with emotion.

"But what if he asks—what if he asks why he can't—" Before I can finish my sentence, before Malachi can advise me, the warehouse fades and an ocean appears.

"Calamity?" The raspy timbre makes my heart catch and release.

My face is so full of heartbreak that I don't dare turn. This cannot be the only way I get to be with him.

"Calamity!" Tarian's voice froths like the waves lapping against the rubble of my chest. "I dreamt that you'd found me." He must be moving toward me because the slats creak and quiver beneath my poppy-red stilettos. "Did you?"

I try to banish my grief and resuscitate my trodden optimism, but tears trip down my cold cheeks. How can I tell him the truth? It'll break his spirit. What if a broken spirit shatters what's become of his heart?

His warm, hurried breaths fray a path across my stinging scalp, and then his hands—pliant and warm—wind around my biceps. "Darling, have you?"

I fist my fingers and do the thing he hates most. I lie. "Not yet."

# SEVENTY-THREE

I *haven't been found…*

Hope is a most villainous emotion—edging itself inside hearts before expanding, filled with nothing, yet taking up so much space that once it bursts, it creates a yawning void.

"I'm sorry, Tarian." Although Calanthe has her back to me, I don't miss the wet shine of her cheeks and the scarlet sheen of her eyes. "We caught Yasmin and Lynch, though."

The air I breathe streams not into my lungs but into my deflated heart. "Are they being interrogated?" I wait. And wait. "Calanthe?"

She starts, as though the use of her real name shot an electrical charge through her body.

"What aren't you telling me?"

She stiffens. "They're not lucid. Or they weren't when I came here."

Again, I show patience. And again, I'm rewarded with silence.

I slide one of my hands to her navel and splay my fingers there, anchoring her to me. She sucks in a harsh breath.

"What is it?"

"Bruise," she murmurs.

"Why do you have a bruise?"

"Because I haven't been healed yet."

"I meant…"

"I know what you meant, Tarian."

"Then how about you give me the answer I want?"

"Because you don't want *this* answer."

I spin her toward me. "I want *all* the answers."

"The bruises are courtesy of your captors. The blood—"

"What blood?"

She touches her cheeks, then inspects her fingers. "I must've imagined the blood."

She's lying. "You're bleeding back in the real world?"

Her breath catches, and then her bottom lip begins to quiver. "No."

"Whose blood"—my jaw kinks from how hard I'm clenching my molars—"is it, then?"

"Electra's. Lynch shot her."

"Tell Dorian and Malachi to keep the sergeant and Yasmin alive for me. I want the pleasure of dismembering them."

Her throat constricts.

I slide my hands to the small of her back. "Does this feel all right?"

She nods.

I step into her body, needing to feel her flesh against mine. Although slow to soften, the tension in her body eventually eases, and she exhales, pressing her cheek against my pec.

"There's more, isn't there?"

Her lids lower as though a delicate partition of flesh could dissimulate her thoughts.

"I want the truth, darling." I tuck an errant curl behind her ear. "Even if it's ugly. Even if it hurts."

A tear traipses across her freckles. "Yasmin and Lynch fired bullets laced with dust from your magical mine. They shot Malachi, Ines, Dorian, and Electra with them."

That's why my girl is distraught. Because she thinks Yasmin managed to kill my people.

The relief that swamps me is so potent it swells my airways. "They'll live."

"I know. Mal and Ines already woke up. It was just really"— she ensnares her trembling lip before croaking—"frightening."

"I can imagine." I smile to reassure her. "My father and uncle created those bullets when I was still a kid. After trying them on regular Atlanteans, Saul insisted on trying one on me, but Father didn't want to take the risk. I ended up testing it on myself."

"You shot yourself?"

Funny how she forgets that I'm immortal. "I wanted to know what it would do to me. After all, knowledge is power. Anyway, I shot myself in the foot and lost consciousness for six and a half minutes. Symeon timed it."

We lapse into silence. One fraught with thoughts. Where other instances of my past replay on the canvas of my lids, Calanthe must dwell on something more immediate and urgent because her pulse flogs her neck.

"Why so agitated?" I caress the sharp sweep of her cheekbones, connecting one freckle to the next.

"Do you realize how much information you gave Symeon, Tarian? He knew how long those bullets affected you! He knew what your blood was made of! He knew *everything* about you."

My smirk wanes, and my hand freezes on her cheek before falling to her neck. "He was my little brother. My flesh and blood. I never imagined he'd use that knowledge to betray me. To be honest, I didn't think anyone *could* take me down." I pop my jawbone to relieve it of tension, but it's just as tight when I open my mouth to add, "I'm glad my magic took the decision to end his life out of my hands, because I don't think I'd have had the courage to erase him from our world."

"Your magic didn't kill him, Tarian." Annoyance slashes her cheeks in color. "It rid him of his runes, but not of his blood."

"Is that an educated guess?"

"No. It's not a guess. Yasmin confessed to draining Symeon after—" She stops talking suddenly.

"After...?" I prod.

She rumples her nose. "After Symeon tried to abscond with your paralyzed body."

"I stung him, even though he was trying to save me?"

Her cheeks dimple, and not with a smile. "He wasn't trying to save you."

I crook a finger under her chin to carry her gaze back to mine. "What was he trying to do, Calanthe?"

"He wanted to make you disappear. To sink your body to the bottom of the ocean. Where Yasmin and Lynch wanted runes, he wanted you gone forever. I know you feel guilty at having withdrawn his magic, but your brother...he wasn't a good man."

"I feel many things, but not guilt. Not anymore. Not after what I witnessed after you vanished from our last dream."

"What did you witness?"

As I recount the scene, I fasten my gaze on Calanthe's red shoes, willing them to anchor me to this dream. "I wondered if it was a fabrication of my mind to offset my guilt, or an overheard conversation between my captors." Now I wonder if it wasn't some boastful last confession of my brother's.

"I'll ask Saul."

"Absolutely not."

"He was there, Tarian. And he's alive."

"I said no, Calanthe," I grit out. "I don't want him to hurt you."

Her pretty, plush lips round with understanding.

"Even if Symeon was ultimately the one to hammer the nail into our father's coffin, Saul's silence cost Father his life. Once you find my body, or once I wake up—whichever comes first—I'll get to the bottom of what truly happened."

Her lashes begin to beat, turbulent like the ocean surrounding us.

"You're keeping something else from me, aren't you?"

Her pulse goes wild beneath my thumb.

"Calanthe…" My growl makes her jump.

"You stung Yasmin." Her words slingshot out of her. "She lost her magic."

"Well, that's fucking fantastic news."

Calanthe's bottom lip quivers so hard that she clamps her teeth over it.

"Since I doubt you're distressed about Nora's daughter, I take it someone else was shoved into me." My mind goes to the three people who've been guarding her. Could my magic have hurt them? "Who else?"

"No one else." She squints at the sea, her eyes filling.

"Was anyone else besides Yasmin and Lynch complicit in my abduction?"

She shakes her head, which shakes the tears loose. They collapse down her cheeks and around her mouth before tripping down her chin and bleeding along my wrist.

"And you truly caught them?"

"Yes."

"Then why the fuck are you so distraught?"

A whimper escapes her teeth-tortured lips. "They stopped your heart. That's why you're not waking up."

"I'm an Atlantean, darling. Even if they've packed my veins with dust and staked me with shards from the mine, my magic will eventually evacuate it all. It's just a matter of time."

More tears dash across her freckles. Too many to sweep away.

"Darling, as long as I have my runes, my heart will eject anything they've injected into me." When that fails to calm her, I ask, "I do still have my runes, right?"

"Yes."

"Then why the bloody hell are you grieving?"

Her raucous sobs rend the air.

"Calanthe, I can't help if you don't tell me what's wrong." I frame her face between my hands. "Tell. Me."

Her vivid eyes fly open, the eddies of color wide and wild. "Symeon put you inside a diamond synthesis machine!"

I frown.

"He managed to—to—to…" Her throat bobs. Her chest quakes. "He managed to crystallize your blood."

My confusion deepens.

"That's why your runes glow blue, Tarian! Because your blood solidified, which stopped your heart!" Her shrill shout careens over the tempestuous landscape. "Or maybe your heart stopped first, and it made your blood harden. The point is, your heart doesn't beat, so it can't evacuate anything."

"My brother transformed me into a blasted diamond?"

"Yes."

"Do I fucking twinkle?"

"I-I-I… That's what you're focusing on?" Her eyelids twitch. "Whether you *twinkle*?"

"Do my people still have their runes?"

Her brow furls. "Yes."

My heart may be out of sorts, but as long as I have my magic, then I'm bound to recover. Unless… I dismiss my shirt and pivot. "Read both sentences out to me, from the nape down. I want to see if the wording changed."

As she sounds out the words that are still foreign to her, my lungs empty, filling anew only once she's done.

Not bothering with conjuring a shirt, I whirl. "My awakening spell hasn't morphed."

"Did you expect it to?" Her voice is as stippled with emotion as her complexion.

I shrug. "I just wanted to make sure that my brother's experimentation hadn't fucked with my magic." I delicately pinch her wrist to carry her hand to my chest. At her whimper, I spring my fingers wide. "What?"

"It's just sore."

I slide my teeth. Crack my neck. I will do far worse than dismember Lynch and his daughter. Far, far worse.

"My other wrist is fine." She presents it to me.

I barely squeeze as I lift it to my heart and flatten her fingers against the thudding muscle. "You know what I believe, Calamity? I believe that the mere graze of your skin will galvanize my stone heart."

Her throat pumps out a whimper that she fruitlessly tries to impede by crushing her lips together.

"Have faith, darling."

Tears fall. I kiss away the salt of her anguish before attempting to chase away its muted din, but it keeps resonating through her... through me.

I clasp the back of her head and roll our foreheads together. "Believe."

That only provokes her torment. Sobs crash out of her like the waves against the beach I summoned into existence.

"Why won't you believe?"

She laces her arms around my neck and crushes her mouth to mine, eclipsing the world around us. For a beautiful moment, there is only her and me. But too soon, the ocean roars and the air rumbles with voices. I think I recognize my uncle's, Malachi's, and...is that Ines? Could they have found me?

Keeping my arms locked around Calanthe's waist, I hunt the land rising toward my father's...*my* house. "Do you hear them?"

She tucks her head into the crook of my neck, and although her breaths are ragged, her tears have finally subsided. "I'll see you soon, Tarian."

I splay my fingers on her waist, careful not to put too much pressure on her battered skin, and hold her against me. I hate farewells. I cannot wait for them to end. *Find me. Wake me.*

"I love you," she murmurs, pressing a feather-soft kiss on my pulse point.

When she fades out of my embrace, my heart tightens. Hardens. Deadens.

I roll my fingers into fists that bang listlessly against my thighs and raise my face to the sky marbled with clouds.

*Find me. Wake me.*

"Son?" My father's voice ignites my runes and pebbles my bare flesh. "Your mother and brother await."

"For what?" I glance over my shoulder.

My father stands in front of my brother and mother, hand outstretched. "For you."

A chill sweeps across my spine.

Mother sidles over to Father and threads her arm around his waist. "Come, baby."

The pier mutates into a conveyor belt that propels me toward the threesome I'm not ready to join. I begin to run in the opposite direction. The belt speeds up.

My nostrils flare, and I gnash my teeth. I'm not fucking ready to die.

"None of us were ready, sweetheart," Mother says. "But such is life. Such is death. Come to us."

I stop sprinting forward, but only to gather the strength to lunge sideways into the ocean. Into the unknown.

*Find me, Calamity.*

*Wake me.*

*Save me.*

# SEVENTY-FOUR

I jerk awake on the backseat of an SUV. My head spins from how briskly I sit up, and my wrist... I bear down on my escalating whimper.

After a prolonged gawk at the driver and a rapid glimpse into the empty trunk, I focus on the man in the passenger seat. "Where's Tarian, Mal?"

"In Ines's car." Malachi offers me a placid smile that does little to quell my anxiety.

"Why not in this one?"

Saul's knuckles whiten around the steering wheel. "Not enough trunk space."

"Ines will keep my cousin safe, Callie."

Malachi's reassurance does nothing to squash my anguish. "What about Dorian and Electra?"

He sighs. "They're also with her. They're still out for the count, though."

"And Yasmin and Lynch?"

"Dead." Saul's voice is as dull as the sky.

I meet his stare in the rearview mirror. "I know they're dead, Mr. Hadez. I meant, where are their bodies?"

"In one of the cars behind us," Saul replies. "Along with Bryn."

Although wind no longer wallops the island, and rain no longer striates the sky, the sun has yet to encroach on the heavy clouds.

I inspect my bruised, swollen wrist before resting it on my lap. "Were you really going to help her father start a new life?"

"No, but she wouldn't have reached out to him if I hadn't made that promise." After a beat of silence, he adds, "So you can communicate with my nephew when you sleep?"

I nod.

"Is he aware of what befell him?"

I purse my lips. "He's aware that he was abducted and that his heart no longer beats."

Malachi's fingers curl around the center console. "Did he have any suggestions for reversing the damage?"

"Tons."

"Really?" Saul startles, which makes the car swerve out of the white lines.

I flatten both hands against the seat to keep my body from listing, and holy shitballs…my wrist. I grimace.

"He knows how to liquefy diamonds?" Surprise disturbs Saul's tone.

"It's Tarian we're speaking about, Father. Of course he'd have ideas."

Saul's dark eyebrows are peaked. "I'm eager to hear them."

*I bet you are, Saul.*

"Do share, Miss Bloom."

"I'll tell Mal later."

"How about you tell us now?"

*How impatient you are, Saul…* "How come the council didn't try and stop Yasmin and her father?"

Saul's eyes taper on mine in the mirror. "I gave Bryn a cell phone, didn't I?"

A cop-out, if you ask me.

Malachi sighs. "You wanted to use Calanthe to negotiate Tarian's release. You can't expect her to trust you."

"I was trying to get my nephew back."

Was he, or was he trying to get rid of me? I can't decide whether Saul actually cares about Tarian or not. After all, he let his own brother perish.

I'm dying to bring up Barak, but since I promised Tarian I wouldn't, I bite my tongue. "Joslyn must've been worried when Bryn left the house earlier."

"She trusted her ex wouldn't harm their daughter," Saul grits out.

Mother of the year, that one.

I think of my own mom. Even though I want news of her day, I decide not to bring her up in Saul's company, because yeah, I don't trust the guy. "How's Catalina taking her granddaughter's death?"

Saul stretches out one of his hands. "Badly. She was very attached to the child, but she said she wouldn't press charges against Electra."

"Charges?" Malachi's eyebrows stoop so low they tangle with his lashes.

"Electra not only killed an Atlantean, but she also desecrated Yasmin's body," Saul says. "We don't murder without a trial."

"Are you fucking joking right now?" My spine is taut with disbelief. "Yasmin fucking abducted your nephew!"

"Watch your mouth."

"Or what?" I'm now sitting on the edge of my seat, my good hand clamped around the *oh-shit* handle. "You'll put me on trial?"

"You wear one of our runes, so yes, you could very well be tried."

"I wear one of *Tarian's* runes, not *yours*," I spit out.

"Relax, Callie, no one's putting you on trial." Malachi's eyes taper on his father's profile. "Stop trying to intimidate her, Father. As for Electra, she killed Yasmin on *my* orders, so if anyone were to be trialed, it should be me."

Saul slows as he approaches the gates of Tarian's estate. "That child will never grow up if you and Dorian keep coddling her."

"She isn't a child." Malachi's voice is low and rough. It roughens some more when he adds words in Atlantean that I don't grasp. I catch Ines's name, but that's it.

It must've been quite the conversation, because the gates open and close twice before Saul finally guns the SUV past them and up the short drive. The men don't talk again as they both exit the vehicle. Where Saul marches straight into the house, Malachi draws my door open and proffers his hand. I wince as I climb out.

"Where does it hurt?" Malachi asks.

"Where doesn't it hurt would be a better question," I mumble.

"Show me."

I gesture to my hairline. "Bryn's bullet scraped my scalp after Electra headbutted me."

He delicately presses my curls aside. Was it only this morning that Electra healed me from a similar wound? It feels like a month has elapsed…a whole freaking year.

"The council's not actually going to press charges against Electra, right?"

"No."

Once he's done healing my scalp, I unzip my jacket and hike up my black tank top, flashing him an abdomen that's an ombre shade of purple and red.

"Does Tarian really have a solution?" he murmurs as he makes the spilled blood trapped beneath my skin retract like an oxalis bloom at dusk.

"He thinks…" My throat and nose begin to sting with a new wave of emotion. "He thinks my touch will somehow wake him."

Malachi's palm stops emitting heat for a long moment.

"I couldn't bring myself to tell him that I've already touched him—that you did, too—and that nothing happened."

He sighs before focusing on my ribs. "We'll find a solution, Callie."

I don't know whether he's saying it to reassure himself or me.

"Any more injuries?"

"Shoulder." I toss the soiled leather jacket onto the backseat of the car. "Dorian took the bullet out, but it still hurts like a bitch."

As he heals my tender skin, three more black SUVs careen up the driveway.

"Anywhere else?"

I prop my wrist up. "I swallowed some of Electra's blood when she was shot. What will that do to me?"

"As long as you wear Tarian's rune, Atlantean blood shouldn't affect you anymore than regular blood."

Bryn emerges from one of the cars. Our eyes meet and hold for a minute, but then she shakes her head and streaks toward the house.

"What will happen to Bryn?" I ask once he's done setting my wrist bone.

"Her memory will be cleansed as soon as her pill wears off."

I readjust my tank top. "Good." When I spot Ines circling one of the vehicles, I rush off to meet her by the trunk. "You told everyone not to touch Tarian, right?"

"Not everyone. Only the colleagues I like."

I blink at her. She tilts her head, her mouth poised in an impeccably straight line. I'm starting to think that the woman *does* have a sense of humor, but it's as dry as potpourri.

Malachi ambles up to us. "Ready?"

Ines nods and shifts to the side, raking me backward. Using magic, the Atlanteans float the coffin out of the trunk. I hate that Tarian's still confined inside. Malachi gives orders in Atlantean and two guards rush into the house. Seconds later, the windows of the first floor are thrown wide and the coffin sails right through. When he pivots on his heel, I start after him, but Ines calls out my name.

"Thank you." Although her skin is caked in blood and her eyes rimmed with fatigue, there's a softness to her expression.

"He's not awake yet."

"But he's safe."

I peer into the car. "Are Dorian and Electra still out?"

"Yes. I dropped them off at the gatehouse." She rubs her temple, which makes me wonder if that's where Lynch shot her.

"Why did you knock Electra out and dump her at a motel?"

"She looked in dire need of a little R&R." Ines's lips curve around what is clearly a lie.

"Thank you for trying to keep her safe."

Her mouth straightens, which kicks up my curiosity. "I'd love to stay and chat, but I have to shower before Symeon's memorial."

I startle. "It's still happening?"

She backs up, her unshaded gaze scrolling over the imposing façade of Tarian's house. "Saul wanted to spare Tarian the need to attend, especially since Paloma Fablez insisted on honoring her daughter's life at the same time."

"Honoring?"

"I suggested a compost ceremony, but Malachi told me it was in very poor taste."

A surprised chuckle vaults out of me. "You and Electra are almost the same person."

My comment creates such an odd tension on her face that I think I've hit a nerve. Unless it's a truth? Could Electra and Ines be related? Sure, Ines's skin is a honeyed-brown, and Electra's, a peachy-olive, but maybe they share a common ancestor? Someday, I'll get to the bottom of their tangled history, but not today. Until Tarian awakens, I won't expend an ounce of energy on anyone or anything other than his curse.

Ines must see me staring at the window the coffin vanished through, because she says, "He'll wake up, Calanthe. Tarian Hadez is far from done terrorizing the lesser folks of this world."

I decide that I like Ines, dry wit and all. Which does beg the question of what she's doing at the service of Saul. But again, a question for another day.

I finally enter Tarian's house, climb his stairs, and tread his navy runner. If I had any doubts as to where I'd find his bedroom, they disappear the second I spot the guards stationed along one hallway. I count five men and one woman. I wonder where they came from? Did they fly in from Boston? Are they Saul's people? Tarian's? New recruits?

I glance at each of them, undecided as to whether I'm comforted or alarmed by their presence. I suppose that until Tarian can defend himself, he has no choice but to be protected by others. God, he'd hate this so much.

The last guard sweeps open the door for me. Like the others, he doesn't make eye contact or ask for identification. I imagine Malachi briefed them but can't help but wonder what they were told.

As soon as the door closes, my gaze skips over the bedroom. It's identical to the one in Tarian's dreams down to the blueprint of the aircraft carrier, the striped navy-and-white curtains that Malachi is closing, and the navy shee—

"Malachi!" The shrillness of my voice makes him whirl and rush to Tarian's bedside.

He moves so fast he's a blur of limbs. "What?"

"Did you touch him?" Anguish knits my heartbeats together.

"Have you forgotten that I've already touched him?"

"No, but—" I lick my lips. "Just be careful, all right?"

"I lifted him out of the coffin with magic." He sticks his hands inside his pockets and gazes down at his sleeping cousin.

Once my pulse eases, I ask, "What have the guards outside been told?"

"To let no one in without your permission."

"I meant, about me?"

"That you're Tarian's special friend."

I smile. "'Special friend,' huh?"

He returns my smile as he ambles toward the door. "Suite's

yours, Callie. Relax. Bathe. Sleep. Watch TV. Read." He sweeps his hand toward a wooden bookcase made from the same white timber as the ceiling beams. "I'll get you a new phone in the morning. In case you need anything, Barak had a bell installed here." He points to a glowing red button on the nightstand closest to Tarian. "It rings the gatehouse. Alternately, you can ask the guards outside to fetch you anything you need."

He ambles around the bed and crosses the vast room toward where I stand rooted by the door. "I'm tempted to hug you, but I imagine Tarian wouldn't approve."

"Yeah, he hates—*Actually...*" I throw my arms around Malachi who releases a surprised *oomph*. "Is he moving?"

"No."

"Maybe hug me back." When I feel his hands settle on my waist, I twist my head as far back as my neck will allow to glance at Tarian. Although his lids don't lift, his runes spark very blue.

"How devious, Miss Bloom."

I pull away from Malachi and go to the dreamer haloed like some fallen saint, then lay my hand on his chest. When nothing beats beneath my fingers, I feel like weeping.

Malachi must realize that our hug was in vain because he sighs. "I'll come by after the memorial."

I want to ask him whether he's going by choice or by duty, but the lump in my throat is too large to squeeze out the question.

After the bedroom door snicks shut, I trail my knuckles over the steep cliffs of Tarian's cheekbones to the deep hollows they shadow. I reassure myself that he doesn't mind my touch. Especially considering my intentions are pure. Not that I think he'd mind if my intentions weren't.

My gaze trawls over the duvet cover pulled up to his pecs, down the body concealed beneath it. Would touching him *elsewhere* make him stir? I wrinkle my nose, shoving the consideration far and wide. I will *not* molest a sleeping man. Not even in the hopes of jumpstarting his heart.

But what if it did?

*No, Callie*, I chide myself.

I pull my hand back and escape into the ginormous bathroom. My heart lifts at the sight of the oval bathtub enthroned in the middle of a mosaic that seems to have been lifted from some ancient temple. The colors are faded, but the design is spectacular, made even more so by the navy walls and soft lighting.

Although the tub calls to me, I'm so bone weary that I end up in the giant shower. I empty a bottle of shampoo and a bottle of soap, lather, rinse, then wrap myself in a fluffy navy robe emblazoned with a scripted white "H." I contemplate the bed a long while before giving in to the lure of the soft sheets. They're even silkier than they looked. And the pillow... God the pillow is perfection. I'm still groaning and complimenting its plump featheriness when the mattress dips.

My lids fly up, and I meet the most dazzling umber stare in the entire world.

# SEVENTY-FIVE

"You're awake!" I climb up onto a forearm so fast that I topple over and smack my face against Tarian's rock-hard pec.

"I am." He threads his fingers through my hair as I prop myself back up. "I had a nightmare."

"That you didn't invite me to partake in?"

"You were there."

I frown.

He flips onto his side, his fingers trailing over my shoulder and down my arm before settling on my waist. My *bare* waist. My eyes fill with tears. Unless I threw off my robe while sleeping, this isn't real. Tarian didn't wake up.

"Malachi had his arms around you," he says, while I bite my trembling lips, desperate to subdue the sob. His fingers stiffen, and his pupils shrink. "What? Did it truly happen? Did my cousin…?"

My tear ducts heat.

"You said there was nothing between you and Malachi." His conclusion remodels my grief.

"Oh, Tarian…" I shut my eyes, about to set him straight, when the weight of his hand vanishes. I sit upright so fast that my blood whooshes between my temples. "Tarian?"

One wall of the bedroom falls away. The others turn a lurid shade of pink.

"Tarian!" I try to toss my legs over the side of the bed, but I'm strapped into a silver bodycon dress that looks like something off a runway but feels like something out of an asylum. "Shit, shit, shit."

I can't believe he vanished thinking I have a thing for Malachi. I wriggle and roll. Instead of rising from the bed with a modicum of grace, I flop right over. "Fuck."

I try to change out of this ridiculous garment, but a nasal voice makes my mind veer right off my accoutrement. I shoot to my feet, suddenly a whole lot lither. Who knew anger was good for agility?

"You can put the Badinguini here." Mackenzie traipses into the bedroom, six faceless men rushing after her, staggering under the weight of an outsized painting. "I said *here*." She points to one of the pink walls.

The men unveil the canvas. I gawk at it for a full minute because… What the actual fuck? It's a painting of a naked Mackenzie lolling in a mussel shell as big as a car, mounds of spaghetti artfully arranged around her perky boobs and crotch.

She barks out orders to center it on the wall. "Farther left. Not *that* left." Under her breath, she mutters, "Idiots." Once the painting is hung, she twirls on a pair of gaudy pink heels that match her velour leggings and crop top.

Out of everyone, why did I have to dream of her? Unless this is Tarian's dream?

"What the fuck are you doing in my room, Calla Lily?"

I don't engage because, one, she's a figment of someone's imagination, and two, I need to locate Tarian.

"Tarian?" I call out as I march past her.

When I see her sneering at my bare feet, I buckle on a pair of fantastic black booties made of black lace and leather that make her stilettos look like something bought off a department store sale rack.

Yes, yes, I realize I am the creator of both pairs of shoes, so it's totally petty, but it gives my morale one heck of a boost.

Also, *my* dream.

"Tarian!" I call out.

"He's in a work meeting."

"Where?"

She crosses her arms, stepping right into the middle of the area where a wall used to stand. "What do you want with *my* husband?"

My heart clobbers my ribs. *Not real. Tarian hasn't gotten hitched to Macrazy. This nightmare is courtesy of your insecurities.* My pep talk calms me a fraction. What calms me a tad more is swapping Mackenzie's shoes for mussel shells held together with duct tape. *Take that, you absolute bitch.*

And then I shoulder past her down a hallway adorned with a pink runner. I officially hate the color pink.

Mackenzie shrieks. I smile. Until I start noticing the framed photos on the wall—all of them of Mackenzie and Tarian. Together at the Met Ball. At the Oscars. In a private jet. On a yacht. At a runway show. In a pool. Under a crystallized arbor, wearing wedding attire.

I'm not smiling anymore. I'm furious at my mind. I want out of this nightmare, but first, I need to find Tarian to explain that there's nothing going on between Malachi and me. My mind finally conjures a door. It's pink. I hate it.

I flick the handle and step into an oval room decorated with more paintings of Mackenzie in various stages of undress.

"May I help you, Calanthe?" Tarian's terse voice steers my attention off the unpleasant art.

"You disappeared before I could finish my damn sentence, and now I'm imagining you married to Barbie Fielding."

"Her name's Mackenzie." He shoots me a smile that's as tight as my stupid dress.

"Really, Tarian? Really?"

He studies the silver bondage material that has risen so high from my brisk walk that I grip the hem and yank. "I'm in the middle of a meeting." His eyes linger on the small vee cutout between my breasts.

"Adjourn it. This is more important."

"What is more important?"

"The conversation we're about to have."

He reclines in his leather armchair, his long fingers folding his shirt cuffs. My mouth goes dry as he unveils his lean, corded forearms decorated in magical black glyphs. How is forearm porn not a thing?

"I don't like Malachi," I blurt out.

"Ouch," says the man I just shunned. *Of course* he's here…

"I care about you, Mal, just not in the way Tarian thinks."

"What way do I think?" Tarian drapes one gorgeous arm over the back of his seat cushion and hooks an ankle over his knee, revealing a pair of pink socks.

Gritting my teeth, I swap them out for black socks. "Amorously," I bite out.

"Tarian, honey!" Mackenzie stumbles into the office on her mussel-shell shoes.

I'm so riled up by this nightmarish fantasy that I don't even get a kick out of her clumsy entrance. But Tarian does.

One corner of his mouth tucks up in time with a single eyebrow. "Can we make something perfectly clear? Even if you dumped me for Malachi, I wouldn't approach Mackenzie Fielding with a thousand-foot pole."

"Mackenzie Hadez," the woman says.

He sighs. "Calamity, banish her already."

Mackenzie's mouth rounds with an offended pout as she winks out of existence, leaving behind a fishy smell. I banish Malachi next. And then I drain the canvases of ink and paint the walls navy.

If Tarian's dark smile is anything to go by, he's enjoying my jealous outburst immensely.

I thrust my chin up and tug at my infuriating hem.

He cradles the side of his head between his thumb and forefinger. "What you're doing is futile, darling."

I frown as I reach him. "What I'm doing? You mean attempting to convince you that I'm bonkers about you?"

"No. I meant about the dress. Let it go."

"If I let it go, it's going to end up around my navel."

"It'll end up around your navel whether you let go of it or not."

When I realize what he's implying, my temper calms, and I return his smile.

Tarian leans forward. "Hands off that spectacular dress."

My lips curve as I curl my fingers around the hem. I ease it up and up until the silver material bunches around my waist and reveals a matching silver thong.

A nerve feathers his jaw as his eyes lock on my underwear.

"They're crotchless," I add with a wink that he doesn't catch since his attention is grafted to my nether regions.

His runes begin to glow like a beacon summoning me forward. I take the three last steps separating us, knock his foot off his knee, then sit astride his lap. He snaps out of his daze when I lower myself onto the massive erection trapped against his zipper.

"Get my pants off." His hands slap my ass and squeeze.

"Nope."

"Calamity…" he growls, his fingers tensing.

When I begin to rock, he snarls. Between that noise and his hard-on, I go from wet to soaked in under a second. Heat builds in my core, billows through my veins, and tightens my nipples to peaks that drill the bands of silver fabric.

Hips pistoning now, Tarian palms my ass with one hand and

snares my décolleté with the other. He yanks, freeing my breasts, then curses so low in his throat that it vibrates his Adam's apple. I want to lean over and kiss it, but his mouth hits my nipple first.

"Gah…Tarian." My head falls back.

He returns both his hands to my hips and sets a rhythm that is both punishing and fantastic.

"I'm going to come," I mewl.

"Not yet." He slaps his open palm against my tingling crotch.

I groan from the tiny spark of pleasure, then rumble when it dulls. I seek friction against his palm, but my asshole lover cups his hand, putting space between our flesh.

"Tarian."

A zipper purrs, and then the man whose lap I straddle fists his engorged cock. Before I realize what his plan is, his hand is off my crotch. "I know I said I wanted to wait to penetrate you, but I can't —" He chokes when I make the tip of his dick vanish inside of me.

"Good, because I am dying"—I glide down—"to come all over"—down—"your mammoth dick."

"Fuuuuuck."

The word echoes through me, a heady encouragement to sheath him in fully. When his pubic hair grazes my clit, a bead of sweat drips down my spine. I haven't reached his root. In all honesty, I'm not entirely sure that I can.

His hands are clamped around my hips, but instead of using them to drive me low, he uses them to buoy me. "Take your time, darling."

My pussy feels like it's made of the same material as my dress, barely capable of stretching around his girth. I must breathe too hard for his liking because he's suddenly lifting me. I catch his wrists and sit. All the fucking way down.

He gasps. I don't have air in my lungs to gasp out.

We stare at each other, connected through flesh, but also through so much more.

He cups my face, dark eyes sparkling. "I don't think you understand just how deeply I love you."

My heart beats in time with my eyelids that are trying to chase away the surge of emotion his words stir in me.

He leans over and slants his mouth over mine in the sweetest, softest kiss. A tear trickles down my cheek as I rock forward, then back. Forward then back.

I cry because of how illogically and completely I love him back.

I cry because I want him to wake up.

I cry because I never want either of us to break out of this dream.

Loud banging erupts against the door.

"Don't let them in," he snarls, pistoning his hips now.

"Miss Bloom?" I don't recognize the voice calling me.

"Stay with me, Calamity. Don't leave me."

However hard I clutch his shoulders, the knocking rips me away from Tarian. My lids don't lift, they bang up. And then I glare at the door against which knuckles are still rapping.

I turn toward Tarian, kiss his stiff cold cheek, and murmur, "I'll be right back," in his ear.

And then I fling my legs off the bed, readjust the belt on my bathrobe, and stalk to the door. This better be of the utmost importance. "Come in!"

A guard pokes his head in. "Sorry to disturb you, Miss Bloom, but your friend insisted on bringing you a tray of food. Can we let her in?"

My annoyance softens an iota at the mention of food, and I say, "Yes," before wondering, *What friend?* Has Electra regained conscious—

Heels click.

My visitor is no friend.

# SEVENTY-SIX

I blink at my platinum blonde visitor who passed herself off as my friend when she's really anything but. As per usual, Mackenzie Fielding is dressed in pink, from her strapless satin dress to the tiny pink Chanel bag strung across her chest like her beloved pageant sashes.

"I bring sustenance." She nods to the silver tray she carries.

No wonder I dreamt of mussels. Wisps of steam curl off a huge mound of spaghetti topped with that particular shellfish.

"I'm sorry, Calanthe." She sets the platter on the bronze side table that stands between a brown leather chaise longue and the bookcase.

I'm still blinking, attempting to untangle real-Mackenzie from dream-Mackenzie. Also… *"You're* sorry? About what?"

"Being a bitch to you. I was jealous."

"Jealous of *me?*"

She sighs and nods. "Anyway, I was hoping we could start over."

"Start what over?"

Her heavily mascaraed eyes widen. "Our friendship."

"We never had one."

"Well, I'd like us to have one."

Do I get a choice in the matter? Because I'm not all too keen on cultivating any form of relationship with Bryn's sister.

"You saved my sister, and she's everything to me."

Saved Bryn? Who the hell told her that? Saul?

Mackenzie's irises shimmer as though she were about to weep. I didn't think Mackenzie's ducts were capable of producing tears. "Poor Tarian. I can't believe the helicopter crashed. It's a miracle he's still alive."

So the story is a helicopter crash.

She flips back one of the locks framing her face. "I've been praying that he'll wake up from his coma. Even went to church with Mom earlier."

"I didn't know you were a churchgoer." I rake a hand through my hair that's still damp, and from the feel of it, horribly snarled. Where is Electra and her conditioner when I need it?

"You don't know a lot of things about me." She perches on the edge of the chaise, then pats the spot next to her. "Come sit, and I'll answer your questions." When I don't cross the room, Mackenzie nibbles on her lip. "Bryn mentioned I'd be wasting my time and breath, but there's no achievement without effort, right?" She runs a finger under her lash line and sniffles. "I know Tarian wired you money for the engagement ceremony's floral arrangement, but I also sent you funds. Double what we'd negotiated. And I canceled Fleur-de-Lys. I was hoping… I was hoping you and your mom could do Saul and Mom's wedding?"

Is this another dream? I pinch the skin over my knuckles—although how useful is this trick when I feel everything the same way in my dreams?

"Please give me a chance, Calla Lily?"

My stomach growls. She must hear it, too, because she smiles and pats the seat cushion beside her.

"Fine. Whatever. Just drop the nickname."

"Consider it dropped." She grins.

With some reluctance, I set off in her direction. I may be ravenous for food, but I'm not particularly ravenous for a rapport with Mackenzie Fielding.

"I hope your pasta isn't cold." She grimaces. "Cold pasta is the worst."

"I'm surprised you have an opinion on a dish you never eat."

"I eat pasta, but the gluten-free type." She smooths one hand down her skeletal thigh. "I know my relationship with food seems awful, but I never want to be fat again."

"Again?" I pick up my fork and begin twirling it. The aroma that surges from the dish is as mouthwatering as the lobster from lunch. I still can't believe that meal was mere hours ago. "When were you ever fat?"

"I was a size six in my late teens."

I set down my fork and gape at her. "Mackenzie, a size six is *not fat.*"

"I have very fine bones." She nods to me. "On people with larger bones—like yourself—size *whatever you are* looks great."

I glance down at my legs that peek out of my bathrobe. I never gave bone width much of a thought before, but now I'm wondering if my skeleton is thick.

"Besides, you have the boobs to go with your figure. Mine are almost nonexistent. I've been thinking of getting implants. Mom says I should, but apparently breastfeeding is harder, and I want to be able to breastfeed if it's important to my husband." Her face gyrates toward the bed and the man lying on it, whose runes spark as she stares.

Although the walls don't pinken and no giant clam painting appears, my molars clench. She better not be contemplating being married to Tarian, because that will *never* happen. I spin my fork with such gusto that the tines scrape the bottom of the dish, then scrape my tongue as I shove the bite of pasta inside my mouth.

My annoyance must reach Tarian because his radiance intensifies and swoops toward me. It twines over my lap, my torso, my throat. I'm about to ask Mackenzie if she sees his light when I find her watching it skip around my face.

"Do you believe in fairytales, Calanthe?"

I swallow, then swallow again because it feels like my forkful is still lodged in my throat. I reach out for the glass of water on the tray and upend it. My tongue begins to tingle, my throat to itch, my lips to swell. I release the glass. It falls silently on the rug.

"'Cause I do." She cocks her head. "Something wrong?"

I try to cry out for help but manage only a thin yelp. Even with their superhuman hearing, I doubt the guards outside will hear me. My eyes begin to water. I try to scoop up my glass to toss it at the door, but Mackenzie catches me eyeing it and kicks it out of my reach.

"Food allergies are the pits." She says this with a congenial mien.

My rune heats, yet I shiver…shudder.

God, I'm such a fool for swallowing down Mackenzie's scallop-infused peace offering hook, line, and sinker.

Tarian's magic thickens, cloaking all the places my own magical fire can't reach. It slides into my throat and presses against its puffing lining as though to beat it into submission.

Except my flesh doesn't submit. It keeps distending.

*You can't die. You're immortal*, I remind myself because I'm feeling extra mortal at the moment. What if Tarian can only save me from death by magic?

I lurch to my feet and dash toward the door, but Mackenzie trips me, sending me sailing face first into the thick rug. I pray the guards outside will hear my body thump and wonder what the fuck is going down in Tarian's bedroom. The door doesn't fly open. Did my fall make so little noise?

I heave my body onto my side, gagging, choking.

"My favorite fairytale was "Sleeping Beauty." I have *all* the lines memorized. My favorite was this one: *And from this slumber you shall wake, when true love's kiss, the spell shall break.* I know, I know. You probably think I'm delusional, but I'm a great believer in the power of true love."

I try to say, "You're not delusional. You're heartless and insane," but the words stick to the swollen lining of my throat.

When she makes her way toward Tarian, anger and adrenaline spur me onto my knees. I grab the fork off the tray, climb to my feet, and stagger toward her. She's so focused on my man that she doesn't sense me coming at her.

I plunge the fork into the tissue connecting her shoulder to her neck. I pray she yells since I can't, but she only sucks in a breath, spins around, and slaps me. I weave.

She pulls the fork out and lobs it toward the chaise longue, blood spurting down her shoulder blade, staining the pink satin.

My lungs are an inferno. They burn hotter than my spine, but not as hot as my rage. My vision darkens, fragments. I blink hard. Light filters back into my corneas. I almost wish it hadn't because Mackenzie's bent over Tarian, and her mouth is on his.

I want to throw up, to shout, to cry, to tear her head off her shoulders.

I want her to die.

She gasps.

Because he woke up? Even though I don't want her kiss to rouse him, I'm not selfish enough to wish his curse to endure.

His lids are still clasped.

His features, motionless.

His glow, blue.

Mackenzie's hands fly to her throat, and she gurgles. I realize, as the blood leaches from her face, that Tarian's magic must've punished her for hurting me.

Recalling the button on his nightstand, I grab fistfuls of his comforter and force my numb legs to shuffle.

Mackenzie stumbles toward me, claps my arm. "Help."

I shrug her off. She collapses, retching, the blood on her shoulder is now black, just like the veins forking beneath her insipid skin. The world grays again. I blink. This time, no color returns, only shapes. And dull ones at that.

I reach the nightstand and blindly pat its side until I feel a protrusion. I jam my finger against the button, praying my call for help will reach someone. The ground shifts beneath my feet, and I list, sinking onto the edge of the bed.

Tarian must've been wrong about his rune's power to keep me alive. Or maybe it was keeping me alive just long enough to find him. Now that he's been found…

I fold myself over him. Although my head and throat hurt, the ache in my chest is the most excruciating. I want to whisper one last, "I love you," but I've no air left to power the words.

So, I think it. I think it with all my might as I rest my lips over his.

I'm suddenly back on his lap in that oval office. Kissing him. I think I'm dreaming but realize I'm dying when he fades and reappears on the pier. And then the silken walls of the boardroom rise up around us. But they, too, vanish. Just like the flower shop filled with carolers. Just like the net suspended in the sky, and the train, the circus, the deck of the *Amapola,* this bedroom.

I relive the car crash and then our first meeting.

Everything is reversed.

The sting of his rune comes first, then the glow of his mesmerizing stare, his inebriating scent, his raucous timbre. Pebbles crunch beneath my cowboy boots and the sun swathes my skin as he backs up from me, tugs down his sleeves, refastens his cufflinks, shrugs his jacket back on, and folds himself into his sleek car. The car reverses, and the air whirs before turning quiet.

Too quiet.

The words *come back* stick to the lining of my throat.

My lips wobble.

My throat aches.

My lungs cramp.

I expect my parents and Bryn to show up next, but I'm wrong.

Tarian's Bugatti winds back toward me.

Tarian emerges from the car with that air of danger and darkness he wears like armor.

He steps toward me, one veined hand working the buttons of his jacket before rising to his shirt collar and unfastening it.

"Calamity Darling, I'm home." He prowls toward me. "I've missed you."

"Missed you more."

"Impossible."

I stare up at my achingly beautiful beast of a man, tears making his face shimmer.

What is this? One final dream? A small mercy from the mine to allow me to say goodbye to Tarian?

Unless…unless this is the afterlife?

He grips my wrists and carries them to his neck. "Kiss me, wife."

*Wife?*

That breaks whatever fragile dam I'd erected around my heart, and tears spill down my cheeks. This is the cruelest dream of all because it's everything I want and will probably never have.

Tarian sighs, peppering my face with his affection. "These naughty babies. Reaping such havoc." His palm suddenly sweeps against my abdomen that is so swollen it brushes against his hard stomach.

"Babies?" I squeak.

"Three."

"I'm pregnant?"

He smirks. "You sound surprised by the potency of my sperm."

I close my lids and sob.

Tarian threads his fingers through my hair to cradle my scalp. "Look at me, darling."

I do.

"Do you love me?"

"More than—more than life itself."

"Then come back to me."

I drift again. I must end up in a bed because there are rumpled sheets beneath me.

I sigh when I feel a firm, warm body pressed against mine, then sigh once more when Tarian's intoxicating fragrance glides into my lungs.

He strokes my face this time, not my belly.

"Calamity?"

I wonder if I'm pregnant in this dream.

"Darling, wake up."

"I like dreaming."

He kisses the corner of my mouth. "I know, but I need you to wake up."

"No."

"Calanthe."

My lungs ache. "As long as you can't, I'd rather sleep. I'd rather dream."

"I'm awake."

"How I wish that were true."

"It is, my love." His pliant lips press against mine, and his hot breaths coil into my tight lungs.

I skate my mouth off his to rasp, "I love you."

"It's a prerequisite for the woman of my dreams."

Even though my heart smarts, I smile.

His mouth chases that smile before targeting other parts of me: my jaw, my throat, my collarbone, my—

When he kisses my navel, his long fingers unraveling the ties of my bathrobe, my lids slam up and I gasp. "Tarian?"

"Hello, Sleeping Beauty."

I crane my neck and gape as he applies a tender kiss to my scar, followed by an agonizingly slow lick.

I groan, flopping back onto the pillow. "If this is the afterlife, then we need to spread the word about how awesome dying is."

When he traces my slit with one finger, from clit to ass and back, I thread my fingers into his hair that's a little stiff and a lot snarled but still the most perfect hair in the world. Then again, everything about Tarian is perfection.

He sinks his digit inside of me. As my spine arches, loud voices erupt around us. Tarian clicks his fingers, muttering something beneath his breath.

"Open the door immediately!" Dorian shouts, while Electra—sweet Electra—swears and yells, "I can't believe you idiots let that bitch inside."

I hear one reply, something about *food* and *friend*.

I prop myself onto my forearms while Tarian keeps fingering me.

"Door's locked, Serran," one of the guards says, while I blink from the door to the crooked smile tipping Tarian's lips.

"Well, fucking blast it open," Dorian growls.

Tarian smirks, then presses that smirk to my center.

"You're...? You're really...?" My breath catches because he's doing something with his tongue which is mind-numbingly divine. "You're awake?"

He jimmies himself up, his gaze—and mine—clocking his rigid cock. "Very."

Dorian huffs and puffs and mutters stuff in Atlantean I don't understand.

"I woke you?" My heart is drilling my ribs now.

"You woke me." He settles back onto his stomach. "Seems like my body was retrieved. When were you planning on mentioning it?"

"When I found a way—"

He adds a finger.

"—to wake...oh my god."

"Forever and always. The only one you're allowed to worship from this day on." He pulls his finger out of me, then sucks it clean. The sound that rumbles in his chest makes my thighs quake. He rises to his knees and parts my thighs farther. "Shall we get back to that dream you abandoned me in?"

If this is real, then that must mean…

Tarian catches my chin to keep my stare on his. "She's gone."

I imagine he means dead.

"For fuck's sake, Dorian," he barks, "stop destroying my house."

The creaking and banging halt, and the air grows rife with silence.

"Tarian?" Dorian's timbre trembles.

"Yes?" Tarian laces his hands around my ankles and raises my legs, then glides his hands to my thighs and scoots me close.

I'm so shaken that all I can do is gawk at the roguish male backlit in the brightest, palest gold, a primeval illumination come to life.

"Y-You're—you're back?" Dorian stutters.

"I'm back."

"Is Calanthe safe?"

"She is now. Please see that the idiots Saul hired are dismissed and collect the corpse outside my window." He rubs himself against me, and although I shouldn't be turned on, not after the mention of a corpse, my walls tighten in anticipation. "I hear Paloma's holding a memorial for the dearly departed. Get the cars ready."

"You want to go?" I hiss.

"Only to make sure I wasn't forgotten." His smile smacks of violence. "Oh, and, Dorian, load Mackenzie into one of the cars. Electra, find Calanthe something to wear."

"Everyone in this house is a size zero." I wrinkle my nose. Also everyone in this house is a Fielding, and the last thing I want is to sport clothes that belong to them.

Tarian pushes an inch of himself inside of me. "Calamity, Calamity, Calamity…do you really think I'd make you recycle a dress? We're Atlanteans."

"It's the middle of the night."

"We're Atlanteans," he repeats, as though that were a perfectly adequate explanation. "Whatever we want, we get." He rocks his hips, sheathing himself in several more inches. "Can you guess what I want?"

Him…this…us all feels wildly surreal. Even though he no longer glows blue, I raise my palm to his broad chest to make sure the muscle beneath beats. And it does. It pounds.

"Hmm." Reassured, I rake my nails down his chest, down the runnel of his abs before tracing each brick of muscle. "Starts with an 'R' and ends with an 'E'?"

A frown touches his brow.

"Revenge."

"Ah, yes. I do desire plenty of that." He cants his hips, stretching me. "But do you know what I desire more?"

"Starts with an 'S'"—I suck in a sharp breath—"ends with an 'X'?"

That drags one corner of his mouth up and up. "A charade fiend, I see."

"Says the man who"—I gulp in air because *that girth*—"branded me with a palindrome."

He chuckles, and the unctuous sound resounds through my veins, through my bones, through my marrow.

Tarian releases my legs, plants his palms on either side of my head, and leans over, his mouth brushing against mine. "What I want starts with a 'C' and ends with me."

# SEVENTY-SEVEN

"You don't need a seatbelt," I whisper into Calanthe's curls, hooking her waist and pulling her onto my lap in the backseat of the G-class. "You've got me."

She twists her head, swallows my soul with her forest-fire stare, then plants a kiss on my cheek.

I thumb her hip bone through the marvelous black jumpsuit that hugs her curves to perfection. "On a scale of one to a million, how thrilled do you suspect Saul will be to see me awake?"

Dorian's gaze meets mine in the rearview mirror. If I were to take a wild guess, I'd say his answer was in the single digits.

"Depends on if you demand he greet you with a hug," Electra quips.

While Dorian hisses at his sister, I smile to myself.

"Will you?" Calanthe's voice feathers my smooth jaw.

Although a shower and a shave felt stupendous after my week-long imprisonment, especially since the shower came with a glorious hand job, the grime of the past week still clings to me. It runs in my veins like poison, inflames my heart like a virus, and pollutes my skull like a migraine.

"I think I should." I tuck an errant curl behind Calanthe's ear. "What do you think?"

"I think it might eliminate his magic," she murmurs.

I hold her stare, my fingers growing still on her hip. When she frowns, I look out at the stars that glow as brightly as Dorian's runes.

"Actually, it probably won't." Electra sounds disappointed. "After all, Saul wasn't behind the abduction."

Dorian flicks on his blinker, and the vehicles bracketing us follow suit, carving the night with their bright beams. When I mentioned an escort was overkill, he leveled my opinion with a fearsome scowl and a muttered, *"Remember what happened the last time I let you go off on your own?"*

Calanthe reddens her coral lip with her teeth, which makes my tux trousers pinch at the groin.

"Better stop biting your mouth." I steal her hand and carry it to my swelling cock.

She raises an eyebrow and gives me an indolent stroke. "We're discussing death and punishment."

"We're discussing justice."

"You *really* like justice."

"I fucking adore justice." I shift on the seat to allow her hand better access to my bulge since she doesn't seem opposed to petting me there.

She runs her knuckles across my imprisoned length twice before relocating her hand to my shoulder. I narrow my gaze, making sure to silently communicate how thoroughly she'll pay for teasing me once I get her out of her jumpsuit. Actually, I'll keep her clothed while I play with her.

A small voice murmurs, *She may no longer want to play once you tell her.*

"Saul might not have ordered the abduction, Elle, but he knew all about it," Dorian murmurs, steering my thoughts off the problem I'll contend with *after*.

I recline further into my seat, my hands banding around the fragile woman on my lap. "If Saul doesn't lose his magic for his complicity, he'll lose it for killing my father."

Dorian whirls, which makes the car swerve onto the curb.

*Right.* I forgot to mention my dream.

The hand Calanthe rested on my shoulder creases the black wool. "Next time you share earth-shattering news, can you do so outside of moving vehicles?" Her knuckles remain clamped even after all four tires bang back against the flooded road.

May she cling to me always.

"Saul killed Barak?" Dorian sputters as water rises in an arc across my window.

My storm really did a number on the island. "Saul *and* my brother. Well I assume they did, for I dreamed it." I tell all. This time, I even disclose Joslyn's presence, and the footage she captured.

Calanthe gasps. "That's why Saul's marrying her!"

"Where was Ines?" Electra asks.

"Visiting her ex-husband," I reply.

Electra's jaw slackens. "Ines was married?"

Dorian shoots me an eloquent look in the mirror. I was all for protecting Electra from the truth while she was a child, but I believe it's time she found out. Not that I'll tell her. It's not my place to divulge another family's secrets.

"Do you hold his complicity from a reliable source?" Calanthe's voice is calm, even though her pulse isn't.

It takes me a moment to understand that by "his," she means Saul and not Ines's ex. "Yes." Thanks to the woman on my lap, I do.

Her eyebrows quirk as she waits for me to elaborate.

"You know"—Electra swivels in her seat—"I think you should

shake everyone's hand tonight, Tarian. Human and Atlantean alike."

Calanthe hisses. "His touch might kill, Elle."

Dorian's sister bobs her head. "Only the ill-intentioned people."

She's right.

"I doubt Bryn will feel all warm and fuzzy toward Tarian once we unveil Mackenzie's body," my girl mumbles.

I delicately pinch her nape to angle her face toward mine. "Mackenzie tried to kill you, darling."

My muscles strum with both ire and horror, because she didn't only attempt to end Calanthe's life, she succeeded. The ecstasy of awakening to Calanthe's body draped over mine morphed into sheer terror when I realized that her heart no longer beat.

My magic didn't make her immortal, only magical.

With a sigh, she whispers, "Except she failed, Tarian."

I slide her close and lock my arms around her before she reads the truth on my face. Once the mine inks runes onto her neck, I may tell her that I retrieved her soul from the underworld, but until our visit to my homeland, I'm keeping her in the dark about her mortality.

Dorian has been made aware, though. I want him alert while we navigate the crowd of Atlanteans tonight.

"Are we sure the guards weren't in on Mackenzie's plan?" Electra asks.

"Yes." Dorian flexes his jaw, beating himself up over not having been there. Poor guy was under the spell of mine dust. He wasn't even conscious. "You should fire me."

"And miss out on further grizzling your hair?" My jibe earns me a smile from both women. Dorian proves a tougher audience, but he does eventually grace me with an unamused snort.

The conversation in the car dithers after that. I tuck my face into Calanthe's neck and breathe her in, gathering her honeyed, wildflower scent deep.

"How long can Diego stay with Mom?" Her timbre titillates my nose.

"He'll stay for as long as you need him," Electra says. "I sent him a message while I waited for the shopkeeper to open the boutique, and he told me that he's never been so pampered in his life."

"Diego, huh?" I run my nose up and down Calanthe's throat. "Is he back in the picture?"

"No." Dorian's tone is far too succinct to be truthful.

"You know what? I *should* fire you. Now that Electra's all grown up, she can take over."

Dorian swerves again, making Calanthe's muscles lock up. I knead the ones I can reach to assuage her tension.

"Electra's headed back to college," he finally says.

Even though there's no one I trust more than Dorian—save for Malachi—I don't want him to wake up someday with regrets, so in Atlantean, I say, "After our trip to Atlantis, I'm giving you leave for the rest of the summer. You get to choose your replacement."

"No."

"Did it sound like a suggestion? Because it wasn't."

He grumbles the rest of the way to Paloma's estate, mostly to his sister, who keeps needling him with a grin reminiscent of the abhorrent man who fathered her.

Floodlights pour over the property I haven't visited since Saul and Nora sold it to Catalina's daughter. Nothing's changed. The hedges are still manicured within an inch of their life, and the house, an architectural cube of glass, is just as see-through as ever.

I sit up from the thrill electrifying my blood. "Neither of you called ahead, right?"

"Only to inform them that I'd be bringing the Fielding girl," Dorian replies.

The bridge of Calanthe's nose furrows. I hope it's with disgust and not compunction, because Mackenzie Fielding's rapid death was far too kind a fate. If my runes hadn't spread a toxin through her veins that converted her blood to ash, I would've called her soul back for another ride around my ruinous carousel.

As Dorian and Electra hop out of the vehicle, Calanthe smooths her hands over my satin lapels. "You're glowing."

I peck her lips. "No, *you're* glowing."

She gives her head a small shake. "You know what I mean."

I do know what she means. "What can I say? I'm eager to reap revenge on all those who voted for me to become one with the mine."

"Are there many?"

"Twelve."

Dorian gets my door, and I set Calanthe on her pretty heels.

My hand reflexively brushes her spine before twirling her body into mine. I kiss her deeply, thoroughly, and don't halt my assault until the tension in her body liquefies. Only then do I break our kiss and pivot toward the glass enclosure, hunting the sea of slack faces for the twelve cowards who dispatched two kids and one mortal to sedate a beast.

"What would you like to do with the Fielding girl's body, Tarian?" Dorian nods to the open trunk of the SUV.

"The guard awaits my signal. Electra, Dorian, I want a permanent shield around Calanthe."

"Already done, boss." Electra sidles close, her magic fluttering Calanthe's long hair. In Atlantean, she asks, "I've been meaning to ask…what does Calanthe's rune read to you?"

Her question tightens my gut. Instead of replying, I ask, "Is there a reason you're asking in a language Calanthe doesn't grasp?"

"Obviously."

"What did she ask?" Calanthe side-eyes Dorian's sister.

"She asked what your"—my throat tautens—"rune reads to me."

A devastating grin spreads over her lips. "Nice try, Elle."

"I helped save your life. Telling me what's written on your back is a very small ask."

The curve of Calanthe's mouth deepens.

I know Dorian's desperate to send his sister back to college come fall, but whatever happens tonight, Calanthe will need to be protected.

"I know what you're thinking, Tarian, and my answer is no." Dorian materializes at my side, the runes on his neck glowing as he fortifies Electra's shield.

I cock an eyebrow. "Do tell, what am I thinking, Serran?"

"That you want to offer my sister a permanent position at Calanthe's side." His voice is low, I imagine to keep his theory from reaching Electra.

I stare at him for a good long while. I shouldn't be surprised by how well he knows me, yet I am. "She'll need someone."

"I had an idea."

"I'm listening." Is it me or does a blush streak his cheeks?

He tugs at the collar of the black T-shirt he wears beneath his suit jacket. "Diego."

"What an intriguing idea."

Dorian doesn't meet my stare.

"If he wants the job, it's his. But he starts *after* the summer."

Dorian swings his head in my direction.

Before he can growl that he's not taking a vacation, I tug Calanthe toward the glass doors, which I blow open with a breath. How I missed my powers.

Calanthe glances between my mouth and the house, the arch of her eyebrows high. "Did you just— With your mouth?"

"Blow a door open? Yes."

"Can every Atlantean do that?"

"No." When the bridge of her nose rumples, I slow. "What is it?"

"Just thinking that if I hadn't been with you in the car that night, they would never have been able to capture you."

"My hubris doomed me. You, darling"—I spin her toward me and take her face between my palms, then press our foreheads together—"saved me."

# SEVENTY-EIGHT

When we step into the open foyer, we create quite the stir. Or rather, quite the silence.

"What a send-off," I say, my eyes locking on the two bodies swathed in white and sprinkled with petals.

My brother looks so small in death. Then again, he died a small man.

I search for Ines and Malachi, the only two people forewarned of my wakefulness and of our imminent arrival. I find them already fording through the lavish crowd toward us. Where relief glosses Malachi's irises, Ines's sparkle with anticipation.

She extricates her cell phone from the breast pocket of her tailored blazer and calls out to the man of the house. "Mind if we change the music, Mr. Hassek?"

I smirk at her congeniality since we'll be commandeering the stereo, whatever Paloma's husband's answer.

"What's going on?" Calanthe asks.

As Hassek's complexion turns as green as the potted fern beside which he sits, I murmur, "Malachi's recording."

She frowns.

I'm aware it's Calanthe's, but no one outside our little circle has any business learning the true source of the taped confession.

When Saul and Catalina's voices leak from the ceiling speakers, Calanthe nestles into my side. "Didn't think you wanted to get rid of me so fast."

It takes me a second to compute her inference. When I do, I release her hand and wrap both my arms around her. "I never want to be rid of you." I pull her flush against me and kiss the crown of her head. "*Never*," I repeat, praying the feeling is mutual.

As I hold her, my gaze surfs over my compatriots. I'm pleasantly surprised by the look of confusion that crosses many a face. When the recording ends, Atlanteans swivel toward the illustrious members who've been sitting on our council for far too long.

"I didn't know." Marek's tone writhes with nerves that contradict his claim.

"In that case, my magic won't hurt you, for it only stings those who wish Gaea and myself harm."

His palms come up. I think it's to readjust his signature fedora until a magical gust bangs against the wide glass chandelier over my head, merely glancing off the shield the Serran siblings have erected around Calanthe and me.

"I'll be right back. Electra, Dorian, do not let her out of your sight." Runes bright and no longer blue, I exit the magical cloche just as a bullet plinks against it and another pings against my chest.

Calanthe screams.

I shoot her a wink over my shoulder. "I'm bulletproof tonight, darling."

Her eyes remain wide, her pupils dilated.

"Please reassure her, Dorian," I say, as a few more bullets glance against my body. With a sigh, I crouch and scoop them up, then hold my palm to my mouth, whisper to the bullets to find their way into the bodies of the shooters, and blow. Gasps and yelps rise as metal pierces flesh. "Any more ammunition sent my way will be coated in my blood before being returned to sender. Do I make myself clear?"

No one makes a peep as I stroll toward the departed, streaming fire onto the linens swathing their wretched bodies. Once they both lie naked as the day they were born, I peruse their flesh for the runes that slipped my blood and entered theirs.

I find Symeon's immediately, for it's stamped on his bloodless chest. I reach out and trace the "X" wrapped in a circle that eliminated his immortality. The rune pulses, and then before my very eyes, the symbol stretches and rearranges itself into a word—the original one—before brightening and fading. I frown as I lift my finger, then suck in air when my shoulder tingles, right where the missing rune used to sit.

Many gasp, but it's Calanthe's intake of air I hear over all the others. My lids shut a moment, and I breathe in long and deep before affixing my attention to Yasmin's hand. Like Calanthe saw in her train dream, an "X" emblazons the ridge of her left pinkie. I trace the rune, which, like Symeon's, mutates back into a word before sinking into my blood.

My thoughts stray to my father. Would it lift from his skin if I were to exhume his body? What's the point in dwelling on something I'll never do, though? The same way I decide never to root around for the reason Gaea rid him of magic, I decide to leave this mystery unsolved.

"Tell me, Uncle, who came up with the idea of transforming me into a fucking diamond?"

"Your brother," he says, without hesitation. "It was all Symeon. You remember how crazy he was about his inventions."

I nod at Ines. "Play the recording again." Once it finishes, I say, "I wondered how Symeon and Yasmin managed to keep me hidden on an island crawling with Atlanteans." I speak in English so that Calanthe can grasp the part of the recording that Malachi didn't translate. "I suppose that when one has the support of the entire council, it does make flying under the radar simpler."

"I-I didn't know what S-Symeon had planned." Saul shakes his head vehemently. "I swear I d-didn't know."

I don't bother with his false contrition. "Was Yasmin aware of the reason the council was so enthusiastic about her plan to abduct me?"

"She knew the risks." Catalina's expression is so tight that the frame of her face looks fashioned from steel beams. "You're clearly here to punish us, Tarian. Why drag it out?"

"Curiosity and closure. But you're right. The introvert in me is quite done with this party." I stop in front of her, wrapping her in a forcefield that pins her arms to her sides and her feet to the floor.

Before the next sweep of her eyelashes, my hand cinches her nape, and I whisper the undoing spell. Her eyes flare in time with her nostrils and skin. And then all of her dulls and pleats until her face resembles the melting stalks of wax at my family's dream dinner.

"I'm tempted to let you live out your mortal life, for I know how squeamish you are about aging, but a woman scorned and all that." I shift my gaze to her chest, fist my fingers, then spring them wide.

She gasps when her heart explodes, then collapses in a heap of designer cloth and pallid limbs.

"Next!" I call out.

Predictably, no one rushes to get in line.

I sigh. "Fine." I call out the names of the eleven council members, picturing their despicable bodies engulfed in flames.

The crowd in which they sought refuge disperses. I snuff out the flames that did a number to their clothing but left the rest of them intact. I truss up their bodies with the same gusts that put out their flames.

"Tarian?" Calanthe's voice streams against my eardrums like a wind-snapped ribbon.

I turn to find her pushing against Dorian and Electra's magic to get to me. "Mal, get everyone lined up."

As he and Ines gather the council members, I stride toward the woman whose scowl unsettles my beating heart. What was I thinking, to bring her here and let her observe my monstrosity?

I roll my lips, flex my jaw. "Yes?"

"I understand you're the only one who can do this, but do you *have* to touch them?"

"I can only purge their magic through touch."

The emerald tint of her hazel irises eddies, usurping the gold and gray. "I don't want you to lose more runes."

*Ah.* After contracting, my heartbeats space out anew. "My runes only rub off when I'm unintentionally spellcasting. Besides, I salvaged the ones on Symeon and Yasmin's skin."

My words dash against her mind and ripple, spawning only shallow furrows and moving shadows.

"How?" she finally asks.

"Death cancels the usefulness of my magic."

The shadows churn. The furrows deepen. "I meant, *how* did you do it? How did you recoup them?"

"My skin sopped them up."

"You've touched my rune multiple times."

"I'm aware."

Her dimples suddenly poke free as a smile that is as devastating as it is heartrending digs into her cheeks. "Are you saying that unless I die, the rune is mine to keep?"

I don't nod. I don't speak.

"It gives *till death do us part* a whole new meaning, doesn't it?"

My Adam's apple bobs, which erodes her joy. Before she can ask the reason for my distress, I fit my mouth to hers and fold her into my embrace, my heart clamoring, *I'm still yours. Forever yours.*

A throat clears and pitches me out of the little bubble that belongs only to her and me. I pare my mouth from hers, thumb her freckles, then tread away. Her gaze warms my shoulder blades as I go through the motions of removing everyone's runes, including my uncle's.

Some beg for mercy. Others spout out vapid apologies. Too little, too late.

"Malachi, Saul's fate is yours to decide. Everyone else, Gaea will choose whether you live or die. May repentance reign in your hearts."

Ten sets of eyebrows bend, then jolt when I instruct the newfangled mortals to touch me. All flinch, but none flee thanks to my magical shackles.

One of them—Ramir—has the gall to try and justify his decision. "Catalina said Gaea came to her in a dream after you killed Barak. She said it warned her that you'd annihilate the rest of us if we didn't—if we didn't bring you back to Atlantis…to the mine. That's why I went ahead with the vote."

"Well, now my abduction and subsequent torture makes so much sense." I give a humorless chuckle, even though neither his gullibility nor Catalina's deceit is remotely comical. "If only Saul hadn't lied to Catalina." All eyes swing toward my uncle. "If he'd told her—and me—the truth of how my father died, perhaps you would've all been capable of less bias and more intellect."

My uncle sucks in a breath, eyes so wide they look about to burst from his skull. "I didn't kill him." Yet he glances sideways, toward Joslyn, who's shaking her head.

"You did. Accidentally, but you did. Symeon was the one who told you not to call me. Symeon was also the one to drain Father so that his soul couldn't be shepherded back. Terribly sorry for ruining your blackmail scheme, Jos." I shoot her a cursory glance. "On the bright side, you no longer have to marry one another now. Anyway, where were we? Ah yes. Ramir, hand out."

His complexion is so pale that he seems fashioned from the same cotton as his dress shirt. "Y-Y-You've already taken my magic. Please, Tarian, d-don't—"

With a sigh, I force his hand from behind his back. The reek of urine stains the air. I take a step back to avoid the puddle widening around the fashion sneakers he paired with his dark suit, then lift my hand to his. The instant our flesh meets, the blood in his veins becomes leaden. He succumbs to my magic like Mackenzie.

Only one former councilmember survives the grazing of my skin—Ariana. I knew I inspired fear, but loathing to the point of impenitence? Even I'm surprised. Admittedly, I'm more surprised by Ariana's exoneration.

"Look at that." I lower my hand. "Gaea's forgiven you, Ari. You may return to your family."

The blonde Atlantean, who immigrated to Europe three decades ago and took over the energy sector, skims her finger beneath her mascara-smudged lash line. "I hope that someday I can earn my runes back."

I don't bolster her hope as I signal the guard to carry Mackenzie inside. I'd been planning on a big reveal, but I'm exhausted from spellcasting and troubled from the talk I need to have with Calanthe.

"Will you elect a new council?" someone asks.

"Eventually, but I'll be handpicking its members. And I do mean that in the most literal sense of the term." Although I skim the crowd, I don't look at anyone in particular. Not until I've pivoted fully on my heel, and my stare knocks into autumnal irises.

"I was played just like you were, Nephew." The sob that lurches from Saul's throat makes me glance away from the object of my obsession and affection.

I stretch my neck. "You may not have known the specifics of what they planned on doing to me—too busy trying to contain the truth about Father—but your inaction when Catalina explained what she and your fellow councilmembers had done makes you complicit in their scheme."

He falls to his knees on the buffed black marble. "They were using weapons soaked in your blood as a deterrent."

"Yet Dorian, Malachi, Ines, Electra, and Calanthe still came to my rescue." I step closer to him. "A mortal girl, but not my own fucking uncle. Then again, why am I still expecting anything of my family?"

Saul's lips tremble. "I'm so s-s-sorry, but Barak…" He cranes his neck to look up at me. "He killed Nora, and then he chemically castrated me for years."

"He killed Mother because she planned to steal Tarian." Malachi crouches in front of his father. "As for the other thing, I agree it wasn't right, but Barak did that, Father, not Tarian."

"Because of your lie, I didn't dare touch anyone for months, Saul. Fucking months. And when I did touch someone"—I gesture to Calanthe—"I was certain she'd die because of me."

"But if we'd told you, *we'd* have died!"

Malachi rises from his crouch. "How did keeping it a secret work out for you, Father?"

A thud followed by a feminine scream shreds the air. My heart misses every beat until I spot Calanthe standing between Dorian and Electra, unscathed.

# SEVENTY-NINE

The guard dumps Mackenzie's gray corpse on the marble floor. Joslyn screams again, stumbling out of the crowd toward the lifeless body.

Bryn, on the other hand, remains still and silent, but it's not a passive silence. No, it's a contemplative, disturbing silence. The type that festers, that mutates, that condemns. Although she hasn't approached me, choosing to remain at her mother's side, her eyes have strayed to mine often.

She watched me watch Tarian stop Catalina's heart. She watched me pour questions into Electra's ear, asking the Atlantean for translations and explanations. She watched me take refuge behind Dorian when the crowd's attention became a little too insistent.

"You monster!" Joslyn wails, hiking up her black pencil-thin dress in order to kneel. It takes her several tries to yank the stiff material far enough to allow her joints to bend. "You killed my daughter! My beautiful, sweet daughter."

Tarian sighs. "Mackenzie killed herself."

Bryn raises her chin. "My sister wasn't suicidal, Tarian."

"Your sister touched me without my consent."

Bryn purses her lips. "*Before* or *after* you magically woke up?"

"What exactly are you getting at, Miss Fielding?" Tarian asks.

"Wasn't Calanthe in the room with you at all times?"

My heartbeats duplicate and divide until there isn't a silent interval between them. "You think *I* pushed Mackenzie into Tarian?" I try to plow past my bodyguards so I can have an unhindered view of Bryn, but Dorian and Electra's protective forcefield herds me right back.

"Is that so far-fetched?" Bryn asks. "You knew what would happen if a mortal touched his skin."

"Tarian's magic was unstable, and I was worried his runes would peel off. I didn't *know* his touch could kill someone until I recovered from my anaphylactic shock."

"Hmm. How did that work exactly? Did Tarian have an EpiPen laying around his bedroom?"

"I cured Calanthe with magic." Although Tarian's tone is flat, his stare is all serrated edges.

"So, let me get the timeline straight. My sister poisons Calanthe before *accidentally*"—she sketches quotation marks while looking straight at me—"bumping into you. Calanthe goes into anaphylactic shock while Mackenzie drops dead. *You* then wake up *from* the dead and morph into an EpiPen?"

"Not that I owe you an explanation, but you've summarized the event brilliantly, Miss Fielding. Though I do feel the need to add that I did not shapeshift into an EpiPen."

"Why didn't you save my sister?"

Tarian snorts, which intensifies Bryn's scowl.

"Resurrect her!" Joslyn combs back Mackenzie's hair. "Resurrect her, and I'll give you the footage of your father's death."

"I've already seen it once. I've no desire to see it twice."

"I'll sign over all my rights to the baby."

"Why in the world do you think I'd want your unborn child, Joslyn?"

"I was talking about Saul. I'll give him full guardianship against a very small amount of money."

A vein thunders along Tarian's temple.

"For free!" she amends, sensing Tarian's lack of interest. "I'll give him the baby for free."

"That's a conversation you need to have with him. Not with me."

"I'll do anything." Joslyn's voice fractures. "*Anything* if you resurrect my sweet, beautiful girl."

*Can* he resurrect her?

"Calanthe, please." Bryn finally takes a step, not toward me though, toward her mother and sister. "Tell him to bring her back. It's the least you can do after I saved you."

My heart skips a shocked beat. "Mackenzie tried to kill me."

Bryn purses her lips—because she doesn't care? Because she's not convinced?

Tarian closes the distance between us. "This conversation is utterly pointless since I can't resuscitate her."

Even though the room is filled with people, they all stand still and quiet.

"You can't, or you won't?" Anger and grief dapples Bryn's complexion.

Tarian halts.

When his fingers ball and his gaze clocks Bryn's chest, I shove hard at the forefield surrounding me. "Tarian, no!"

He doesn't react to the sound of my voice.

I'm about to call out to him again when Joslyn shrieks, "Let him try, you selfish twat."

Tarian's gaze bangs into Joslyn.

Before I can explain what I was trying to prevent, his fingers unspool. Joslyn chokes and then her eyes reel to the back of her skull, and she flops face first against Mackenzie's body.

Saul staggers to his feet and teeters toward Joslyn. "My baby! You murdered my baby."

"You're right. That's unfair." Tarian walks over to Joslyn and presses two fingers to the back of her skull before pressing those same two fingers to the base of her neck. "There. I'd get her to a hospital, though, because she'll need to be tube-fed from now on." Tarian rises to his full height, which makes Saul shy away. "Feel free to send me the medical bills." And then his gaze wheels over the crowd, and he says something in Atlantean that includes Malachi's name before calling to me.

The magic around my body loosens. Fucking finally. I almost trip over my own feet as I rush toward him and stab my fingers through his. He stares at my face, then at our hands, before finally curling his fingers around mine with a firmness that eases some of my qualms.

In silence, we return to the car. Like on the way to the glass mansion, I end up on Tarian's lap. His touch is gentle this time, his temper dissolved, nevertheless, he isn't calm.

Is he troubled by his people's connivance? By his uncle's lack of remorse? By what the future holds?

As Dorian swerves out of the driveway, I point out that Electra's not in the car. I imagine he noticed, but like Tarian, he seems preoccupied.

The taillights of the car preceding us splash Dorian's haggard features. "She'll come home later."

Right before we barrel off the property, I peek back at the house, shuddering when I meet Bryn's cold, violent stare. In spite of the distance, it licks and pricks my skin like an icy current. The only thing that reassures me is that she's human and I'm a little more.

Tarian rubs my pebbled arm before threading our fingers together and docking them on my abdomen. "Pump the heat up, Dorian."

God, I love this man. I curl my body into his.

"I'm surprised you still want to touch me after the spectacle I subjected you to tonight." Tarian's voice scrapes my skin like sandpaper.

"Your magic doesn't scare me, and neither do you."

He raises our clasped hands to his mouth and places a kiss on my knuckles, his skull-shaped cufflinks—a gag gift from Malachi for a past birthday apparently—sparking like my pulse.

"And before you say anything, it's not the rune talking. It's me."

His mouth grows rigid against my skin, his breaths, sparse.

"What is it?"

He gives me a smile that's so slight, so tight it fills me with anxiety. "We'll talk at home."

The heat gusting from the vents bounces against my skin without penetrating. "That sounds ominous."

His lashes flutter. I hunt through the thick fringe for a hint of what we're about to discuss. Does it have to do with him and me? I don't prod, partly because he's asked me to wait and partly because my gut churns with uneasiness.

Although he keeps popping his jaw the entire way home, he doesn't let go of my hand. If he were about to break up with me, he wouldn't bother touching me, would he? When we reach his bedroom, he blows the door shut. The latch falls into place softly, yet the click echoes like a thunderous bang.

"Now you're scaring me," I say. "Please just…just spit it out."

Tarian unbinds our fingers. "You're free to leave, Calanthe."

"And go where?"

"Wherever you want. The building that houses your shop belongs to you and is debt free. I've also set up a bank account in your name. And like promised, I'll repair your mother's memory come morning."

I frown.

"Taking you with me tonight was… It was selfish." Tarian begins to pace. "I shouldn't have exposed you like that. Even though no Atlantean will risk my wrath for the foreseeable future, I've painted a target on your back, so I'd still like to give you runes —but if you don't want magic, know that you'll have a guard for the rest of your life."

"Why wouldn't I want supernatural powers?"

"Because it'll tie you to me and to my world."

"I'm already tied to you."

Tarian halts his manic pacing and stares at me for a long, long while. And then he shrugs out of his tuxedo jacket, feeds the golden skull out of his right cuff, and rolls up his sleeve.

The unbroken strand of runes on his gorgeous forearm glimmers gold in the subdued lighting. I don't think he stripped for my viewing pleasure—after all, his fingers aren't working on his second cufflink—but damn if it doesn't chase away some of my dread.

When he stabs his hand through his black hair, tussling the gel-tamed locks, my body temperature shoots up another few degrees.

"I was trying to decide how best to tell you." He takes a step in my direction. Stops. Takes another step.

I narrow my eyes because it almost seems like approaching me is torture. "How best to tell me what?"

He stops close enough for me to count his lashes, yet too far away for me to touch. "That you're free. Of me."

My head rocks back. "Wait, was this…was tonight all a dream?"

His throat jostles. "No. It was real."

"Then I don't—I don't understand."

"You're free, darling."

"Why do you keep repeating that word? *Free.* Like I was some caged animal before."

"Not an animal." He takes another step and raises his hand to my cheek. "But you were caged by my magic." His touch, like his voice, judders.

I've seen Tarian go through a kaleidoscope of emotions in the past week, but never did I see him tremble. It's almost more alarming than the words that keep dropping from his mouth.

"Oh my god." I suck in a breath and take a step back, as though adding distance could stop him from reaching for my rune and siphoning it away. "Now that you know how to recoup runes, you want to take mine back!" Something dawns on me. Something that makes me take another step back. "Shit, were you really planning on killing me?"

He blinks. "What?"

"You can't take your magic back from a live body." I blink, a little pissed and a lot hurt.

"Calanthe, that's not—" He ruffles his hair again.

"I saw our future."

"When?"

"Like, two hours ago. We have three kids, you asshole. Three. And all of them at the same time."

He straightens his neck, narrows his eyes. Nothing on his person trembles now. He is the picture of confidence and poise. "How does that make me an asshole?"

"Because *three* babies, *one* pregnancy. That's bound to do more damage than any Brazilian wax." I point to my nether regions. "But mostly, you're discussing getting rid of me."

He scoffs. "I'm not discussing getting rid of you."

"Sorry. *Freeing* me." I bite out the word.

His jaw ticks.

"You seemed plenty happy in the dream. Plenty proud, too. What changed your mind? Did you see someone tonight that you fancy more than me? That's it, isn't it? Why would you stay with a frumpy mortal when you could have any gorgeous Atlantean?"

"Fuck." Before I can stagger back, he closes the distance between us and bands his arms around my waist. "Calanthe, what you saw wasn't a vision of our future."

"Some of my dreams have been premonitory," I mumble, desperately trying not to shatter, even though only his arms are keeping me in one piece.

"It was a chemical hallucination. When a person dies, they don't only see the past flash before their eyes. They also see the future they long for."

"Wh-what?"

He works his jaw from side to side, the vein in his neck swelling and shrinking like his pupils. "My magic didn't make you immortal. It only enchanted your sleep."

"What?" I try to pull away, but he won't let me.

"You woke me with your last breath."

This time, I shove so hard against his thudding chest that I manage to lean back. "I. Fucking. Died?"

A corner of his mouth traipses up.

"Of course you'd find my death amusing, Hades. You're named after the fucking god of the underworld. For all I know, you're actually him." His smile gains traction until I say, "So, what? While I was dead, you recouped your precious little rune?"

His lips flatten. "I didn't realize I'd gotten it back until after our shower. I was a little distracted until then."

I shake my head. I'm not sure why I shake it. I just know that it's moving left and right, left and right. "I want it back!" I suddenly shrill. "I want my rune back."

"I can't. I don't know how to."

I contort my arms to unzip my jumpsuit. When my fingers skid off the zipper, I seize his forearm and stick it against my brutally pumping chest. I wait to feel the bite of his magic, wait to feel its sting as it slides under my skin, wait to feel its heat when it glows.

I don't feel any of those things.

"I'll give you runes tomorrow."

"I don't want just any runes, Tarian! I want *your* rune. I want to be yours. I want our dreams back." My manic grip slackens around his arm. "I want your triplets."

His mouth curves as he gathers me against him. "You don't need my rune to be mine. All you need is my love, and you have that for all of eternity. If that is, in fact, what you truly desire."

"Why in the world would you think I'd want anything else?"

"Because I'm a deeply flawed and fucked up man."

I roll my hot eyes and palm his neck. "You have no flaws." In spite of my sky-high heels, I have to press up on tiptoe to reach his mouth.

Our kiss is feral. All tongue and teeth and heart. Our touch, frenzied. Our coupling, beatific.

It is only after, as we lay replete against one another, our sweat-slickened skin cooling, that the answer to a long-ago mystery dawns over me. "It isn't magic."

Tarian caresses the edge of my arm. "What isn't?"

"Our absurd chemistry."

In the subdued glow of his runes, I see his lips hitch up. "Feels pretty fucking magical."

I plant my elbows on either side of his head. "But it isn't."

"I know, darling." He caresses the small of my back, his thumb moving as though to trace the letters that used to blaze there, as though to imprint them back into my flesh.

How I wish he could. "I'm going to miss sharing our dreams."

"You get to share my life now. Although, I'm not sure that's much of a gift."

I kiss him. "I can't wait."

"You're truly not frightened?"

"Of you?" I grin. "If it turns you on, I can act terrified." I palm my mouth and squeak, "Tarian, you beast! Please don't torture me."

He pops my ass. "I meant about touching me?"

"No, Tarian. I'm not afraid."

The bones in his face rearrange, sharpen. "Swear never to leave me? Especially for another man."

His jealousy is frankly perplexing. He's the god of gods, a man with so much power and wealth and beauty that he could have anyone in the entire world.

"I swear." An idea crops up in the back of my mind, one that makes my dimples dig deep and his eyebrows slant low. After my visit to the mine, I'll be heading to a tattoo parlor and getting the word *mine* emblazoned on my spine, for old time's sake.

"What's with the smile?"

"It's a surprise."

"I don't like surprises."

"Of course you don't." I press my smile against his hard lips until they soften. "But you'll like this one, my beast."

# EPILOGUE

The sky is so blindingly blue that it seems surreal. A lot like this past week. A lot like the man sitting beside me in the helicopter that Dorian and Electra are flying over the Boston skyline. The man who grips my hand as though worried I might slip away like I would from our dreams.

My heart gives a painful little thud at the loss of our magical connection. Tarian may fear losing me, but I fear losing him so much more. I barely dared to sleep last night, afraid that I'd wake in a cold bed to a man who'd changed his mind. He may still worry about touching others, but the truth is, he can, and I hate it.

His fingers open so suddenly that I startle.

"Why did you let go?" Could I sound more desperate?

Because I don't have supernatural hearing, he shifts my headset aside. "You seemed in pain."

I rethread my fingers through his and carry them onto my lap so he can't steal them away again. "I'm not in pain. I'm in fear." *In fear…* Is that proper English? It doesn't sound right but I can't bother to care.

"I won't hurt your mother, Calanthe."

His fingers are solid and long, still so pale from having been bled and held in captivity.

"That's not— Well, it is…" I lick my lips and glance out at the ocean shimmering like a bolt of raw silk around my brick and glass city. "I'm currently *in fear*"—still sounds wrong—"that I'm going to wake up from this dream, Tarian."

He cups my cheek. "This isn't a dream, darling; it's our reality. Now and forever."

I sigh as he sweeps away my insecurities with a brush of his lips. I'm aware I'll have powers before the day is out—the first human in three decades to be given magic—nevertheless, I worry that an inscription on my neck will only heighten the absence of the one that adorned my spine.

A handful of minutes later, Dorian lands the helicopter on the roof of Marion Tower. It takes everything in me not to ask Tarian— for the hundredth time—whether he's certain his magic won't harm my mother.

He promised it would be fine. Swore that even if she didn't adore the Hadezes, his magic wouldn't damage her. After all, he's the one who's going to be touching her and not the other way around.

Yet as Tarian helps me out of the chopper, my nerves remain as frayed as the hem of my shorts. As always, he senses my disquiet, because when he sets me down, he cups my cheeks and vows—for the hundredth time since sunrise—that his magic will cure her.

"My heart knows this, Tarian. It's my mind that's having trouble believing."

His jaw clenches. Is he self-flagellating himself again for having brought me to last night's soul-weighing party? "We can put this off. Revisit it in a few days."

"No." I grip the lapels of his pale linen blazer, push up on my spectacular black stilettos, and kiss him.

His arms come around me, creasing my white, tissue-soft Fleetwood Mac tee. Did I hesitate to recycle the fancy jumpsuit? Yes. Especially when Tarian stalked out of his closet dressed like some debonair gazillionaire about to embark on a private yacht.

In the end, I chose casual over dressy, considering the amount of traveling Tarian intends to do in one day. Also, I suspected a swanky outfit would weird my mother out a little. Especially once her mind cleared.

*If it clears.*

*If she doesn't drop dead.*

I'm not sure who's more nervous on the elevator ride down. It's a tossup between Dorian and me. Where he keeps drumming his fingers on his thighs, I keep playing with the frayed threads of my shorts.

"Very apropos." Electra nods to my T-shirt.

My brow furrows until I realize that the word *Dreams* is printed in technicolor beneath the band's name. The sight of it roughens the lump in my throat. Even though I didn't have piles and piles of clothes, I had four other T-shirts. Why did I have to pick the one reminder of what I've lost?

As Electra frowns at my odd reaction, Tarian slides his palm under my breasts until his thumb and index finger obscure the bottom-half of the word and then he tucks me into his side. I don't know whether he does it because he senses the title of the song unsettles me, or just because he wants me closer.

The sad irony of my shirt flits right out of my mind when the elevator dings and Dorian unlocks the door. Diego greets us with a dimpled smile that becomes an odd mix of restrained and unnerved at the sight of Tarian.

"She was doing well until about an hour ago when I suggested a game of Scrabble. I'm sorry, Miss Bloom." He rubs the side of his neck until his caramel skin reddens. "Mrs. Murphy only told me after my blunder. I compelled it from her mind, but she's still troubled."

I blink back the heat welling up behind my lids that are still bloated from yesterday's emotional rollercoaster. "You couldn't have known."

"I should've checked with Mrs. Murphy."

So he stops beating himself up over this, I touch his arm. "Thank you for keeping her safe." And then I tread past him, Electra on my heels.

"What's the story with Scrabble?" she murmurs.

"That's how Dad proposed."

"Aw, shit."

I stop at the sight of Mom sitting in a dining room chair angled toward the window. She's watching gulls soar over Boston Harbor, stretching wings they had probably kept folded while Tarian's storm raged.

"If this works," I murmur, "my father leaves her forever."

Electra's odd-hued gaze travels over my tense features. "It'll work."

I nod, even though a part of me can't help but remain skeptical, and another, apprehensive.

A toilet flushes somewhere in the apartment, followed by a familiar clanking of keys and the heavy shuffle of slippered feet. A second later, my neighbor's chirrupy voice fills the quiet living room. "Lisa, look who's back!"

Mom turns away from the gulls. When wrinkles fan around the outer corners of her chestnut eyes and the wide mouth I inherited from her thins, I realize she can't place me.

"She was doin' well until the—" Mrs. Fiona's head tips back. And back.

Tarian must've made his appearance.

"Lord almighty." She crosses herself and shrinks back.

Tarian comes to stand right behind me, his body as solid as mine is not. "Mrs. Murphy, Diego tells me you've been saving up to purchase a house in Ireland." He splays his hand on my hip.

She gulps once, twice.

"My friend"—he gestures toward Dorian—"is arranging for you to tour the land of your ancestors with a real estate agent until you find your dream house."

Mrs. Fiona's jaw slackens as though fashioned from old rubber instead of bone. "*Why?*"

"Because I'd like to thank you for your kindness toward the Blooms."

"By makin' me tour houses?"

"By buying you one." Tarian's fingers begin to stroke.

Her alarmed gaze drops to my hip, to the hand I placed over Tarian's. "A whole house?"

"Usually, people prefer whole houses to halved ones," he deadpans, which makes a smile warp the tense line of my lips.

Mrs. Fiona's lids smack down, reel up, smack, reel. "Y-You're T-Tarian Hadez."

The name ruffles Mom's brow.

"I am."

"*The* Tarian."

"I don't believe I have exclusivity on the name." Tarian's breath tickles my scalp.

Her chest is lifting with such hectic heartbeats that her lanyard of keys clink as hard as Bryn's bangles. The sound slots the memory of my friend's icy stare back into my mind, sending a wave of goosebumps coursing over my bare limbs.

Tarian gathers me against him, his hand moving to my squirming abdomen, and though his touch and heat ease the ache of having lost a friend, they sadly don't expunge it.

It suddenly dawns on me that he could remove Bryn from my mind. He could remove himself. He could remove this week. He could take it all away from me. Anyone could. My impatience to visit the Atlantean mine transforms into a primordial need.

"Fi, choose something big because you *know* Nick, Callie, and I will be stopping by for visits." My mother's crystalline voice shears through my thoughts.

"I hear they've got castles for sale." She eyes Tarian as though expecting him to squirm at her threat of spending a ton of his money.

"Whatever your heart desires, Mrs. Murphy." Tarian's voice resounds with an amused lilt that doesn't charm my guarded neighbor.

The Holy Hunters' crusades to make humans distrustful of Atlanteans has clearly borne fruit. I imagine Tarian's generosity will end up wearing Mrs. Fiona down, but what about the rest of the world? Does he care how they perceive him and his people? Maybe he actually enjoys inspiring terror.

Mom stands from her chair and ambles over to us, readjusting the belt on her knitted cardigan. "I didn't realize my daughter had a new man in her life." She throws me an eloquent look, one that says, *What about Lucas?* Or maybe it says, *Someone has been keeping a secret.*

"Mom, I'd like you to meet Tarian." I crane my face to look up at him. "My…"

"Your…?" She prompts.

"Her Nick," Tarian says, startling a rogue tear clinging to my lashes.

As it tracks down my cheek, Mom folds her arms in front of her chest. "Really? Those are big shoes to fill, Mr. Hadez."

Mrs. Fiona sidles over to Mom, crossing her arms in solidarity. "Real big. Massive. And yes, you've got large feet, but my friend meant this figuratively."

Electra snorts.

"How long?" Mom's pixie cut is backlit by the morning sun, making the strands appear a deeper shade of brown.

"How long what, Mom?"

"How long have you two been—"

"Canoodlin'?" Mrs. Fiona's word choice makes Electra puff out a giggle.

It's so out of character that it momentarily distracts me from the million and one nerves crackling beneath my skin.

"I'm sorry," she wheezes between more giggles, which she tries and fails to stifle with a palm.

"So?" Mrs. Fiona flips her chin up another notch until she's staring down her nose at Tarian. Well, at me. She's still staring up at Tarian because of the almost two-head size difference.

"A week," I finally admit, even though it feels like ten. Like I've never *not* had Tarian Hadez in my life.

He says something in Atlantean to Dorian that makes Mrs. Fiona's pupils distend. "Dorian would like to go over the details of your trip, Mrs. Murphy. Why don't you follow him to the kitchen?"

Mrs. Fiona's arms fall from their knot, and she marches away.

"Your eyes," Mom gasps. "What did you do to her?"

"It's called compulsion, Mrs. Bloom."

I grimace because I sense the only reason he's explaining this is because he's about to wipe her mind.

"I'm going to use it on you now. You have nothing to fear from me or from my people, Mrs. Bloom."

The inside of my mouth becomes as dry as chalk when Tarian steps away from me, then drier still when his nape blazes and my mother's eyes glaze.

Fingers lock around mine, stilling their spastic tremble. "You're about to get her back, Callie."

I clutch Electra's promise like I clutch her fingers as Tarian sets his palms atop my mother's head. When his long fingers begin to radiate that blinding light that can both end lives and make them begin anew, a whimper flits past my chattering teeth.

Tarian murmurs something in his tongue, or maybe he speaks in English. It isn't as though I can discern anything over my frenetic pulse. Mom's pupils spread wide before contracting. Her nostrils, too, flare. Is it me or are her veins shimmering? Is that normal?

I check Tarian's expression—calm focus—then Electra's—captivated awe. Although my heart still feels like it's about to stumble out of my chest, my lungs no longer feel like the crushed hood of a car. I inhale, one breath, two, three. The air hits my blood so fast that I grow dizzy and slightly woozy.

"Hold her," Tarian growls.

I blink hard. Why does Mom need to be held? Did something go wrong? When Electra's arm wraps around my waist, I realize that the "her" he was referring to was me. My mother isn't shivering like a leaf in the dead of autumn. She is calm and poised, hands open and relaxed, mouth soft, throat slack, pupils wide and…reflective.

Is *that* normal?

When she sucks in a startled breath, my heart stops.

Tarian lifts his hands. She blinks. Her eyes remain lambent. Lambent and guarded.

She raises a hand to her forehead and kneads her furrowed brow, her eyebrows arching as she regards Tarian, the living room, Electra, me. "Callie, baby, where the hell are we?"

"At a friend's house, Mom."

She glances between Electra and Tarian, then peers farther. Can she see Dorian, Diego, and Mrs. Fiona, or is it just their voices she hears? "Well, are you going to introduce me?"

Electra holds out her hand. "I'm Electra Serran. You can call me Elle."

Mom offers her a guarded smile. "And you know my daughter how?"

"I met her through Mr. Hadez." Electra nods to Tarian, who's taken a step back, but whose gaze has remained riveted on Mom.

"Tarian, ma'am," he says, his gaze skipping between her eyes and pulse point.

"And how did you come to meet—oh. Silly me. Bryn must've introduced you." Her eyes spark. "Her mother's marrying your uncle, no?"

"I believe the wedding's been canceled, but yes, that's how I met Tarian, Mom. Through Bryn." The stubborn lump that appears at the mention of Bryn's name bloats my throat anew.

"Is she here, too?"

I shake my head. "We had a bit of a falling out." I add this in case Bryn stops by the flower shop.

Shit, what if she does stop by? What if she decides to take her hurt out on my mother? I must pale, because Tarian closes the distance between us, his arm replacing Electra's.

I peer up into his face. "Can Mom come with us to Atlantis?" What I don't ask is, *Can you give her runes, too?*

"That is up to her, darling, not up to me."

"Well, it's a little up to you," I murmur. "Since you're the conduit and all."

He presses a feather-soft kiss to the corner of my mouth. "If she wants runes, they're hers. Why don't you sit down with her and tell her everything while I go check on the evolution of Mrs. Murphy's trip?"

"Everything?" I sink my teeth into my bottom lip. As much as I want to disclose all my secrets, I don't want her mind to be toyed with.

My forever attentive god murmurs into my ear, "Everything, Calamity. After all, her grandchildren will have magic. She's allowed to know all." He kisses my stunned lips, then calls out to Electra to follow him into the kitchen.

"Darling…?" she murmurs.

My neck cracks from how rapidly I look at Mom, only to realize that she was parroting Tarian.

"Runes? Atlantis? Conduit? Tarian Hadez? We have a lot to talk about, don't we, baby?" She rubs her chest which makes my breath frizz.

"What's wrong? Does something hurt?"

"Just my heart." She must sense my rising panic because she takes two steps in my direction, cups my shoulders, and whispers a *shh* that does squat to repress my alarm. "Nothing's wrong with it, Callie."

"Then why does it hurt?"

"Because the way that man looks at you reminded me of your father. Of the way he used to—" Her voice catches. "Of the way he used to look at me."

Heat simmers on my lash line, blurring her features. "I wish he was here, Mom. I wish he could've met Tarian."

"I know, baby." A gentle smile tips her lips. "But I have no doubt he's watching you. Probably with binoculars and a tumbler of whiskey."

"Creepy," I croak between sobs.

"Make that a full bottle. His little girl, his biggest treasure, has not only found love but with an Atlantean."

"We should probably sit down for this conversation."

"We have a transatlantic flight ahead of us. We'll be doing plenty of sitting then."

"You're coming?"

She glances past me. "Of course, I'm going. I don't want my daughter vanishing on some exotic, enchanted island. Especially after I just got her back from…" She frowns.

My heart holds still.

"When did you graduate from college?"

"Two years ago," I say.

Her frown deepens. "So odd. It feels like…yesterday."

"I know. The last two years have been rough on you."

She inhales raggedly. "Yeah. I'm sorry, baby. When your father died, I just…checked out."

My chest trembles.

"But I'm back now."

I throw my arms around her and clutch her tight, yet it doesn't feel tight enough.

"So, Atlantis?" Her fingers sail through my hair as I lay my head on her shoulder. "We're not going there to work on our tans, are we?"

Although Tarian stands by the front door, conversing with the Serrans, his eyes are on me. Always on me.

*My Dark Beast*

"Do you believe in magic, Mom?"
"Is this when you tell me it exists?"
"Yes. This is when I tell you it's real."

# EPILOGUE

I approach Calanthe's mother in the galley of the private jet taking us to my homeland. "How are you feeling, Mrs. Bloom?"

Physically, she's exactly like the woman I met in Calanthe's dream; emotionally, she's vastly different—accepting and curious.

"Please, Tarian. Call me Lisa. As for how I'm feeling..." Her soft brown eyes rest on her daughter, who's smiling and shaking her head at something Electra shows her in one of those magazines that my pilots stock. "Better than I've felt in a long time. Calanthe mentioned I had you to thank for this."

"It was nothing." I twist the cap off my bottle of Evian and drink the whole thing down.

Lisa smirks. "You have an odd definition of *nothing*, sweetheart."

The term of endearment catches me by such surprise that I

crush the empty bottle. My heart is many things, but not sweet. "Have you decided whether you'll be visiting the mine?"

She returns her stare to her daughter. "Calanthe wants me to."

"But what do you want, Lisa?"

"Is it reversible? In case I ever want to…leave?"

"Yes. The day you decide you're done with this life, I can rid you of your runes."

"And you would? Even if my daughter begged you not to."

"I would never force anyone to live."

Lisa bobs her head a few times. "Then I guess my nape is yours to decorate, Tarian." She smiles, but the curve is edged in sadness. I may have brought her back, but I failed to retrieve that part of her that disappeared the day her husband died. "Do you believe that Bryn will try to harm her?"

"Bryn's mind will be thoroughly wiped, so no. But I do believe many people will try to harm your daughter as long as she stays with me." I try to screw the cap on the empty water bottle but can't seem to match the grooves to the tracks. "I hesitated to erase everything from her mind last night but I…I couldn't do it." My muscles clench as I stare at the girl who chose me. Who woke me. "I hope you can forgive me for my selfishness, Lisa."

"Selfishness? Sweetheart, that's called love. Do you know how rare it is? How precious?"

"Calanthe would still have been safer away from me."

"I don't believe that. I believe the only thing she would've been is miserable, Tarian."

"She wouldn't have remembered."

"She would've remembered the feeling. She would've known something was amiss." Lisa sets down the pastry she'd come to fetch when I waylaid her. "When you find that person who makes your heart beat harder and faster and longer than anything in the world, you hold onto them. You cherish them. You never, under any circumstances, cast them away. And if you ever separate, you make that decision together."

My heart grinds to a screeching halt. *Separate?* Fucking never. Apparently, the water bottle still had some air left inside after all.

Calanthe frowns at me, then untucks her legs and stands from the divan she shares with Electra.

"I'll leave you two to talk." Lisa grabs the whole tray of pastries and walks back to her seat.

I catch her exchanging a passing look with her daughter. Probably a silent warning to tread carefully around me.

The second she reaches the galley, Calanthe palms my granite jaw. "Why do you look like someone just kicked the mine?"

"Separation isn't an option, so never put it on the table."

Her head rears back. "Well, damn. Here I was coming to suggest it."

I don't laugh. No, I stew. And I crush the plastic some more.

She hits the button that slides the galley door closed, extricates the flattened plastic bottle from my fingers, then links her arms around my neck. "Want to tell me where that came from?"

"Your mother," I huff.

Her eyebrows slide toward one another. "My mother advised us to separate?"

"No. She said that if we ever *wanted to*," I grit out, "it has to be a mutual decision."

"Well, obviously."

"*Obviously*?" The plane jounces, which makes Calanthe's grip tighten.

"First, my love, please don't crash the plane. Second, if we *both* wanted out—keyword *both*—it would be a cruel and unusual punishment to stay together, no?"

"You made my fucking heart beat, Calamity. It will probably stop again if you ever try to leave me."

Her dimples make an appearance. "I'd sure hope so, 'cause I'd really hate for it to beat for anyone else."

I'm torn between growling and fucking her. I end up doing both. After buffeting the varnished wood panel with a sound barrier, I snap the button off her shorts, plunge my hand inside her thong, and work her clit until she's soaked and gasping my name against my shoulder.

Only then do I unzip myself. "Get rid of the shorts and the thong. Keep the—"

"Heels?"

I grin. She grins back. And then I cup her ass and hoist her up. Her arms return to my neck as she glides home. To think I considered sending her away with no memory of me... I shudder.

She doesn't ask me what's wrong as I begin to rock my hips. She merely digs her heels into my backside and stares into my eyes while I stare into hers. The colors ringing her pupils eddy— the green bleeds into the gold before usurping the gray.

"I love you, my beast," she murmurs, her words fisting my heart, making it pound harder, faster.

No wonder she converted stone to flesh. The ascendancy she has over me is nothing short of supernatural.

My thrusts align themselves with my pulse. I balance her gorgeous body on one forearm then reach between us to thumb her clit. I wait for her to come before I allow the fire basting my spine to surge out of me and into her.

I bury my face in her neck as my dick weeps and softens. "*T'adoshek, me belesa*," I murmur against her wildflower skin.

Her fingers loop my short black strands, tugging deliciously at their roots. "What does that mean?"

"I adore you, my beauty."

Her throat contracts along with her slick walls, hardening my heavy cock but softening every other corner of my dark being. Eyes gleaming like faceted jewels, she cradles my jaw and fits her mouth to mine.

I lose myself in her one more time, the thrumming in my blood amplifying as we near the land that shaped an innocent dreamer into a creature of nightmare.

Yosef and Malika Serran meet us at the airstrip in open-top vehicles. In spite of the magic running in their veins, this week has aged them—drained their smiles of vigor and whittled their sun-burnished skin. I imagine it's changed all of us. Even little Electra seems to have grown up.

Whereas they greet me with a solemn nod, they hug Calanthe and her mother with just as much warmth as they show their kids. How I loathe Symeon for having robbed me of our father, yet I don't loathe him enough to deprive him of being buried beside the man and woman who created us. He's the only corpse I repatriated. Well, Ines and Malachi brought him back since I didn't want him aboard my jet.

"Is he in the ground?" I ask Yosef as Malika leads the way to the cars.

"Yes. They're already waiting for you by Gaea's mine."

Calanthe, who holds my hand, squeezes my fingers tight. She knows how conflicted I am about Symeon's passing. After all, she's had a front row seat to the depth of my love for the boy he was before malice and jealousy uprooted all the good from his soul.

I toss my jacket in the front passenger seat, then climb in the back with Calanthe and let Yosef drive. As we take off down the dirt road of my youth, her eyes are huge. I tell Yosef to take the scenic route, the one cut into the limestone cliffs that ring our speck of land.

Her lips part in awe as the Atlantic muscles the white stone, spraying salt so high it glimmers like tossed glitter, refracting the last rays of the dying sun. Unlike our neighboring countries, Atlantis is rugged and inhospitable, all frothing waters and fierce currents, with year-long gusts that claw at the squat trees and stubborn shrubs. It was an island reviled by most, aban-doned by many. Until the mine revealed itself to the world. Everything changed after that. Every country in a thousand-mile radius salivated to incorporate the valuable landmass under their flag. I may hate the council with every rune on my body, but it's thanks to them that my island remained a sovereign state, and for that and that alone, I'm grateful to its original members.

Yosef starts down the lone road around which our entire town is built. Dozens of small clapboard homes branch out from the paved strip, their facades eroded by the elements.

When I was three, that road felt treacherous. When I returned as a teenager, it felt stunted. Now it feels…formidable.

"Which one was yours?" Calanthe asks, tearing my gaze from the graveyard with its sloping headstones shaded by stocky olive trees.

I nod to the one-story white house taken hostage by an ancestral fig tree.

"Malika and I readied the bedrooms. In case you decided to stay the night," Yosef tells us as he eases the car to a stop on the side of the road.

I want to thank him but my blood burns too hot and my lungs clap too hard to produce any words. My legs feel all at once wooden and woolen as I climb out of the vehicle, the stiffness in my joints increasing as I lead Calanthe through the thickets of rubbery shrubs toward the well in the earth that I fell into thirty years ago.

I've been back, but never with an unmarked. I begin to worry that the rules will have changed. That the mine will refuse to imprint magic into Calanthe's skin. And then I worry that it will strip me of mine. All these thoughts coalesce to a discordant crescendo when we reach Malachi, Ines, and the twenty or so brave Atlantean souls who chose to stay when so many others left.

After quick introductions—made by Malachi—my compatriots back up.

"How do we get down?" Calanthe observes the crevasse that's no wider than a manhole.

"We float down," I say.

She snorts. "Of course we do."

I fashion a platform made of air and guide her onto it. As I lower us into the entrails of the earth, her eyes lock on mine, sparkling gold and then blue.

"Breathe," I murmur as we sink and sink.

The aquamarine shine of the mine's walls dances on her skin, catching on the lips she keeps biting and the lashes she keeps batting.

"You fell all this way?" She peers up, then down. "How did you not die, Tarian?"

"I did. Gaea retrieved my soul."

She gasps.

"Did I forget to mention that?"

"Um, yes."

When our feet touch the ground, Calanthe twirls on herself sending her hair fanning out around her. It slaps my jaw and tickles my neck.

I fist it, lever her head back, then against her mouth, I ask, "Ready?"

"Are you?"

"I'm ready to spend the rest of my immortal days with you."

She swallows, and then she kisses me, a gentle, barely-there graze that I deepen before steering her to the wall that blazes with stacked verses of glyphs. My fingers tingle, my runes glow, my blood rages.

"It'll sting," I warn her as I lace my fingers through hers.

"I remember."

At my frown, she says, "Have you already forgotten my absent rune?"

How could I when I've prayed since daybreak for its return. Although she slept in my arms, my night was terribly lonely, my dreams terribly dull.

I breathe in slowly, then breathe out even slower, and then, only then, do I press flesh to stone.

The jolt of power that runs through me irradiates my entire body. It races through my veins and jerks into Calanthe's, electrifying her blood. Her nostrils flare and her lips tense, but she doesn't whimper.

I think it's over when a fiery blade cuts into my spine, swooping and curving as though inscribing words into my skin. Fuck. I try to lift my hand, but it's fused with the stone.

*I am not done, my son.* Gaea's eerie whisper knocks into my breastbone and tosses my heart.

Calanthe sucks in air, then licks the perspiration off her upper lip. I squeeze her fingers, reassuring words forming and dying on my tongue. I will not tell her that this is normal, because it isn't. I may have been three when I last transmitted power to a human, but I remember it with perfect clarity.

The glyphs on the wall flare before darkening, marking the end of the transition. I pull my hand away, then spin Calanthe and hook her hair off her nape.

"Did it work?" she asks.

The runes '*I am awakened*' brighten her skin, but so do other runes. I hike up her T-shirt, tug on her bra strap, and gaze in wonder at what Gaea has done.

"Okay, you're freaking me out a little, Tarian. Did I not get them? Because it felt like I got a lot of them."

I reverently trace the sentence on Calanthe's spine that ends just above her tailbone.

"Tarian?" She tries to look over her shoulder, but the bunched cotton keeps her from glimpsing the trail of light.

I finally read the verse out to her, and then I begin to translate what it says, but she doesn't need a translation. Not only has Gaea given her magic, but she's given her the comprehension of our tongue.

"*You are awakened, little bloom*?" She smirks. "Your goddess has a sense of humor."

The glyphs on the wall ripple.

"*Our* goddess." I contemplate the words on my girl's spine a while longer, committing them to memory. *From this day forward, you will thrive in my son's soil in slumber and in wakefulness. Forever his. Forever mine.* I smooth down Calanthe's bra and T-shirt and rasp a quiet, "Thank you."

The veins of diamonds brighten as her voice echoes between my temples. *Your souls chose each other, Tarian.*

"Do you think this means dream-sharing is back on?" Calanthe wheels around, her eyes glowing with joy but also with magic.

I do. Nevertheless, as I unbutton my shirt, I elect to remain cautious. "We'll see tonight."

"Um. They're all waiting to come down. They're probably all *looking* down." She cranes her neck and waves. "Yep. All looking."

"I'm not taking my shirt off to seduce you, Calamity."

"Then why are you getting undressed?" she hisses between clenched teeth, still waving at the others who await my command to join us.

"Because I think Gaea carved new runes into my skin."

Calanthe's head swings back my way so fast that her shimmering neck clicks.

I display my back. When a muted gasp rents the air, I glance over my shoulder.

"She did," my woman whispers, tracing the iridescent swoops nestled between my shoulder blades.

"What do they say?"

Calanthe's voice, like her gleaming stare, brims with affection and wonder as she sounds out my new runes. *"Forever hers. Forever mine."*

# Afterword

*Although **My Dark Beast** was supposed to be a standalone, I've decided to write another story in this world. Whose story will it be? Download the bonus epilogue and find out...*

Either enter this link in your browser:

**https://bit.ly/MDBbonus**

or scan this QR code:

*Grab your bonus content here*

# Acknowledgments

Well, this has been a labor of love and insanity. Chaos, even. But by god, did I enjoy the ride.

I started writing *My Dark Beast* back in 2022. It was a side project, a book I'd work on between other books. I'd publish episodes a tad erratically through Kindle Vella, until fast forward to September of 2023 when I decided to give my gods and monsters my full attention.

I *adore* retellings. What I don't especially adore is *Sleeping Beauty*. Then why did I draw inspiration from that particular tale? Simple. I wanted to write a story about dreams, because I have *a lot* of those. Every night. And they're all crazy eventful. I've woken up laughing, sobbing, breathless, panicked, and shocked. In truth, my nocturnal life is way more exciting than my diurnal one.

You may still be wondering why I didn't like *Sleeping Beauty* (or not, but you're about to find out either way). Even though I don't discard the existence of love at first sight, I'm not sold on love at first kiss. Imagine waking up to a stranger with their mouth on yours. Be they a royal or a regular Joe / Jane, that'd be odd, and undoubtedly, grounds for sexual assault. Not very romantic.

I hope you've enjoyed my take on this age-old tale and grew to love my new gods as fiercely as I did. Thank you to every reader who nurtured Calanthe and Tarian into the characters they became.

Thank you to Lexi and Rachel for working their magic on my

manuscript. Especially to Rachel, whose comments along the way never failed to make me laugh. I heart you so much, lady.

Thank you to my author friends, Miranda Lyn and Jenny Hickman, who not only took the time to read an early copy of my book but also to advise and comfort me when I began to doubt everything about this story.

Thank you to my extraordinary mother—my role model and book packing fairy—and to my devoted father—my favorite storyteller (Can you believe I managed to place your high school "squid mating tale" inside a book? I still can't. ).

To my siblings, my extended siblings, my tribe, how lucky I am to have such a loud and supportive family.

To Katie, I've lost count of the number of metaphorical corners you've dragged me out of over the years but I haven't lost count of how many margaritas I still owe you.

To my children—Adam, Gabrielle, and Estée—thank you for keeping me grounded when my stories tear me away from the real world. You are, and always will be, my most beautiful creations.

Last but never least, thank you to the man of my dreams. You are my Nick, my Tarian, my everything, Jon. Forever and always.

*xoxo*

*Olivia*

# Also by Olivia Wildenstein

**PARANORMAL ROMANCE**

*The Lost Clan* series

ROSE PETAL GRAVES

ROWAN WOOD LEGENDS

RISING SILVER MIST

RAGING RIVAL HEARTS

RECKLESS CRUEL HEIRS

*The Boulder Wolves* series

A PACK OF BLOOD AND LIES

A PACK OF VOWS AND TEARS

A PACK OF LOVE AND HATE

A PACK OF STORMS AND STARS

*Angels of Elysium* series

FEATHER

CELESTIAL

STARLIGHT

*The Quatrefoil Chronicles* series

OF WICKED BLOOD

OF TAINTED HEART

*The Kingdom of Crows* series

HOUSE OF BEATING WINGS

HOUSE OF POUNDING HEARTS

HOUSE OF STRIKING OATHS

HOUSE OF SHIFTING TIDES

**CONTEMPORARY ROMANCE**

GHOSTBOY, CHAMELEON & THE DUKE OF GRAFFITI

NOT ANOTHER LOVE SONG

**ROMANTIC SUSPENSE**

*Cold Little Games* **series**

COLD LITTLE LIES

COLD LITTLE GAMES

COLD LITTLE HEARTS

# About the Author

Olivia is a *USA Today* best-selling author of romantasy. When she's not swooning over her characters' steamy escapades, or plotting their demise, you can find her sipping wine and crafting her next twisted, romantic masterpiece, all while trying to convince her children and leading man that she loves them more than her laptop.

WWW.OLIVIAWILDENSTEIN.COM
INSTAGRAM: @OLIVES21
TIKTOK: @OWILDWRITES
FACEBOOK READER GROUP: OLIVIA'S DARLING READERS